DEDICATION

This book is dedicated to those who struggle but never give up.

ACKNOWLEDGEMENT

Over a period of four years that took me to write this book, a number of friends read it, supported it and encouraged me to finish it. Thanks are due to, Mary Anne Pogany, Megan Hartman, Darlene Randolph, Bill Woods and Judy Schuler who edited it. And, of course, my wife, Skylar, who inspired me to write and edited the first draft. The team at Create Space who helped in formatting and printing deserve my appreciation.

PROLOGUE

After the partition of India, the violence that engulfed his surroundings, the harsh realities of the world around him and the insecurities in his life stole Saleem's childhood away. He no longer enjoyed the things he used to. His father still bought him new shoes for special occasions, but they did not excite him anymore; he now looked at them as a piece of clothing that needed replacing periodically. His cherished festivals, the reason to feast and a chance to celebrate with the family and friends, lost their luster. Eid, a festival that was celebrated with new clothes for everyone, toys for children, and presents in the form of money, fell during the period when Father was in prison. That year there was no feast, and gloom replaced the celebrations. Within a year of the partition of India, the sense of well-being he felt during the early years had left him and he felt unprotected and insecure. All that happiness in his life belonged to a different era, the era of his childhood, which seemed buried somewhere far away in the past. And he was only ten years old.

CHAPTER 1

Lying in bed, Saleem heard his mother say to her visiting neighbor that the most unfortunate thing for parents was to watch their child withering away, dying, leaving them to suffer the loss and grieve for the rest of their lives. For him, that was reason enough to pull through and get well. He certainly did not want his father or mother to be in long-lasting pain because of him. When the doctor tried to assuage his fears and convince him that he was soon going to be healthy, Saleem believed him. Illness was not new to him. During his short life, he had been unwell a number of times, and each time he had fought for recovery and bounced back.

The idea of dying never ever crossed his mind, for he was convinced that to die you had to be old. He was not old. He was young—too young! The look on his mother's face was a cause of concern, but as for him, he was not troubled by his current state. In a way, he was happy that he was getting yet another disease out of the way.

Typhoid fever, according to the doctor, was to last over twenty days. Once his condition had been diagnosed, Saleem understood that he was going to be in bed for several weeks. Resigned to tackle yet another ailment, he just lay there looking at the ceiling when he was inside and the more interesting sky, where an occasional bird floated by, when his bed was outside.

At times, he found himself staring at nothing, especially when he had a high temperature. While his mother was worried about his declining health, oblivious to her fears, his worry was that he might be falling behind in school.

He was, however, troubled by the anguish that hung around him—everyone tiptoeing, murmuring in whispers. It was so depressing.

Saleem was in the fourth grade when one day he suddenly felt tired, a slight headache came onto him, and he felt cold. He realized that he should take off and go home. His teacher advised him to leave. Walking home, the cloudless sky was letting the heat of the September sun soak his body, but for him the sun had lost its heat; he continuously felt cold. By the time he got home, he could tell he was sick.

When his mother saw him come home early, she knew something was wrong. His looks told her he was unwell. She cupped his face in her hands; it felt hot. She took him directly to his bed and gave him a thermometer to stick under his tongue. It showed a temperature of 102. She made him tea, thinking he was coming down with cold.

Two days passed but the fever would not break. In addition, he started to have stomach cramps. These symptoms led the experienced local physician to believe that this time his disease was typhoid. When his mother heard the diagnosis, she cried. Although she had witnessed several cases in the family where people had recovered from this disease, she knew he was physically not strong, and feared this harsh illness might take him away from her forever.

At night, she would come by and check on him several times, put her hand on his forehead to gauge his temperature. In spite of the assurances from the doctor and what she had known about this illness, she was worried to a point that she imagined the angel of death was lurking in her house. Before going back to bed, she would sit next to her son, whisper a prayer to her God, beg him for her son's life and blow air from her mouth on to his body and all around him. This was her way of driving away the evil spirits that were making her son ill and threatening his life.

His father hardly ever sat down on his bed, or if he did, it was never for very long. Once during the day Father would stand by Saleem's bedside, check his pulse and ask him how he was feeling, expecting his son to have his chin up and answer in a positive manner of being well. Not that he was not worried or was negligent in providing care; he just did not want to come across as an over-concerned parent like his wife. At times, when he was unable to control his emotions and his concern got the better of him, it came out as anxiety.

One day, when Saleem wanted a drink—he needed a soda that day—his father personally went to the market and brought a bottle home but could not find an opener. Soda was not something the children drank often. In his hurry, he tried to open it with his bare hand. The sharp edges of the bottle top cut into the muscle causing it to bleed, and then in his frustration he tried his teeth. His wife, who was watching his agitation, took the bottle from him before he did more damage to himself and opened it with one of her kitchen knives. That day Saleem realized that his father did care about him but hid his feelings; a show of inherent manliness was a part of his parent's upbringing. That was where Saleem had learned to answer he was well, when he was in fact hurting.

When he was alone, his mind would wander and most of the time his thoughts lingered on different foods that he would one day be allowed to eat once again. These days the little he ate was rice with *dal* or yogurt.

His parents recorded his temperature every morning, afternoon and at night. The mercury thread of that delicate instrument seemed to be stuck at 103. The doctor, who had prescribed a liquid medicine for him to take every four hours, would visit every third day, review the temperature chart and examine him, look at his throat, his tongue, press his fingers on his stomach, sometimes too hard, and ask him if it hurt. This went on forever—that was how it felt to Saleem.

After three weeks, as the doctor had predicted, his temperature broke. He was weak but finally out of danger. The day the thermometer read normal for his temperature was a day to rejoice his health in the family; the gloom lifted and a smile returned to his mother's face. Normalcy moved back into the household. Gradually, he started eating normal food of meat, *chapatti* and different vegetables his mother made especially for him. And finally he was healthy once again.

Because of his illness, he missed a whole month of school. His tutor had always kept him so far ahead of the class that when he returned he was able to catch up in no time. In school, kids now treated him with some respect, as he was one of the elite members of a group who were "survivors of serious illnesses", although not known by this name, but recognized for their tenacity to fight off diseases.

Saleem's childhood was filled with different illnesses as if someone had singled him out for the punishment. While he was an infant, he got whooping cough, which nearly killed him. His mother blamed herself for his suffering, as she thought his cough was a result of her indulging in ice cream while still nursing him. Before he entered his teens, he had eczema, malaria and typhoid. He would break out with eczema on his arms and legs every year at the beginning of summer. One year, it was so severe that he could hardly walk; his father had to rent a *Tonga*, a horse drawn carriage, to take him to school so he could take his final exams, required for the promotion to the next class.

He had been plagued by so many diseases that he started to wonder if he ever would be like other children—normal and healthy. To fight his infections, he received so many injections in his early years, that he thought he might have more chemicals in his body than blood. In the beginning, he feared the needle, but as the practice continued, he lost that fright. He could even look at the sharp pointed instrument and not flinch as the doctor punctured his arm.

He had suffered just about every childhood disease of the area with the exception of smallpox. Many of the boys he knew had scarred faces as a result of this malady. Their skin reminded him of the surface of a grinding stone, like the chiseled one his mother used to crush spices. Because pockmarked faces were such a common sight, it would not have bothered him if he wound up looking the same. Of course, it would be a different matter if he was a girl. A scarred face on a daughter would make parents worry that no one might want to take their child as a wife.

Every year, some part of the town experienced a cholera outbreak. One year, Saleem's mother learned that the cholera was spreading into an area Saleem had to walk through to go to school. She got him inoculated, but still not convinced, she sent the servant to buy some camphor. She then wrapped a small piece of the chemical into a strip of gauze and tied it to Saleem's arm. Camphor, with its smell, was her way of driving away bad spirits, germs, or anything else that was dangerous and harmful to her children.

During his illnesses, Saleem had seen many doctors. After examining him, one of them answering his health concerns told him that he need not worry, once he was over eighteen years of age, he would be as healthy as anybody else. This gave him hope and he started looking for that day. It turned out that doctor was right. As he passed his teen years, he never got sick again. He speculated that either he had filled his quota of illnesses or he had developed a universal immunity. He was happy that finally his body was no longer prey to the microbes of his world.

CHAPTER 2

One of Saleem's childhood memories was the family sleeping outside on the roof of the old house during the summer months, looking at the countless stars, and he marveling about the moon that floated across the sky changing its shape every night. The moon was his friend; it followed him when he ran.

The concrete floor upstairs would get very hot during the day. Saleem's father had arranged for a man to climb the stairs in the evening and spray cold water from a nearby well out of a *mashak*, a leather bag. By the time it got dark and the family went to bed, the floor would have cooled down, enough that Salem could walk barefoot on it. Up on the roof, unlike the courtyard down below where rooms and verandahs obstructed the cooler night breeze, it was comfortable for everyone to sleep.

Every evening after sunset, a servant would make beds on the cots with *dhurries*, thin cotton carpets, lined with white bed sheets. Father had the largest bed. Mother, before she went to her bed, would pull the sheet of Father's bed from the sides and then from the top and bottom to get those wrinkles out of the cotton, which seemed so hard to take out, especially when the ironed sheet had been slept on. Her last action was smoothing the bed sheet with her palms spread out. All this she did because she wanted to. He had never asked for a wrinkle free sheet and did not know there was so much effort put in making his bed. He got so used to the fact that if he would see a wrinkled bed sheet he would notice it, the unwrinkled one he would only glance at and pass as usual.

Saleem's smaller bed lay next to his mother's. Occasionally, when they would see a meteorite shooting across the star-studded sky, he would ask his mother about it. Every time the question came up, his mother would tell him that the devil was trying to get into heaven and God shot him down with a flash of fire…once again. And occasionally when there was a meteorite shower, to them it was a night when the devil was pushing the limits.

In Saleem's mind, he could visualize how the evil spirit, dressed in black clothes, hiding in the darkness of the night, would try to sneak in. God sitting up with his long flowing beard on his throne, making all the important decisions, did not want this fiend to come and corrupt the good souls in his paradise. He was doing enough damage on Earth.

Another unforgettable image from childhood that was imprinted on his mind was of his mother getting up early in the morning and reading aloud from the Qur'an. He did not understand a word of what she was reciting; he was certain his mother did not either. But it had a soothing effect on him and he assumed on her as well. As he got older, he came to realize that the tranquility they experienced was a result of the recitation being in Arabic, not so much because of the lyrical nature of the narration but because it was a language of heavens they did not understand. And mother believed she was communicating with her invisible God in his vernacular.

He wondered, if he knew Arabic, would the mystery of the words and their magical effect be lost. God the mysterious had to speak in mysterious ways.

Saleem's father never sat down to read the scriptures and hardly ever went to the mosque to pray as some of his neighbors did on regular basis. Instead, he was content to go for solitary walks away from the town early in the morning before sunrise, where he sought closeness with nature and drew his strength from it. Father was so tied up with his morning routine that if perchance the heavy rain made it impossible for him to get out for his outdoor exercise, he did not know what to do in the early hours of the day. He felt caged by an element of nature. He would be fidgety, get up and walk a few paces, look at the sky, check how the clouds looked and inform his wife that they needed rain for the crops, make small talk.

His wife would notice his restlessness and prepare breakfast early that day. Once he had had his milk, his day had started; he was ready to go out, even if he needed an umbrella. Go to the town library to read his newspaper, meet his friends and discuss politics.

Saleem, an early riser himself, one day got up at sunrise just as his father was ready to leave for his walk. He asked if he could come along. His father preferred to walk alone, but he made an allowance for his son this morning and the two left together.

Clutched in his father's right hand was a cane with a carved wooden handle, which added a sense of dignity to the image of the tall man. Since there was no small walking stick in the house, Saleem had no choice but to come along empty handed. However, this did not diminish his ecstatic feelings. With a spring in his step, chest swelled, walking next to his father without holding his hand, he experienced a new stage in his life; it made him feel grown up—suddenly.

They did not encounter many people on the road, but the few they saw seemed to know and respect his father. They walked a short distance through the quiet town and then continued silently along a narrow path through the chessboard of fields.

Saleem would remember this morning all his life. It was the month of June when days got hot, but it was nice and cool early that day. Some birds in the sky were testing their wings and a few farmers were already out watering their crops. Saleem noticed that some of those working on their fields also knew his father.

Away from the path in the empty grounds, Saleem noticed men squatting on the farmland with a small round metal pot beside them. He wondered what they were doing, sitting all alone under the open sky so early. His father explained that not all had toilets in their homes and people came to the fields to relieve themselves.

"They carry along a pot of water to cleanse afterwards. When they go home, they clean everything by scrubbing their hands and the pot with a small amount of clay and rinsing them off with plenty of water. Most of them will then bathe; some will even wash their loincloths. This ritual starts the day for most the Hindus in small towns and the neighboring villages," his father said.

Father seemed impressed by the habits of hygiene in the Hindu culture. As a Muslim, he knew that they were generally not as clean. He also knew the importance in their faith was being *pak* or *napak*. What was *pak*, meaning clean, or *napak*, meaning unclean, was prescribed by the religion. Those who said prayers did wash their hands, faces and feet a number of times during the day, but those who prayed only occasionally did not feel the need to wash or bathe very often.

Sweat and dirt was not *napak*. If they bathed once a week on Fridays, they felt they were clean.

Father, with his long legs, was a fast walker; it was difficult for his young son to keep up with him. After all, Saleem was only six years old and his small legs soon got tired. He was falling behind. Besides, it was more interesting for him to stop and watch a little bird here and there, or admire a little bug carrying a load larger than its own size.

Not only was it his first time walking with his father, it was his first time in the open air so far away from home where he could see sky meeting the earth and could toss a stone as far as it would go without hitting anything. He picked up a small rock and threw it just to see how far it would land and then he picked up another one to check if he could hit the small tree in the distance. When father saw his son running through an empty field with his arms stretched, waving like the wings of the birds overhead, he knew his morning walk was not going well and it was time to cut it short to be home in time for breakfast.

Breakfast usually consisted of tea and biscuits, except for his father who always had a bowl of hot milk with sugar. For him, the sweet white drink provided all the energy he needed to start the day. During the winter months, the children would also get an egg with their tea.

As a tradition in the family, at the age of six, Saleem started school. For this purpose, Mr. Mahmood, who tutored the children at home, accompanied Saleem to the school located on the outskirts of the town. On foot they covered the distance of half a mile in less than thirty minutes. As they approached the school, his angst rose, his senses sharpened. Although Saleem had been on this road several times before, he noticed things he had never seen. Noticing his anxiety, Mr. Mahmood talked to him about things other than studies. Once they arrived, they directly went to the admissions office.

School always started on July 7, except for those years when the date fell on a Sunday. The month of July was into the monsoon season, but it was not raining that day; it was just cloudy, hot and humid. Several times before, he had passed by this red brick structure, where a row of classrooms stood on a raised ground protected by a verandah in front. A central area for assembly of students separated the two wings. When they approached the school, Saleem was suddenly awe struck. Never before he had felt overwhelmed by a building as he did this morning.

Once inside the school grounds, still a little nervous, his mind was busy imagining how he would be coming here every day, learning new things and making new friends. He did learn different things every day at home from Mr. Mahmood, but it was not exciting like it would be while competing with other classmates, taking exams and getting a new teacher every year, as he would advance to higher classes.

To begin the process, they walked into the office, a windowless room with a solitary light bulb hanging from the ceiling, a worn out desk and chair. The door and the single light bulb were the only source of light. The dusty files were piled up wherever space allowed, on the shelves as well as on the floor. The middle-aged clerk who occupied the chair slowly raised his eyes to look at the visitors over the rim of his spectacles. His old reading glasses kept sliding down his nose as he peered at the two.

It appeared to Saleem that the clerk did not know Mr. Mahmood. But as soon as he heard Saleem's full name, a smile spread over his wrinkled face, revealing a set of bad teeth.

He politely said, "*Adab Arz*", a greeting used between Hindus and Muslims. A Hindu greeted another Hindu by touching palms and saying *Namaste*, while a Muslim greeted another Muslim by saying *Salam Alekum*. In the present situation, there was no chance of making a mistake. Since the clerk knew Saleem's father; he used the proper words.

Unquestionably, when a man and a child arrived on the first day of school, it meant they had come to apply for admission. The clerk did not even ask about the nature of their business.

Saleem watched the man behind the desk as he opened a brown file, carefully licked his index finger and picked out a blank form, which he held toward the two of them. Mr. Mahmood, being the older one who at this point was a guardian figure, took the paper. He then pulled out a fountain pen and filled out the blank spaces with information such as name, age, date of birth and the like, without asking a single question from Saleem. He did not even ask him his date of birth. Not that Saleem knew his birth date. He was simply too young and too wound up by the whole situation to care what the man was writing on the document. And he was made to believe that older people, especially teachers, know everything. Little did he know that at that moment, he was being assigned a date, correct or incorrect, that would become his birthday for the rest of his life.

From his tutor, Saleem knew that he would have to take some tests before the process of his admission was complete. The new students started to lineup for the required evaluation. Since this school started from the third grade, each one, including him, was there seeking entrance into that class.

Everybody knew that the third grade teacher, Sharma Gee, was a man of strict rules. Saleem's older brothers and cousins, who were now in the upper classes, had forewarned him about Sharma Gee and his thin cane, which he always carried with him and used on students freely—whenever he thought it was time to discipline or impress upon them who was in charge.

Since Saleem had come to join the line, more children of his age arrived and stood behind him. An adult accompanied each child. They all stood outside in a line when Sharma Gee was inside the room in no hurry, administering the tests and interviewing, one pupil at a time. Grown-ups had started chatting with each other, but children, worried about the upcoming ordeal, were standing quietly waiting for their turn. The teacher took his time to examine each student to judge whether the child was worthy of his class.

At last, it was Saleem's turn to enter. Sharma Gee sat on a chair with his famous cane, the instrument of his power, resting within easy reach on the table in front. Papers in hand, ready to get in, Saleem turned around to see if the tutor was still there. Mr. Mahmood gave him an encouraging nod and smiled.

Saleem straightened his back and walked into the classroom. Suddenly remembering his cousins telling him that Sharma Gee did not like young pupils looking directly into his eyes, he focused on the table in front; looking up above the teacher's head would be disrespectful. No greetings were exchanged. Saleem, fearful of the unknown, handed the papers to the teacher. Paying no attention to the student, Sharma Gee studied them for a while and then with an expressionless face he glanced at Saleem.

"I know your father," Sharma Gee said. "I also know you have a tutor at home. Let us see how well he has prepared you for this school."

Sharma Gee's voice was not as harsh as he had expected. Saleem's nervousness diminished as he grew more confident and comfortable. He was handed a children's book in English, opened randomly to a page by the teacher to read aloud the first ten lines. Because he had already studied this book with his tutor at home, he was able to read the passage with ease. Then he was asked to recite tables of five and after that to solve a problem in addition and one in subtraction on separate pieces of paper. Still a little anxious, Saleem dutifully sat down on a small chair by a desk and worked out the arithmetic as best as he could. As he handed the papers back to Sharma Gee, he so much wanted to see the expression on the teacher's face, but remembering the advice of his siblings, he decided he better not. He could look up as far as the desk where Sharma Gee was evaluating his work. Keeping his head down, he stole a look and found the older man with a grim face, his eyeglasses at the tip of his nose, not looking at him.

Saleem hoped that in spite of his anxiety he was able to get the correct answers. Sharma Gee looked at the test papers and the application form and asked, "Are you ready to start the classes at the K.M. English High School?" "Yes, Sir!" replied Saleem.

Sharma Gee looked at him. His expression had not changed a bit since Saleem had walked in. He picked up his pen and put a big check mark across the application, signed it and handed it back to Saleem. "Take these back to the office."

When Saleem came out, he was relieved he would not have to face this teacher on a one-on-one basis again. If admitted, Sharma Gee would become his classroom teacher, but he would be just one of many students.

Exercising his right as the older person and tutor, Mr. Mahmood took the papers away from Saleem and looked at them. The check mark was a good sign—check marks always carried a positive message. His heart lit up with pride, but his face showed no expression; he did not believe in praise.

Together, they walked the short distance back to the admissions office and returned the papers to the clerk, who after scanning them, looked up and said, "Sharma Gee must have really liked you…look at the size of the mark on your paper…so large…so bold. Normally, he would make a small mark in the corner. You are now definitely accepted as a student to the K.M. English High School…just as soon as I can collect the tuition fee."

Mr. Mahmood, who had the money, paid.

After a receipt was written, the clerk continued, "You should be here tomorrow at nine o'clock in the morning. Your teacher will inform you about the rules and regulations of the school and assign you a desk. The regular classes will start the day after tomorrow."

Hearing what the man in the office said, Saleem felt he was starting a new life with some achievements. Counting his recent accomplishments, he recalled that he first successfully passed the test of a tough teacher and then Sharma Gee had given him a big check mark!

After completing the admission formalities, the clerk pointed a pen he was holding toward a blackboard on which were listed various items for students to bring to school. Mr. Mahmood and Saleem both read and copied the list onto a piece of paper. The list contained names of textbooks, number of notebooks, pencil and eraser for drawing class, and a pen for writing. Ink would be provided by the school.

CHAPTER 3

Saleem always got new clothes and new shoes for weddings and for *Eid,* a yearly Muslim festival, celebrated at the end of the month of fasting, *Ramazan* (Ramadan in the Arab world). Of all the new clothing items, he derived the most pleasure from shoes. Among several shoemakers in town, there was one outstanding craftsman; he had come from Kanpur, the shoe capital of that region.

One year after he started his school, when there was a wedding coming up in the family, for his new shoes this artist let Saleem browse through a book with pictures of different styles to pick out whichever model he liked best. For him this was the first decision of some significance that he had to make. He looked and looked. Finally, he saw a pair that he had seen in the photographs of the leader of the political party his father belonged to. He had noticed him wearing the two-tone shoes, white and brown. His mind was made up. He was going to ask for a similar pair.

His father thought it would be difficult to keep the white of the shoes clean, but Saleem insisted and promised that he would keep them nice and white. Father relented and let him have his pair of shoes. It was a challenge for the shoemaker, but he agreed to make them. The price he wanted to charge was high, but the family could afford it.

For the land they leased from him, farmers paid Saleem's father in the form of money and a share of their crop, mostly wheat. The family also owned properties in town that were rented out. As a result, Saleem's parents were never short of money. In fact, they were considered the affluent family in the community.

Saleem's father, as influential as he was, had his enemies. Some of them even wanted to hurt him physically. Among his land properties were a few villages. A village in that region comprised a small group of farmers living in huts. They worked on the land, and split their crops and earnings with the landowner.

Twenty-six years ago in one of these villages, all was not calm. A family of thugs started terrorizing their own and the neighboring farmers. Murders were not uncommon in these remote areas. But they were usually revenge-oriented honor-killings and the murderers were never for hire. These villains were mercenaries and robbed and killed people for their gain, people they did not even know.

The village elders approached Saleem's father to ask him if he could do anything to help them get rid of these scoundrels. Using his influence and his friendship with the police, he got them all arrested. They were tried in the court. The leader got a death sentence and his two younger brothers were exiled to a remote island in the Indian Ocean for twenty-five years. Time passed and the two brothers returned. They had suffered hardship because of one man and they knew who. They wanted revenge.

The night was dark and Saleem's father was leaving to attend one of the more important out-of-town political meetings when he got a note from one of his resources that the two brothers, now free, were plotting to attack his home and his family. They had acquired guns and help from a local group of troublemakers. He did not want to change his schedule but made sure that the family was protected. For this he sought help from the police and the neighbors, who would keep a vigil at night and a close watch during the daytime.

Nothing ever happened. The children, who were terrified by these threats, asked when Father returned as to how they should protect themselves against these bad people.

"You need not worry about your safety as long as I am alive," was all they heard from him. But when his wife asked about her concerns he told her, "Well, these people who were coming to harm us changed their mind and went to rob another village. And when they were trying to distribute their loot, they had a fight and both brothers were ambushed and killed by their friends. In fact, their heads were all police could find the rest of their bodies were never located."

"We did not have anything to do with it. Did we?"

"The investigating authorities don't think so," he answered as he left the house.

CHAPTER 4

Most of the small towns and villages in northern India had majority of Hindu population. The town of Jampur with a population of nearly twenty thousand was no exception. Here Saleem's father and his family had made their home. In this small city, sixty percent of the population was of the Hindu faith and the rest were Muslims. On the outskirts of this town, as in most of the towns in the region, lived a community of untouchables, ignored by both Hindus and Muslims.

Religion and social groups divided Jampur into different sections where Hindus and Muslims lived in separate areas. In this town, which was inhabited by two different religions, the two communities were as far apart as though physically separated by a wall. The main reason was that Muslims ate meat and in the Hindu religion killing of animals was against their faith. For most of Hindus, anyone who ate meat was impure and not to be touched, unless it was absolutely necessary. This had pulled the two communities apart to a point where they lived separate lives. The only contact was through the business they did with each other—mostly man-to-man.

Except for Saleem's family and Mr. Singh's family, where women occasionally met each other, there was no social association between women of these two faiths in this area. And this was true of most of India, particularly North India. The only commonality between the two groups was their patriarchal nature, where most women had little to do in making important decisions in their homes.

The communities were so unlike that they not only had different eating habits, prayed to different gods, celebrated different festivals; they even had separate systems to treat their sick. Hindus practiced a system known as *Ayurvedic*; Muslims treated their illness by getting advice from medicine men called Hakeems, and they subscribed to the *Yunani* (Greek) system. Although both systems used the local herbs, they had different names for them. The patients never crossed the line to go to the other system unless they were desperate and all else had failed. Saleem's father used modern medicine for his children, but for himself he preferred the advice of the local Hakeem for his health issues.

One paved main street ran through the town, not very well maintained, but wide enough so two *tongas*, the horse carriages, could pass. It ran straight through the middle of the city and at the north end it branched. One road went to the railway station while the other went to the wholesale market. Some of the side streets were laid in brick. The poorer areas had dirt roads. The only car in town belonged to a Hindu *zamindar*, a landowner. Whenever it was brought out on the road, which was not often, children would run to catch a glimpse of it, to touch it if possible, and if not, just to get a whiff of the fumes.

Of the two ethnic groups, Hindus were more prosperous and more educated. Their leaders had the foresight that, to make progress in India and to learn new sciences and technology, they had to learn English. Consequently, rich Hindu property owners and merchants all over the country had set up English schools, schools where Indian teachers taught English, mainly reading and writing, with an accent of their own. The other subjects were schooled in the local languages. K.M. English High School, the city's only contact with the west, was one of these institutions located in Saleem's town. Except for the one teacher who taught Urdu, the language spoken by Muslims, all the others were Hindu. Only a few students in each class learned Urdu as their first language and for that they went to a small classroom where this subject was taught, while the majority of students stayed in their homerooms to study Hindi with Pundit Gee, the Hindi teacher.

The next day after his admission, when Saleem started school, he knew that there would be all new children in his class. So far, he had had little contact with Hindu children of his own age. In fact, he did not have contact with any other children besides the ones in his family. Family, to Saleem, was everyone who was a relative. Of course, his parents knew how they all were related, but Saleem was too young to understand.

With the help of his mother he packed his newly bought books, notebooks, pen and pencil, which he could carry in a bag that had his name written on it. She made sure that he ate before he left. He walked with his older brother to school. On his way, he kicked a few stones just because he wanted to and no one was there to tell him not to do it. His brother did not care; his parents were the ones who did not want him to scuff his shoes. As they got closer to the school building, he started getting cramps in his stomach. He was nervous that his brother was leaving him soon to go to his class and he would then be on his own to face this new world he was stepping into.

His father had always reminded his children *they were Pathans, originally the tribal people from the northwestern part of India. And Pathans could face any situation without fear because they were strong and brave. They would always keep their heads up high as they had in the past and face every situation boldly.* Trying to remember his father's words took his mind off the alarm and apprehension that was numbing his body and mind.

When he arrived at the door of his classroom a few minutes before nine, a few students were already there waiting for the teacher. One by one, other children came and stood quietly beside him. By the time Sharma Gee appeared, the group had swelled to a small assembly. Sharma Gee, cane in hand, walked to the door at nine o'clock sharp amid the students who parted respectfully to make room for him to enter. A few who were whispering were now quiet. Their instinct told them that they had to wait until the teacher told them when to come in.

After Sharma Gee entered the room, he sat on a chair, opened a register on the table in front and started calling names from a list provided by the office, a list of students with their first names arranged in alphabetical order. Everyone in the class was there for the first time. As the teacher called a name, the young boy went in and sat at a designated place—a sturdy wooden desk that had an indentation at the far end for a pen and an ink well in the far right corner. Each desk had its own chair. The process of assigning desks and seating students lasted for some time—Sharma Gee was in no hurry. His occasional look was enough to quiet those who showed impatience outside the classroom.

Saleem's name came up toward the end as his first name started with an S. By the time Saleem got in, most kids were already at their assigned places, sitting at their desks in silence. With everyone seated, Sharma Gee closed the register, looked at the faces of his new students and said, "Let us begin."

He started the class with a short lecture where he emphasized the significance of being on time. He also told the boys the importance of discipline in school and that he would not tolerate any disobedience from anyone in his class. To elaborate, he said that the students were not to talk to each other when seated. If they needed to ask for something, they should always stand up and seek permission to speak before saying anything. These rules applied to everyone during the class hours.

"You all have a desk and a chair. It is yours for the whole year. Do not write your name on it or mark it in any way because next year there will be someone else sitting here." He further added, "If any one of you does not follow the rules, I will not hesitate to use this cane." He pointed to the thin long stick lying on his desk. As if not all this was enough to put fear into the hearts of the little children who were already insecure and uncomfortable in their new surroundings, he picked up his cane, and to make his point hit it on the table.

"I will be your teacher during the first two periods. Each period would last forty-five minutes". Sharma Gee emphasized. "In the third period, all of you in the classroom would take out sketchbooks, pencil and eraser, and walk to the art class where the art teacher would instruct you how to draw. At the end of drawing class, you would come back to your homeroom and have another lesson with me".

"In the sixth period, all those who are taking Urdu as their first language would go to the classroom where Mr. Ghani teaches Urdu. Those who have Hindi as their first language would stay in the room and Pundit Gee will come and teach that class. I would then again be your teacher in the seventh period. Remember, when you walk from one class to another, you always walk in a line. And no talking," he reiterated.

At the end of his talk, he did not ask if anyone had questions or did not understand what he said. He just got up and told the kids to make a line outside the room and follow him. Sharma Gee walked in front with all the kids behind him. They passed a few classrooms where students were sitting quietly listening to the teacher. Sharma Gee stopped in front of the door to an empty room that had drawings and paintings stuck to the walls. He pointed his cane toward the door and said, "This is the drawing-room where you are supposed to come for your art class in the third period."

He then walked a little farther with all the children following him in a line once again, turned a corner, arrived at a small room with only a few desks, and pointed out for the benefit of those who would be taking Urdu as their first language to come here for their lessons. Then, they all walked back.

Once they were back in their homeroom, Sharma Gee asked them to sit down and said, "One more thing that you must remember is that if you are not here on time, you will return home and be marked absent for that day. If for some reason you cannot come to the school, your father must write a note to me explaining why you are unable to attend. September is a month when many children get malaria, but I should be informed that you are sick and cannot be present. If you are absent without my knowledge, you will be fined and your father will have to pay extra money to keep you in school." He also reminded, "You must bring everything you need with you when you come in the morning. And as for examinations, there will be two—one, the half yearly, in December and the other, the Final, in April. For your promotion to the fourth grade you must pass the final."

The first day of school went by quickly. It was exciting, but full of anxiety. After having received their class schedule and the rules of behavior, the students were dismissed. Saleem knew his way home. He did not wait for his brother and walked back all by himself, thinking about those things that happened since he left home. While walking home, Saleem wondered if they would still have seven periods in school when not all the students were there. He had heard a gong go off every forty-five minutes, when he knew the classes had not been following their regular study schedule that day.

Saleem had noticed a long, narrow flat iron bar strung from a thick tree branch. To announce the start of a period, a man would walk up to the tree that could be seen from Saleem's classroom, stand next to the metal, and hit it a number of times with a small hammer. To declare the start of the second period, he would hit it twice, and three hits on the bar announced the start of the third period. For recess, he hit it several times rather quickly, causing a different sound effect altogether. This was the beloved sound everyone was waiting for at the end of the third period. The start and end of the school day was announced by the ringing-of-the-bell, which was striking the hammer on the bar in quick succession for at least half a minute.

His mother was surprised he came back so early, but she was glad to see him safe.

Fridays were unusual, because they were the days of prayer for Muslims, and school closed at twelve o'clock. They still had all seven periods, but they were much shorter. Instead of Hindi and Urdu as the first language, on Fridays, students had them as a second language. Saleem would learn Hindi on Fridays and the others who normally had Hindi at that time would learn Urdu. This would be something new for Saleem, since his tutor at home had not taught him any Hindi so far.

CHAPTER 5

On the second day of school, the morning started with an assembly of students in an open central area between the two wings of the school building. The gathering was very orderly. The students stood side by side in rows according to their grade. Saleem was directed by his teacher with the new children in the first row in front. That was the third grade. The last row was for the tenth grade where the boys were much taller and older than Saleem.

On cue, the children started singing a Hindi song. Every voice had its own tune; still the devotion of the singers blended it together into one. Saleem did not join in because he did not know the words; it sounded like a prayer to him. He just stood there quietly with his head bowed, hands folded in front, as his tutor had told him to do. After the recital was over, the headmaster welcomed the students to the school and left. He was a man of few words who believed that no one who talked much would command the esteem of his audience.

Everybody respected the head master, mostly because of what he was. His serious composure generated fear in all the students, and possibly even in most of the staff of the school. He was a scholar and a poet of Hindi language. The Hindi prayer that the students sang every morning was a poem written by him.

The Morning Prayer would be a daily ritual throughout the school year, Saleem soon found out.

The school was now officially in session and the students went to their classrooms. Saleem and his classmates walked in a line to their room, sat down at their assigned desks, and waited for the teacher.

Sharma Gee briefly talked with the other teachers before coming in. As he entered, the entire class stood up until they were asked to sit down. The teacher called each name from a list. Every child responded with a "Yes, Sir" in English as he stood up. After all, this was an English school—certain things had to be said in English.

Saleem memorized the names of some of the other students during the roll call. He paid special attention to the names of the boys sitting next to him on either side. On the left was Ram Chandra, and sitting on his right was Suresh Dutt. They all seemed friendly enough, which put Saleem at ease. He also got a chance to talk to some of his classmates during recess and found out they all feared Sharma Gee; he was not the only one.

Within a few days of attending classes, Saleem made friends with a number of students in his class. For some, it was useful to get to know him, because he would help them with their homework during recess…sometimes. Other times, he would just play with his classmates. All they did was run around a flat grass-covered area. Occasionally, a student would bring a soft rubber ball from home, and they would play catch or try to strike one another with the ball. The teachers frowned upon any game where one student would hit another.

And so the days went by. In the beginning, Saleem came home tired, but soon he got used to the routine. After a few hours of rest in the afternoon, Mr. Mahmood would help him with his homework and prepare him for the next day's lessons. Thus, he always stayed ahead of the class. Whenever teacher asked a question, he knew the answer and raised his hand.

It did not take long for him to discover that Sharma Gee not only punished young boys, he also humiliated them if they did not learn their lessons well. Frequently, he would start asking questions from one end of the classroom. When a child answered the question, he had to stand up. If the answer was correct, the teacher would allow him to sit down. If he did not know the answer or answered it wrongly, he would continue to stand and the child who answered the same question correctly would come down and slap him. This, Saleem thought, was humiliating for everyone. Once in a while, every student suffered this disgrace, but for some who did not have self-control, a habit to sit down to revise their lessons and complete their homework, this shame was a daily gift of the system. He hated it, but he also knew that the opinions of a six-year-old did not count. He did not want to slap anyone, and he intensely disliked it when someone slapped him. But, this was how Sharma Gee ran his class.

Soon, Saleem stopped raising his hand, even when he knew the answer to a question. However, on occasion, he still had to slap one of his friends. He would feel so badly afterwards that to make up for it, he would intentionally say that he did not know the answer so someone could slap him as well. This way, he felt no one would turn against him; everyone would be equally embarrassed and therefore stay friends.

Although slapping was a way of punishment, commonly administered by an angry frustrated parent, it usually came as a surprise for the child in the privacy of home and not in an anticipated form while he waited for it as it did in this classroom in front of his peers. Here, when Saleem was the subject of this smacking, he could see it coming. When a hand of another boy came down on his cheek, he could feel the tingling even before it hit his face. He would wince and his eyes usually closed before the impact. They did not slap each other very hard, but the teacher, whose aim was to humiliate and not so much to inflict the physical pain, overlooked this aspect of the punishment.

Only four students attended Urdu class with him. Two of them were Muslims and two were Hindus. The other Muslim boy was a cousin of his. Hindu students in his Urdu class came from the liberal families that loved Urdu poetry and the Urdu language. To most Hindus, Urdu was a useless language of an alien culture.

Saleem soon recognized that most of the Muslim boys who were in the school were his relatives. One day, he asked his tutor why it was so. Mr. Mahmood explained that the K.M. English High School was a private institution that charged tuition. Most of the Muslims who lived in this town were poor and could not afford to pay the monthly fee, especially when they had more than one child in the family.

Also, some Muslims were of the *Wahabi* sect and the influential people in their group discouraged them from going to English schools. They feared that the learning of the English language would corrupt their faith. They sent their children to a *Madrasah*, the local religious school, where mullahs and imams taught religion, the only subject of study. For they were true believers who were convinced that all knowledge needed for humanity was revealed through scriptures and to learn one did not need to go to any other source. To them learning of the English language was nothing more than to imitate the conquerors.

Saleem's father was of the opinion that this brand of education did not benefit the younger generation. Rather than opening and expanding them, he felt that such methods would lock the minds of children against accepting new ideas. However, his belief that an open mind was the only road to progress had little effect on people of the *Wahabi* following. In fact, they did not approve of him for promoting Western ways.

He was, however, able to convince several of his relatives and friends to send their children to the English school where they would receive modern education and be better prepared for the future. That was the reason there were so very few Muslim students in the K.M English School, and most of those who were there came from Saleem's family.

All this time when Mr. Mahmood was telling him about his father's interest in teaching the English language to the children, Saleem wondered why his father was different from others in his thinking. Mr. Mahmood, realizing his curiosity mentioned, "Your father worked with the British Army. There he learned about the British ways and their language." This made sense to Saleem.

Saleem's father, by working with the British, developed a progressive outlook. He thought that those who did not learn the English language, in which most of the modern scientific and technical knowledge existed, would be left behind. Although some members of his own expanded family felt that learning of the western language would lead to the destruction of their centuries-old culture, Saleem's father was able to convince them otherwise with his argument: "The children must be taught the ways of those who are the rulers, because they obviously possess better know-how than those whom they conquered. And if the younger generation does not learn the new ways, their knowledge and skills will always be inferior, resulting in their suppression by the groups with better technical know-how. That is reason enough to try to acquire knowledge the foreigners have and get to know their ways, which will come only through their language."

As Saleem grew older he learned the history of his family partly from his parents and mostly from Mr. Mahmood.

When his father had hired Mr. Mahmood as a tutor for his children at 50 rupees a month (the family counted money's value in gold: one tola or 11.7grams of gold was worth 20 rupees in those times) with free accommodation and three meals a day, his job was not only to help the children with their school work but also to educate them about the customs of the society, the culture, and the ancestral background. He expected that at certain point when the children became curious to know about their family's past, Mr. Mahmood would provide them with that knowledge. The tutor knew a little about the lineage because he was the son of a close friend of a relative. His own parents had recently died, and that was why he had taken the job. He came to work with a burden of his own and a responsibility for his employer's children. He had a younger brother and a sister. The older sister was taking care of the brother, but the family's financial support fell on Mr. Mahmood. The money he made was important to him.

Saleem's father wanted the tutor to know everything about the family and pass it on to his children, who would be better off learning from him than from the outsiders and the intrusive relatives. He further instructed Mr. Mahmood to use his discretion and filter out what he thought was not proper for their age. Mr. Mahmood realized the seriousness of his task, but at the same time appreciated the trust put in him by his employer.

The father had wealth, he had knowledge, and he had the foresight that made him understand what was going on in the country. The tutor had also noticed his employer was old to have young children. His curiosity led him to discover that the mother of the children was his employer's third wife. His first wife had died in childbirth; his second wife could not bear any children and was living away in the ancestral village. His present wife was much younger and an intelligent woman who had taken charge of running the household, which allowed him to devote his time and energy on the political interests he cherished.

When the tutor saw that there was enough money in the family to live in comfort without economic worries, he wanted to explore the source of wealth. The information was easy to get; how true it was he had no means to verify. From the people of a small town where everyone knew everyone and just about everyone knew Saleem's father, he gradually learned that Saleem's great grandfather and his three brothers were Pathan-mercenaries who had helped the British army fight and suppress the 1857 uprising in India. As a reward, they were given large pieces of land comprising several villages. The eldest brother, the head of the clan, did an excellent job not only to control what he was awarded, but also turning the arid land into green fields of wheat and rice. He had thus established a well-run estate.

Over the three generations the land had been divided and subdivided, some members losing it through mismanagement, some to women, gambling and other extravagant spending habits. Saleem's father inherited three villages and properties in the town, which he administered. He managed them well. He did not live only on the income of his inheritance; he had gone out and won contracts with the British army to supply them what they required during the war and helped them in any way they needed. There he had come in contact with the British officers and learned their ways. During this period he had met and befriended a young Hindu, Mr. Rao Singh.

In his youth he was able to not only establish himself as a man of importance in town, he also had accumulated wealth in terms of more real estate. For a short time when his first wife died in childbirth, he lost direction. Grief distracted him and he indulged in drinking and visiting dancing girls. But, being wise and having varied experiences in life, he soon realized and corrected his course.

During these unsettled years his parents got him to marry a woman in the family, the woman who could not bear any children and had little education and no ambition. Most of her life she had stayed with her parents and then in a house of her own, which he bought for her in the ancestral village. He was now in his early forties. Needing a family of his own and a compatible companion in his middle age, he married a young widow who was intelligent and beautiful. With the help of his third wife, with whom he was deeply in love, he pulled back to the path he deemed proper earlier in his life. Saleem, his three brothers and a sister were all born of his last wife.

Mr. Mahmood, equipped with all this knowledge gathered over a period, passed it on to his pupils a piece at a time. Saleem always wondered how Mr. Mahmood knew so much about his family when he knew so little. But then the teachers always knew more than everyone else, he thought.

The tutor decided not to tell the children about the details of their father's personal life, which he had picked up through the gossip in town. He did not tell them that the older woman whom they referred to as Aunty Zaineb was in fact the second wife of their father. He also avoided telling them that Aunt Raisa was actually their stepsister from the first wife, a stepmother they never knew. In his opinion, if the parents were not revealing this information to the children, he should respect their rights.

With changing circumstances in his life and the political atmosphere in the country, the father directed his energies to the less fortunate members of his Muslim community. He made it his mission to bring them to realize what would be in store for them when the British left. In his new role, Saleem's father turned into a big proponent of learning the English language and, to a certain degree, the ways of the British people in general. He strongly believed that the British were better educated and technologically more advanced than many other populations. The knowledge and their ruthless ways, combined with diplomacy, allowed them to become powerful to the point where they were able to defeat and take over a country as large as India without ever fighting a real war. Their strength was not in numbers, but in their methodical way of doing things—in the way they processed their thinking.

He wanted Muslims of India not to dwell on the past, forget that they ruled India for many years, and try to understand why it was that they lost their power. He wanted them to realize that Muslims never had the benefit of being a majority in India, even at the time when they ruled the country. They were a ruling minority over a vast Hindu population.

Soon the British would leave, and the void thus created would result in a power struggle. Of this, his father was convinced. He believed that the suppressed majority, who were of Hindu faith, would emerge to dominate the political future of India. Through his knowledge of history, he could see that when and wherever a group of suppressed individuals, especially if they were the majority, got a chance to exercise their power, reprisals and ugly incidents followed.

It was common knowledge that Muslim rule over India was during an era in the past. The present generation of Hindus had not experienced any of the grave injustices done to them during that period. However, a group of politically active individuals kept reminding the populace of those historical events to serve their own agenda. Saleem's father understood how easily crowds could be manipulated by bringing up old historical grievances in order to incite hate. The ruling British government did not discourage activities and movements that caused animosity or rift between the Hindus and Muslims. It was in their interest to keep the friction alive, enabling the crown to rule a population divided.

The negative forces, he suspected, were somehow in line with the laws of nature, and they easily overpowered the positive efforts that required a lot more energy and hard work. As a result, the destructive tasks had always been easier to accomplish than the constructive ones. Keeping all this in mind, he was convinced that hard times were looming for Muslims in India, especially in the regions where they were the minority. And unless Indian Muslims prepared and planned accordingly, they were fated to be the victims of history. In his thoughts, the only way to awareness and success was through modern education.

Saleem's father was aware of the fact that many Hindu leaders were already preparing themselves to take over after the British left. Hindus had recognized the importance of learning the English language. Moreover, they had started to introduce the British system of organization into their political plan. Their system had produced leaders like Gandhi, who was not only trying to win independence for India; he was trying to instill a sense of pride in the Indian nation. Unfortunately for Muslims, he was a Hindu and his way of life exemplified his faith. This led people like Saleem's father to believe that, in spite of Gandhi's sincere efforts to reconcile the differences between Hindus and Muslims, there would be problems between the followers of these two religions after the British relinquished their authority.

He could see that Gandhi's conviction and practice of nonviolence had already won him respect in the educated, influential Western world. However, not all his followers in India had accepted his philosophy of passivity and his tolerance of others' religious beliefs. The majority of Hindus revered him as a saint, but a group of fanatics wanted India to be free of all foreign influences. In their views, Muslims were foreigners who must change their ways of life to be in conformity with the Hindu culture. Because of the basic differences in their religious beliefs, their lifestyles were different. Hindus resented that Muslims ate meat, especially beef. A cow to them was a deity to be worshiped, not killed for food.

Saleem's father was convinced that it was high time Muslims organized themselves and prepared for the future. Although he was not a religious man, being born as a Muslim, he had a life that was culturally different from Hindus and he wanted to preserve it. He did not think it was impossible to live in peace, side by side with Hindus in India. He had a number of Hindu friends. Most of the farmers who worked on his land were Hindus, who often came to seek his advice and had a good relationship with him. His best friend in town was Mr. Rao Singh, a Hindu. They tolerated the differences in their cultures and, instead of using diversity in their beliefs to create a gulf, they used it to enrich their friendship, their lives, and the conviction that a common culture would evolve one day, which would bring the two communities closer together.

CHAPTER 6

Saleem never had to be coaxed to go to school and arrive on time. He found school to be interesting and he was learning new things every day. In his first year, he learned the history of his town, who founded it and when. He learned about ancient wonders of the world. Most fascinating of all these wonders, to him, was the Hanging Gardens of Babylon. In his mind's eye these gardens were somehow suspended in the air with the help of ropes and swayed with the winds. The fact that they were trees and plants growing on high walls destroyed all those captivatingly fascinating images his head had created.

He practiced his mathematics, which at this stage were addition, subtraction and multiplication. He also improved his reading and writing skills. Sharma Gee was quite happy with his progress, showing it now and then by ruffling Saleem's hair when he happened to pass his desk. At the end of the year, all students were tested on what they had been taught. Saleem did well enough to secure the second position in his class of twenty students. His friend Suresh got the first position.

The school closed for summer vacation at the end of April. Everyone got a two-month break.

Raisa and her husband, a police officer, lived in Naini Tal, a city in the hills of northern India, which was also the summer capital of the state, the United Province. The government of the state moved from Lucknow, the winter capital, to Naini Tal during the hot summer months, as a number of senior officials was British, and in Lucknow the temperature was unbearable for them during that time of year.

Raisa was much younger than Saleem's mother, but they had a close relationship. All he knew about Raisa was that she was brought to his mother's home as a baby. She was one of those children whose mothers died during childbirth, and the children never found out where they came from or who their parents were until they got older. Saleem's grandparents took her in and raised her as their own.

Raisa loved children but could never have of her own. She had invited Saleem to come and stay with her for a vacation. Previously, his mother had been reluctant to send him to stay away from home because of his young age. It would be too much work for the younger woman to take care of him. Since, now he was old enough to go to school, tie his own shoes and put on his clothes without any help, his mother felt he was more responsible and would not be much of a burden to his aunty. He might have a good time away from home somewhere where the weather was cooler. Saleem's mother trusted Raisa with her children. She treated the kids as if they were her own—by now she knew how they were related to her. She was comfortable if they called her aunty rather than sister. Her husband also enjoyed having kids around, especially those who could take care of themselves.

Saleem's father decided to take him up to Naini Tal himself. The town was located at an elevation of nearly seven thousand feet. To reach there, Saleem and his father took a train for the first leg of their journey. Their train trip ended at a small town called Haldwani. At the start of their journey Saleem was told that trains did not go all the way to Naini Tal; the last few miles were too steep to be accessible by rail.

By the time the father and son arrived in Haldwani, the sun had set. A friend of Saleem's father met them at the railway station and together they walked to his house.

This was the first time for Saleem to stay with people who were not his relatives. When Saleem's father wrote to his friend that he and his son would be visiting and staying with them overnight, he perhaps forgot to tell him that his son was only seven years old, because there were two large cots with clean white bed sheets waiting for them in the guest quarters under the open sky.

The father and his friend talked about things that did not interest Saleem. He was getting bored. He gathered from what he heard that they were talking about the war. He could hear words like Germany and Japan. He knew there was a war going on, but at his age it was not important to him. As far as he knew, neither he nor any of his family members was in any way affected by it. He had noticed, however, that the trains were exceptionally crowded; he thought they were crowded because everyone was going on a vacation like him. His father had to explain that it was wartime and all trains were transporting things related to the war. Many of the British army were moving from one part of India to another, some by trucks and some by train. "We were lucky," he told Saleem, "to get seats in the train for our trip."

Dinner was soon to be served; Saleem could tell from the smell of food reaching him through the air floating from inside the house. He had not eaten since they left home except for a few biscuits his mother had given him. A servant brought some water to wash their hands and a towel to dry them. Saleem's father, his friend, and then Saleem washed and dried their hands in that order. He was getting some idea about the protocol: Guests first, children last. With hands washed, the host led the two guests into a small room. A clean sheet of cloth with a printed area in the center was spread out on the carpet in the middle of the room. Saleem knew not to sit on the printed area, that part was for laying out the food.

With their shoes off, the three of them sat around the sheet with the host facing across from father and son. A young boy, who like a good obedient servant never looked up, brought in several covered dishes on a tray, placed them in the center on the printed portion and withdrew to the side of the room. Saleem could smell the aroma of spices coming out of the freshly cooked hot food as the host uncovered the dishes. He then asked Saleem's father to serve himself; Saleem watched as his father put a small portion from each dish onto his plate and then looked briefly at his friend, who nodded, indicating that he should serve his son, also a guest in the house. When both visitors had food on their plates, the man finally helped himself.

Saleem was hungry. The food tasted different than what he ate at home, but it was good. He ate one whole *chapatti*, the thin flat bread, and most of the spicy meat and potato dish that was on his plate. However, he could not finish everything. He was glad that his father had given him small portions, so not much was wasted.

Saleem was not paying attention to what the men were talking about during the meal until he heard them discuss hunting; then he was all ears. He listened to them talk about tigers, deer and leopards.

His father's friend said that the meat they just ate was from a deer he shot yesterday. Saleem quietly listened, wondering if the deer meat was the reason why some of the food tasted so odd to him. After the plates were removed, the drinking water was served in metallic tumblers. They had rice pudding, decorated with a film of silver topped with almond slivers, for dessert. Once the meal was over, they all got up, washed their hands once again, and moved outside where Saleem's father and his friend talked about their families, the political situation in the country, and all that eluded Saleem's interests.

Saleem had noticed that there were no women around, but it was no surprise to him since he knew that women did not come out in the presence of men from outside the family. He wondered if he was old enough to be a male-stranger as well. Just as he was thinking about these things, a servant appeared and told his father that Saleem was wanted inside the home. This meant that the women and children wanted to meet him. Saleem was not keen to be all by himself with women he did not know, but obeyed his father who told him to go in. He had no choice, so he braced himself and followed the servant. They went through a corridor that opened into an enclosed courtyard. Under the open sky, beds of different sizes were laid out in a line, all ready for the night. Saleem assumed that the smaller beds were for kids and the larger ones for adults, like in his own home.

A woman, whom he took to be the wife of the host, seemed to be in charge of the household asked him to come and sit down on a small stool next to where she was sitting on a bed. She asked him his name, his age and in what class he was in. She told everyone around what a nice boy Saleem was as she ruffled his hair, which Saleem took as a sign of affection. She slipped her hand under her pillow, pulled out a five-rupee note, and gave it to him. He would not take it at first, and only accepted it after she explained that it was a custom of the family to always give a present to a child who was visiting their home for the first time. As he took the money, he thought that he would tell his father about it and let him decide if it was proper to keep it or not. Two small children standing nearby, approximately of his age, were staring at him. The lady nudged them to take Saleem and show him their toys.

The boy and girl were young like him and definitely not bashful. The boy led Saleem by his hand to a room where he saw the playthings scattered on the carpet and dolls on a small table in the corner. The boy demonstrated his toys, especially the new ones. Some were old, obviously hand-me-downs from older brothers. Most of these objects of amusement for young children were cars, trucks and soldiers, which needed winding up to perform their acts. The girl wanted Saleem to look at her things, but her brother brushed her away saying that boys were not interested in dolls.

He then pulled Saleem over to a board game, "Snakes and Ladders". The boy explained that the game was played by rolling a dice. The player was to advance his or her chip on the board by the number displayed. Each player had a different color chip. The board that had one hundred squares had several snakes and ladders drawn in different sizes. If the chip landed at the base of a ladder, it would climb up, but if the chip landed on the open mouth of a snake, it would be swallowed and brought down to where the tail of that snake ended. Whoever reached the hundredth square first won the match.

Saleem liked the game. He wanted to play it with these children, but just then, servant came to tell Saleem that his father would like him to sleep so they could catch the early bus. Saleem was sleepy by this time anyway, so he took permission to retire from the lady of the house and went outside to where his father was ready to go to bed. Both father and son were tired from their trip and slept well through the cool night.

Early next morning as Saleem woke up, there was enough light that he could see the mountains in the distance. They were green. He assumed the green color was because of the cover of tall wild grass. He imagined himself running, trampling, hiding in the wild growth.

After breakfast, the host walked them both to the bus station, a servant carried their luggage a few steps behind. After they bought the tickets, their bags were stored on top of the bus and secured with a rope. They climbed in and found two seats together. Saleem sat by the window next to his father so he could watch the scenery outside. Father and son were on their way to Naini Tal, the famous hill station at Himalayan foothills. As they pulled out of the town, the road twisted and turned like a snake while it climbed into the mountains.

Saleem was having a good time. The green growth on the mountains he thought was grass turned out to be tall pine trees.

From the sputtering and groaning sounds that were coming out from the engine, it appeared their vehicle was using all its power to drag its load uphill. Load of its own weight it could perhaps pull, but the burden of the bodies riding appeared too heavy on it. They had not been travelling for too long when the driver announced that they would be coming to a scenic point where everyone could get out and walk around and enjoy the fresh cool air of the mountains. As soon as the driver pulled off the road, he turned off the engine, jumped out and lifted the hood for the motor to cool down.

Saleem and his father climbed down, as did all the other passengers. Father pointed to a small waterfall close to where they stood. Saleem had never seen one before. He could make out a flow of water rolling downhill going around the stones and making gentle noises as it fell from one rock to another. His father took Saleem by the hand and guided him to a tiny pool at the bottom of the fall. He showed him how to cup his hands and hold water. As Saleem bent down to catch some in his small hands, he got a spray on his face. It felt icy cold and tasted better than what they drank at home. He noticed he was not alone, tasting the cold spring water. Some even splashed their faces, touched their palms and bowed to the stream. Father explained that the melting snow somewhere on a mountaintop was the source of this frothy stream and that was why it was so chilled.

Next, he saw his father buying raspberries from a boy nearby. The berries came in cups of folded leaves. Fruits growing on higher altitudes were different from what he was used to. Raspberries were something new for Saleem. He did not like them very much, but he ate them anyway as they were part of this adventure. After they had been looking around for a while, they heard the driver blow his horn to inform the passengers it was time to leave. Everyone drifted back, at their own pace, to their seats and once again the bus resumed its strenuous slow climb.

It was Saleem's first journey so far away from home and it was exciting to be traveling with his father and experiencing so many things for the first time, the winding road, crevices of valleys, and loftiness of mountaintops. After another half an hour, they reached their destination—the town of Naini Tal.

The house where Raisa lived with her husband was not far from where they got off the bus, but it was high up on a hill. They hired a man of the several waiting to carry the passengers' luggage. Saleem noticed the man looked different than what he was used to seeing where they lived down in the plains away from the mountains.

His features looked more like those of the people from China that he thought he had seen in pictures.

Sensing his son's curiosity, Saleem's father explained, "They are mountain people. They are strong and they work hard."

Saleem noticed the way he carried the luggage; it was different as well. He had the entire weight on his back, tied together with a band that went around his forehead. When he walked, he stooped forward. The idea of carrying heavy weight in this fashion fascinated the young lad. Once he got older, he thought, he would like to try that.

They walked up the slope. In his excitement Saleem ran, and although it had only been a short distance, he was out of breath and had to slow down. His father had him sit down on a rock for a moment and rubbed his back; a back-rub seemed to be cure-all in his family. When he coughed his mother rubbed his back, when he cried as a child they rubbed his back and now when he was out of breath, his father was again doing the same. As a father who always wanted to pass on to his son what he knew, he explained that the air got thinner at higher elevations. Since air was the source of oxygen, they all needed to breathe deeper and more often up here in the mountains. This could cause a feeling of breathlessness. And to teach wisdom he added, "Just as it is difficult to climb a hill, it is also difficult to climb up in life to succeed." The man carrying their luggage caught up with them and asked Saleem to walk slowly like him and hold on to his father's hand.

They finally arrived where Raisa and her husband lived. Raisa, who was waiting for the two of them, came out and picked him up. She was strong, Saleem thought. She came over and stood by his father, who put his hand on her head to bless her, patted her back, and asked her how she was doing. She was teary-eyed and did not say much for the longest time. Her husband was not yet back from his work. She had food ready for them, which they all ate together and then talked about their trip. To Saleem it felt like he was home.

The house on the top of a hill offered an impressive view of the surrounding peaks. In the distance, Saleem could even see the snow-covered Himalayas. It was much cooler here than where they lived.

The next morning, his father took Saleem for a walk around the area. Although the sun was out, it was still cold. Saira helped him put on a sweater. Now that they were in a foreign territory, no one knew his father.

People walked by without greeting or acknowledging him.

They walked up to the lake. For Saleem it was a continuous series of new experiences. He encountered things he had not seen before. He noticed that the lake was located in the middle and the town was built around it. Several boats were sailing on the smooth water while some people were busy rowing their crafts. He had seen pictures of similar scenes. For the first time in his life, he saw white people, the British his father often talked about. He was amazed how evenly their white clothes blended with their skin to where he could not tell where one began and the other ended.

One side of the lake had a paved road, on the other side there was a trail, which wound upwards. They climbed up on this unpaved path until they could see the entire lake down below. As they took it all in, his father told him, "This lake has significance in the ancient Indian mythology. The legend being that the lake was one of the sixty-four sites where parts of the corpse of Sati fell on earth while being carried by the grieving Lord Shiva. In the location where the left eye of Sati fell, a lake was formed and came to be called Naini Tal (lake of the eye). If looked upon from the high surrounding mountains, the lake appeared as if it were an eye lying deep in the mountains. The name of this town was derived from two words: *Nain* (eye) and *Tal* (lake)."

As Saleem was listening to the story, he wondered and asked, "Who was Sati? And why were her body parts falling off?"

His father, being a Muslim, did not know all details of the account, but he knew that Sati was Lord Shiva's wife who immolated herself through her yogic powers after she lost the affection of her father. This enraged Lord Shiva, who in his rage ran all over with her charred body, her body falling apart. He told Saleem what he knew. They both were looking down at the lake now when his father asked him, "Does it look like an eye to you from here?"

"No! It is too big," Saleem added as he looked up to his father, "but I like the story."

From above, the boats appeared as if they were wooden chips floating in a bathtub, moving at snail's pace. After a good one-hour walk where his father tried to answer most of his son's queries, they slowly climbed back, looking at the blue-green water of the lake, which played hide and seek with them, sometimes in full view, sometimes hiding behind rocks and at times trees blocking the view. His father held Saleem's hand all the way up and all the way down.

CHAPTER 7

The only way to cool down and fight the heat during hot summer months in Jampur where Saleem and his family lived was by a hand-held fan. Several such fans were in the house and they came in different sizes. Saleem recognized that flapping a fan created movement of air, which cooled the body.

Rather than having things explained to him, Saleem had always liked to draw his own conclusions. He correctly came to believe that the waving of a flat object, like a fan, caused air to move. He then noticed that whenever a strong wind was blowing, the trees around his house were swaying. He extended his theory and concluded that the movement of the trees, just like the fan, was causing the wind to blow. In one of his classes, the teacher was explaining how strong winds in the desert could shift a whole sand dune from one place to another. Saleem was confused and could not understand how there could be strong winds in the desert if there were no trees to blow the air. He wanted to ask the teacher, but then decided to hold back. He needed some time to think about it to work it out himself. He could not come up with an answer, so the next day he asked the teacher as to how winds formed in the desert where there were no trees. The teacher elaborated about heat affecting air pressure in an area resulting in air transfer from one place to another and how this caused winds to *blow* not only in deserts, but everywhere in the world. "And then the earth is moving which also drags air. This you would learn in a higher class," he added. This concept fascinated Saleem: a question resolved by a scientific explanation!

Saleem was growing. He was taller now, but he was still young and his body was not very strong. At the age of eight, in September, the month of tropical ailments, he had bouts of malaria, which was a common illness in that part of the country. After the monsoon, a lot of rainwater accumulated in ponds and fields, which served as breeding grounds for mosquitoes, the blood-sucking carriers of the malaria parasite. Not everyone who was stung by these insects caught the disease. Saleem, however, did and suffered.

The malaria attacks came every third day. He would feel it coming. All of a sudden, a barrage of shivers and chills would storm his body and then a high temperature would set in, sometimes as high as 104,105 degrees. The episode would last three to four hours, mostly in the afternoon. At the end, when his temperature was down, he felt extremely tired and his whole body ached.

In the beginning, his parents got very worried and called the doctor every time the thermometer climbed over 100. When he lay sick in bed, and two chairs were placed by his bedside, Saleem knew that the doctor was coming. The town physician would arrive with his black bag; contained therein were the tools of his trade. He and Saleem's father would sit on the chairs.

First, he would check Saleem's pulse, his throat and his tongue, and then he would pull out a thermometer from a slim metal tube. The device was stuck under Saleem's tongue for one whole minute while the patient kept his mouth closed. The doctor would read the temperature by slowly rolling the instrument between his index finger and the thumb, to find the proper position for reading the mercury thread.

The whole procedure fascinated Saleem, especially the shaking of the thermometer after every time it was used. And when the entire process of taking the temperature, checking his pulse, and putting the instruments back in the bag was over, Saleem's father and the doctor would talk about his condition and a prescription would be written, which invariably was for quinine.

The doctor told Saleem's parents that if the temperature started to rise above 103, they should try to bring it down by cooling his head with ice-cold water pads. The only medicine for malaria was quinine, available in the form of pills or a solution. His mother thought the solution was more effective than a pill. He had to drink a dose of this liquid medicine three times a day to fight further bouts of the disease. It was so terribly bitter that he would remember this taste for the rest of his life.

CHAPTER 8

A large section of Muslim population in India demanded a separate state for their community when the British left the region. The concept of Pakistan as a separate country thus evolved. Saleem's father learned that the man leading the struggle for the formation of Pakistan was a lawyer from Bombay named Jinah. Like Gandhi, he had studied law in England, but unlike Gandhi, Jinah maintained a Western lifestyle. Once back in India, Gandhi was able to shed his suits and ties in favor of clothes of a poor local Hindu, whereas, Jinnah preferred to dress up like a barrister-at-law in England. It might seem ironic that a number of Hindu and Muslim leaders who were in the forefront of the self-rule movement had received their education in England. The politicians who were familiar with the British system of government and British law thus led the struggle for independence in India.

Jinah was not fanatic about religion like some other Muslim leaders were. Saleem's father shared Jinah's vision of a country where Muslims could live in freedom in accordance with the axioms of their culture. The new country would be created for Muslims, but it would be a secular state and accept people of all faiths. Little did they know that one day, intolerant zealots would exploit religion to gain control and seize power.

As he grew older Saleem came to know that all Hindus opposed the division of India. They considered it their holy motherland, but splitting of the country was essential for the formation of Pakistan. A number of Muslims were also of the opinion that India should stay undivided, but Saleem's father had made up his mind and was not going to change it. He actively defended the creation of Pakistan and campaigned to get support for the cause. In spite of his political views, his friendship with Mr. Rao Singh remained intact; they just did not discuss the politics of the region.

Tensions were on the increase between those who wanted a separate state for Muslims and those who were against the partition of India. The boys in his class had little knowledge of the issues involved; still they fell in line of their fathers' political views. With passing time, Saleem noticed a developing tension in school among the Hindu and Muslim students. In his class of twenty-five, there were only two Muslim boys. And this was the situation in all of the classes in school. The outnumbered Muslim students had little power and no say. He could not change schools because there were no other schools in the area that taught English. Since everyone knew whose son he was, he became the target of frequent mocking and scorn.

One day, coming back from school, he suddenly found himself surrounded by a number of boys his age, including some he recognized from his class. They must have been hiding because he did not see them follow him. They were all carrying sticks, not the thick kind that caused serious injury, but still thick enough to hurt. For some reason, they did not block his way and he kept on walking. He was scared. He had learned from his father to never show fear and never run. "They will chase you like a predator if you ever run from those confronting you. You can make noise, but don't ever let the enemy know you're afraid," his father had told him repeatedly. This was easier said than done. He wanted to run, but he knew he would be chased. He kept on walking. Another hundred yards or so and he would be safe—he would be in area where people of his religion lived.

As he walked, the boys started taunting him and calling him names. One boy hit him with a stick on his legs, hit him as if he deserved it. It did not hurt because he was wearing pajama-like long pants. The hit triggered a nerve, instead of running, he turned around and stared at that boy—this boy was the classroom bully. Standing behind him were some youngsters who once had been his friends. He looked at him and his one-time friends who would not look back at him. His mind was actively working to find a way out of this situation when he heard the tinkle of a bicycle bell.

At the sound of an approaching bicycle, the boys dispersed and Saleem found himself standing there all by himself. It turned out to be Sharma Gee, who was riding home. He did not stop to ask Saleem about the confrontation and appeared withdrawn, lost in his own thoughts. Nonetheless, his purposeful ringing had put an end to an ugly state of affairs, at least this time. Fortunately for Saleem the incident did not repeat. He gave credit to his former teacher, who perhaps had talked with the parents of the boys involved.

The time was fast approaching for the departure of the British and the end of their rule over India. In the meantime, the Muslim leadership, headed by Jinah, was successful in persuading the rulers to support the creation of Pakistan. The election results clearly indicated the Muslim population's desire for the division of India to live in a country of their own.

The war was long over and India was well on its way to independence. It was the middle of 1946 and Saleem was in the sixth grade when the news of the sectarian killings in the Eastern part of India started trickling in. In certain areas of the country, the majority of the region was trying to wipe out the minority. Neighbors started murdering neighbors. Revenge and counter revenge became the chain events on an agenda. Daily news was about looting, burning and killing that further fanned the fire of hatred over the land. Riots erupted all over the country and atrocities became the order of the day. The violence reached a level where the law enforcement lost control of the situation and got out of the way of those trying to kill each other.

Though the communal riots and killings spared the town of Jampur, the tensions between Hindu and Muslim communities ran high and did not spare the school. This took a toll on Saleem's psyche. He was now afraid to go to his classes. Mr. Rao Singh, being an influential member of the Hindu community, knew several teachers including the headmaster. He talked to them about the fears and plight of Muslim students in general and Saleem in particular. The authorities assured him that as far as the school was concerned, studies would go on without any interruptions with serious efforts to curb communal feelings in the student population. The school would not only punish those who disturbed the peace; the principal would expel them from the institution.

Mr. Singh and Saleem's father sat down and explained the situation to Saleem. They told him that the schoolteachers would keep everything running as normally as possible and protect all the Muslim students as best they could. Although there were some isolated incidents, the teachers and parents alike were able to keep trouble-makers at bay and things never got out of hand.

People were of the opinion that although times were bad now, they would most likely get worse in 1947, after the departure of the British and the formation of Pakistan, which would divide the country.

The town of Jampur was relatively small; the general population was not overwhelmingly in favor of one ethnic group or the other. And the local leadership was sensible enough to realize the dangers of the communal unrest. They appealed to the public to maintain peace and cautioned against grave losses of life and property associated with public violence. In spite of all the efforts, no one could feel at ease—nervousness and anxiety had taken hold of the town. Tension was increasing by the day; lawlessness was spreading all over the country. No community was safe and not one individual could claim being spared by the feelings of fear and danger.

As a precaution and in response to the prevailing conditions, Saleem's father organized a group of young Muslim men to patrol at night, so that a possible attack from a neighboring village would not catch them unprepared. Armed with a flashlight and his cane, he would walk most of the night among the streets of the Muslim section of the town, talking to people and encouraging them to keep some light in the house. This, he thought, would keep the intruders away as they would realize that not everyone was asleep. They took turns staying on watch all night.

CHAPTER 9

Saleem grew up in a culture where the first-born son was the privileged child of the family. He would get the best of everything his father could afford. Parents always emphasized that the oldest brother was similar to a father. Being second in command, he considered this privileged position as his birthright. He could mistreat his siblings without being punished. Although they respected the custom, the younger children resented the advantageous status of their older brother.

Uncle Shams was one of those fortunate children in his mother's family. Uncle Shams's father, Saleem's maternal grandfather, had spared no expense in educating his oldest son. He had borrowed money against his property to send him to college and then to law school.

For the lack of money, Sham's younger brother Sharif could not go to college. And Saleem's mother, who could read and write at an early age, was prevented from formal education, victimized by a society where few girls were sent to school in those days.

Uncle Sharif ended up going to a school where he earned a medical degree after two years of high school. This was inferior to the M.B.B.S., the medical degree where one was a qualified medical practitioner. In a two-tiered system, L.S.M.F., the degree Uncle Sharif obtained, allowed him to practice medicine and treat common ailments, such as colds, upset stomachs and malaria. He could write prescriptions, which were dispensed in the same building by a *compounder,* the chemist, who was an employee of the doctor. Stored in the compounder's room was an array of jars with liquid solutions prepared in advance. These were the mixtures marked with Roman numerals prescribed by the doctor for the ailments of his patients. For those who could afford them, injections were available and were delivered through a glass syringe, which sat in a tray of boiling water.

Uncle Sharif did well in his profession. It was a common sight to see a large number of people sitting on benches in the morning, waiting in front of the doctor's office. Uncle Sharif treated everyone in the order in which he or she had arrived, until of course, a relative or an important member of the community came in. Since most of his patients came with common diseases, he could write prescriptions very quickly. Sometimes, the prescription, a mere Roman numeral, was ready long before the patient had finished talking about his symptoms.

Uncle Sharif lived in the same town as Saleem's family. He and Saleem's father, however, did not see much of each other. Whenever they met at family gatherings, they were polite, but not friendly. From Mr. Mahmood he later found out that Uncle Sharif was against widows marrying again. He did not approve of the marriage of his sister to Saleem's father.

Uncle Shams, on the other hand, was everyone's favorite in Saleem's home. He read enthusiastically, and he was a great storyteller. Next to his parents, Uncle Shams had had the greatest influence on Saleem. Whenever he was in town, he would come and visit for a day or two. Saleem's mother, Uncle Shams' only sister, must have been his favorite. The way they greeted each other and the way he put his hand on her head to show his affection declared his feelings for her. The children in the house, though, were of much interest for him. He came to visit them as much as he came to visit the parents. He liked an attentive audience and in the children of this house he found it. He acted like a preacher with a pocketful of seeds of wisdom that he wanted to sow in the young minds of the new generation. On those occasions, Uncle Shams told many a story, some yarns, but others genuinely thought-provoking accounts of incidents in his life. Saleem would stay close to him, not wanting to miss any of his wonderful anecdotes.

Uncle Shams had serious doubts about the legitimacy of religious beliefs. He would go to Friday prayers more to socialize than to pray. Recalling one of his experiences, he told Saleem that one Friday when he was in the mosque, the imam, to drive the fear of God into the hearts of his audience, started to describe in detail the conditions in hell, a place of eternal punishment for the damned sinners. The account was so vivid that Uncle Shams could not restrain himself from asking the man on the pulpit if he had been there personally. This question upset the imam to a degree where he raised his voice and blamed such insolent thinking on the influence of Western education. Saleem had to laugh when he heard this story, and so did his uncle.

He made Saleem understand that he would learn by questioning, and not by believing everything he was told. Only through questioning and analyzing would he be able to find the right answers and get to the truth. The reason Western countries were so advanced, he said, was because they had started to question and challenge the political and religious authorities.

He felt that queries about faith and beliefs were a taboo in the so-called God-fearing families because parents were reluctant to answer them. They were afraid a logical response might lead to other questions about their faith. Therefore, an inquiring child was told that it was word-of-God, and one must trust God. To top it all, such answers were usually given in a harsh tone to discourage further inquiry. In a matter of time, the child's inquisitiveness perished in its infancy and along with it died his chances for achievement and success. Over generations such behavior eventually resulted in an ignorant, backward society. "The evidence is all around us," he would add.

Uncle Shams had a very critical mind; one could even say he was a cynical man. He disregarded claims that conflicted with his thoughts. Over a period, he had formed his own opinions on life. He believed that since nature had provided human beings with a brain, they should use it to solve the problems and come up with their own solutions. According to him, believing in anything without a valid reason was not only a blasphemy, it was against everything that nature had equipped the human mind with; and those who did so were not in harmony with life and God. Nature was his god and elements were his soul. To him, nature did not control or play any role in the everyday life of humans. "You-sow-you-reap" was his philosophy.

He did not believe God dropped Adam and Eve on earth to start the human race. He also did not believe that morals and ethics originated from religions. His contention was that, as societies evolved, people learned what worked and what did not. This method of trial and error grew into a value system we call laws today. According to him, human values were not a monopoly of any religion, but were a universal law. His sister, Saleem's mother, would hear what he was teaching her son, but ignore it as men-talk. Her own life was angels and devils and, of course, God. Only men could rebel against old age beliefs—women, they found security in the old religion, culture and things only they knew.

Uncle Shams had an opinion about everything. Since he was a lawyer and a well-read man, he was able to present his opinions in a convincing manner. He was not a supporter for the formation of Pakistan, but in spite of his verbal skills, he could not influence Saleem's father to change his mind. Saleem would hear them talking and arguing, but in the end, neither Father nor Uncle succeeded in changing the other's political views.

CHAPTER 10

The long awaited month of August 1947 finally arrived. This was the time when the British were officially transferring power to the local leaders. Pakistan came into existence on August 14, and India got its status as an independent nation on August 15. For many, this was a day of celebration. Saleem was happy for his father that his dream of an independent Muslim nation, Pakistan, was fulfilled in his lifetime. However, what followed was the most uncertain period of his life.

Since Saleem's family had actively campaigned for the formation of Pakistan, they were not considered friends of the Indian government and were labeled as adversaries. Although there were no specific rules, the majority of Hindus wanted all those who had supported the partition of India to leave the country and move to Pakistan.

The pro and con mentality sparked new waves of violence all over North India as well as in Pakistan. The harassed minorities were slaughtered by the thousands. To escape the atrocities, people were trying to relocate to more secure regions. Ruthless hateful crowds stopped the trains in isolated areas and butchered men, women and children without mercy. These passengers were cut down regardless of their age and gender. People who did not believe in killing killed; people who needed no protection died protecting their loved ones. Madness had taken over. The worst of the worst came out in the best.

Aliens in their own country, Saleem's family became the target of racial and religious slurs. Where his father was once a man of influence, he now became a person besieged with animosity and hate. The very people who had enjoyed his generosity turned against him, with the exception of his friend, Mr. Rao Singh and his kin, who never wavered and supported his friend and his family during the worst of times.

A large number of Muslims who lived in Saleem's town were poor and uneducated. His father knew that the poorest of them were the most vulnerable. As if he had a calling, he felt that he should lend support and help them to organize themselves. Most of these people had voted against the formation of Pakistan. They had followed their religious leaders who did not approve of Jinah because of his secular Western ways. During this period of madness, political views no longer had any significance. Religion was the dominant element that alienated the communities. The safety or peril of one's life now depended on which religion one was born into—merely by an accident of nature.

One Hindu faction in town stood fiercely against Muslims. This group of extremists gained strength through airing news of the latest atrocities committed in the new country of Pakistan against the local Hindu population. They were preaching hate and wanted to get rid of the Muslims from amongst them—from an India that now stood split because of them.

"When Muslims came and occupied this country, they converted many of the local population to their religion. Let us now bring them all back to their original faith!" said one Hindu leader. "They cannot hide. We can always tell where they are. They look different because most of them grow beards. We can even tell those who shave by the clothes they wear. The ones who shave and wear Western clothes, we will pull their pants down and check what they are hiding. You know what I am talking about...?"

"Their circumcision!" a voice boomed from the crowd and everyone laughed.

These people wanted to take India back to where she was centuries ago, when the Hindu culture and religion dominated the area. A sizeable portion of the Hindu population supported this ideology. These trends troubled Saleem's father. Through his life experiences, he had learned that the evil forces resonate and feed on bad times. And these were bad times indeed.

Recognizing the uncertainty of the situation, Saleem's father met with small groups of Muslims regularly and advised them to spread the word that everyone should avoid travel, stay in town and be vigilant.

"You and your family are not safe away from home. You especially do not want to be on a train these days. Trains have turned into death traps for many people. Staying together makes us safer. Let us stay home and hope bad times will be over soon." He told them. "These times will pass—time always moves on," he would always add.

To boost their morale, Saleem's father would always point out that this town was once a peaceful place to live. Now, the region was going through a period of turmoil. Outsiders had moved in and were inciting the local population and preaching hate. Although he knew that not all the hate mongers were from outside, he still tried to emphasize that the local people were good people. "You have lived and worked in harmony with your friends and neighbors, and one day you shall again live with them in tranquility."

Mr. Rao Singh, a prominent Hindu in the community, because of his friendship with Saleem's father, was an important link between the two religious groups. He was largely responsible in reducing tension and promoting peace in town.

Saleem's father had considered moving to Pakistan for the safety of his family, but he decided to stay until the situation improved. Everything he owned was located in this region, and he knew that the government would not let him sell his properties and take the money with him. Without the resources, he would not be able to provide for and educate his children. Education of his children and welfare of his family were of foremost importance to him. Furthermore, he felt he had a certain responsibility toward the locals in general, and the Muslim population in particular.

CHAPTER 11

Saleem's father was unaware that his name was in certain government files where he was marked as one of those who actively supported the division of India, and hence labeled as an enemy of the state.

One day, to his surprise, police showed up at his house and the inspector presented him with papers signed by the highest district authority to search his house. He was to declare any arms that may be in his home. On this form, he put down a twelve-gauge double-barrel gun and a twenty-two-caliber rifle that he used for hunting. He had a government-issued license for both. He and the police inspector knew each other well. The inspector, a Hindu, treated his father with respect. The search was not viscous, but it was never revealed what they were looking for. When the search was over, he left with the weapons.

The day the police searched the house, Saleem's mother felt not only violated, but also disgraced and humiliated. The security wall the family thought was around them—a wall that no one else but they themselves had built by their social and economic stature—crumbled that day. Their home was no more their castle. Strangers who trampled the peace and quiet of their lives seem to have legal power to do so again whenever they chose or wanted. The doors now could be pushed open by the strangers who would not only walk around freely but get into the privacy of homeowners and look at them as if they were naked, stripped of dignity and respect just because they had aligned with a cause different than those now in authority. Some had become powerful by sucking it out of those who were now powerless.

This episode devastated the little confidence the family had in the present system and the people who were now in position of influence. The guns in the house, an umbrella of protection for the family, were gone now. Saleem's mother believed that the authorities had treated them like criminals, although they were the voice of peace in town. She wished that her husband had not been active in politics, so the family would not have to undergo this humiliation. But it was too late now. And after she calmed down, she had to admit that she had given him and his cause her full support.

A couple of days after the house search, Saleem noticed a crowd of people in front of the police station as he was coming home from school. He found it to be unusual for he passed the station daily on his way to school and back. As he got closer, he recognized several of the men in the crowd. Most of them were his father's friends. He saw his father sitting in the courtyard of the station talking with police officers. Saleem did not give it much thought, as his father was in the habit of discussing with them about his efforts to keep the town safe and, besides, he was a friend of the police inspector.

Saleem lingered a moment and was about to turn away when a man came up to him and said, "Nothing to worry about, everything will be fine." Wondering what it meant, Saleem walked home and one look at his mother's face told him that not everything was fine at all. He could tell that she had cried. She sat down with him and gave him something to eat. While he was eating, she told him that his father had been arrested and would have to stay in prison until he would sign an oath of loyalty to the government of India and an apology for his political views. Saleem and his mother both knew that his father was not going to do either one of these things. The situation was unsettling for the family, but Saleem's mother put up a bold face and told him that the family would endure and survive.

Saleem's father argued with those who had powers to enforce the law that he had not done anything illegal. His efforts, since India became independent, had been nothing but trying to maintain peace in town. He only espoused political activities that were legal. He felt he should not be singled out to sign an oath of loyalty, if the general population was not required to do the same, but he never got a chance to argue his case in the court of law.

Mr. Rao Singh tried to impress upon the local authorities that it was important for his friend to be freed in order to preserve calm in town. He was told that it was out of their hands. The following day, Saleem's father was moved from the local police station to a detention center thirty miles away from his hometown. One section of this prison housed mainly political detainees. The majority of people in town, Muslims and Hindus, thought that the arrest was unfair. Many Hindus did not like Saleem's father; they felt that he represented those who advocated splitting of the country. In spite of this, they all admired him for his courage and for what he had done to preserve a sense of tranquility in town.

During this trying time, Mr. Rao Singh staunchly supported his friend. He visited Saleem's mother every day to see if she needed anything. This he did without fail until the day Saleem's father was released to come home. Saleem's mother did not require any assistance in running her household, but it was reassuring to know that her husband had a loyal friend whom she could count on in case of emergency. The only change Saleem noticed in his mother was that she did not laugh anymore and was praying more regularly now. Saleem thought she was hoping to get in touch with a God she could not see but strongly believed in. She was either seeking divine intervention for the release of her husband or asking for strength to survive this ordeal.

Two other prominent Muslims in that district were also in prison with similar political charges to Saleem's father. During this time of isolation and hardship, the three had bonded in friendship. After two months of confinement, one of them signed the papers, which included the oath of loyalty and the apology for his political activities. He was let go. Before he left, he tried to persuade Saleem's father to do the same. He boasted of his connections on both sides of the border that would make it easy for the two of them to move out from India to Pakistan safely with their families and all of their belongings. In Pakistan, some of his friends occupied important government positions; these friends should be able to assist him and his friend to establish in the new country.

"Every new country is a land of opportunities…especially if you know the right people. And I know the right people. Having been imprisoned for supporting the creation of Pakistan, we will be treated as heroes," he whispered as he was leaving.

Saleem's father declined. He planned to visit Pakistan one day and was proud to have contributed, in whatever modest way, to its creation. However, he felt that signing these documents would be an admission that he had done something wrong. It was against his principles to admit to wrongdoing for a cause he believed in with all his heart. He would remain in jail and wait until someone would come to reason and would let him go home.

Saleem's father wound up spending six months in confinement. Prison took its toll. He lost weight. He ate foods he was not accustomed to and slept on the floor. The people in power thought that hardship would break his spirit and that he would do as asked. However, they had underestimated his conviction and strength of character, which Saleem's father was known for. He was a stubborn man who did not intend to sacrifice his principles. He often said that a hardship could only hurt you if you let it. For him to endure a hardship was a sacrifice he would make to uphold his principles.

Saleem's father was still in prison when a militant Hindu extremist whose religion enjoined him not to eat meat because it involved killing of animals, hated Gandhi's conciliatory policies toward Muslims and Pakistan to a point that he felt no remorse or guilt when he gunned him down. The news shocked the nation. The public began to realize that the violence and inciting of hatred had gotten out of hand. It had claimed the life of a revered pacifist, the man who was the real father of the independent Indian nation. Many cried, but for a few it was a time to rejoice.

Deeply disturbed over this tragedy, the government of India woke up from its passive mode and started to deal with the hostilities. Change was in the air. Random killings subsided. It was as if someone had dropped water on a wildfire. The fire that was burning all around the nation was quenched by the blood of one man. Unashamed, some claimed "mission accomplished."

Together with the support of Mr. Rao Singh and help from the tutor, Saleem's mother was able to run the household without change of routine. Saleem's schooling went on uninterrupted. Most of his classmates at school knew that his father was in prison, but they never brought it up. And those who used to say that he and his family should leave India and go to Pakistan, stopped doing that as well. With time, the state of extreme tension slowly gave way to a degree of normalcy in its new form.

Muslims were always a minority in the area Saleem grew up. Only when India became independent did he understand what it meant to belong to a group with little control and no power. In the new India, Saleem felt more insecure. He was no longer safe in certain areas of town. Things had changed—something he felt but could not intellectually explain. He sensed he no longer belonged where he lived.

He reasoned with fear that the people who put his father in prison might do the same to him or anyone else they did not like. He wished he were somewhere else. He wanted to feel safe again. He understood that the income from their various properties was the family's sole means of support. Moving to Pakistan meant losing all they had.

With time, Saleem had learned to live with hostilities, which would jump out at him most unexpectedly, especially in school. Two friends he made the very first day he attended school, the two boys, Suresh and Ram, who sat next to him in the class, stayed his friends even in the bad times. Among other fellow students, he observed a spectrum of attitudes. Those who were his casual friends now avoided him and some who never liked him were now openly hostile. They would talk among themselves and say things that Saleem found offensive. And they wanted him to hear what they were saying.

He was aware that he was not physically strong enough to win a fight against those who were always challenging him. He also knew that if he ever decided to confront, it would not be one on one; it would be him against many. He felt unsafe after school hours when teachers were no longer responsible for his wellbeing. The instinct for survival now controlled his mind and to protect himself he desperately wanted to make friends with Hindu students. He wanted to learn and mimic their ways. But his pride would get in his way and not allow him to do any of those things. His insecurities at certain times, unconsciously made him act in a manner that could be interpreted as an appeasement of the majority around him. His mere trend of thoughts, his unintended sense of capitulation made him uncomfortable. He was frustrated as he was brought to bear more and more hardships in his young life and he could do nothing to change it. Most of his problems he blamed on his minority affiliations. To weather it all meant that he had no choice but to learn to live with it.

CHAPTER 12

The new government of independent India passed new laws. The abolition of the *Zamindari* system was the first legislation that affected Saleem's family. In this system, a typical *zamindar* like Saleem's father owned large parcels of land, leased it to the farmers and paid a land tax to the government. The British had inherited this system from the Mogul era and retained it as a way to collect taxes from the peasantry.

With passage of this new regulation, complete control of the land went to the farmers. Saleem's family lost ownership of their leased land, which was the family's main source of income. In return, the government paid the *Zamindars* like Saleem's father, a meager sum, a fraction of the value of the land, in bonds payable over forty years. In short, the landowners, who were affluent property owners during the British rule, could no longer maintain their former lifestyle of privilege and ease. Times were changing and so was Saleem's life.

Saleem's mother, being a wise woman, adapted to the new conditions. Monetary worries were dealt with in a way that the children's lives were least affected. Finances were never discussed in front of the children and their education remained the primary goal of the parents, just as before.

To cut expenses, changes were made in the household. Saleem's mother took on the responsibility of preparing food when the cook of many years was dismissed. The woman who came to sweep the floor and clean the house continued working, but the boy who used to run errands and went to the market to buy fresh vegetables was let go. Not that the family was destitute, they were just not as prosperous as they used to be.

To reduce expenses further, his father did consider getting rid of the tutor, but because of his interest in his children's education and since over time, Mr. Mahmood had become a part of the family, he could not bring himself to do that. The tutor was aware of how the situation had changed, so he started helping out with chores outside the house. Thus, everyone sacrificed, and conformed to the economic changes in their lives.

As time passed, the ethnic tensions between the two communities subsided, but did not go away. After the partition of India, the violence that engulfed his surroundings, the harsh realities of the hostile world and the insecurities in his life stole Saleem's childhood away from him. He no longer enjoyed the things he used to. His father still bought him new shoes for special occasions, but they did not excite him anymore; he now looked at them as a piece of clothing that needed replacing periodically. His cherished festivals, the reason to feast and a chance to celebrate with the family and friends, lost their luster. Eid, a festival that was celebrated with new clothes for everyone, toys for children, and presents in the form of money, fell during the period when Father was in prison. That year there was no feast, and gloom replaced the celebrations. Within a year of the partition of India, the sense of wellbeing he felt during the early years had left him and he felt unprotected and insecure. All that happiness in his life belonged to a different era, the era of his childhood, which seemed buried somewhere far away in the past. And he was only ten years old. He tried in vain to bring back those days when the little things were a source of joy.

He was aware of the changes that had taken place since the British left, but he did not understand why they affected him the way they did. Then it occurred to him that he must have suddenly grown older.

To Saleem, older people never seemed to get excited about things and they did not appear to enjoy events to the same degree the children did. Now, as he was growing up, he started to understand what older people missed in their lives. He was somewhere in between his childhood and his adulthood. As a result, he could no longer have fun with things children enjoyed, yet he was not old enough to sit down and discuss the political issues and the problems of life and humanity with his elders. As his parents discouraged his going out of the home for security reasons, he had time on his hands, and his mind, when he was not tutored, would wander beyond the borders of reality and travel into the imagined future, which with his limited life experiences was carved out of books. The storybooks of fantasy turned real in his mind. Knowing well they were far from true, his mental agility, his visualization, created a world, maybe unreal, but fascinating. His thoughts would soar into the future, which lay far away from the turmoil of the land he lived in and thus the seed was put in his mind that would take him to places far away from where he was born. Reading he enjoyed, and it became his new world and an escape from the current despondency.

His favorite book was *Bahadree Ke Quissay* (*Stories of the Brave*). They were about a man called Rostam who was so powerful that he was never defeated. He fought evil on the side of righteousness. He had arrows, which could find the enemy no matter where they were; his sword could cut through any armor the opponent wore, and his horse could outrun any beast that challenged it. He conquered evil, as it appeared in the form of dragons and snakes. He walked through burning forests and stormy deserts. He singlehandedly defeated the armies of invaders. Saleem knew that these were all tall tales. Still, they inspired him. Rostam was his hero. He wished he had Rostam on his side, especially when certain people were threatening him or his family.

When Saleem was not studying, he would sit in the kitchen and watch his mother cook. She always let him taste a tiny portion of whatever she was cooking. Usually, it was a piece of spicy meat, or if she was preparing vegetables to cook, she would ask him to wash them for her. As he cleaned carrots, cauliflower and peas, he would nibble on them and wonder why they need to be cooked—to him they tasted better raw. While mother and son were doing these kitchen chores, he was able to absorb much of life's wisdom from his mother's stories—the things he would not ever learn in any classroom.

Occasionally, a worker would come and repair things in the house. Saleem noticed that his mother always asked about the cost of materials and labor before she allowed the person to start. Once the price was agreed upon and the task completed, she would have the money ready and pay him. She told Saleem, "A worker should be paid immediately after he completes his work. That way, on one hand he is happy that he got money to buy food for his family, and you, on the other hand, do not have to worry if you have enough to pay him.

Remember this Saleem, it is a good principle because it makes the people who work for you happy, and that will bring joy in your life."

Saleem was a bank of his parents' knowledge and they used it as repository whenever they had a chance. As a result he accumulated know-how that comes only through experience.

CHAPTER 13

With time things changed and Saleem began to feel safer in school, revived his friendship with some of his old friends, his Hindu classmates who were now more responsive. His teachers were nice to him for he worked hard and did well in class. Periodically, when the test results were announced, Saleem's name always came up in the second place, whereas his friend Suresh would be in the first position. This was a constant source of frustration for Saleem. In one of his exams, he noticed that he had scored ninety-six in math, but the teacher had lowered it to ninety, which put him once again in second place.

When he confronted his teacher about the unfair grading, he was told that he had solved the problem with a method different from the one taught in class. Although his method allowed him to find the correct answer, it was inferior to the one he was supposed to use. In his heart, Saleem knew that was truly unfair; he felt victimized. In his mind, he should have been rewarded not punished for his innovation, but he did not want to argue and accepted the teacher's explanation.

No matter how hard he worked, or how clearly he understood the subjects, he could never reach the desired pinnacle, the first position in his class. When he complained to his mother, she said, "We know you are the best." But that was not good enough for him. He wanted to receive his deserved recognition in front of his peers and teachers, but it would not happen. The gods must be against him, he thought.

During the summer vacation, Saleem kept on going to his Aunt Raisa's house. He had a chance to go visit different places where the uncle's work took him—to the smaller towns where he was a part of the police force now. Raisa's husband enjoyed Saleem's company and he would take him along when he was going out on short trips. Saleem was twelve years old when his uncle invited him on a hunting trip with friends. Saleem was excited and could hardly wait for the night to fall when the party would depart. When all the hunters had arrived, they piled into small bullock carts, two men plus a driver per vehicle. Saleem and his uncle shared one cart and the caravan got under way. Everyone, except for Saleem and the cart-drivers, had a shotgun. The way they were acting, it became obvious that the men planned to hunt all night long. That was exciting for Saleem—for him it was a great adventure—a first in his young life.

Slowly, they moved through the countryside. Although there was a half moon, it got dark and very quiet. No one was talking. The only sound was the dirt crunching under the wheels of the carts sluggishly moving on the bumpy unpaved road. The hunters had brought long powerful flashlights, which they started to shine into the shadows of the wilderness. Saleem had never seen eyes of an animal at night before. To see them glow in the dark like two burning candles when light reflected on them was unnerving, but the most amazing sight he had ever known.

As they chugged along, the beam of the flashlight suddenly reflected two sparkling big eyes from the bushes not so far away. The eyes of a beast were staring back at them, Saleem thought. The men whispered amongst themselves, trying to identify the animal. All of them, the experienced hunters, could not decide what they were looking at.

"The eyes are big and too far apart, so it cannot be a small one," said one.

"Could it be a tiger?" the other asked.

"No, tigers' eyes are red," retorted another.

The carts had come to a full halt now and everyone was busily guessing what kind of an animal they had encountered. Due to the size of the eyes, they finally agreed, it had to be a tiger. They had not brought any rifles with them, and they all agreed it would be hard to kill a tiger with a shotgun. If they all fired at the same time, they could kill an elephant, someone suggested. Saleem was listening and thinking about a book he recently read, *Man-Eaters of Kumaon,* by Jim Corbett. The writer was an avid hunter who had been commissioned by the Indian government to kill the man-eating tigers. In his book, Corbett had described vivid scenes of trying to chase a tiger while, at the same time the tiger was stealthily trying to ambush him. He pointed out several instances wherein a wounded tiger would ferociously attack the hunter.

Saleem's roving imagination was now on the loose. Now he could see the entire body of the creature, including the tail and the stripes on his back. A growl or a roar he was expecting any minute. Thinking of an injured tiger attacking their party was making him nervous. Scared, he sat there with his uncle. Still, somewhere inside was the feeling of the tingling adventure he had never lived through before. He wished the hunting party would decide against firing at the wild animal and look for something else to hunt. He kept quiet. He knew that no one wanted his input. A child among grownups was, at best, tolerable. But a child with suggestions might be unacceptable. He quietly hoped and prayed that they would all move on.

The hunters kept the light fixed on the eyes lest the animal moved away and get lost. At one point he half expected them to start shooting, but their reluctance to confront the beast, if it did not die, kept them mulling. All talk and no action of these so-called experts proved annoying to this object of interest mesmerized by the beam of light. It got up. To Saleem's surprise, what he thought was a ferocious tiger with stripes turned out to be a harmless cow standing quietly in the bushes, wagging its tail.

A heavy silence fell upon the group. In the distance an owl hooted as if making fun of the hunters. Finally, someone spoke, "You don't know how happy I am that you guys decided not to fire your guns. It would be hard to explain a dead cow riddled with gun shots in the morning."

"What do you mean…you guys? You were the one who suggested we all fire at the same time," said another.

Saleem's uncle realized that everyone was as embarrassed as he was and started to laugh. They all joined in and the tension melted into amusement. The drivers got the carts moving again and they were on their way to the next adventure.

Finally, they came upon some deer. This time there was no doubt as to what they were looking at. Even Saleem, who was no expert, could tell what was before him staring back at the shining beam. The hunters were able to shoot one of them. They cleaned up their trophy and secured it at the back of one of the carts. They had come quite a distance and hoped to make it back home by dawn. So they turned the carts around and drove back at their usual leisurely pace.

It was quiet and dark all around. The moon that was shining earlier was gone and the stars of varied sizes and brightness now decorated the sky. In the starlight, he could see the outline of the trees in distance and quiet all around—a novel experience for a twelve year old. The grownups in the convoy were missing this display of nature, or they did not seem to care; Saleem noticed some had dozed off. The hunting trip had been a success.

In the distant horizon, Saleem noticed a glow of light. The darkness of the night was fading away. From his geography class, he knew that in some far away land, the sun was preparing to set, just as it was getting ready to bring daylight to the land where he was now. His uncle told him, "It will be at least two more hours until the sun comes out. In the early hours, we may see some partridges. This will be an opportunity for all of us to get off the carts, stretch our legs and walk a little, and shoot some birds." He suddenly looked at him and said, "Saleem, you are old enough now to use a gun. Let's see in the morning, if you can hit what you are aiming at."

Saleem was excited. *So, the hunt isn't over yet,* he thought. He had wanted to fire a gun for some time. He craved to get the feel of it against his shoulder. It would be such an adult thing to do, he thought.

The caravan of carts crept along the dirt road, carved by generations who had traveled this path before to their fields, used this course to transport produce and bring back wood from the forest.

Gradually, the stars were losing their brightness; the smaller ones in the east disappearing first, their faint light swallowed by rising sun. Saleem now could see his surroundings. Trees, the dry fields, and grass surrounded him. The grass was brown and the earth parched— monsoon season had not started yet. In the distance Saleem could hear a rooster crow, announcing the dawning of a new day.

Saleem figured Muslims were living in the village nearby. He had taught himself to notice little things around him, as it might one day save his life. The rooster meant that there would also be chicken and eggs. Only Muslims ate eggs. Hindus living in rural areas were strictly vegetarians. They did not eat chicken or the eggs.

There was a little padding lining the cart, but Saleem could not sleep. The ride was too bumpy and uncomfortable. Also, he did not want to miss out on anything that he might see. Soon everyone in the group was getting alert.

Birds had started chirping and he could see some were now flying. Then he heard one partridge calling another. For the hunters, this call meant there was something worth shooting in the area. They all got off their carts. Saleem's uncle gave him his gun and told him how never to point it toward another person and keep the barrel facing down. They all walked in a file. A partridge was in the air; one of the hunters took a shot and missed. The uncle told everyone that it was now Saleem's turn to shoot. Saleem, accompanied by his uncle was now walking a little ahead of everyone.

His uncle gave some last minute instructions about how to hold the gun. "Your hold has to be firm, against your shoulder and against your cheek, when you are trying to aim. Make sure the gun is held firmly," he emphasized the last word once more, "otherwise it will recoil and hurt your shoulder and your jaw."

Saleem was impatient. He already knew all this, but he still appreciated his uncle's concern for safety.

A partridge took off in front of him. He aimed, but his moves were too slow and unsure. Before he could get it in his sight, it was too far gone to shoot. His uncle told him that there was nothing to worry about and suggested that he fire once in the air, just to get the feel of it. Saleem raised the barrel of his gun toward the sky, the butt pressed against his shoulder, holding it as firmly as he could aim at nothing, and pressed the trigger. He heard a loud thud, his eyes flinched. It was much louder than when others had fired their guns. He felt the kick against his shoulder and against his jaw. It felt as if the smooth wooden stock was trying to leap out of his grip. He held it there. He had fired his first shot and he was thrilled!

The blast was noisy and several birds flew out of the bushes. One of them was a partridge. One of the hunters shot it just as it took off. It came down like a stone, straight to the ground. The hunter felt good; a partridge was dead.

The sun had come out now and it was time to go home before it got too hot. They all went back to their carts and the drivers coaxed the bullocks into action once again. On their way back Saleem thought about his experiences during the night; he recalled how he watched the excitement of a possible tiger hunt that fizzled out. He remembered the killing of a deer, which lay on one of the carts, and how a partridge's life was cut short by a gun. Overall, he was happy to have participated in the all-night hunt and that he could fire his first shot.

When they got home, Aunt Raisa was expecting them. She suggested that they should bathe and then have breakfast. Breakfast consisted of eggs, some freshly prepared *parathas*, the fried flat bread, and tea. Both Saleem and his uncle were tired and hungry and everything tasted good. Afterwards, Saleem fell into a fitful sleep and did not wake up until his aunt called him to afternoon tea.

CHAPTER 14

With the new independence, times changed in India and so did the education system in his school. The authorities eliminated Urdu, a language mainly spoken by the Muslim population, from the curriculum and Saleem was asked to learn Hindi instead. He had learned the Hindi alphabet earlier, but now he had to learn to read books in the Hindi language. The stories he had to read were about the Hindu mythology and their gods. Saleem wondered if the new system was trying to teach him a language or if it intended to convert him to the Hindu religion. Whoever had picked these books as part of the program definitely did not even pretend to be secular. They were teaching him religion in a non-parochial school. In the beginning, he disliked these lessons, but soon the stories became fairy tales to him and he started to enjoy them.

At home, they all spoke Urdu, the language of their culture, but it was not very different from spoken Hindi. In fact, they were so similar that the spoken language in the area was a mixture of the two, and understood by everyone. Since the structure of the sentences and most words in Hindi and Urdu were the same, he quickly discovered how to substitute a few words in his sentences to convert them from one language to the other. Many of his friends in school were Hindus and they were constantly using Hindi words in their speech. And as he started to pay attention, he was able to speak Hindi in no time. However, the scripts of the two languages were entirely different. Urdu script, derived from Farsi, was written from right to left, whereas the base of Hindi script was Sanskrit, which was written from left to right. With some practice and his knowledge of the alphabet, he soon was able to read and write the Hindi language.

By the time Saleem was in the tenth grade, the highest grade in school, all students in lower classes knew him by name. The younger boys looked up to the students of the uppermost class in school with awe, and he felt as if he was now one of the gods in the land of little people. Even teachers treated the tenth graders with certain respect. He found it thrilling that finally he was a member of the elite, the senior most class. At this point, he was completely oblivious to the fact that he would soon be at the bottom again upon entering college.

When Saleem was preparing for the final examination to earn his high school diploma, he knew that this exam would be conducted by the Board of Education and not by the school itself. Since the United Province, which was now *Uttar Pradesh*, was the most populous state in India, the Board of Education tested thousands of students. He, along with the other students was assigned a roll number, which he was to use on his answer books instead of his name. These notebooks had numbered pages and each page was stamped. The teachers with undisclosed names prepared the questions and the Board, for grading anonymously, picked the teachers at random and never disclosed their names. A lot of planning and work went into this examination. And keeping everything secret added to its importance and the mystery that surrounded it.

As the day of the final test approached, the preparations to take the exam got underway at school and at home. Saleem's class arranged to have a Hindu ceremony to bless all the students. Saleem, who was the only non-Hindu student in the class, decided to stay there and be a member of the group as a passive participant. He sat in the back as a quiet spectator. They had a Brahmin come over and recite Sanskrit mantras while everyone sat around a fire lighted especially for this purpose. The ceremony lasted over an hour and the Pundit blessed all the students to get good grades. At home, his parents got him new pens and pencils. His mother prayed for him, but then she always did.

The *SCHEME* was finally announced. This was the schedule of high school examinations, which students had to follow all over the state. Under the supervision of teachers, the school's employees cleaned the desks and arranged them in rows with some distance in-between to minimize cheating during this trial of evaluation. Each desk had a small paper pasted on the top right hand corner with a roll number. This was the desk where the student with the assigned number would sit and take all his tests. The list of roll numbers was posted on each classroom door which was kept locked. A day before the examinations started, Saleem went to school to find out where he would be sitting.

Finally, the important day arrived. Saleem got to school early that morning. The doors were unlocked ten minutes before nine o'clock, the time when the test papers were handed to the students. Saleem found his desk and sat there with his eyes closed to get rid of the jitters. His ten tests were spread over a two-week period and covered languages, sciences, math, history, geography, agriculture and general knowledge. Once the examinations got started, everyone was busy and the days passed in a hurry. The grueling two weeks of tests were finally over. On the last day, as he said good-bye to his high school he felt the ending of an era in his life. Once at home reflecting on his performance in the examinations, Saleem thought he had done well. Summer vacation started for all the tenth graders. This year, instead of going to his Aunt Raisa's house, he decided to stay at home and wait for the results.

It took a month for the whole process of grading the notebooks and compiling the data. A special evening edition of the newspaper was to announce the results. One evening, Saleem learned that the anxiously awaited special edition had come out and was available on the street. He and his whole family were keen to find out how he did. Mr. Rao Singh had gotten hold of a copy and was bringing it to Saleem's house when he encountered the boy and his tutor who were on their way to buy the paper. Saleem was nervous, but he wanted to look for his roll number right at that moment. The numbers were printed in rows in small print. And there were pages and pages of them. Fortunately, there was an order to them. In the mean time, it got dark. They all stood by the street light and started to look for 71181. A number he could never forget. It was etched on his mind.

Saleem was tense. With every passing moment his heart beat harder and suddenly he felt anxious, and his mouth was dry. This was the most important examination of his whole life. At last, they saw the number they were looking for! The letter F stood in front of it. When he saw that F, his heart missed a beat or two; he thought he had failed. His tutor, however, pointed out that those who fail do not get their roll numbers printed; F meant the First Division.

Mr. Mahmood was excited and almost shouted, "Look, Saleem there is also a small m in front of F. This means you earned distinction in Mathematics."

They all started patting his back. Whosoever passed by wanted to know how Saleem had fared. When they learned that he had passed the examination with First Division and distinction in Math, there was quite a celebration right on the street. Mr. Singh thought they all should go home and let the parents know, because they were waiting to find out as well. They should be informed immediately.

They quickly walked home to bring the good news. That evening everyone was full of praise for Saleem and congratulated him again and again on his good work. Saleem was embarrassed for receiving all this attention, but in his heart he was happy that he had made his parents proud of him.

"Tomorrow we will distribute sweets to celebrate and announce the good news to our neighbors, friends and relatives," his mother announced.

"Many people already know about the result. A lot of them were there when we were looking at the newspaper on the street". Saleem told his mother.

On the following day, the proud parents ordered sweets to be distributed to friends and relatives. They were so happy about their son's achievement; they wanted everyone to know. Some relatives even sent money to him. Saleem felt he was smart and was happy that the Board of Education recognized his ability this time by placing him in the top 1% of thousands of students who took that examination.

CHAPTER 15

Going to college was the next step in climbing the stairs of his life. It was not optional; it was part of the process of living his life charted out by his parents; the details they needed to work out. In his case, he knew where the step was; he also knew he had to climb it, but where this step would take him was the decision his parents would make. It was their job to decide what he would study and where he would study it.

Saleem's parents, especially his father, started considering different colleges for him to attend. Choices included a University in Aligarh, the Aligarh Muslim University, where the majority of students were Muslims. A man called Sir Sayed Ahmad Khan established this institution fashioned on the model of Cambridge and Oxford. He was one of the very few Muslim leaders in India who at the very early stages of the British rule understood that people of his religion should be exposed to the Western ways and get an English education. He had successfully campaigned and convinced the British to help him start a college where Muslims could learn English. Mohammedan Anglo-Oriental College was thus born and over a period evolved into a full university with many different faculties. For his vision, the British Crown knighted him.

Orthodox Muslims opposed Sir Sayed's views and condemned him as a lackey of the rulers. However, in the end it benefited the entire Muslim community of North India. Some Hindu leaders did not look at it favorably because they considered it the place where the movement for the establishment of Pakistan and division of India got its beginnings. Saleem's father had emotional ties with this institution; he had contributed to the drive for its expansion and its stability.

He was, however, concerned about the quality of food served there and its effects on students' health. He surmised that, in an effort to keep the costs down, Aligarh campus would provide lower quality meals to the resident student body. In spite of his attachment to the institution, he did not want to put his son's health at risk.

The other two choices were a Christian college in Lucknow and a Christian college in Agra. After the University in Aligarh, Christian colleges were his father's second choice. In his opinion, a Christian institution would be impartial and fair to both Hindu and Muslim students and the communal rivalries would be minimal. After considering all options, St. John's College in Agra was picked for Saleem for his higher education. The college accepted him readily because of his good grades.

Saleem's mother was worried that Saleem was too young to be all alone so far away from home. But, at the same time she understood how important it was for him to go to a good college. Being away from home was an education in itself, she thought, it should teach him to take responsibility for his actions and bear the consequences if and when he made mistakes. His mother decided that it was time to let go of her son for he would have to face the world all alone eventually and his training for this task had to start at some point.

Considering all this, preparations were made for Saleem to leave for Agra. His father bought him a trunk to carry his clothes. There also was a canvas carry-all, which would contain his beddings that included a *dhurree*, a thin carpet like sheet, which was the first thing that went on the cot, white bed sheets that would go on top of the *dhurree*, and a pillow. A bed-cover to place on top when bed was not in use was also included. Saleem got new shoes, new clothes and new toiletries. Packed with all these necessities, ready to step into a new life, he boarded a train and left for the college. His tutor came to see him off at the railway station.

This was different from how he had felt when he went to get admission to his high school. He was much younger then and his parents were only a short distance away should there ever be a need. This time, he would be on his own. His parents would be supporting him, but they were not physically there to help, and a tutor would no longer be there to supervise his studies or assist him. He was to make new friends and learn to get along with different people.

His parents had decided that he should study medicine and become a doctor. Saleem did not know exactly when this decision was made. It could have been as early as when he went to high school, or even before that. He remembered hearing his parents talk about his fragile health and that they felt he should enter a profession where there was less physical stress. As a doctor, he could practice medicine in his hometown, and at the same time, look after the family properties. Circumstances had changed; there were hardly any properties left to manage. His father was no longer rich. Medical college education was expensive. Regardless of the changed situation, the idea for him to be a doctor stayed on.

As the train was approaching the city of Agra, he caught a glimpse of the Taj Mahal. A child sitting not far from Saleem seemed disappointed. He was telling his father, "You told me it was large, but it is so small… I only see a small one. There… there you see…!" His father calmly explained, "We are miles away from it. Wait till we get there." Only a small number of passengers were paying attention; not everyone was coming to Agra for the first time.

The train slowed down before it got to the main station. Railway tracks started to multiply. Soon there was a web of lines crossing each other, going in many directions. All lines were not empty, some had moving trains, and some had boxes of rail cars just standing idly as if waiting for an engine. The train slowed down considerably before it came to a halt next to a concrete platform. Saleem had finally arrived in the middle of a hot afternoon at the Agra railway station.

As he disembarked, a *coolie* (porter) helped him get his luggage out onto the paved floor. Once away from the train, he looked around and realized that this was a much bigger station than the ones he had known. It had several platforms. Passengers had to walk over bridges to go from one to another. A high metal roof sheltered part of the area where the trains came in. Originally, it might have had a metallic luster, but now it was weathered, dull and black, possibly because of the smoke and soot from the steam engines.

Saleem noticed that in spite of the summer heat, the area was bustling with activity. The passengers, some carrying their luggage on their heads, some hauling heavy loads of the trunks in their hands, their faces covered with sweat, were frantically pushing each other to get by. He saw women dressed in colorful saris and his senses were assaulted by the heavy odor of still hot humid air in a crowded area. Some people simply stood there in small groups, separated from the crowd. Those were obviously members of a family, waiting to welcome the arrival of their guests. When he looked around, there was not a face he recognized—not that he was expecting someone to welcome him—still…

A few fans hung from the ceiling lazily churning the space, doing little except mixing the air with the exhaust fumes of the steam engine that had pulled the train in. And they were doing it gently so as not to disturb anything. Nearby a bookstall exhibited books and magazines. Prominently displayed were some English magazines, such as *The Illustrated Weekly of India* a weekly news magazine and *Film Fare*, which dished out the latest gossip of Bombay's film industry. The latter was especially popular with young people. The back shelves contained English paperbacks and some Hindi books. The place was noisy and had an atmosphere of a town fair. Everyone was in such a hurry to get in the train or get out of the station that no one was paying any attention to what was going on. He thought he was unique. But no one noticed him; for them he was part of the crowd—one of them.

In a short time, the crowd thinned by the train, enabled the vendors to pander their merchandise to the remaining passengers. They shouted their slogans, their jingles, trying to sell their wares as they moved along the platform. Some were carrying food and snacks in small wooden boxes with sides of glass enabling customers to see what was being offered. Others were pushing food carts with one hand, while trying to wave the flies off with the other. In addition to all this, a tea stand sold beverages, including hot tea, soft drinks and an assortment of biscuits (cookies). Surprisingly, people were drinking hot tea in this hot weather; some who were in a hurry had poured it from the cup to the saucer to cool it down and were slurping it from there.

Some coolies, identifiable by their numbered red shirts and a turban of the same color, were bargaining with the passengers about the price for carrying their luggage out of the station. Parents were holding on to their children's hands so they would not get lost in the crowd. There was so much going on around him, it made Saleem's head swim.

The coolies knew that the young students were the ones who paid the best, since most of them had not yet learned the art of haggling. Saleem hired the coolie who had helped him bring his luggage down from the train to carry it out.

To exit the station, they had to pass through a two-door gate. One door was bolted to the ground and the other was held slightly ajar with a latch just wide enough to let people through, one person at a time. On the other side stood a man in a white uniform, wearing a white safari hat. His job was to make sure that everyone who got off the train had a valid ticket. He looked very much like the ticket-checker he had seen at the railway station in his hometown. Saleem handed him his train ticket. The man in the white uniform looked at it then looked at Saleem for a moment and nodded, which meant he could now leave the station. Saleem was one of the first to come out. Outside the train station, the scene was different. The sun was delivering its sunshine with its glory. Shade was what everyone sought and under a tree everyone wanted to be. Even the *tongawalas* were slow to move to capture a customer. Saleem, an obvious customer, had little effect on their lethargy; his coolie had to ask one of them to come over to help the arriving passenger. Heat had injected laziness in men and their horses. Beaten by heat, horses had their heads down; the only movement was their tails swishing to get rid of flies.

At that time of the day not a leaf stirred, as if at that hour their sole purpose was to provide shade and not to disturb the still air. The mood was funereal until the passengers started spewing out of the one gate manned by the ticket checker. The passengers brought with them some of the energy from inside to the outside of the train station. Prices were negotiated, some tongas were hired, and finally there was a stir in the air. Saleem was not alone haggling over the price.

Saleem settled on a price with the *tongawala* (the tonga driver) before the coolie could put the luggage in. He had never done this before and surely did not know how to bargain; still, he managed to lower the asking price. Though not by much, still he felt satisfied. The carriage had two seats in the back, facing away, and two in front by the driver. Passengers in front looked forward in the direction they were headed.

This was not his first ride in a *tonga*, but not all of these carriages were the same. The one he was riding now had plastic-covered seats. The top was also made of the same material. He assumed the synthetic material must be a sign of progress and the progress had not yet reached his small town. He preferred the cloth-covered seats, especially in summer, because they did not get as hot. He was in a big city now and things were more modern and flashy here, he thought. When he complained about the hot seat, the *tongawala* pointed out that the cover he had was cleaner than the cloth as he could wash it with soap and water frequently.

Once they started to move, it occurred to him that he was not only entering a city, he was now a grownup travelling alone—master of his own destiny. He was out of his nursery planted in an unknown forest—on his own—to grow and carve out a future in this jungle of world.

As they rode away from the railway station, his *tonga* made its way through streets crowded with people on bicycles and on foot. Scooters and motorcycles were also weaving their way through this throng. A few cars, stuck in the crowd were honking, trying in vain to carve a path among all this traffic. Saleem also noticed a few rickshaws. These were large tricycles pulled by men with seats for two in the back. Everyone was going somewhere and hoped that others would get out of the way. As a result, there was a fair amount of noise and confusion. The road was chaos in motion.

Saleem's *Tonga* passed crowded streets lined with shops on both sides and also some areas that were not so busy. Slowly, they wound their way through the shopping area, and after that, the horse trotted along at a comfortable pace. Since Saleem decided to sit in the back seat, his luggage had to be placed in front to balance the weight. Saleem had learned earlier that sitting in front did give you a good view of where you were heading, but then you ran the risk of putting up with the foul gases periodically released by the horses.

After about a half-hour ride, they finally arrived at the St. John's College campus. Saleem had been instructed by the admission office to come a few days early. He thus had time to settle in before classes started. A room had already been reserved for him in one of the hostels. He located the caretaker who was looking for the arriving students. The man walked him to the office of the warden, Mr. Paul, who turned out to be a short dark man with a crop of thick graying black hair. The office was much cooler than outside, the revolving electric fan doing its job well. The warden welcomed him as a new resident of his hostel and recited what Saleem already knew from a small handbook of the college rules sent to him along with his acceptance as a student. Mr. Paul informed him that everyone had to be back in the boarding house by nine o'clock at night. Anyone who needed to stay out after nine should inform him and seek his permission. He also explained about the eating arrangements. The residents were divided into three different dinning groups, one non-vegetarian and two vegetarian. Vegetarian groups were for Hindu students. Pundits who cooked for the vegetarians would do that exclusively for Hindus and for only those who absolutely did not eat meat. All Christian, Muslim and some Hindu students belonged to the non-vegetarian group, where food cooked with goat meat and occasional chicken was served. Looking at Saleem's name, the warden knew that the new student would automatically be a part of the non-vegetarian group.

"Meal time is six to eight at night. Time for lunch is before the classes begin, at nine in the morning. Lunchtime may seem odd, but it does not take long to get used to it. The same people who work for your dining group will also take care of cleaning your room. Since it is too hot to sleep inside during the summer; one of those workers will bring your cot outside in the evening and then take it back in the morning," Mr. Paul explained.

Saleem's roommate would be a Muslim like him. The warden avoided pairing students of different religions, or vegetarians with non-vegetarians in these double occupancy rooms. The other person assigned to his room was also a first-year student. When Saleem and Sharif met, the two young men instantly bonded when Saleem told him that his uncle had the same name. And as they talked to get to know each other, they found that they had many other things in common. They both came from small towns, had led a sheltered lives at home, and their fathers were prominent figures in their home-towns.

The room they shared was small. It was long, but not very wide. Walls and ceiling was painted white. On each side, by the wall, there was a bed—a bare cot. It was up to the occupants to put on their own bedding. There was also a chair and study desk for each student. At night, the only source of light in the room was a solitary naked forty-watt bulb hanging from the ceiling in the middle of the room. Both Saleem and Sharif decided to buy their own table lamps for studying. Two built-in shelves, one on each side of the door, provided space for books or anything else they wanted to display. Saleem and his room-mate decided to keep the books on one side and use the other side to put toothpaste, toothbrush, their shaving kits and other items they used on a daily basis. Facing the door, on the back wall of the room a window with bars poured light during the day. The bars served dual purposes, one of protecting the students from outsiders and, at the same time, keeping them in.

Walking around on the campus, he discovered he needed to cross a public road to go to the other half of the college campus. On one side of the street, was the administration building and the faculty of arts and on the other side was the faculty of science with the department of sciences and mathematics. The building was red, but Saleem could not discern whether it was made of brick or stone. The principal sat in an office located on the second floor of the main building, which was designed with domes and arches to reflect the influence of the historical Mogul architecture in Agra. It had a large window overlooking the lawn and the faculty of science across the street.

The next day, he had an interview with the principal in the morning. Nervous with anticipation Saleem waited in the secretary's office before being called inside. As he entered, he noticed Mr. Mahajan leaned to one side on the armrest of his chair as he sat facing a massive desk. He was a short bald man with thick eyebrows and glasses perched on a long curved nose. He had a deep, resonating voice and spoke English with a British accent. The principal obtained his degree from Oxford University, and for that reason MA (Oxon) always garnished his name.

Although it was summer, Mr. Mahajan wore a light grey suit and black tie. Saleem noticed numerous portraits of somber men staring at him from the office walls. He assumed they were the former guardians of the college. The principal's large office had carpet on the floor and bookshelves lined a part of the sidewalls. A lot more impressive than his headmaster's office in the high school, Saleem thought. Mr. Mahajan looked tired. He, perhaps, had talked to a number of new students before Saleem came in. The principal asked his name, what his family did and if he played any sports in high school. In the end, he asked Saleem why he chose St. John's College, to which Saleem answered that his father had actually picked it for him. He welcomed Saleem and wished him good luck. As he was leaving, Mr. Mahajan asked, "You are going to live in the hostel?"

The tone of principal's voice should have cued Saleem in that it was a question. Saleem did not realize that it was; he thought the principal was approving his staying on campus to which his response was, "Thank you."

The principal did not quite understand the answer and repeated his question. Saleem was confused and thanked him again.

Mr. Mahajan was puzzled at first and then all of a sudden realized that he was talking to someone who was not used to spoken English. He rephrased the sentence and asked, "Are you going to stay in the hostel?"

Now, Saleem's eyes brightened as he realized that the statement was a question. "Yes Sir, I am going to stay in the hostel," he answered.

The principal found the incident amusing, smiled, got up and shook Saleem's hand. The whole experience was very different from his first encounter with Sharma Gee. The principal did not seem to mind when Saleem answered all the questions looking directly into his eyes.

Life in the hostel was different than living at home. He learned to eat with spoons and forks. In St. John's College, the manners were foreign to him, but he had learned to adapt as a child. He had, earlier in high school, adapted to the Hindu customs; he was now adapting to the ways of an Anglo-Indian institution.

Everyone gathered in the assembly hall to start the day at ten o'clock in the morning. The male students took their place on the benches on the ground floor and the girls sat on the balcony. Mr. Mahajan in his resonating voice would recite a philosophical inspirational passage. If there were any announcements to be made, the principal would read them in the morning assembly after which everyone went to their classrooms.

In St. John's College, Saleem experienced the coeducational system for the first time. He, like other boys of his age, liked the girls, but he was nervous and shy around them. For most girls in his class, he noticed, it was no different. It was also their first time to be studying with boys—boys they had never met or seen before.

The assimilation of boys and girls was hard on both sexes, especially for the first year students. Realizing that social contact between the teenage boys and the girls, even in families, was uncommon in the Indian culture, the unwritten college regulation endorsed by the society made them sit in different rows in the classroom. The girls would stay outside by the door and only enter when the teacher arrived, even then, they would sit in the front row—first row seats were reserved for girls.

The novel environment had boys and girls fantasize about each other and Saleem was no exception. That was a major distraction

to him and most other students as well. Soon, Saleem made friends
with some of the classmates who sat next to him in the lectures. Their
common bond—the girls fascinated them. They talked about young
women on the campus as if that was the most important thing in their
lives and if there was another, they were unaware of it. Within a short
time, Saleem knew every detail about all the girls in his class and to
some degree all the good-looking young women on campus. To the
dismay of Saleem and his friends, the girls made up only about one
fifth of the student population on the campus and the good-looking
girls were few. Most of the boys enjoyed talking about the girls, but
they were not yet ready to talk to them.

Life in the hostel was different. The majority of the young men
who resided in his hostel were not new to this college. Gradually,
Saleem got to know all those who lived close to his room and he
made friends with those who ate with him. Once settled in the new
surroundings, he and some his new friends decided to go and visit
the Taj Mahal, the august marble building the town was recognized
for. This was one of those Seven Wonders of the World he had read
about in school when he had just started. Now, he was living only a
few miles away. Anxious to see this wonder-of-the-world that everyone had heard about, they rented bicycles on a Sunday morning and
headed to the historical monument. It was amazing to experience
the way they lost sight of the building the closer they got.

They parked their bicycles outside the main gate guarded by an
attendant. The outer gate opened into a yard filled with noisy vendors. It felt as if they were in a bazaar. They pushed their way through
people hawking trinkets and souvenirs until they came to a large gate
that was the main entrance to the mausoleum. And there it was it in
its entire splendor: The Taj Mahal! It took Saleem's breath away. The
pictures he had seen so many times in the magazines and books; still
he was unprepared for the real thing and the sense of awe that swept
over him as he stood there, taking it all in.

The huge building felt alive. Set in white stone it stood with all its
majesty and stunning grandeur guarded by sentinels of four tall mina-
rets. To describe his experience, he would have to find words he did
not know. He just stood there, letting it wash over him and penetrate
his senses. He was dwarfed by the sensation that over the generations,
scores of people had stood and walked where he was now and many of
them probably had had the same experience and similar feelings that

he sensed at that point. As in a dream, he finally heard his name called by his friends who had already moved ahead and did not want to leave him behind. As he ambled toward the majestic building, he felt as if he was shrinking and the Taj Mahal was getting larger and larger.

He thought that certain things in this world were beautiful in their entirety, and definitely, the Taj Mahal was one of them. Engraved in the walls inlaid with black marble were intricate flower patterns and Arabic writings from the scriptures. And as impressive as the artful details were, they gave way to the overall awe-inspiring presence the entire structure radiated toward its visitors.

Beyond a certain point, everyone had to take off their shoes. Saleem and his friends climbed steps to get to the platform where the main building stood with all its awesome presence. Now barefoot, they entered the central room where the royal couple was buried. Here the mood was somber; people were talking in low whispers as if the ghosts of the past still lingered there—so different from the cheery outdoors. The queen's grave dominated the center of the room and, to one side, was that of her husband, once the emperor of India, Shah Jahan.

The custodian explained that Shah Jahan had dedicated this building as his wife's final resting place and he was going to have a separate one erected for his own, across the river. The memorial that the king had planned for himself was to be in black marble and would have been even larger than the queen's was, had it not been that the treasury ran out of money. And his son had him buried in the queen's chamber. This was why the king's grave was on the side and queen's occupied the middle.

Saleem and his friends walked all around the building. They went up to the museum and looked at pictures of the Taj Mahal in different periods. Saleem wondered what it looked like brand new, right after completion three hundred years ago. But he was thrilled to have seen it when he had the opportunity.

During his four years of college in Agra, he revisited the site several times. He saw it in bright sunlight, wet with rain, under cloudy skies, and finally one October night in the light of full moon. All these visits were wonderful, but none of them ever inspired the same overwhelming feelings that he experienced on the day he first set eyes on the Taj Mahal.

CHAPTER 16

On his way to college he had envisioned his education to be a continuation of his high school years with minor changes in his routines as he would be living in a hostel instead of home. But once there, the enormous changes he encountered baffled him and distracted him from his purpose—his studies.

For the first time, he found he was free to do as he pleased. In college, no one controlled his decisions or his actions. In the new system, no one even asked him or cared if he did or did not attend a class. He had known how to function within the restrictions and guidelines placed upon him by his parents and the tutor. He had followed his daily routine like an actor on the stage of life. He had done very well within the structured settings of home. Now, when there was no one to tell him what to do, he was like an actor without a director. He had tasks to perform, but no one to consult and no one to guide him. He was surprised to discover he did not know how to act or plan his days. Mediocrity was not expected of him when he was living at home and he had stood up well to the challenge. Now, his own desire to excel was muddled by a sense of freedom he never experienced before. Intoxicated with the new perception, he drifted off course. He was free but lost.

To a certain degree, attending classes and observing the rules of living at the hostel put some order and shaped his days. But once the classes were over, he came back to his room and had tea with his roommate; he did not know what to do. He had no idea how to fill his free time with useful pursuits. So, he started to engage in activities he knew deep down his parents would disapprove of and consider a waste of his time.

At home, going to the motion pictures was time squandered. But now, he had no restrictions and watched every movie in town, good or bad, with his roommate. And there were eleven theaters in Agra. Two theaters showed films exclusively in the English language. He and his roommate saw films produced in England and in Hollywood where they did not even understand the dialogue. He would always remember when he watched *Street Car Named Desire* and did not understand a word of the lines spoken by actors. They would go to see the foreign shows just so they could impress their friends by bringing up the names of the actors.

What fascinated him most about the movies was the fact that he would watch things that he could never even imagine; in the darkness of the theater he could watch the beautiful women looking at him from the screen and he would look back into those young eyes without ever feeling shy or bashful—something he had been unable to do in the real life. This was the fascinating world of cinema, unknown to him so far. When they ran out of movies to watch, they would go out to walk with friends in the evening, and all they did was talk about the girls in college.

Thoughts of so many new experiences inundated Saleem's mind that he found himself unable to concentrate on books and lectures. Even when he opened his books, his mind would wander and he could not concentrate on the subject. The consequence of all this wasted time started to show in his test results. His professors and peers no longer considered him a good student. He began to doubt his own abilities and that depressed him. A slow realization started to dawn on him that if things were to continue this way, he would be dismissed from college and sent home as a failure.

It took Saleem several weeks to become aware of the abrupt change that had produced the sense of going astray. He had to remind himself once and again that he was now older and accountable for his actions. In spite of his awareness that he was drifting off course, he found it difficult to change his ways—his disastrous course was taking him where his parents would not want him to be.

And then, one day, the awakening came in a shocking manner. In the chemistry lecture, sitting in the back row with his *cool* friends, he was leafing through a magazine with pictures of Indian movie stars. When the teacher noticed his inattention, he asked him to leave the class.

Being thrown out of the classroom was a first for him. With his head down as he stomped out of the lecture theater, every step he took was like a slap on his face from Sharma Gee, a rare action even from that harsh teacher. That was what he needed to bring him back to the world of reality from his dull dream.

After he got over the initial shock of humiliation, he began to realize what was going on in his life and a sudden insight, a clear understanding of his goals, started to crystallize in his mind. He wondered how someone like him, who used to be at the top of his class had slid down so low—to the bottom. He thought of his parents who had put their trust in him and were providing for his higher education at considerable sacrifice to them. He could not go home for lack of success and disappoint them. He realized that the burden of running his life was now his own and the purpose of him being in college was to get education. The idea started to take a form and he began to focus on his responsibilities.

He now understood why his parents wanted him to be away from home. He needed to learn how to manage life by himself, without supervision. He needed to learn how to function in this newfound freedom by setting goals, and do whatever it took to achieve them. Life was not unlike riding his bicycle on a bumpy road strewn with rocks and potholes all around, Saleem thought. He could ride it with skill, intent on reaching the destination, or he could be careless and wreck it and his life with it. He now understood that discipline was required for the pursuit of one's aspirations. By comparing a bike path with his life he needed to watch for the direction to reach his goal and fight the temptations that would entice him.

During the first year, he went home three times. On each visit, his mother would spoil him with all his favorite foods. He would meet with some of his old friends from school. A few of them were also going to college, while others had started working in their families' businesses. His friend Suresh, who always got first position in the class, was held back by his father to help support the family by finding him a job in a local retail shop. Suresh had hoped to continue his studies and Saleem was saddened by the fact that his friend's personal situation had prevented this star pupil from pursuing a higher education.

On his trips home, Saleem always wore pants and a shirt, as he did in college. This way, no one on the train could tell whether he was a Hindu or a Muslim. Things had been slow to change for the better, and it was still unsafe for a Muslim to travel alone. He avoided talking to anyone, which was not always easy, because he knew that any conversation would lead to an introduction. "What is your good name?" was a common question once two people started talking. The name would be a giveaway that Saleem was Muslim. Circumstances were such that he was afraid of the consequences that, at best, would terminate all conversation, and the other person would turn his back to him, or worse, he might hear slurs directed at him. The best way to avoid talking with strangers was to read a book or magazine during those daylong train rides. He was literally hiding behind his books.

Saleem never mentioned anything about his fears, real or not, when he came home. He thought it would just be another problem for his parents to worry about.

During spring break, Saleem did not have much money left. He wanted to go home, but was reluctant to ask his father for more than his usual monthly allowance. With what he had, he could only purchase a third-class ticket, the cheapest way to travel on the Indian railway system. He knew that that he would be travelling in a very crowded situation and he would consider himself lucky if he found a place to sit. As the train pulled onto the platform, which was now familiar to him, Saleem scanned the different cars as they slowly moved by. He spotted one that was not teeming with travelers, and ran for it. He positioned himself at the door before the train came to a stop. Other people who had noticed Saleem's move gravitated to that same entrance. Then, with some struggle, caused mainly by people trying to get in at the same time as the passengers were getting off, he managed to push his way in. Saleem did not expect to find a seat; he just wanted to be inside. The compartment had two rows of benches by the windows and two rows in the middle. Seating was for about thirty passengers, but there were more than forty people in this confined area, all of them men—mostly young.

The train started with a jolt and all those who were standing had to hold on to something they could grasp. The train slowly moved out of the station and picked up speed. Soon it was tearing through green and brown fields in ever-changing scenery. People were settling into their spaces and were looking around measuring up their fellow passengers. Saleem noted that most of the men wore typical Hindu clothes, only a few had shirts and pants on like him. This was typical for the population traveling in third class. An old man, his facial hair pronouncing him a Muslim, caught Saleem's eye. He seemed to be by himself and sat in a corner near the window. In normal times, the bearded man would not be so odd and out of place and no one would pay much attention. But these were not normal times.

Unfortunately, a rowdy group of young men was sitting near this odd old man. They were on their way to some religious festival or a ceremony, which was evident from the red color on their foreheads. They were laughing and joking with each other. Once the train had picked up speed, they noticed the man who was now sitting with his legs up on the seat. Sensing danger, he had shrunk into himself, as if he were a scared animal in a trap. The young lads, like a pack of wild dogs who had cornered its prey, closed on him. First they jeered the old passenger about his beard and his clothes, then harassed him by questioning his being here when he should be in Pakistan. He was old and frail, while they were young and many. Sensing the hostility around him, he squeezed himself more and more into the corner, as if he wanted to disappear.

"This train is not going to Pakistan, old man. How about if we throw you out the window and you catch the right train to your beloved country," one of them said with distinct disdain in his voice.

Things can easily get out of hand, Saleem thought. He could not interfere. He was afraid, but the father's words *never show fear* kept echoing in his head. He acted as if he was unaware of what was happening a short distance away from him.

The space was crowded and a few older Hindus were watching what was going on, but they kept to themselves. Saleem was shocked when one of the young men lit a match and started to move the flame close to this passenger's beard. The old man was paralyzed, and such was his fright that he would not even raise his arms to protect himself. Saleem caught the man's eyes and in them, he saw a fear that was spilling over to him. He had never before experienced anything similar in his life. He wished to help the man, but worried about his own safety he kept quiet. He felt his own life threatened and all empathy he had was marred by his fears. He was too far away from the emergency chain that was there to be pulled to stop the train. And in no case did he want to draw attention to himself. He feared that, if they discovered he was a Muslim, they surely would have no mercy for a younger man and might in fact throw him out.

Fortunately, for the man harassed, an older man, a Hindu who had been keeping to himself during this ugly display of behavior finally got up from his seat and shouted at the young troublemakers to calm down and stop acting like fools. In spite of the difference in religion and the hostility that existed between the two faiths, a certain sense of decency and commonality of age had brought out an old Hindu to save an old Muslim man.

The elderly Hindu passenger lowered his voice and said, "You should be ashamed of your conduct. Look at you. And look at him and his age." Now, this voice was the only sound in the compartment. The young men were not expecting it. They were trying to be "men" out to prove something to themselves—a crowd mentality had taken them over. It all melted away with that father-figure voice which continued, "You should be helping an old man, not insulting and scaring him. Behave yourselves. Leave the man alone."

To Saleem's surprise, they listened and obeyed as if they were relieved that someone was there to stop them. The moment passed, everybody quieted down and the group let the old man be. They resumed their joking and laughing among themselves as if nothing had happened, or they had done anything wrong to the man and whatever they did, he had it coming. With an atmosphere of apathy around him, the old man with the beard remained motionless in his corner. Saleem could not imagine what was going on in the man's mind. Scared himself, he stared out at the rolling blanket of scenery.

When Saleem arrived at home, he was still distraught over what he witnessed in the train. His mother noticed and asked if he was all right. Since he did not want to worry her, he answered that he was tired from the trip. Ever since leaving home for college, Saleem had decided that he would fight for his own survival and not bother his parents with things that were beyond their control. And his parents for their part never asked him how he was doing in the college. Either they were certain that he was doing well, or they had confidence in his ability to handle the problems that might present themselves. Saleem appreciated this trust and was grateful to have such understanding parents.

During these vacations, Saleem mostly stayed home. To keep him busy, he had brought some books to study in his spare time. Occasionally, he would sit by his mother's side as she cooked all his favorite foods and talk with her about his college life. She was worried about his eating habits away from home and wanted to know every detail about the meals served at the hostel.

Discussing girls with parents was culturally prohibitive. The topics he and his mother talked over were so completely different from the things he would gossip about with his friends at the campus. He found that talking with his mother and being with his father restored his calm and energized his mind, whereas at college it was just the opposite, most conversations with his friends drained his psyche.

As the vacation ended, Saleem was mentally recharged and looking forward to getting back to college. During conversations, his parents would point it out that college life was but a small sample of what the future had in store for him.

By the end of his first year, Saleem was content with some structure in his life. His roommate, however, was still struggling with issues of freedom from parental supervision. Part of the problem was that his father sent him too much money. Saleem and Sharif attended different classes during the day. Their classrooms were in different buildings separated by the busy public thoroughfare, so they hardly ever saw each other during the day. Back in their room at night, however, they would talk about the activities of the day. Sharif was always telling Saleem about his new friends. And that he even had talked with some girls. Saleem was impressed and thought that was quite an achievement for someone who grew up in a small conservative town—like him.

At the end of the year, the final examination was held and he did manage to pass all his tests. He was no longer a top student, but he was promoted to the next higher class, the second year of college.

CHAPTER 17

Over one hundred years of tradition and history defined the culture of the St John's College, an institution established by the Church of Missionary Society of England. Because of its past affiliation with the West, diversity existed where the Western lifestyle blended with Indian culture. St. John's College provided certain social freedoms that were not common in a typical Indian Institutions; coeducation was there partly because of the Western influence. The school authorities did not frown upon boys and girls mingling together. The students had dubbed a passage covered with shady trees, between the two wings on the campus, as Lovers' Lane where boys and girls met regularly for rendezvous. From time to time, Saleem had seen Sharif talking to one girl or another in that area.

Over a short time, the roommates had learned a lot about each other. Saleem thought that Sharif was a bit too reckless, but he usually got away with it because he was athletic, handsome and had a winning personality. It also did not hurt that the boy had extra money to spend. and for that he attracted an assortment of fellow students, many of whom Saleem did not approve of.

Saleem and Sharif were now in the second year of college. They were sharing the room again. Sharif had played tennis during the first year and he had played it well enough that he was picked to play on the college team. Now, everyone who was interested in sports knew of him. The girls noticed him.

Saleem learned that among his roommate's numerous new friends, there was one good-looking girl. Her name was Geeta and almost everyone on campus knew that she was the daughter of a prominent doctor at the medical college. There were not that many girls on campus and pretty ones were few. She had many admirers and many boys were secretly in love with her. She came from a Hindu family and Sharif was a Muslim; this was a circumstance bound for trouble. And trouble Sharif found.

"I think I am falling in love," Sharif declared one day.

"Does she know about it?" Saleem asked. "It is Geeta, isn't it"?

"Yes, to both of your questions," Sharif answered with a smile.

"Whatever your plans may be, I hope you realize the difference in the religion between the two of you. Times have changed but not that much. This kind of relationship has little chance of success. Even in better times, the mixing of the two faiths in a man-woman relationship was frowned upon. But these days, it is outright dangerous. You be careful. And besides, you are both too young anyway." Saleem kept on rattling thoughts he had bottled up inside him for some time, even though he knew Sharif was paying little attention to his words. But Saleem could not stop himself. He felt it was his duty, as a friend, to warn his roommate about the risks, about the dangers of such a relationship.

The subject was never brought up again. Saleem was busy with his studies, but he knew that his friend continued to see Geeta. He wished he could somehow make him understand the hopelessness of the situation, but Sharif was in teenage-love and no one could talk any sense into him.

CHAPTER 18

The second year in college was ending. Saleem had adapted to living away from home. He had also learned to manage his money and tried to get by with as little as possible because he knew that his father did not have as much as he had in the past. On his last visit home, he had also noticed that his mother was cutting down on her personal expenses. She was no longer wearing new shoes and clothes, and he could tell that she missed that. His father had also become more frugal, yet both parents hoped the children would not notice or feel there was any need to lower their standard of living. Saleem started to save some of the money he received from home so he could bring to his mother some of her favorite things next time he came home during the summer vacations.

It was springtime now and Saleem was occupied preparing for the final exams. One day, when he was studying hunched over his desk, Sharif walked in and excitedly announced that Geeta had invited him to come over to her house and meet her parents.

Saleem asked, "Did she tell them you're a Muslim?"

"She wants me to meet them first and then, once we get to know each other, she will tell them. Her father, she says, is an educated man and he is above all these petty prejudices," Sharif said in a tone that sounded as if he was trying to convince himself of his words.

Saleem wanted to warn his friend one more time that what he was doing was dangerous. He also wanted to tell him to grow up and think like an adult. He felt that this romance had nothing but trouble written all over it. He wanted to tell him a lot more but, again, closed his mouth and held his thoughts. Saleem had learned by now that in certain circumstances, people only listened selectively. They just heard what they wanted to hear. And so, he simply said, "Good luck, I'd be careful if I were you."

Geeta's brother knew that his sister had befriended a Muslim boy. Though he could understand how a girl like Geeta would fall for someone like Sharif who was good looking and was on the college tennis team, he was unable to entertain the idea. As her brother, he tried to reason with Geeta, but she brushed him off and told him to mind his own business and not to spy on her. Then he took up the matter with the mother. Geeta's mother was an open-minded woman, but she could not imagine having a Muslim son-in-law. She had a talk with her daughter and tried to make her see the difficulties associated with such a friendship. But no one brought it up to the father. The doctor was a busy man, no one in the family wanted to mention such matters to him that would distract him from his work. In addition, they knew what he would say. He did not believe in religion. In his opinion, human beings were above that sort of thing and one religion was as bad as another was.

Geeta was her father's favorite child. In her mind she was certain that her father would be charmed by Sharif, once he met him. Sharif was well mannered, good looking and of fair complexion. Except for his religion, everything about him was a good match for her. And, above all, she was in love with him.

Sharif dressed up and looked good when he left in the late afternoon to meet his friend's parents. He did not return to his room that night. Knowing where his roommate had gone, Saleem was worried and drew the warden into his confidence. Mr. Paul was alarmed as he understood the gravity of the situation. The college authorities were nervous because, living on campus, Sharif was their ward; they were responsible for his safety and his wellbeing.

Geeta also missed her classes next day, but she was safe at home. According to her, Sharif was supposed to come to their house and meet her parents. She and the family waited for him and were disappointed when he never showed up. This was not like him. She was fearful that something bad happened to him. She knew that her brother who was a violent man had found out about Sharif and her. She also knew that he did not approve of her meeting with Sharif and had repeatedly told her so, but she had consistently ignored him. She was not aware of the fact that his friends were teasing him about getting a Muslim brother-in-law, which infuriated him. Her brother had had several quarrels with his friends on this issue.

The college authorities, suspecting foul play, reported it to the police department. After an hour, the police inspector called the vice-principal of the college and informed him that a young student was admitted to the college hospital with facial and head wounds as if someone had roughed him up. However, according to the attending doctor, the injuries were not life threatening. The hospital had reported the case to the police that night. The vice principal wanted to talk to the attending surgeon and because of his status at the college, they were soon connected by phone. He wanted to make sure that the patient was in fact Sharif, and needed to know the medical status of the student. Again, the doctor reassured him that the patient Sharif was indeed hurt, but was expected to make a fast recovery. He also mentioned that a piece of paper was found in Sharif's jacket with the words written on it: "Stay away from her." Mr. Barbosa, the vice principal, then informed Sharif's father of the unfortunate incident in the neighboring town.

The police inspector arrived at the hospital in the morning to launch an official investigation and learned that Sharif's father had been contacted and was arriving sometime soon.

As soon as Saleem found out about his friend, he pedaled as fast as he could on a rented bicycle to the hospital. A tall good-looking man dressed in the western style, was there talking to the doctors. He easily spotted Sharif's father—his son looked so much like him. He walked up to him and introduced himself. The father was concerned about his son and he was angry. The doctors had convinced him that Sharif needed to stay in the hospital for at least three days and, after that, he would have to rest for a few weeks to recover. "Most likely there will be no long term effects of the injuries," he was told. Sharif's father had a few friends in Agra where he could stay until his son was able to travel home with him. The father wanted to get to the bottom of this and find out what really happened to his son.

The nurse led Saleem to Sharif's bedside. His friend's face had bandages over his nose and forehead, but he was able to talk to Saleem. "After I left you that evening, I thought I would walk. I hadn't gone very far when I noticed three young men following me. Suddenly, one of them attacked me, hit me on the head with a stick while the other two jumped me and struck me in the face. They never said anything. It all happened so fast. I didn't know who they were. I had never seen them before. After I fell down, I must have passed out because, the next thing I remember I was in the hospital and there was some discussion about admitting me. There were questions about who would pay for treatment and the room. Once I was able to tell them I'm a student at St. John's College, I heard someone say, 'If he goes to that college, his father must have money.' And so they decided to take care of me and asked my name and my father's name. Soon the doctor came and told me that my father had been informed of my accident and the hospital I was in."

As Saleem listened, he became angry with those who hurt his friend. He felt helpless and did not know what he could do.

Sharif continued, "They must have given me a sedative because I fell asleep after they cleaned and stitched all the wounds. Now, I feel pain all over again."

Saleem could see that Sharif was hurting. Soon the nurse came back and asked him to leave so they could change the bandages.

Sharif's father was a businessman of means. First, he wanted to find out who was the one responsible for his son's injuries. He was determined to even the score with this person or persons. "If the police are not going to take care of this, I will," he told Saleem. During the conversation with Saleem, his friend's father found out that his son was on his way to meet a girl named Geeta. At once, he concluded that it was a Hindu-girl-Muslim-boy problem. The people who beat Sharif up, he surmised, had to be Hindus and could be Geeta's relatives or just someone who liked her and did not want another person getting close to her.

Sharif's father met with some of his Hindu friends and asked them for help. It was not his town and for that reason, there were factors that limited his ability to do what he really wanted to do. Since he was already in the hospital, he thought he might want to meet with Geeta's father who was a senior physician there. The doctor was busy, but he found time at three in the afternoon to see Sharif's father. Geeta's father already knew whom he was meeting and expressed his regrets that some hooligan assaulted his son on his way to their house. Sharif's father asked him if he knew of anyone or could find out who would hurt his son because of his friendship with Geeta.

The doctor thought for a moment and said, "Mr. Ahmed you understand how the situation has been in the past few years. There are still elements around us who exploit any situation to arouse bad feelings between the two communities to accomplish their own agenda. I cannot tell you what they get out of this, but they will try to use any situation to anger and incite their supporters. This is the only way they get to use their influence. I am not in your position, but I understand how angry you must be. If I were in your situation, I would go and personally kill the bastard and, if you did, I would understand. However, if you ask my opinion, I would suggest you leave the matter to the police. They will investigate and I hope they will find some answers soon. I will cooperate with them, for Geeta's sake, in any way I can." He also told him how concerned and hurt his daughter was when she found out what happened. She had not eaten anything or slept since she learned of the incident.

Mr. Ahmed, Sharif's father, appreciated what the man had to say, but he was not satisfied. He realized the complexities of the situation and he felt powerless. He knew that the police would not do anything because all the people he talked within the police department were Hindus. They said how sorry they were for what had happened to his son, but he could read on their faces and in their mannerisms that they felt his son was burned because he was playing with fire. They did not say it in so many words, but imparted upon him the impression that he should be thankful his son was alive. Mr. Ahmed was not the one to let things go by easily. He thought he would stay in town until his son was better, then take him back and review the situation from his home base where he knew the right people. He did not get to be a successful man by being pushed around.

Sharif had finally recovered to a point where he was well enough to go home. He left all his belongings in the room with Saleem. Before he left, he told Saleem how angry his father was with him and how he was frustrated with the whole situation. "I'm sorry I didn't listen to you, Saleem. I should have been more careful. I'm still in love with her and I know that will never change. Once I'm home, I'll write to you," and then Sharif left with his father.

After a few weeks, everyone had forgotten about the incident. Saleem saw Geeta in college, but she was not the same girl anymore. The vivacious girl who walked with a spring in her step now walked with a slump and had her head down as if someone had robbed her of her happiness. She was sad and quiet. Saleem got a letter from Sharif. He reported that he had made a full recovery and, except for a small scar on his forehead, there were no signs left of the injuries. He had started taking part again in physical activities and was playing badminton with his younger brother who was in high school. His father had not yet made up his mind whether he could return to college. He seriously doubted that he would ever come back to St. John's College. There was talk between his parents about sending him to England for his education. He did not mention Geeta in his letter.

Mr. Ahmed was one of those people who did not forget things easily. If someone did him a favor, he remained indebted for the rest of his life. But if someone harmed him, he remembered that too. He was hurt and the anger was eating him up alive. Some days he was so angry that all he wanted to do was to wipe out those who had harmed his son. If someone had hurt his son because he had done something bad, his father could understand. He would not only have understood he would actually have punished him himself. But he could not see anything wrong in what his son had done. He did not get a girl pregnant; he was just a young boy who thought he was in love. Was that a crime to be beaten up for? Mr. Ahmed's mind constantly returned to these thoughts, and he wanted to get even with the responsible party. After his conversation with Geeta's father, he concluded that the doctor did not have anything to do with the incident. He was certain that he would find out through his resources in Agra the name of the person responsible for this ugly incident. He had not decided what he would do, once he knew who the culprit was. At this point, he just wanted to kill him.

Mrs. Ahmed, Sharif's mother, was a gentle woman. When she saw her son come in all bandaged up, his face all black and blue, she wanted to take him in her arms and protect him from all his enemies. Like her husband, she was angry and hurt that their child was brutally assaulted just for being a Muslim boy in love, but then she soon managed to get over it. She was grateful that Sharif was well and healthy once again.

She was more concerned about her husband's rage and his thirst for revenge that was consuming him. She did not know how to convince him to put it behind him so they could get back to their normal lives. She wanted him to forget it all. But her soothing words simply washed over him, unheard. What worried her most was the knowledge that he was capable of getting people killed. If any of those attackers were harmed or murdered which, in her opinion they deserved, the authorities would come back after her husband. He would be their prime suspect. And he was a Muslim; it would not take much to convince a judge or any other authority in government to destroy him. His destruction would be the death of the whole family and all those who depended on him.

Sharif woke up one night and overheard someone crying in the room adjacent to his where his parents slept. He recognized the voice as that of his mother's. She was begging his father to get over his rage and let it go. "Do not destroy us all. We depend on you. Our son, the one you want to avenge, will also get hurt. He needs you. We all need you. Please don't throw it all away. I understand your pride and your feelings, but I beg of you to get over it."

It finally dawned on Sharif what he had put his parents through, and he felt guilty. He was sorry and felt ashamed. He wanted to go to their room and apologize for the pain he had caused, but he also knew that it was not the right time and place.

It took nearly two months for Mr. Ahmed to find out all the details of assault on Sharif. He believed that if he did, so could the police. He had learned that Geeta's brother was not directly involved in the attack on his son, but his friends were. They wanted to teach him a lesson and left a note in his pocket for just that purpose. He wanted to do the same to them. But he told his men not to do anything for the time being. In these past two months, he had thought about the problems that could arise from any reprisals, and he respected his wife's judgment.

His anguish over the loss of his vanity was not as acute now, and the thought he might have to swallow his pride and let go for the good of all those close to him had become more bearable with time. He knew he could never forgive or forget, and he knew he would always regret letting the villains get away with it. But then, times had changed, and perhaps he should too!

CHAPTER 19

After Sharif's departure with his father, a man came to pick up his belongings. He let Saleem and the authorities know that the boy would not be coming back. Since the school year was ending, the warden did not assign another person to the room. It was his first experience of living alone. At home, the entire family always slept in one room during winter or in the courtyard in summer; only Father had his own bedroom. Saleem liked the freedom and privacy of being all by himself. He enjoyed his space. He decided that this was what he would try for next year, to get a room without a roommate—a space for himself.

Although he cherished the present situation of being alone, he often thought about Sharif and wondered if they would ever meet again. He did not see Geeta on campus anymore and had not heard what happened to her. With time, the whole incident of Geeta and Sharif was forgotten and became just a vague faded memory.

Where he grew up in India one knew swimming was a talent that enabled one to stay afloat, move in the water and survive. Only those who lived in the areas that got flooded by an overflowing river had to learn this skill. For them, it was a necessity for survival. But in St. John's College it was an exercise; it was a sport, and it was entertainment. And for this purpose the college had its own swimming pool on the campus. Living in the hostel, he had an opportunity to go there in the summer mornings to try it out.

Accompanied by some friends who promised to teach him the art, he ventured out wearing a borrowed swimming costume. In spite of the rumors that some swimmers urinated in the water, he got into the shallow end of the pool and held on to a smooth round metal bar that ran along the inside. Holding the bar with both hands he moved his legs up and down which to his surprise brought his whole body to float. It was an exciting experience, but an attempt to float without holding the bar failed no matter how hard and how fast he moved his arms and legs. There was no lifeguard on duty to save him if he ever drowned was the fear that lingered in his mind. With the help of his friends and with his continued drill, in two weeks he was able to swim across the length of the pool.

One morning, as he was recovering from a cold, in an attempt to swim the whole length once more, someone crossed his path and broke his rhythm, he almost drowned. Though he recognized it worked his muscles so it must be a good exercise, the experience taught him swimming he did not need to survive, and it did not entertain him. That day he developed fear of water. He reasoned he perhaps did not have those needed genes to make swimming a learnable activity—he had to let it go until another time, which never came.

The next two years in college were uneventful. Saleem, according to the wishes of his parents, was to go into medical school after he finished at St. John's College. He knew that this would be an expensive commitment on his father's part when the family no longer had the same financial resources they had earlier. Knowing his father, he understood that if he went to medical school, his father would support him by selling his properties. And Saleem did not think that was right.

So, he chose to continue his education and get a Master's degree in chemistry instead. To make things easier for his father, he moved to Aligarh Muslim University, which would cut down his expenses. It was also a safe haven for Muslims in North India. At the university, everything was larger than what he had seen and experienced in the college in Agra. Since there were lot more students in the hostels, the food was served in a large hall in metal plates and bowls. The food was not as good as he had in college, but it did not affect Saleem's health.

Muslim leaders of the world visiting India would always stop by Aligarh. During his two years of study at the university, Saleem saw the likes of the Shah of Iran and Queen Soraya, Sukarno of Indonesia, and King Faisal of Saudi Arabia. Accompanying these dignitaries were Indian leaders: Pundit Nehru, Indira Gandhi and several other less known figures of the Indian government.

After he finished his program at the university, as far as Saleem was concerned, his studies were over and the next step was to find a job. The employment situation was difficult in the area where his family lived, and more so for the Muslims. Everyone in the family, including his father, was of the opinion that Saleem should not be wasting time looking for work in India. He should head directly to Pakistan, the country for which the family had sacrificed much, including the father's imprisonment. Moreover, there might be more opportunities, in a young country for a young man like him. His older brother and a cousin were already living in Karachi holding good positions.

Moving to Pakistan was no longer an easy matter; Saleem needed a passport, a difficult task for a member of the minority he belonged to living in India. Saleem's father had to ask his friend, Mr. Rao Singh, to intervene on their behalf with the influential people he knew in the government. It took several months of persuading the authorities to grant Saleem the permission to leave the country. Finally, one day to every one's delight, Mr. Singh brought him his passport. Those who looked at it wanted to see his picture rather than what was written in the thin booklet. For him, the passport brought a sense of freedom.

Within a few days, he was on the train to Amritsar, the city bordering Pakistan. The customs officials at the Indian border checked his papers and searched his luggage. Finding everything in order, they let him board the train to Lahore, Pakistan. Saleem was excited about the prospect of heading toward the country of his dreams. Heading to the Promised Land filled him with awe and joy. From childhood, he had witnessed his father campaign for its creation. His family had lived in fear and lost most of their possessions for the establishment of this new state.

The train finally crossed the Pakistani border where he saw the flag. His heartbeat went up a few notches. He was overwhelmed with anticipation. Finally, the train came to stop at the Lahore railway station where the passengers had to go through customs again. Passport in hand he moved forward with an expectation of a warm welcome, but awaiting him was a rude awakening.

The scene at customs was complete chaos. The arm-waving uniformed officers who spoke Punjabi, a language Saleem was not familiar with, were herding the helpless *Hindustanis* (Indians) over to the tables so their luggage could be searched. Not so much to see if they had brought in any illegal substance but to find what could be taken away from these vulnerable men and women. Although Saleem was not a refugee seeking asylum, he was made to feel he was one. Here everyone was treated equally—badly. He was a *nobody* here.

He wanted to tell someone that his family sacrificed to create Pakistan. He wanted to say, "My father spent time in a prison for sake of this country. If persons like my father did not exist, there would be no Pakistan today and you, Mr. Customs Officer, would not be treating me like this." But that someone was not there to listen.

He went through an hour of humiliation for coming to the country of his dreams. During this time, the customs' bureaucrats behaved toward him as if he were a foreign intruder. They searched his luggage as if he were a criminal.

Saleem watched another person going through a search by a man in uniform. This man had brought in some mangoes with him. The inspector wanted to take them all away from him, but then out of goodness of his heart, and to be just he took only his *fair share*. Saleem saw how this government representative divided the fruit taking one for himself and the other for the Hindustani until he had half of them.

In that one first moment of entry, the harshness of reality shattered all the idealistic images formed early on in childhood. He remembered, when he had gone out on the streets with grownups shouting: *Le Ke Rahenge Pakistan*, (we will take Pakistan), he had no idea what he was demanding. A country? For him and his family? That was all he could imagine.

Now, when he entered the state he thought he had helped create, the people around him had no idea he had built that haven in his imagination. They did not seem to care, either. His dreams marginalized, he sat there watching people who had gone through the same ordeal he had. They all looked beaten. Disappointment and disillusion engulfed him and those who journeyed with him. He was angry. An oasis he had come for, a desert was all he had found. He wondered, was this what his father and those who thought like him wanted to create, and was this supposed to be a sanctuary for Muslims from India? These disturbing questions occupied his mind within a few hours of setting foot on the soil of this new country. That a dream he had built, a love he had cherished since his early days, would be soured so abruptly was hard for him to cope with. The only comforting thought in his mind was that the majority of people around him were Muslims and he was no longer a part of a scared minority. His life was probably safer here than it was in India. But after what he experienced, he was not quite certain of even that.

Once the ordeal of going through customs was over, he was allowed to enter the main railway station, a station not very different to the one he encountered in Agra. To his delight, waiting for him were his relatives his father had arranged to meet with him. They had reserved a seat for him for his travel to Karachi. Being with people who were living a comfortable life in Lahore and did not have to experience what he went through earlier during the day abated his worries to a certain degree and he felt at ease once again. They took him to the restaurant at the station and paid for his lunch. They stayed with him until he boarded the Awami-Express, a train which had only one class of compartments, for Karachi, the city to which his older brother and a cousin had emigrated earlier.

As the train tore through nearly seven hundred miles of land, passing through green fields and barren desert, stopping several times on stations that were foreign to him, his mind drifted back to what he had experienced at the border. He understood that Pakistan was created for the Muslims of India. Why then was he maltreated and received like an outsider? Why did this country, created for and by the Indian Muslims, seem to favor only those who were already living there?

In Saleem's mind, there was something gone wrong with the entire concept of this newly formed state…unless his thinking was flawed. He doubted that. He also doubted that Jinah, the father of the nation, who had brought Pakistan into existence, had visualized this. When his father campaigned for the formation of the new country, he was asking for a country for the Indian Muslims and not for the few who lived in certain regions. He felt that people using religion for their benefit had already hijacked the country. Then, it dawned on him that this country was no longer for Muslims of the Indian subcontinent, but for only those who were there and they were now the masters—running it according to their whims. He felt he and his family were cheated out of their rights, which he thought they had earned by making sacrifices.

During the long hours on this train, he had time to reflect on matters that came to his attention since he crossed the border into the new land. What he saw let him down. Finally to his chagrin, he accepted that the icons created through one's mind were fantasy; survival was the important thing, and the high-blown ideals do nothing but disappoint people. In the back of his mind he had always known that. And now his experience had confirmed his belief. So, he took a deep breath and pulled himself up in his seat. He was in Pakistan now. He must learn to survive with the new facts of existence, together with real people. Pakistan was a concept, but Pakistanis who lived there were reality.

Next day, the train arrived in Karachi. Saleem had heard that it was a large city, bigger than any he had visited or lived in before. By now, he was over the initial disillusionment of entering his dreamland, and was happy and excited to see his brother and cousin waving at him at the platform of the Karachi City Station. In the excitement, he almost lost his luggage. Once everything was sorted out, they left for his brother's house, which was located in Nazimabad, a newly built section on the edge of the city. The distances here were large; they used a cab—no tongas in this metropolis. Most people who moved to Pakistan from North India and spoke Urdu settled in this area. This place did not seem as foreign as where he had entered the country. The home had two bedrooms, since there were no children in the house. Saleem was given one of them.

Saleem came to learn that people who had moved from India to Pakistan were called *Mohajirs* (migrants), he was now a *Mohajir*—again a minority. Was he destined to be a minority no matter where he went? he wondered. On the other hand, he was aware that it only mattered if he cared. Minority was just a label, he mused, assigned by the majority, so that there was someone who had to obey their rules in the name of democracy.

His cousin or his brother, whoever had time, showed him around the city and explained the local transportation system. They gave him a brief breakdown on different means of conveyance available starting from taxis to motor rickshaw to buses was the order of expense, taxis being the most expensive.

When they took him to the beach, he saw the ocean for the first time in his life: a vast expanse of water touching the horizon. So far, his knowledge about these large bodies of water was from maps in his geography class. Being here, at the edge of the world, so to speak, was awe-inspiring. He loved this open space and just stood there, listening to the sound of the breaking waves and breathing in the clean ocean air. They all rolled up their pants, took off their shoes and walked in the shallow water. Experiencing water and sand between his toes was an unforgettable experience, he felt his world expanding. It was intoxicating and yet calming at the same time.

Once he knew how and where to catch a bus, he started traveling on his own to augment his knowledge of the city and its roadways. At the bus stops, in the crowded areas, he noticed beggars some with twisted and some with missing limbs, their faces distorted, their bodies covered with dirt, the likes of which he had never seen, crawled around as sub-human mutants appealing to the sympathy of the passengers and pedestrians. The sight troubled him for the first few days. But soon, as his mind put up a screen to protect his feelings, their grotesque physical state became a part of the scenery and no longer raised any emotions in him. Like all others who walked by them, he hardly noticed or was distressed by their condition anymore.

Shortly after his arrival, Saleem applied for Pakistani citizenship. What he thought was his inherent right turned out to be a big hurdle. He could not even get an application form without knowing someone in the office, or paying for it—he paid for it. If it was not for his cousin, who knew a number of people working in that office, he perhaps would never have been able to legalize his status of a resident. Still, it took a year to complete the process. While he was in the process of legitimizing his stay through the maze of bureaucracy, he started looking for a job. He went on a few interviews, but nothing came out of them because they needed a person with experience that he did not have. In the meantime, he had learned how to use the city buses. To get into a bus was a task. There was no line and if there was one it dissolved, at the sight of the arriving transport. In the morning hours he had to fight his way in. With time he was finding it easier to move around in his new surroundings.

Exploring the city he discovered that not far from the Sadar area, the upscale part of downtown Karachi, was a cluster of offices and government buildings. In front of one of them, Saleem saw a sign identifying it as the Pakistan Council of Scientific and Industrial Research. He mentioned what he saw to his brother the next day and learned that the British had originally established the Council in India. And following the establishment of the new state, it was now called the Pakistan Council. It was a place of research and development of new products for business and industry. He suggested that Saleem should apply for a job there.

The following day, Saleem got started early in the morning, put on a clean, nicely ironed shirt and white pants. He carefully polished his black shoes and left home to catch a bus. Getting into a bus in the morning took skill and physical courage. He was lucky that day; the first bus that came had enough room for him to get in—getting in did not mean sitting down. He was careful not to mess up his clothes on the way to the office where he was hoping to find work.

Halfway through the bus ride, he found an empty seat. No longer looking for a place to sit, his mind drifted to the upcoming possibility of a job interview. Only then did he realize that he had forgotten to bring along the application he had prepared. This was in the form of a letter to the director wherein he had stated his academic qualifications and his desire to work in the research section of the Council. He could get off the bus and go back, but decided against it. He reasoned it would take too long. If he could not accomplish anything that day, he would at least find out where exactly the offices were located, he thought.

At his destination he walked toward the buildings where he had seen the sign the other day. To his relief, it was right around the corner, not far from where he was standing. It was still early and people were coming in for work. To his surprise, he noticed the director of the Council, Dr. Kazmi, whom he recognized from a picture he had recently seen in the newspaper. The director got out of a chauffeur-driven Datsun in front of the gate with the sign. Saleem watched him go in. He waited for about two minutes to enter through that very entrance. Inside, he found himself standing in front of a man sitting at a desk. For a second he thought he was back in high school when he went to get admission with his tutor. Same scene, different person.

Saleem, a little nervous, got hold of himself and managed not to show any anxiety. He walked up to the man, greeted him and asked to see Dr. Kazmi, as if he knew the director. Either his demeanor or his clothes must have made a positive impression because, instead of dismissing Saleem, the man asked him about the purpose of his visit. Saleem explained that he was there on a personal business. The man at the desk gave him a piece of paper to write down his name. He then briefly looked at it and went through a door on the back wall. Saleem was certain that this man had no clue that he was here looking for a job. If he had brought along that application, the series of events that unfolded would have undoubtedly not been the same. The man came back and held the door for him to go in. As Saleem entered the office, he saw Dr. Kazmi was alone, still standing and looking at some papers on his table. The man shook his hand, pointed toward a chair, and asked him to sit down. After Saleem was seated, Dr. Kazmi asked him about the purpose of his visit.

Saleem, very briefly but explicitly, explained that he graduated from Aligarh Muslim University in India last year. He had recently arrived in Pakistan and was looking for a job where he could utilize his knowledge of chemistry. The director knew a number of professors who had taught Saleem at this university in India. Before accepting a job with the Council, he himself was briefly a professor at this institution of higher learning. He talked about the place in a fond, reminiscing way and asked Saleem how soon he could join, as someone in the chemistry section was looking for an assistant and he was also a graduate of that same university. Saleem could hardly believe his luck. Dr. Kazmi picked up a pen, wrote a few sentences on his pad, and handed the paper to Saleem to give to his secretary in the outer office. Saleem took the paper, thanked Dr. Kazmi for seeing him and left.

As he was leaving, Dr. Kazmi said, "Go and see Dr. Jamal tomorrow morning. He is the one who needs the new assistant."

In the outside office, Saleem found the man who had let him in to see the director, handed him the paper and waited to see his reaction. After looking at the paper, the man asked Saleem to sit down. He called Dr. Jamal to set up an appointment for Saleem at the council laboratories the next day at ten o'clock in the morning.

When Saleem came out, he was in a daze. The possibility of securing his first job, making money for the first time was going to be an experience new to him in every sense of the word. He could not absorb or believe the events of the past fifteen minutes. He wanted to share his feelings, his elation, and his excitement with someone, but there was no one there to listen. He needed to sit down somewhere.

He recalled that there was a coffee house not far from where he was. Wrapped up in his thoughts, he walked to the place, went in and found a seat near a window. The place was not crowded at this early hour. Only a few tables had customers, people who were on their way to work or meeting other people for business. No one was talking loudly. This was the right place for Saleem to sit and reflect on what just happened. As he waited for coffee, he tried to rationalize the series of events: He got a place on the first bus; he forgot his application; he arrived at the office at the best possible time, and someone needed an assistant. The chances of all that happening were extremely rare, but still it happened. He decided it must be his lucky day. He felt he needed to celebrate, so he ordered another cup, with heavy cream this time, and a pastry to go with it.

That night he could not sleep well. His job depended on how he fared with the doctor who was to employ him. He had no idea what the nature of the project he needed to work on was, or even if his knowledge of chemistry was enough to answer the questions during the forthcoming interview.

The next morning with all his apprehensions, he left home early but at that hour the buses were all crowded with people going to work. He decided to hire a motor-rickshaw instead, which got him to the laboratories located on the outskirts of the city at half past nine. The buildings housing the research labs were temporary structures spread over a large area. Still, there was an entrance gate secured by a man whose job seemed to be directing people rather than guarding the premises. He directed Saleem to where the chemistry section was located. After a few more inquiries, he was at Dr. Jamal's office. Dr. Jamal turned out to be a tall gray-haired man. When he noticed the new face, he got up from his chair and extended his hand to shake. "You must be Saleem. I was expecting you. When did you leave Aligarh?" Dr. Jamal showered him with questions about Aligarh.

They talked for an hour all about the city where he had gone to the university in India; they had a common bond, being alumni of the same institution. Dr. Jamal did not ask a single question about his experience or his knowledge of chemistry. He talked about the campus life as a man starved for news.

Saleem found out that Dr. Jamal was born in Aligarh while his father taught at the university. His entire childhood memories were of that place. No wonder he was so keen to talk to someone who was there so recently, Saleem thought. When he had walked into the office of Dr. Jamal, he was not greeted like one who came to look for the job; he was treated like a messenger from the past. All through the questioning and evaluation, Saleem felt he was talking to a member of his family—the alumni. A perception new to him. When he had moved from the college to the university, he had no idea how this change would help him secure his first job.

Dr. Jamal was a man who chose to like or dislike a person the moment he met him or her. Luckily, Saleem fell under the first category. This Saleem could tell by the way he smiled and laughed while talking to him and the way he heartily shook his hand. After the interview was over, Dr Jamal introduced Saleem to the other five members of his team as the new addition to the group. Now, Saleem knew he had a job. All his fellow workers were organic chemists. He felt as if he was back in his college days.

Saleem filled out the necessary forms and left them in the office.

The next day he started working in the lab, something he enjoyed doing. It took him some time to get to know what everyone was involved in and how he would fit into it and be useful to the group, where the research was focused on isolation and characterization of the compounds isolated from the herbal plants. The first project he worked on was in collaboration with another assistant who needed help. For the first six months, he refluxed; he filtered and distilled the liquids and solvents. He used the skills he had learned in college for extraction of the products from the plant seeds used for healing mental illnesses. During this time, he familiarized himself with the system and had an opportunity to learn about those who were there. He found Dr. Jamal to be kind and helpful that made him feel comfortable and at home.

At work, he ordered his lunch from the cafeteria nearby and for the first time paid for his food with his own money. He was so thrilled by the feeling of spending his money that he carried the cash he was paid monthly in his pocket, always handy when he needed it.

These were the days when penicillin was still a newly discovered wonder drug, and the natural products isolated from different mold and fungi were of great interest as antibiotics. The botany department of the council drew Dr. Jamal's attention to a new species of fungus isolated by one of their scientists. With the prospects of finding new chemicals of medicinal value, growing this new species and isolating products from there became a main concern of his section. The task of separation and identification of the compounds produced by this fungus fell on Saleem. Under the direction of Dr. Jamal, he was able to isolate a white powder, which turned out to be a mixture of several compounds. Later he managed to separate three from this mixture in pure crystalline form. Since they all came from the same source, in Dr. Jamal's opinion, they probably had related structures. If he could establish a composition for one of them, the structures for the other two most likely would be easy to determine.

During his work in the lab, Saleem found out that in chemical research one fails a lot more often than one succeeds. Every time he failed, he was disappointed, but all he could think of was trying once more. Over a period, he developed a tolerance for failure. He anticipated that success might only come by changing parameters and conditions of the experiment, which meant starting all over again. Saleem now had been working within the group for almost a year and a half, and he had dedicated himself to this particular project for the last twelve months. He was slowly getting a feel for what he was doing. During the last six months, Saleem had been trying unsuccessfully to break down a complex molecule to a simpler form, which would then be identifiable more easily.

Breaking up an organic molecule could be achieved in several ways; the most common method was to treat it with different acids and bases. He carried out several experiments and accomplished nothing meaningful. The only acid he had not tried was the concentrated sulfuric acid because it charred organic matter. He suggested a few times that he wanted to try this acid on one of the products. Everyone he talked to always discouraged him; consensus was that sulfuric acid would destroy the material. Saleem had accumulated enough products through an isolation process that he and his supervisor had developed in the lab.

One day, without telling anyone, he took a small quantity of one of these compounds, the compound that he had in the largest amount, placed it on a clean watch glass and carefully added one drop of concentrated sulfuric acid to it. Nothing happened, which Saleem took as a good sign. The reaction mixture did not turn black, which meant it did not char the material and turn it into carbon. And since there was no visible change, Saleem concluded that it needed gentle heating to bring about a reaction. The best way to achieve that, in his opinion, was to heat some water in a beaker and set the watch glass on top where the rising steam would slowly warm the mixture. After this was done, he left the lab to get some lunch. Upon returning, he could not believe what he saw. Needle-shaped crystals now covered the entire bottom of the watch glass. Like the petals of a bouquet of white flowers, they were staring at him.

Excitedly, he rushed to Dr. Jamal's office to show him what had happened. Dr. Jamal's first reaction was that of a typical organic chemist, "It seems to me that the acid you put in evaporated and you recovered the material you started with. But to make sure we should determine the melting point and the mixed melting point, which should tell us if there was any change in the structure of the original compound."

Saleem was disappointed at the possibility that nothing had altered. He performed a few quick tests to establish whether the original compound had been affected by the acid treatment and, within a few minutes, he knew that his instinct was right. They had possibly broken up the molecule, or at least had modified its chemical structure. When Saleem told Dr. Jamal what he observed during the melting point determinations, Dr. Jamal got up from his desk, without a word grabbed his lab coat, and hurried over to Saleem's workbench.

He did some other tests to confirm the new findings. During his PhD research in England, Dr. Jamal had come across a compound of similar properties. He went back to his old box where he had been collecting and saving chemical samples from his student days. They had been cataloged, organized, and lay in neat rows. It did not take long to find what he was looking for. He pulled it out, looked at it, and decided to compare its infrared spectrum with the spectrum of the compound Saleem just made. The whole procedure took another hour. In the end, they found that the two compounds were identical. Their hard work had paid off. This was a eureka moment for both of them.

By that time, it was dark outside and everyone had gone home. Dr. Jamal said, "Well, we did some good work today. Let's close everything and lock up, and I will drive you home." Dr. Jamal insisted on driving Saleem to his house, even though it was far away from where the doctor lived. On the way, Dr. Jamal told him what a nice job he had been doing. He felt on that day Saleem had taken the first step in the direction of chemical research and let him know that he could achieve great things if he set his mind to it.

Saleem felt very proud of himself. The experienced scientists had told him his idea was wild, but oddly enough it had worked. He understood it was going to bring him recognition of his abilities by others. It made him feel for the first time that he was capable thinking on his own, independently, and get results.

He was savoring his success of the afternoon, when he heard Dr. Jamal say, "You are PhD material. You should apply either to some university in England or in the United States. I will strongly recommend you and help you in any way I can."

Saleem did not know what to say, he simply thanked his research director for his support and his compliments.

Saleem had met a number of people since he had joined the Council Laboratories who had gone abroad to obtain their higher degrees from England and other countries in the West. Whenever they had extra time, these scientists would tell stories about their student days in foreign universities and their accomplishments there. When they compared their present situation to the facilities they had visited abroad, it appeared that they were almost sorry for themselves in their present situation. It came across as if they were sad that they had come back. Saleem had been paying attention to these accounts. What became clear in his mind was a need for him to visit these advanced facilities in the Western world. On the other hand, if he never went, he would not know what he was missing here in Pakistan, and thus would have no regrets and sorrows of coming back. These two conflicting thoughts occupied his mind for the longest time.

He understood that a higher degree from abroad could open up new doors for him, but he was happy and content in his present situation in the research job he liked. He kept putting off applying for admission anywhere abroad, in England or in America. But soon came a time when all his friends, who had the same level of education as he did, started leaving Pakistan for higher studies to the countries in the West. One of his peers, who left for Canada, gave him a list of the American universities, where according to his research, there was a fair chance of getting admitted to graduate school with an assistantship in the chemistry department. Saleem put the paper in a drawer and promptly forgot about it.

Saleem had been working for nearly two years when he took a week off to go and visit Lahore, the historical city where he had entered Pakistan. He had relatives there who invited him to stay with them for a few of days. They had been living in Lahore for a number of years, and had learned to speak the language of that region fluently. They took him to a number of historical buildings that dated back to the Mogul period. Saleem enjoyed seeing the places he had read about in his history class. He thought of the trip as interesting and educational. Because he could not speak Punjabi, the regional language, people referred to him often as *Hindustani* (Indian) which took him back to the time he first entered Pakistan when people had called him by the same name. Being typecast again as a foreign minority bothered him. He felt that he might as well go and live in a more advanced country and be a minority there, instead of being mislabeled in Pakistan.

The minute he returned from his trip, he looked for the list of addresses that he had so carelessly tossed earlier. He proceeded to handwrite a letter to each of the twelve universities on that list, applying for admission to the graduate program and an assistantship in the department of chemistry. In response, he received proper application forms from six of these universities. Wasting no time, he filled them out and sent them back.

Then came the rejection letters. The first one bothered him the most. One by one, he read them and threw them into the wastebasket. He was discouraged. The image in his mind of him working in a lab in an American university was fading away. He quit reading the last ones altogether.

One of his friends noticed an unopened envelope from the University of Oregon lying on Saleem's desk. Being curious, he asked, "Saleem, why you haven't read your mail.

"I already know the contents of the letter—it is just another rejection".

His friend picked up the envelope, looked at it and put it back. Just as he was about to leave, his curiosity got the better of him and he could not resist asking for permission to open it. Saleem only shrugged. His friend unfolded the letter, looked closer and then jumped up and shouted, "Saleem, you are going to America!"

In the letter, the university had offered him an assistantship and admission to the graduate school. He took the letter and as he read it his body was awash with emotions he had never experienced before. Suddenly, he could sense his life change. He felt as if this news had elevated him to a higher level, not only that it put wings on him, it also had put wind beneath them. If he wanted to, he could fly now— in his mind, he actually was.

He yearned to go out and tell everyone; instead, he just sat at his desk trying to absorb what the letter had meant to him and his future. After he got control over himself, he went and sent a telegram to his parents, giving them the good news of his upcoming studies in America. Next, he needed to look up Eugene on the map. So far, America to him was New York, Chicago, California and Texas. Oregon he knew nothing about. The city of Eugene sounded like his small town, Jampur, insignificant in the universe of a large country— important to him, noticed only by a few.

CHAPTER 20

Saleem's trip to the United States was by a cargo boat, the cheapest way to travel for a student. Several others, some from Pakistan and some from India, had chosen the same carrier for their trip for higher education. As they sailed away in the afternoon from the port of Karachi, a crowd gathered on the shore to send the ship off on its long journey. Passengers who had their relatives standing ashore waved goodbye. Saleem's brother was not there to bid him farewell for he was needed at his work. He waved to the crowd anyway. He waved at people he did not know; they waved back to wish him good luck. He wanted to believe they did.

This was his second move in the past five years to a different country. When he was coming to Pakistan he was elated, but travelling overseas, so far away from everything he knew, so far away from the security he had created around him, scared him. The feelings were similar to the emotions he had had when he was sent to college in Agra to face the new challenges in a place at a distance from home. Now, once again he was traveling to be a student in an entirely new system of which he knew nothing. Uncertainties and apprehensions surrounded him. At the same time, he understood that the decision was not forced on him; he had welcomed the opportunity; he had invited the challenge. He imagined that these doubts and fears would not leave him until he was face to face with them. And now it was up to him to face the responsibility, embrace the unknown that lay ahead and make the experience worth its while. With these thoughts in his mind, he moved toward the new world, toward a country he knew only through movies and books. He could hear a land across the oceans beckoning him.

The sluggish Liberty ship, built during the Second World War bringing a load of iron ore from Australia to New York, was now his carrier. It crawled, fighting some heavy storms, where sea sickness did not spare even the young and the healthy, for nearly six weeks before it reached the shores of his destination. The third day into the journey, it stopped in Djibouti, a port in French Somaliland where all students got off and toured the city. Why they stopped there, the captain never told, but being responsible for their safety he sent a shipmate along for some offshore time for his passengers. It was a hot day in the middle of August. The group, guided by the man in uniform, came upon a small restaurant where the young men wanted to get ice cream, but the officer from the ship dissuaded them from eating anything; it might make them sick he was afraid and there was little medicine on board, he said.

The second stop was to cross the Suez Canal, which could be entered only in the early morning hours. The ship got there in the late afternoon and had to wait its turn until the next day. Many Egyptian vendors, taking advantage of the passengers stranded on the vessel waiting to go across from red sea to the Mediterranean, brought their merchandise to sell in small boats. Saleem was surprised to note the vast difference between the asking price and for what they would settle; of course the buyer had to know the art of haggling.

Two days into the Mediterranean, the weather, so different from the Red Sea, was cool and the air was crisp. Saleem saw mountains in the distance. And the ship bustled with activity. The crew had clean clothes and the deck was cleared and appeared washed. The atmosphere was festive. To be a part of the ship community Saleem shaved and put on a clean shirt and pants. The vessel moved toward land and anchored. This unannounced last stop before leaving for New York was on a Greek island, which was a surprise for the passengers, but not for the crew who seemed ready to party. Here the boat docked away from the shore and boatloads of women came on board to meet the sailors. These women did not look anything like the Hellenic wives he had seen in Zorba the Greek. These were ladies dressed in short skirts. They were buxom and their faces were painted with heavy makeup—some were young, some not so young. The rumor was that they were families, though families with no children were an oddity for the young students. Still, they accepted what they were told. The captain discreetly threw a party for his guests on board to keep them out of their cabins. Saleem did not think much of it until he went back to his sleeping quarters and found the linen, the towels, all changed. A strange smell, the smell of human sweat and cheap perfume hung in the air whispering a different tale—a tale of bodies and not a chronicle of family reunion.

After leaving the shores of the island, the ship embarked on long voyage of over a month. During his trip Saleem saw the Indian Ocean, the Red Sea, the Mediterranean Sea and finally the Atlantic Ocean. He saw sunrises and sunsets, full moon and new moon, calm and stormy seas. During the storms in the Atlantic Ocean, the hills of water challenged the advancing ship again and again. The high seas crashed into the bow, drowning the deck with the foam of salt water. The young students aboard, awash with a sense of immortality, never felt fear and enjoyed the fight between the turbulent sea with its angry waves and the stubborn progress of their Liberty ship.

He saw so much of Old Man Sea for so long that by the time he was in New York he had seen enough to last him his lifetime.

Finally, to everyone's relief, the boat approached New York harbor; the first sight was of the Statue of Liberty. Then through the light fog they could see the New York skyline—an awesome sight to behold. It was exciting for the young people to finally see and feel the vibrations of an approaching city they had so extensively read about and seen in the pictures and Hollywood movies. Most of these educated men, who were headed for different universities, were now unconsciously in competition, trying to outdo each other as to who could name more of these tall buildings, the skyscrapers of New York. And Saleem was no exception. Everyone, of course, was familiar with the Statue of Liberty and the Empire State building, the tallest of them all.

Saleem was to spend one night in New York before boarding the plane for Portland and from there to Eugene. He had befriended two other students who were going to stay overnight in New York before leaving for their final destinations. After exchanging words of farewell with the crew, which for some was emotional, the passengers went off to set foot on land. It was a strange feeling to walk on terra firma where the surface under their feet no longer wobbled and swayed. The homely dry earth was supporting them once again.

At customs, after the passports were checked, luggage was examined, and x-rays were looked at, the students were allowed to leave the port. Saleem and two of his friends decided to stay at the same hotel for the night. As they rode through the city in a cab, they could not see the tops of the buildings. All they could see were cars, big cars, and so many. The cab entered a tunnel. Saleem was amazed at the brightness in this underground passage, where lights were reflected from the white tiled walls. He had always thought of the tunnels as dark or, at best, dimly lit passages. But this was a whole new world and this particular subway had so much light that it appeared brighter inside than it was outside.

The hotel was located near the famous Times Square, a place all three young men had seen in enough movies to recognize the minute they arrived. It was different and yet familiar.

The gargantuan buildings touching the clouds fascinated Saleem. The first thought that came to his mind was why people built such high structures. Was it because there was not enough land for people to spread out, or were they just competing with each other to see who could look down on whom? Whatever the reason, to him and his friends, it was an impressive display of superb bold architecture, a sign of the verve of the country.

Saleem had heard the expression "a picture is worth a thousand words". He had seen pictures of New York in magazines and in films, but he never realized how tall these buildings really were. The structural enormity of it all could not be felt in the depictions, no matter how panoramic; it had to be experienced in person. Saleem had been overcome with that same sense of awe just once before in his lifetime, when he had first seen the Taj Mahal in Agra where he attended college. There too, he had seen many pictures of the famous marble monument prior to visiting the site. And there too, he had been overwhelmed by its immense size and beauty.

Saleem was glad now that he had decided to come to America rather than going to England. England attracted many students from India and Pakistan for higher education because of her earlier ties with that region. But in America he was going to have novel experiences and New York City, which was his doorway to this country, had already surpassed all expectations.

When he obtained his student visa back in Pakistan, Saleem had seen a film on the American lifestyle at the US Education Foundation office. Also, he was handed a booklet, which was to acquaint him with the customs, traditions and habits of Americans. During the voyage, he had plenty of time to study this handbook. Whoever had prepared it must not have lived in a university town or as a foreign student, because the advice therein would prove useless for Saleem throughout his days at the university. But on this very first day in New York City, he faithfully followed the instructions.

The three friends deposited their luggage in the hotel and ventured out to explore the metropolis on foot. On the boat, the Greek captain had admonished his passengers not to wander alone in a big city. He had suggested that especially those who were first-time visitors to the country should be extra careful. "Avoid walking alone after dark and, if you must, stay on well-lit streets," he had advised.

Mindful of the captain's advice, they ambled into downtown New York. The wide clean roads were filled with traffic, but to their surprise the sidewalks had very few people. They unanimously decided that everyone was riding in the cars. The size and number of vehicles on well-lit streets awed them. The traffic was moving on the road in an order. Here the lanes were traffic rules to be followed, not mere suggestions as he had seen in Pakistan. Even the stores and office buildings that had closed for the day had light shining through the windows. As they walked along the store fronts, the abundance of merchandise on display in the large windows captivated them all.

Saleem was self-conscious and felt that everyone would somehow know that this was his first day in the country. But after walking for a few minutes, he realized that no one was paying attention to him or cared about where he came from or where he was going; this eased his worries. Walking made them hungry, but no one wanted to go to a fancy place for fear of high prices and the possibility of having unfamiliar codes of behavior.

After some searching, they came upon a small eatery with seats by a long narrow counter. Along the wood-paneled sidewall, there were tables for two. Only a few people were eating inside at that hour. A big, tall black man dressed in a chef's hat and white apron stood in the back and looked at them curiously. Judging from their body language, the cook could tell that the three young customers were tourists or students new to the country. He sensed their uneasiness, so he occupied himself with cleaning the tabletop and attending to other chores.

The newcomers sat down at the counter and looked at the menus, which listed items completely unfamiliar to them. To mention a few, there was chili and there were hamburgers of varied names.

Saleem wished that the booklet he had received from the consulate in Karachi had some recommendations about what to eat. After realizing none of the three had any idea about the food offered, Saleem gathered up courage and told the man that they were students who were in New York for one night to connect with flights to different places. Being new, they did not know what they should order.

The man leaned across the counter and kindheartedly welcomed them to America. All three were delighted he could understand their accent and in addition he seemed to be polite and helpful. He suggested that they should try hamburgers. All three of them called out, "But we do not eat ham!"

"This is not ham. The word is derived from a town in Germany named Hamburg. Hamburgers are actually made from beef." He emphasized the words *ham* and *beef*.

Two of them turned to look at Jaipal, who also went by the name Jay, and being a Hindu was supposed to be a vegetarian. Jay, ignoring their looks, kept staring at the menu. Finally, they ordered deluxe hamburgers with lettuce, onions and tomatoes. The man in the white apron soon placed large plates heaped with food in front of them. The large round sandwiches—hamburgers—sat in the center on the plates and French fries heaped up on one side. The sandwiches had brown bulging tops with sesame seeds wedged here and there. Between the two pieces of bread, a patty of meat was barely visible, hiding behind the lettuce leaves sticking out around the edges. Saleem wanted to pick up the top and look inside, but he feared that it might be improper or even rude to check the food in this manner.

The man standing by the cash register was watching them and noticed they have not touched their food. He realized that in the excitement of welcoming these new foreign students he had forgotten to give them silverware and the napkins. He apologized and brought over a napkin, a knife and a fork for each one of them. Just as he was moving away, he mentioned that eating hamburgers by picking them up in your hands was quite acceptable in this country, and they could eat the fries with their fingers as well. They all felt relieved and thus ate their first meal in America. The food tasted great, especially after what they had been eating on the trawler, a cup of alphabet soup as the first course, pasta with meat sauce for the entre and invariably a piece of watermelon as dessert.

While they were eating, the cook came over to their side to chat and to provide them with tips on life in the U.S. They in turn told him about where they were from and where they were headed. He commended them on how well they all spoke English and wished them success.

Then the bill came, which was in the form of a slip of paper with 3 X hamburgers written on it and a price in front. There was no charge for the drinks as they all had water. All three chipped in and handed the money to the man who returned their change. According to the booklet, ten percent of the price of the bill in a restaurant was to be added to the total cost of the food. As all of them got up to leave, the amount, the suggested percentage, was left discreetly hidden under a plate.

They had not walked more than a few yards when they heard the man calling them, "Hey fellows."

Their first reaction was: what did we do wrong?

The cook walked up to them with long steps. He offered them the money they had left on the counter and said, "You forgot these coins. You are students. You will need all you have and more. Don't go on forgetting your money here and there. If you were trying to tip me, I don't accept tips from kids. You go and work hard and get your degrees."

None of them knew what to say. It seemed pointless to explain about the little book from the American Embassy, and so they just thanked him and pocketed the money.

They thought that their first day in America had been splendid. They had seen skyscrapers, wide roads, and shiny cars; to top it all they met an honest man who advised them what to eat and then would not accept a tip for they were students.

On their way back to the hotel, Saleem looked at Jay and said, "I didn't know you ate beef. When I lived in India, I had several Hindu friends, and a number of them ate meat, chicken, goat or lamb, but none of them ever ate beef."

Jay was quiet for some time then answered, "Well, my father served in the British army. During his service, he was all over the world and ate whatever was available during the war. Most of the time, he did not even know what he was eating. But one thing he learned was that you should not make life difficult by drawing more and more lines around you that you may not cross." His father had counseled his son as he was leaving for America, "Do not isolate yourself. Try to absorb what you can learn, and only then will you grow."

"I am going to follow my father's advice," said Jay. "I am here to learn, not to teach. I will probably not cook beef, but if I am ever in a situation where it is easier for everyone that I bend the rules of my culture and religion, I will. And all said and done, what we just ate did not come from an Indian cow."

They all laughed at this and Saleem admired Jay for his honesty and his views, which so resonated with his own.

The following day, they had to leave for the airport for each to catch a flight for his final destination. The hotel had arranged transport to the airport. They boarded a bus carrying other passengers traveling by different airlines. They drove through the streets of New York City once again. Saleem was so absorbed in looking at everything that time passed quickly and before he realized it, they had arrived. He was flying with Pan Am. It was something he had always hoped to do because he had seen their office in Karachi. It had the largest sign on the ground floor of a hotel building in the center of the upscale part of that town. The heavy glass doors were always clean and when he had gone in to purchase his ticket, the air conditioned indoors had surprised and impressed him. English was the only language he had heard there; he had felt that he was already in America.

As he got off the bus, the driver handed him his suitcase. He was now on his own. His friends stayed on the bus, as they were headed toward different airline terminals. He carried his bags to the check-in counter and received a boarding pass. This was not entirely new to him, as he had already flown a couple of times in Pakistan. The woman who gave him the boarding pass saw his ticket and must have noted that he had purchased it in Karachi. Looking at his young face and clothes, she realized that he was a first-time traveler in this country so she spoke slowly and clearly. She directed him to the gate where he would find his plane and told him it would soon be ready for boarding. Saleem found the gate and walked to another counter which displayed the flight number, the same as the number printed on his boarding pass. Hoping the woman there would guide him to the plane, Saleem showed it to her.

She looked at the paper and pointed toward an aircraft and said, "Your plane is right there and they are boarding."

She could not have known that this was his first flight in America and he needed more help. Saleem could see the Pan Am airplane through the glass wall, but did not know how to get into it. The other two times that he had flown, he had boarded a bus, which carried him along with the other passengers to the plane that stood at a distance from the terminal building. As they got off the bus, they climbed a ladder to get in where a hostess ushered him to his seat.

This Pan Am aircraft was parked very close to the terminal, but there was no bus in sight. There were no stairs to climb and above all, there was no usher to guide him. Saleem realized that not all his earlier experiences of flying were going to be of any help here. He did not know what to do. He saw some empty chairs in the lobby, where he sat down, trying to figure out how to get on this plane. According to the departure time on his boarding pass, the flight was leaving in a little over twenty minutes and he was still outside. Five minutes passed. He finally decided he should seek help and walked up to the woman at the counter, showed her his boarding pass once again, and asked how he could board.

The woman answered in a voice where Saleem detected irritation, "You should be in your seat. They will close the doors in fifteen minutes. Go up the stairs and get into the airplane."

He then noticed a platform that was accessible through a staircase. Saleem climbed up and sat down on another chair, hoping someone would see him and come to get him—no such luck. Another five minutes passed and no one came. He noticed a door close to where he was sitting, but there was no sign on it. Was there a restroom behind the door? he wondered. He could tell that it was an entrance, but he was not sure to what. People had been going in and no one had come out.

By this time Saleem was wracked with anxiety; he decided to take some action. He picked up his handbag and, with considerable courage, pushed open the door and dared to go through it. This mystery door did not open into a room, but into a dimly lit narrow passage. Saleem ventured along and to his amazement, he found himself at the end of the walkway where an attendant greeted him, looked at his boarding pass and let him into the plane to find his seat. The rows of seats divided by an aisle lay on both sides. Music was pleasant and as soon as he seated himself a woman came up and offered him plastic wrapped candy. He knew he was in the right plane where he found a place by the window, put on his seat belt and settled down for his trip to Portland, Oregon.

In a few minutes, the attendants closed the doors and the plane was cleared for departure. Saleem remembered how on earlier flights he had enjoyed the take-off the most. After maneuvering through left and right, they approached the runway, stopped, and then with roaring jet-engines the Boeing 707 took off. Saleem watched the runway go by faster and faster as the aircraft sped along, and finally there came the moment when it left the concrete to embrace the sky. They were airborne and soon were flying over those tall buildings of New York. Within the last twenty-four hours, he had seen these buildings from three different angels. First, he saw them from the side as he sailed in, then again, as he walked through the streets, and now from the top as he flew over them. As he looked down, all that was visible were the skyscrapers of New York—the creations of an advanced human civilization, but human life he could no longer see. Creations here dwarfed the creator. This aerial picture he had seen on a postcard.

As the captain announced that they were flying at 30,000 feet, some passengers lighted up their cigarettes; Saleem just pushed his seat back and let his mind wander about things to come.

Until now, except for the last few minutes at the airport, all his experiences had been thrilling. He knew that soon he would have to apply himself at the university. After all, that was what he came for—to work hard and learn, Saleem mused. He remembered his father once telling him how success was like climbing a mountain—hard work. He knew from experience that anything worthwhile came at a cost. He was ready to pay that price and meet the challenges ahead. He had made up his mind; he was not going to disappoint those who had put their faith in him, especially his parents who expected him to succeed.

After the takeoff from New York, there was a stop in Chicago. The plane landed there late in the afternoon and everyone had to get off. It was a one-hour stop. Once Saleem was in the lounge, he walked around to take it all in. The first thing he noticed was the several vending machines lined against the walls. Fascinated and intrigued he stood there and watched them. Contained in some was an assortment of fruits. He saw shiny apples, fresh bananas and oranges sitting there waiting for some hungry traveler. Other machines offered sandwiches and food items wrapped in plastic.

For some reason, it took him back in time to the railway station in Agra when he had gotten off the train when he arrived there for the first time. There had also been food items offered by the vendors. And the platform was crowded by passengers hurrying to get to their destinations. Here at the airport there were not as many people, and the vending machines had replaced the vendors. It was cooler and everything was well lit and clean. In spite of the similarities associated with travel destinations, he was able to appreciate the unique differences in the two countries. He felt things were at a more advanced level here, but in spite of the disparity, they were alike in nature, as if they were at two different stages of evolution.

As Saleem settled in a seat, he heard several announcements; some he could understand and some he could not. One of them, the only one important for him, he failed to catch. The aircraft had developed engine trouble and the airline had cancelled the flight. Only when it was close to the time of departure and Saleem wanted to get on board was he informed of the fact. Until now, everyone had been very polite to him, but this man behind the counter was clearly annoyed that Saleem had not been paying attention to the announcements. The airport employee told Saleem that the next plane to Portland, Oregon would not take off until the morning.

"A while back, the staff was giving tickets to the passengers of this flight for an overnight stay in a hotel. Now, I don't see anyone here. You may want to go and talk to the Pan Am station manager. Maybe he can help you."

Saleem found this unsettling and puzzling. He asked the man if it was all right that he stayed at the airport and waited until the next morning. The man had no objection. He actually showed signs of relief. Saleem was relieved as well.

Saleem spent his second night in the new country sitting on a bench at the airport. He was so excited discovering new things that he did not find it troubling. There was a long night ahead, but then he had spent nights without sleep earlier. He decided he would read some, watch people around him, and maybe learn a thing or two in the process. He was familiar with the American magazines. In preparation of coming to America, he had been reading *Time* magazine and the *Readers' Digest* regularly for the past year. He bought a copy of *Time* and read it from cover to cover. The printing paper of the same magazine in Pakistan felt much thinner between his fingers and it had almost no advertising.

After each hour or so he got up and walked around. As the time passed, the airport became quieter; some of the shops turned off their lights and closed for the night. He noticed a handful of passengers like him, waiting for their flights; some had stretched out in an attempt to sleep; some were sitting and some were reading. The bright lights of the vending machines were beckoning. Saleem was hungry and tempted to purchase a sandwich, but he was afraid to tackle the equipment he had never touched before, and he did not know how to use it.

This was Saleem's first night in a foreign country in a public place and he found it educational. He sat there, staring at what was going on around him. During the night, he saw several people walk away, leaving whatever they were reading on the seats…except for their books. A man carrying a copy of *Life* magazine came and sat not far from him. The man was smoking and his cigarette would dangle from his lips when he browsed through the magazine. The way pages were turning, he was not reading anything; he was looking at the pictures, reading a few sentences, if anything at all, to get an idea about the images he could not make out through a glance.

He stayed for about half an hour turning the pages and then finally read an article or two. When he left, the magazine remained on the seat. Saleem wanted to get the man's attention to tell him he was forgetting something, but then decided not to. He was new here and had no idea how to approach a stranger. Now, Saleem could pick it up to read it. But it was not his.

A new magazine would give him something to read. He knew *Life* always had nice pictures to look at.

But would it be proper thing to pick up something that did not belong to him? The man might have left his reading material behind by mistake and come back for it.

These thoughts were going around in his mind when a cleaner came by, picked it up along with other papers, and threw it in with other trash. To Saleem, this was such a waste, but it seemed perfectly normal to everyone else around him.

After a few more hours, it was the dawning of the new day. With the onset of daylight came activity; the rising sun had brought new vitality and movement to the quiet surrounding him and soon there were many people in the lounge. The place was coming alive. He went to the restroom where he washed his face and brushed his teeth. He now felt ready to tackle another day. He had not slept all night, yet he was not sleepy or tired. The excitement of being in a new place had energized him.

The workers at one of the restaurants started arriving and he could tell that the place was to open soon. Once they started serving, with his bag in hand, Saleem stood there watching how people got their food. Everyone who came into the restaurant would pick up a tray, place a knife, a fork and a paper napkin on it then slide the tray toward where there were pans of hot food. As the person passed a food container, if he desired some of it on his plate, he would point to it or ask for it. At the end of the line, a woman calculated the price and charged for what was on the tray. He stood there learning, and absorbing what was going on. There was no line; still he was waiting for his turn, his mind telling him he was not ready. Eggs, toast, pastries, coffee and milk were the items he recognized. Others he could not make out.

After a few minutes, Saleem was confident that he could do this and get some breakfast to eat. He proceeded to do like other customers he had watched and got a nice breakfast of scrambled eggs, two pastries and a cup of coffee on his tray. He would have preferred tea, but there was no teapot in sight. When he sat down to eat, he enjoyed the food not only because he was hungry, but also because he considered it an achievement to have successfully managed the whole process of getting everything on his tray without making any mistake. For a moment he felt he was in command.

This morning, he did not want to miss any flight information and so he carefully listened every time an announcement came over the speaker system. Some of the messages were garbled and difficult to understand. It was not clear to him whether the system was distorting the announcer's voice or it was the accent that was causing the problem for him. However, he was able to grasp the one about his flight. This time he was at the right place and right time to board the plane. This time, he knew how to get on it too. The takeoff was still exciting, but not like when he left New York.

They got to Portland, Oregon where he caught another flight for Eugene. By the time he was seated on this last flight of the trip, he felt like he was now a veteran flyer. This was a smaller aircraft and the flight was short. As he waited to collect his luggage, a young man of about his age approached him and asked if he was Saleem. Obviously, the professor had gotten the telegram with the arrival information that Saleem had sent from Chicago. Everything was coming together for him.

CHAPTER 21

David, the student who had picked Saleem up at the airport, invited him to stay with him until he found his own place. Rooming together turned out to be an eventful experience. When Saleem was given a cup filled with hot water accompanied by a tea bag, thinking and admiring the ingenuity of the western society that had portion-packed tealeaves for each cup separately, he ripped it open. When David pointed out that the whole tea bag, as it was, was supposed to go into the cup, he was disappointed. He did not want to have paper in his tea. When asked if he would like a cookie with his tea, he declined because he did not know that a cookie was the same as a biscuit in his country.

Later in the evening, he found out that David had two other chemistry graduate students sharing the rented house. All of them were there for the dinner David had prepared that night and were curious to meet the new foreign student. They were amazed he could speak English and they were able to understand what he was saying. When they sat down to eat, the hosts were curious to know about his trip. He described his journey through the oceans and also told them a little about his life in India and Pakistan.

Soon after dinner, the students turned in, as they all had classes or work early in the morning. Everyone had been kind and courteous to Saleem. They wanted him to feel at home in the new country. A sofa in the living room was to be his bed for the night with a sleeping bag to keep him warm. He did not know that he was meant to get into this thing and so he used it as a cover, thinking it was a thick, albeit narrow, quilt. Saleem was tired; he had not slept the night before. He fell into deep sleep as soon as his back touched the soft cushions.

When they got up in the morning, David noticed that Saleem had not unzipped the sleeping bag. He apologized for not explaining to him what he used as a cover was in fact supposed to wrap around him. And he showed him how. Saleem was learning new things every minute.

After breakfast of a cup of coffee with buttered toast, Saleem accompanied David to the office in the chemistry department. The secretary, used to handling new foreign students, took care of all the necessary material to get his class registration, his ID card and the keys to the building. Finally, she took him to meet the professor with whom he had corresponded.

The professor was busy in his office, but took a few minutes to welcome Saleem and told him that classes did not begin for another two days; this should give him ample time to familiarize himself with the department and the building. Back in the office, he was assigned a mailbox where he was to check for his mail and messages. He also received directions to the bookstore where he would buy textbooks for the classes he had registered for. All this started to overwhelm Saleem. There was too much to absorb, too many new things to learn in too short a time. He wished he had a month to get himself acquainted and adjusted to the new conditions. This, however, was not possible. He had to make the best of the situation and hope it would work out.

After he finished his work in the office, he decided to walk around and explore the campus. He had not walked far when he heard someone call his name. He knew it had to be someone from Pakistan because of the tone in the man's voice and the way he pronounced his name. He turned around. To his great surprise and relief, he saw Jafar. Jafar was the young man whom he had met at the passport office in Pakistan a few months before. In the brief encounter, they found out they were going to the US for higher studies, but had no idea they were coming to the same university. It turned out that he was starting graduate school in physics under the Fulbright program. After a few formal words, he asked Saleem if he had a place to live. Saleem told him that he only arrived the day before and had spent the night with an American student named David.

Jafar's sponsor had flown him from Pakistan. He had managed to get there a month earlier than Saleem. He had gotten himself a place to live, and by now, knew his way around. He offered to take

Saleem to meet his landlady and see if she would help find suitable housing for him.

Everyone, Jafar included, seemed to live near the campus. They walked to his place. The property owner, Gretchen, a widow living alone in this big house, had decided to rent two of her rooms to students, but unfortunately for Saleem, both had been rented out for the year. When Jafar and Saleem got there, they found the woman, curlers in her hair, tending her garden. She wiped her hands on her apron and came over to greet the two young men from the land far away. After introducing Saleem to Gretchen, Jafar told her that here was another new graduate student who needed her help. The lady was pleased. To be in a position where she could help young foreign students made her feel useful again.

Gretchen went inside to call her various friends who were also supplementing their income by leasing spare rooms in their homes to the students. Not surprisingly, the homeowners no longer had any available accommodation for the entire academic year. Gretchen, who enjoyed talking with young educated men, invited the two guests in, and acting like a mother, offering each a cup of coffee and a piece of pie. Saleem could see that Jafar had made good impression on his landlady—she was kind to him. And it was because of Jafar that Saleem was getting such attention from her. As they sat together talking about student lodging, the lady came up with a temporary solution for Saleem. She suggested that he could stay in the basement where there was a bed until he found a proper place to live. Under the present circumstances, this seemed like a good solution. Saleem did not want to overtax the hospitality of David and his friends by staying any longer than necessary.

Like a good Samaritan, Gretchen offered Saleem a ride to the chemistry department, where he found David and asked him if he could get his suitcase out of his place. David was gracious enough to say how much he and his friends enjoyed Saleem's staying with them. "We never lock the door. You can go in any time and pick up your things."

Saleem thanked him, shook his hand and promised to call him and his friends over, once he was settled in his own place.

After returning with Saleem's luggage, Gretchen showed him how he could pull a curtain to separate his bed from the storage area and the heating furnace in the basement. The living space was far from ideal, but there was a bed to sleep on and a sink to wash his face. The bathroom located on the first floor was shared by all the guests.

The following day, Saleem went to the department to check if there was anything else he needed to do. He found a note from Dr. Kramer in his mailbox, stating that he would be in his office after ten this morning. Dr. Kramer was the professor who taught the general chemistry class. Since Saleem was going to be his teaching assistant, he had to meet with the professor to get oriented and find out about his duties and schedule. It was only a little after eight in the morning, which gave Saleem two hours to take a walk and acquaint himself with the campus. He marveled at the greenery all around him and the amazingly beautiful flowers planted everywhere. Where he grew up, it was not possible to grow flowers in public places; unless a fence or a gardener protected them, people would pick them and take them home to their families.

It was early and it was quiet, the classes had not started yet. In the hush of the morning he could hear the rustling of the leaves in the gentle breeze. Early sunrays broke through the tall fern trees to light up patches of the green lawns. It was one of those perfect moments when his mind drifted into a state of peace and happiness. When Saleem had left Pakistan, he had no idea what life would be like on the campus in Eugene, Oregon. The rapturous feeling he experienced this morning, he realized, was partly because the scenery was so unexpectedly beautiful. Every moment was a thing to remember, he wanted to take it all in for as long as possible. To describe the rapture, the Farsi words: *Gar Fridaus Ba-roo-e Zamin Ast; Hami Asto, Hami Asto, Hami Ast* (If there is heaven on earth, it's here, it's here, it's here), ascribed to the early seventeenth century Mogul Emperor Jahangir when he visited the Kashmir valley for the first time sailed through his head. He felt like the king must have felt, impressed by the milieu of his surroundings. The Farsi couplet can still be seen engraved on the walls of the royal quarters, *Divan-e-Khas,* in the Red Fort built by his son, the Emperor Shah Jahan in Delhi. In that moment, soaked in the ambiance, he felt he touched the core of happiness. In a state of bliss, he walked around to explore some more.

Saleem enjoyed his stroll on the narrow walkways that crossed grassy lawns. Little did he know that he would seek out these same paths, the same surroundings, during agonizing hours, and again at joyful moments in his student days.

The few people he encountered along the way smiled at him and said hello. After a while, he became conscious of the fact that he was wearing a suit and leather shoes; no one else was. He was different. Saleem recognized that his appearance announced the fact that he was a new foreign student on campus. In his mind, he felt that everyone was being nice to him to make him feel welcome and comfortable. The feelings of rapport on this campus in this foreign country lifted his spirits.

As he walked by the student union, he saw the cafeteria Jafar had told him about. He also found the post office. He had well used his two hours exploring and enjoying the lovely sunshine. He remembered David telling him that the good weather they were having that week was not to last long; the normal rainy wet fall season would catch up with them soon.

Then it was time to go and see Dr. Kramer. Saleem easily located his office and found the door open. The young professor sat behind a clean desk in a white short-sleeve shirt, reading a book. Saleem knocked and entered. Dr. Kramer stood up to greet his new teaching assistant, shook his hand with a firm grip, and asked him to take a seat. First, they made small talk to get acquainted. Dr. Kramer wanted to know when he got into the country and if he had found a place to live. Then he briefly explained the responsibilities of a teaching assistant, and what was expected of him as a student in the department.

Saleem's job was to teach a lab, which included one hour of lecture explaining the experiments students would do that day and three hours in the laboratory, three times a week. In addition, he was to help Dr. Kramer grade the test papers. At the same time, he would be taking his own classes for graduate work. Since this system was new to Saleem, Dr. Kramer suggested that he should soon arrange to meet with the professors who were accepting students into their research groups. The professor of his choice would then be his adviser and guide him throughout the program.

After he left his office, Saleem's impression of Dr. Kramer was that he was a young intelligent man who led a structured life and lacked compassion. He wondered why such a man chose to become a teacher. Saleem's concept of a teacher was an individual who would inspire in his students a desire for learning and not just someone who taught classes and gave tests. But then, who was he to judge an American professor whom he hardly knew? Although he never had a teacher who fit his standard, he was hoping to meet one in America.

After meeting with Dr. Kramer, Saleem headed for the bookstore. He needed to get his textbooks and get ready for work. A number of students in the store, some browsing, some looking around, were scattered in the maze of bookshelves; among them he saw another foreign student. Instinctively he knew that the man must be from the same part of the world where he himself had grown up. This young man appeared to be a few years older than Saleem. He seemed more accustomed and comfortable in his surroundings. Saleem went up to him, introduced himself and asked if he was from India or Pakistan. The man, Kader, it turned out, was from East Pakistan. And he, too, was looking for a place to live. Kader, a new graduate student in the department of economics, was moving to Eugene after spending two years at the University of Wisconsin. No wonder he was so well adjusted in this foreign land, Saleem thought.

After talking for a while, both realized that they had things in common. Their like-mindedness, their compatibility, made them look for a place to live together. With Kader's knowledge of the land, they found an apartment the same day, a little expensive, a little away from campus, but still in walking distance for a young twenty-some-thing. They were able to move in the next day and Saleem was happy to leave his temporary shelter in the basement. The new place on the second floor had a kitchen, a bedroom and a living room. The furnishings did not crowd the area and consisted of a dining table with four chairs, a sofa, a stuffed chair, and a couple of beds. It felt airy and comfortable and, above all, it was now his new home away from home.

CHAPTER 22

The classes started and so did the rains. On his very first day, walking briskly to campus, he got soaked. It took about an hour before he was finally dry to a point where his clothes were no longer hanging like wet rags. He was miserably wet and cold when he attended his first class in completely new surroundings. He had not been in a classroom in over three years. In his previous experience, all his classmates were of the same age group. Being with students of different ages, from different countries was an experience new to him. An equal number of young men and women made up the group. He noticed that everyone was casually dressed. Almost all of them wore canvas shoes. The students sat in various postures. Astonishingly, some even had their feet up on their desks, which in his culture was rude and an absolute no-no. He wondered if he would ever change, enough to where he would one day feel equally comfortable putting his feet up on a desk in a classroom.

Getting back to be a student again, trying to adapt to the system, Saleem got very busy in the following weeks. All his previous schooling had been under a format, introduced in India by the British after their own pattern in England, where the final examination at the end of the year determined one's success and a PhD degree was awarded as an honor for doing an original piece of research. The present system of education was unfamiliar to him. When he had started to plan to get a PhD, all he thought of was doing research and discovering something of value; he enjoyed working in the lab. He did not quite grasp the significance of taking classes, the frequent tests and quizzes under the American system until it was just about too late.

He was anxious to start working in the lab once again. That was his passion. In between classes, Saleem talked with different professors in the department and got a research project assigned, working for a professor he enjoyed meeting. The senior professor who would now be his adviser had many graduate students and about a dozen postdoctoral fellows in his research group, which was thus large and international. Although the interview was short, Saleem felt comfortable talking with the man.

Understanding that in order to obtain his PhD he would have to work hard in the lab and be able to do some original work in organic chemistry—his field of choice—he immersed himself into the research project and would stay up until the early hours. Absorbed in his work, he was learning how to use the sophisticated equipment and mastering new skills. He was enjoying this aspect of his studies. He was working hard and was starting to get some meaningful results.

Saleem envied those postdoctoral fellows and professors who walked the hallways as if deep in thought with a cup of coffee in their hand and a pipe in their mouth, they had already achieved what he was trying to accomplish. Someday he hoped, he would, just like them, be able to mull over a problem without the worry of getting a degree.

Over a month passed since Saleem started attending classes. One day, sitting in the cafeteria eating his lunch, he was thinking about the experiment he finished last night where he for once got results he was expecting. He was happy with his work and with himself that day as he noticed Professor Hayden coming in. He watched the professor ordering his food and bringing his tray over to where he was sitting.

On his way to where Saleem was sitting, the professor's mind was churning to find proper words of caution and warning about the chances of his looming failure, while at the same time leaving him with hope to succeed.

Saleem was surprised, but at the same time felt honored that the professor was coming to eat lunch with him. He started to get up, but his teacher motioned him to stay seated. They started making small talk. The professor asked him if he had ever gone hunting when he lived in India. Saleem had hunted, so they exchanged their stories. Saleem had been unaware that Professor Hayden knew so much about him. The professor mentioned how impressed he was by what

Saleem was doing in the lab on his research project. Saleem was very happy to hear that the professor was satisfied with his work.

However, he soon found out that Professor Hayden had decided to sit with him, not so much to socialize, but to discuss serious aspects of his study program. The professor put on a grim face as he got ready to talk about some grave problems. He said, "The Department and I understand how difficult it must be for you coming from a foreign country with a completely different system of education to adapt to a new method in a very short time. The reality of the fact is, that you are competing here with students who are not only familiar with the system, they are also smart. Here, the grades are awarded on a competitive level and if you fail to earn A's and B's in your courses, you will be disqualified from the program. The research at this level is not as important as you might think.

"At this point, I would like you to concentrate on your courses and improve your grades. Your teachers seem to be concerned about your performance. You perhaps are not aware that all the tests given during the course of the quarter count toward your final grade, and the final examination is not the all-important test that you have in the system you came from. The results of the tests you have taken so far indicate that you are failing the courses and heading for trouble. We have lost some capable students for they were not cautioned in time. You need to gather all your resources and put all your efforts into bringing your grades up to an acceptable level.

"Looking at your old records, I know that you are a capable student and you can do this. If you need any assistance from any of your teachers, they will be very happy to help you and my office has an open-door policy. If you have any questions, do come in and we will talk. I realize that the things I just told you are unpleasant and I hate to spoil your weekend, but we needed to discuss this issue before it was too late. Being your adviser, I consider it my responsibility to tell you early on so that you can correct the problem."

By the time Professor Hayden was finished with his talk, he had also eaten his lunch. As he got up to leave, he added, "I would hate to lose a researcher like you. I see good things in your future." He wished him good luck and was gone.

The professor might have been there to emphasize the priorities, but to Saleem it was a forewarning of failure knocking at the door. With all the new things he had to deal with in his life, the teaching load and the work he had to do in the department, he could not see how he would be able to improve his failing grades. He was in a hole. He was doomed!

He was in shock. He felt as if there had been an explosion around him that had knocked him into a deep dark crevice and he no longer knew where he was or what he was doing. Stunned, he sat there holding his head in his hands. He closed his eyes; he did not feel any different. The darkness had swallowed him so completely that he had lost the awareness of light. It took several minutes before he realized that he was still in the cafeteria with a half-eaten sandwich on his plate in front him. He could not finish his meal. He sat there in a stupor. He needed to be alone. Away from everyone. Why? He did not know. He had to think and work out a solution for this unforeseen obstacle glaring at him that suddenly stood planted between him and his goal. His body felt numb and he was not sure of anything anymore.

He had never before experienced failure staring in his face up so close. He knew things were not going as well as they should have been, too many new things around him had been overwhelming, but he had no idea that he was so close to failing. At this point, a PhD in chemistry was the most important thing in his life and he had travelled far to achieve it.

He did not know that C was a failing grade in this particular program; in the brochure, it stood for "Pass". He had not realized that he had been reading the information sheet for the undergraduate curriculum.

With his head down, hands deep in his pocket and all those ideas churning in his head, Saleem walked around the green lawns trying to collect his thoughts. Like a zombie, he walked here and there, unaware of his surroundings and not knowing where he was going. The shock of the professor's disclosure had been sudden and unexpected. Saleem felt dizzy, his knees were giving out and the world was spinning around him. He sat on a bench and waited for his head to clear.

After a while, it dawned on him that it was Friday afternoon and he had to teach a lab session in half an hour. He really did not feel like educating anyone at this moment, but it was one of the responsibilities of his teaching assistantship. He had no choice; he walked, one foot in front of the other, back to the chemistry building, although he was not sure he could do the job but he had a duty to fulfill.

He desperately tried to push away his worries so he could attend to his students.

Once in the lab, he instructed his class what work they would be doing that afternoon. As the boys and girls got busy with their experiments, they started asking questions. Saleem was one of the more patient teaching assistants who did not mind explaining things over and over again. For this reason most of his students liked him. He was grateful that he had some work to take his mind off his troubles and he was able to settle down.

Finally, it was five o'clock; the class was over and the students left one by one. As he sat there all by himself, thoughts of the lunch conversation, accompanied by a feeling of inadequacy, returned once again. The troubling revelation five hours ago had been so unexpected that he was losing confidence and now doubted his own abilities. Like looking through a dark cloud, his future seemed unclear. With his mind filled with doubts and worries, his dreams, his hopes and his confidence crumbling like an imploded structure, he stepped out into a light drizzle. He was happy for the rain; it had a calming effect on him. Absentmindedly, he put on his raincoat, opened his umbrella, and started walking.

He appreciated Professor Hayden's coming over and talking to him. He was his favorite teacher and his adviser. Nevertheless, he wished the professor had never said, especially the way he said it, what he heard. Reality, however, remained, and he could feel his dreams vanishing. He was still reeling from the shock. In depth of his mind, the words "hate to lose you" echoed once again. To him it meant he had lost without ever playing the game. For the first time he understood why a student in his condition, vanity wounded, confidence at lowest point of despair, all doors to future closed, would consider committing suicide. That route, however humiliating a failure, was not a choice for him. He understood that.

The wet, cold air felt good on his face and had a calming effect on his emotions. Still feeling miserable, Saleem now tried to analyze his abilities and goals. The mere thought of a stumble was paralyzing and draining him of all his energies. Lack of success in school was unacceptable, but under the circumstances he now understood he had no idea how to avoid it. This was compounded by the fact that he was far away from home and continuously overwhelmed by new demands and surroundings in this foreign land. In addition to dealing with depressing thoughts of failure, the disappointed faces of his parents kept flashing in front of his eyes. He attempted to calm himself by trying to recognize his fears—fear of failure and fear of rejection—the two most dreaded conditions. He tried to tell himself that no one who loved him would ever reject him because he had failed. Or, would they? He did not really know.

He felt one part of his mind was losing focus and accepting defeat, while the other was telling him that it was not all over; he still had time. "I can and I will find a way out of this," in an attempt to boost is confidence, he mumbled to himself. In and out of despair, uncertain of his future, Saleem walked to his apartment. *Come what may, I am not giving up. I will do whatever it takes to achieve what I came for*, he finally said to himself.

With this new resolution, he folded his umbrella and let the rain pelt his face. The cold drops felt good and restored his equilibrium. Then out of nowhere, his father's voice was talking to him, "We are Pathans, and Pathans can face any situation without fear. Pathans are not weak; they are strong. Pathans always have and always will keep their heads up high and face all situations with courage." The words that his father had spoken in the past somehow restored Saleem's confidence. He straightened his back, raised his head and marched forward through the rain.

It was Friday evening. With the start of the weekend there were more cars on the road. He needed to watch out. Saleem was still so engrossed in his thoughts that he passed by the small neighborhood grocery store without noticing it. By the time he arrived at his apartment, the rain had stopped. His roommate was not there yet. Saleem felt wet, cold and hungry. After changing into dry clothes, all he could find in the kitchen was leftover chicken from the night before and an apple. As he ate the food without tasting it, his thoughts wandered back again to the lunch conversation. For a moment he was crushed between the failure that loomed ahead and the fear of going back to face those who had put their faith in him to succeed.

When his roommate came in, he found Saleem to be unusually quiet, but did not think much of it. He had eaten a sandwich on the way home. They both talked prior to retiring for the night. Kader did not want to probe and Saleem was not about to reveal what agitated his mind.

Saleem had not slept long when he woke up feeling sick. For a while, still half-asleep, he did not know what was happening. He knew something was wrong but did not know what it was. All he knew was that he had an awful feeling inside his stomach. He ran to the bathroom and threw up. The noise woke Kader who ran over to see Saleem still bent over the toilet bowl, retching and gasping. After watching for a while, Kader could see that his roommate was seriously ill and needed medical care. He called the university infirmary to check if a doctor was in attendance and then called a cab. By the time the taxi arrived, Saleem's stomach must have been empty because the vomiting had stopped. But just in case, Kader did take a paper bag along and sat next to Saleem on the back seat. The trip to the hospital only took a few minutes and Saleem was whisked into an exam room.

Kader explained to the doctor what he had seen, "Saleem ate leftover food and an apple a few hours before the symptoms appeared."

The doctor checked Saleem's temperature, looked into his eyes, checked his stomach and tested his chest with a stethoscope. At the end of the exam, he told the patient and his friend that it was a case of stomach flu, which seemed to be going around. There was nothing to worry about, and the worst was already over. But it would be a good idea if Saleem spent the night in the hospital. A nurse gave him nightclothes and led him to a bed.

There were two beds in the room, but the other one was empty. The nurse brought Saleem a glass of 7-Up with instructions to drink if he felt thirsty. He was tired. The physical ordeal of the day and then his illness had dulled his emotional pain. He no longer had any fears. Getting well was the pressing need. His mind had shut down some functions to take care of the present. At this point worrying was not urgent. There would be time for that later. He sipped some of the liquid by his bedside, lay down and tried to sleep. He woke up several times during the night, but his stomach had settled; he was no longer nauseated.

In the morning he felt better, although still very weak. The nurse wanted him to eat something before going home, but food was the last thing he wanted to look at. And then he did not want to take any chances. However, he did ask the nurse to call a cab for him.

After changing into his clothes, Saleem walked to the main entrance to wait. A girl sitting on a bench was also waiting to go home. Saleem was too tired to notice anything else. When the woman came to tell him that the cab was on its way, the young woman looked up and asked Saleem if she could share the ride to her dorm. She had been waiting for her sister to come and pick her up, but she had not shown up yet.

By the time taxi arrived, they had exchanged some information about each other. She had told Saleem that she was a freshman, studying to be a journalist. Saleem told her that he was a first-year graduate student in the department of chemistry. The only thing the two had in common was that they both spent the night in the hospital with the same disease, the stomach flu.

During the short ride they quietly looked outside. She gave her address to the driver and Saleem asked the man at the wheel to drop her off first and to take him to his address afterwards. At her dorm as she got ready to step out of the car, she turned toward Saleem with her purse open and wanted to pay her share of the ride. Saleem waved her off with a tired smile. She thanked him and quickly climbed up the steps to the dorm door and disappeared.

As the taxi started to move once again, the driver said, "Your girlfriend is pretty."

Saleem was taken aback and told him, "I just met her…only a few minutes back. I don't even know her name. We did spend the night in the hospital with flu…that's all.

The driver was quiet for a while and then said, "Well, she is good-looking…" He emphasized the last word and added, "You should look her up when you feel better."

Saleem was glad to get home. A few words from the driver cheered him up; he thanked the driver and gave him the little money he had as a tip.

Saleem was happy to see that Kader was home. He thanked his friend for taking care of him the night before. Kader, still playing the role of a caretaker, made Saleem a cup of tea and suggested he should go to bed and rest. All Saturday he spent mostly in bed.

The next morning, Saleem woke up feeling a lot better. The shining sun outside promised a pleasant day. As he stood looking out by the window, it occurred to him that he had gotten ill, not so much because of the food he ate, but for what was said during the lunch on Friday. He was still tired from the ordeal of the night before.

He decided it would be best if he stayed home and recovered some of his strength.

He needed a plan to survive. He had to attend to one thing, and one thing alone. As a child he had walked on partially built walls, one step at a time, not looking around. Complete focus, complete concentration. That's what he needed now.

He mentally relived his experiences and concluded that the path in his life had not always been smooth—difficulties he had lived through and survived before. He remembered how he had multiple adjustment problems when he first went to college in Agra. The first year was the hardest, but after certain changes he made, he did well. Looking back, Saleem now realized that he had always had problems adjusting to a new environment. Coping with a new lifestyle seemed to be his weakness. He was learning to adjust to the new life once again; still he found it difficult to be positive.

He remembered that each time there was a crisis in his life, his survival instincts had taken over and his body had started to release those special hormones needed for him to think better and overcome the obstacles. After every ordeal he had come out a stronger person, less sensitive to the vicissitudes of life and more enduring to its hardships. He had been a survivor. And he would survive again, of this he was sure. He must succeed and he must be able to achieve his goal, his degree, that was his promise to himself.

The thoughts flowing through his mind helped Saleem regain his balance. Problems no longer seemed insurmountable. He was feeling better now and his mind wandered to the girl who shared the ride with him from the hospital. He did not know who she was, but she was beautiful—the taxi driver had said so too. Just as the plants and their flowers in the park made him feel cheerful, he recognized she had lighted a spark of cheer in his heart. Just sitting in the car with her gave him the same sense of happiness that he felt while walking in the park, admiring the flowers. This must be a good omen, he thought to himself. At least he wished it were.

During this time of crisis he thought of Jafar and wondered how he was doing in his studies. Did he find the system difficult too? Was he facing similar problems in his studies? Or, being under the Fulbright Program was Jafar better prepared than him? The question remained unanswered as he never got a chance to discuss it with Jafar.

Starting tomorrow, he would adopt a new approach, he decided. He knew he was not wasting any time; he just needed to rearrange his schedule and change his priorities. He made up his mind that he would stop spending time on his research project in the lab, which he so enjoyed, and would concentrate on passing the courses.

CHAPTER 23

For the past month and a half since his arrival in Eugene, Saleem had to contend with many new situations. His mind was occupied with trivial matters, small and inconsequential for someone who lived there, monumental and difficult for one who came from a foreign land, a land very different from where he was now. His exaggerated sense of pride instilled in him by his family made it difficult for him to ask for help. Or, was it his insecurities that made him behave this way? He could not tell.

A simple task, mailing a letter, presented a major challenge. He regularly passed by a mailbox, but for the life of him, he could not figure out how to deposit an envelope in it. He always had to go to the post office. This really bothered him. One day, early in the morning, with a letter in his hand he passed the mailbox again. There was no one around and Saleem thought it was a good opportunity for him to inspect this mysterious container. He slowly walked around it a couple of times, noticing how it stood on its four legs bolted to the ground challenging him reading the letters US MAIL on it. Today was the day when he was not to leave until he solved the riddle of this blue box, the representative of US Postal Service. As he started his third time around this baffling American invention, his curious determination was interrupted by the sound of little feet approaching. Frustrated, he stopped in his track and turned around to see a small girl about six years of age coming toward him. Without saying a word, she pulled on a handle, a handle he could never see because of his height. To his surprise, he saw an amazingly large opening in this mailbox, large enough not only for his letter but also the packages.

Mystery solved. Before he could thank the little girl, she was gone. At a distance, the girl and her mother looked back at him and waved.

In one of his classes, the teacher decided to give a surprise quiz. He had never ever heard of anything like this in his entire student life and was unprepared. To him, it was certainly a *surprise*, and a very unpleasant one indeed. So many unexpected events occurred during the first few weeks that every new problem left him absolutely frustrated. He was constantly reproaching himself for being ignorant. At every corner he felt unprepared and insecure.

Academically unimportant things were cluttering his mind, and preventing him from focusing on his studies. To him it appeared he was coping with a different world now—a world of strange mailboxes, an education system where surprise quizzes were the norm, and eating food he never knew before. In this world even the light switches were upside-down and people drove on the other side of the road. All in all, everything was new—surprises and aggravations waiting for him at every step, everywhere.

He was glad to have at least solved one mystery, the mystery of the mailbox.

A bicycle, a two wheeler transport he knew something about, with its shiny wheels and a black leather seat attracted his attention in a display window as he passed by a shop in town. Now, every time Saleem walked on this street, he would stop and look at it. One day, he decided to go in and ask about the price, which he learned was forty dollars. The storeowner turned out to be a friendly talkative young man who asked if Saleem was going to the university. Saleem told him that he was a graduate student in the chemistry department. The shopkeeper, also a graduate of the university, continued the conversation and mentioned that he had noticed how his foreign customer stopped by regularly to look at this bicycle.

"Are you considering buying one?" the storeowner asked.

"I would like to and I know it would make my life easier, but I cannot afford it at this point," Saleem answered.

"You are a student here…aren't you?"

"Yes I go to the university."

"Since you go to the university, I can let you have this bicycle if you pay me twenty dollars now and ten dollars each for the next two months."

Saleem knew that he had twenty dollars in his wallet. He offered to pay the man right then. The shopkeeper, however, did not want to sell one on display and suggested that Saleem come back the following day and get one that he would assemble for him. They shook hands and Saleem was very happy about the prospect of having an efficient transport starting the next day.

As soon as he could get away from his class schedule, Saleem went straight to the bike shop, handed the man a twenty-dollar bill and, after showing his student ID, became the proud owner of a new bicycle. It came with two chrome-plated baskets, one on each side of the rear wheel, and a headlight. It even had three gears.

As the shopkeeper gave him a pair of keys he said, "I am giving you a lock to keep your bicycle safe when you park it on campus. There have been no reports of bicycle theft, but it is better not to tempt someone with an unlocked one. And one more thing, you should be careful when riding in the rain, as the brakes will not work as well when they are wet; also to avoid the lawns, since lawns may have dips and holes in the ground covered with the grass that would not be visible".

After listening to all these well-meant words of caution, Saleem proudly rode his new bicycle back to the apartment. He felt empowered—he had his own transport.

Saleem was glad to notice that his twenty-minute walk to campus was now reduced to a mere five-minute ride. With his new bicycle, it was so much easier and quicker to get to the class. This fact was a boost to his morale. He felt ready to face new problems as they presented themselves; he was adapting to the new life.

He had noticed that some Chinese students in his class carried a dictionary to follow the lectures. In spite of this handicap, they did not appear to have the problems he had with their exams. They, in fact, were doing very well. One Chinese girl who could hardly speak English scored a hundred percent in her physical chemistry, where the professor declared she was smarter than anyone he ever taught. In contrast, he knew the English language well and did not have any difficulty in understanding what was said in the class. *If they can do it, why can't I?* he asked himself. He decided to talk to one of them and try to find out the secret behind this success.

He who never wanted anyone to show him the way, he who thought he could solve his problems himself was now desperate as he had once been when he was drowning while learning to swim. Someone had pulled him out and saved his life; he needed that someone again. He found that someone in Peter, a Chinese student taking biochemistry class with him. Peter had been in the country for two years and could speak good enough English to communicate. To him, Saleem mentioned his problems, his difficulty with exams.

Peter told him about his own frustrations during the first year, and showed Saleem how he studied now to prepare for the tests. Peter explained that when he read a textbook, after each paragraph he would stop, ask himself if there was anything new in it that he learned and, if so, instead of highlighting the important lines, he would write a corresponding question in the margin. He would repeat this throughout the whole chapter when he read it for the first time. After he finished the chapter, he would go back and try to answer all those questions that he had penciled in. If he found he did not know an answer, he would read that paragraph again until the answer came and he clearly understood the subject. Peter said that he found it helpful in understanding the material and he could review the chapters in no time by answering those questions right before the exam.

A test in biochemistry was coming up in two days. Saleem thought he would try out this new method and see if it worked for him. He studied using Peter's method, made notes in the margin, reviewed the subject before the test and took the exam. He knew he did well, and he scored far above his previous grades. In fact, his answers surprised the instructor who had given up on him. That reinforced his confidence. He felt he had turned the corner. For the first time he now believed that he would be able to improve his grades by the end of the quarter.

CHAPTER 24

By the middle of November, two months into the new country, Saleem was feeling relatively comfortable in his new surroundings. He purchased a raincoat and an umbrella to protect him from the frequent rain. He was now able to face new problems with certain confidence. By this time, he knew where and how to mail his letters, the grocery store still intimidated him but not as much as it did before, and he had the convenience of a bicycle to come and go as he pleased. When he rode his bicycle with grocery bags in the baskets on the rear of his bicycle, he felt connected with the people around him, as if he was one of them. He even had opened a bank account. In general, he felt better managing his life. His grades had improved and his goal, which appeared removed from his reach not long ago, now seemed attainable. The newly learned technique of studying his textbooks was allowing him to retain the lessons and he was content with the results. The lack of confidence defeating him earlier was slowly fading away. His resolve and his persistence were eventually paying off.

Because he had never cooked before he came to America, making his own food was yet another challenge for Saleem. As a young boy, he had observed his mother preparing food for the family. This had been the base for his understanding the concept of cooking. He remembered how his mother would chop onions and fry them in oil or melted butter as a first step in preparing common meat dishes. As the smell of the fried onions wafted through the air, she would add meat to the pot. He could never forget the sizzling sound that erupted when meat fell into the heated oil; to him it sounded like the cheering of a crowd as the master performer entered the

music hall. His mother would then cover the pot for a minute or two
to keep the aroma sealed in and then she would carefully open the
lid and stir the meat. Next, she would add a blend of freshly ground
spices and mix until the air was filled with a wonderful aroma. After
a certain time—his mother must have known precisely how long—
she would put in water and let the whole meal cook for an hour or
two. Periodically, she would check if the meat had tenderized and
the water had not dried up. She knew if the water dried up, the food
would burn. And once in a while it did and soured her mood for
the day. She would always make more than one dish for each meal.
One was always a meat dish accompanied by a vegetable and sometimes even a third plate called *Dal*. The main course was normally
eaten with *Chapatis*, flat bread made out of sifted whole wheat flour.
Occasionally rice replaced *Chapatis*.

From time to time, when Saleem got tired of eating hamburgers,
he would cook for himself. This was not only a pleasant change that
reminded him of home; it was also cheaper than eating out. Through
his friends, Saleem had learned the English names of the different
spices, which were available in the local grocery store along with so
many more he did not know of. He had also bought the cooking pans
and a few plates. Kader had an even larger collection of the pots and
china. Between the two of them, they had enough dishes to invite a
few friends over for a dinner.

Saleem found that the chicken was the easiest to prepare. It took
less time than beef and it was cheaper. He had also learned that his
American friends were familiar with chicken curry. His first guests
were David and his two housemates. This was Saleem's way of thank-
ing them for their hospitality when he had first come to Eugene. He
decided to make chicken curry. While making the rice, when it was
half cooked, he took a pinch of turmeric powder and sprinkled it
on top, let it steam for a bit and then stirred it all together. This way
some of the rice was white and some yellow, which he thought, looked
pretty and unusual. And if the guests did not like the food, he mused,
at least they should find it interesting. He also prepared green beans
with potatoes, and for dessert he bought vanilla ice cream.

Saleem cooked enough food, knowing well the large quantity
the young men consumed. He was a little nervous about the taste of
this meal, but Kader convinced him that he was a good cook, better
than anyone he knew among the students who came from the Indian

subcontinent. This was a big compliment and Saleem felt more at ease. The chicken curry did not come out the same color as it did last time he had made it. In fact, it did not match the color of any of his previous curry dishes, but it tasted good. Recently, he had bought a small can of allspice, assuming that it was a mixture of all the necessary spices he needed, and since he had used it for the first time, he figured that was the reason for the new taste and new color.

It was Saturday evening and the guests arrived around six o'clock. After they were seated, Saleem served his creation. They all had heard of this food, but had never eaten it before. Saleem had avoided using hot chili powder and peppers to keep it mild. The guests seemed to enjoy the food. Looking at the almost empty pots, Saleem knew that his first dinner party had been a success. Since none of them had had chicken curry, and an individual from that part of the world prepared it, they considered it authentic. The guests especially liked the multicolored rice and the potatoes cooked with green beans. By the time the three young men left, they had gotten to know Kader better and had learned a little about the Indian and Pakistani history in addition to the taste of a curry from that region.

CHAPTER 25

As soon as Halloween was over, everyone on campus started talking about Thanksgiving. Saleem had tried to acquaint himself with the American way of life prior to coming to this country. Although he read different magazines, somehow, he had never caught on to the importance of the Thanksgiving celebration.

One of Kader's professors invited the two roommates over for Thanksgiving dinner. There would also be some other foreign students as guests, he was told. Before they went to the professor's home, Kader asked Saleem if he had ever eaten turkey. Saleem did not even know turkey was a bird. The only Turkey he knew was a country. Kader first explained to him about Thanksgiving. He told Saleem that a long time ago there was this group of people called Pilgrims who came to this country. He did not know who they were, but history has it that they planted crops with the help of natives. At the time of harvest, they feasted on turkey and yams plus whatever else they had. And to commemorate this event, just about everyone eats turkey for dinner on the fourth Thursday of November each year. Traditionally, every family in this country observed Thanksgiving with their friends, regardless of their faith. "By the way, turkey is bigger than a chicken and its meat has a different flavor," he added.

The dinner was set for five o'clock. Kader and Saleem called a cab and arrived at the professor's house on time. During the trip, the cab driver, a middle-aged woman, was curious about the two foreigners and asked where they were from. Kader jokingly said she would not know even if he told her.

"Try me," she said.

When Kader replied, "We are from Pakistan," she pondered for a while and said, "Must be somewhere overseas." They all had a good laugh. Thus, there was a cheerful ambiance between the passengers and the cab driver.

The professor and his wife welcomed them into their house. The professor had a white shirt and a tie on that made Saleem comfortable with his suit—he was not overdressed. The professor's wife had a long flowing dress with bold color prints. This was Saleem's first visit to an American home. He had been to Gretchen's house, but this was different. While the other home was more like a guesthouse with the students renting part of the property, the professor's house was a regular family home. It was obvious, that the hosts had traveled widely all over the world; objects from the different countries were displayed, bringing a touch of different cultures in various rooms of the house. Their exposure to diversity had given them a good understanding of foreigners and their ways of life. They were curious to learn more about their guests' backgrounds; they wished to get to know them better without prying into their private lives.

After introductions, the hosts showed them some of the things they had bought in the region where the two young men came from. There was a carpet hanging on the wall and a small model of the Taj Mahal from India displayed on a shelf. It was illuminated with a special light glowing like a pleasant memory from the past. When Saleem mentioned that he had gone to college in Agra, the town where this famous building was located, they all had something to talk about and suddenly there was a feeling of rapport. Saleem wondered about how the material objects of common interest were able to set up emotional bonds between people.

The professor's wife took them on a tour of the whole house. Everything was very clean. All the rooms were carpeted; even the bathroom had a carpet. The rugs at home were thin and had the intricate designs woven in. Here they were all of one color and thick. He felt as if he was walking on a well-manicured lawn. And everyone kept their shoes on, which was so unlike where Saleem grew up; if the house had a floor covering the feet were bare. The students got a chance to look at the outside landscape with its lawn and pretty flowers.

A panoramic view of the mountains in the distance reminded Saleem of his trip to Naini Tal, the place he visited as a child. Then, the hosts talked about places in India and Pakistan that Saleem and Kader had heard about but never visited. Saleem, self-conscious that the foreigners knew more about his country than he did, kept quiet. As if the professor's wife read his mind, she said, "Isn't it true that tourists get to see a lot more places in a country than the locals?"

Soon, the hosts' son and his girlfriend arrived. And then came two more students, one from Kenya and one from Ghana. The dinner became an international gathering. The professor's son was a premedical student and his girlfriend was a psychology major.

The professor and his wife talked about Africa and about the countries on that continent as if they had been there yesterday. They mentioned in passing that the professor had spent a year in Rhodesia on sabbatical, where he had a chance to visit many of the neighboring countries. During that stay, he and his wife set out to learn as much as possible about the natives. Actually, the wife had learned to cook different types of food of that region and she brought it up with some pride. The outfit she had on she had bought during one of their trips of that continent.

They all sat and talked about current events around the world. The professor also suggested some interesting spots for the students to visit in and around the city of Eugene later on in the year, since they were busy in the middle of their studies at this time.

While everyone was talking, an aroma of food was spreading throughout the house. The smell was unlike any that Saleem remembered from his mother's kitchen. It did not smell like the spicy foods from home. Still, this made him think about his parents and his not-so-distant past. He thought of how he and his family would sit down on similar occasions, talk and laugh about things of no importance, and simply enjoy each other's company. Here, he was thousands of miles away in very different surroundings, in the company of strangers, and yet it reminded him very much of home.

The professor's wife asked everyone to come and sit in the dining room. The large table was beautifully set with sparkling crystal glasses, tall candles, neatly arranged plates and silverware. It looked like a picture in a magazine to Saleem. When he saw the wine glasses, he wondered if the wine was part of the dinner as well, but all they served was water. The hostess directed each guest to one of the eight chairs. Saleem was seated next to their son John. She lighted the candles as the professor brought in a large tray with the turkey and set it in the center of the table. Saleem had never seen a bird so large cooked all in one piece. Where he grew up, the meat was always cut up into small pieces before it was cooked. To cook something so big, one would need an oven and there was no such thing in his parents' house. He had heard that some bakeries in the large cities had these appliances, but they used them only for making cakes, pastries and breads.

The professor started to carve the bird with a long knife holding it down with a two-pronged fork. First, he sliced the breast and then the legs. The sliced meat was then placed on a large platter, the breast meat on one side of the plate, and the leg meat was arranged on the other side. The whole process of carving the turkey appeared like a ritual to Saleem, and he liked it. Before food was served onto individual plates, the professor thanked everyone for being there to celebrate this occasion with them.

The meat platter was passed around the table. As it came to John before it got to Saleem, John asked if he could serve him. When Saleem said yes, John needed to know if the guest would like the white or the dark meat. Saleem did not know the difference between the two and assumed that the darker meat came from the legs. He thought the proper thing would be to say that he liked both of them when he had no idea how either one tasted. John served him small portions of each. Next came a bowl filled with stuffing and then there were the yams. Saleem's plate was slowly getting full. He kept watching John and tried to serve himself about the same amount of food each time. Then there were some green beans and cranberry sauce. Finally, there was the gravy to complement the entire meal. With the exception of the beans, just about everything was new to Saleem and tasted different. The lady of the house explained every item of the food on the table for the benefit of the young students from abroad.

Saleem was careful not to take much on his plate. Early in his life, his mother had taught him never to fill his plate with too large an amount of food. He had never forgotten her telling him, "If you are a guest, take only what you can eat. It does not look nice if you cannot finish what you have on your plate, or if you are the last one still eating." He was able to eat every bit of what he had taken.

Once they all had finished eating, John helped his mother carry the dishes to the kitchen. Some of the young guests thought the dinner was over, but their hosts asked them to stay seated and get ready for the dessert. Soon, John and his mother brought in a pumpkin pie and an apple pie. Saleem had tasted an apple pie before. He had also heard a great deal about pumpkins at Halloween, another festival new to him, but he did not know this vegetable could be used for making pies and other desserts. He asked for a small slice from each and since he liked the sweets, he enjoyed both equally and finished everything on his plate once again. Along with the pies came coffee.

During the dinner, the professor kept the conversation going. He briefly touched on the Thanksgiving celebration and then moved on to talk more about the upcoming holiday season, which was to end with New Year's Eve.

Saleem had a separate conversation going on with John and his girl friend and learned about their opinion that anyone enrolled in graduate school had to be smart. He also talked with the students from Kenya and Ghana. They both thought it rained too much in Eugene and that the weather was much cooler compared to where they came from. All the guests, with the exception of Kader, had been in America for only a few months and they all were still learning the ways of life in this country.

When the dinner ended, the group moved over to the living room where the family had already set up a projector. The hosts showed slides of their travels, briefly explaining where they were and what they were doing. For the respect of the professor, and to a certain degree the interesting content of the stories he had to tell about each slide, everyone kept awake in spite of full stomachs and the warm room with its cozy fireplace.

Outside, the weather was changing; it was getting windy and the rain had started to fall. It was almost nine o'clock, and Saleem could feel that the hosts were getting tired. Kader noticed it too, and motioned that it was time to leave. Kader and Saleem got up and asked to use the phone to call a cab. John inquired about the address of their apartment and offered to drive all of them home. He looked at all the four of them and stated that there was enough room in his car to squeeze them in the back seat. As they were driving, the car's light beams were reflected by the wet road, an inky river where pearls of raindrops fell and shattered in the dark night.

John, being familiar with the area—he was born and raised in Eugene—dropped off Kader and Saleem first, and then continued with the other two guests in the car.

The next morning, Saleem woke up to a white wonderland. It had snowed during the night and it appeared as if the entire scenery was painted with white. Saleem had never seen snow before. He put on his raincoat and gloves and went outdoors to explore and experience. To his surprise, it was not cold outside. He carefully stepped into the white powder. He heard the crunching sound the snow made under the leather soles of his shoes, the lone pair that he had brought from Pakistan. His foot sunk into the cold fluffy mass until it touched the concrete. It was slippery. He had walked on slippery mud before and thought he could manage by being careful.

Soon, more snow started to come down, an entirely new experience for him. He could see the snowflakes waltzing in the still air and settling down in the quietest manner. The wet precipitation of rain was always so noisy. He was having fun walking, feeling the flakes brush his face with cold feathers. Alone on the sidewalk, he could see his footprints on the white carpet all the way back from where he had stepped out.

Enjoying himself, he forgot he was on icy grounds. He had not gone very far when he slipped and fell. He wondered if he had been too confident, or had he stepped on a wet spot? He got up quickly, shook off the snow and looked around to see if anyone had seen him fall. Not far from him, on the other side of the street, a man was shoveling the snow, cleaning the sidewalk in front of his house. It surprised Saleem that he did not look up and laugh at him. In India, it was common that if someone slipped and fell, be it on a banana peel or in slippery mud, everyone who saw it would point and laugh, unless the person was old and needed help getting up. He could tell that he was not hurt, just embarrassed. He had learned his lesson; he always walked carefully and never wore leather-soled shoes if there was snow or ice on the ground.

CHAPTER 26

Being accustomed, no more a stranger to the American life, Kader had made many friends in a short time, and one of them was Genevieve, a fellow graduate student in his department. All her friends knew her as Jenny. She taught high school part time. She was from Ohio and had decided to spend her Christmas in Eugene. Since this was a new friendship, Saleem thought she might be staying over to get to know Kader better. The first time Saleem met her was shortly after Thanksgiving when Kader invited her over for dinner at their apartment and Saleem offered to prepare the meal.

Since Saleem had made dinner for David and his friends not long ago, which turned out to be a whopping success, they both felt that he should repeat the same menu. Saleem agreed. It was on a Saturday when Jenny was supposed to come over for dinner. Kader was alone earlier in the day and decided to spend his time tidying up the place. He got the vacuum cleaner from the hall closet and cleaned up the entire apartment, floor, carpet and what have you. He especially enjoyed vacuuming the carpet. It reminded him of his childhood where his farmer uncle let him walk behind him when he was plowing the field; a bullock pulling in front would make those furrows of upturned soil, those lines that marked the hard work of the animal. He got so caught up this morning looking at patterns he made on the green carpet that he not only cleaned the area in the living room but also under the coffee table and the sofa. He even wiped the grime off windows. After he was done, he stood in the middle of the living room, humming a Bengali tune, looked around and admired his own work. Kader then went to the grocery store and bought everything that Saleem had put on the list. All this time,

Saleem was in the library studying and was to come back at three o'clock.

On his way back from the library, Saleem was planning the upcoming dinner and trying to work out in his mind how he would tackle the problem of cooking for Kader's friend. He figured if he started one hour before the guest arrived, he should be able to finish in time and the food would still be hot when they sat down to eat. As he entered the apartment, he noticed that Kader had given the place a thorough cleaning. The whole living area was brighter than he remembered. *Kader must like this girl,* Saleem thought.

Saleem had not been back long when Kader walked in with a bag full of groceries. Saleem was glad when someone else did the shopping for him; he tended to get lost in the large supermarkets. The big neighboring Safeway, a maze of aisles with numerous choices, confused him. It was still fresh in his memory how his first visit to that store had proved to be an overwhelming and testing experience. It would have been nice, he thought; if someone was there to tell him what he needed and where to find it. But that was not to be. Whenever he had to buy things for his kitchen, he did not know where to start and what to get. He would walk bewildered through endless lanes, shelves stacked on both sides, with the cans, cartons and packages of all shapes and sizes. Numerous choices he had not counted on were spread all over the store.

So many times he thought he was buying one thing and when he opened it at home, it turned out be something completely different. Whenever he saw "sugar" printed on a box, he assumed it was the granulated sugar. This was the only type of sugar he knew. When he opened the package, it had turned out to be powdered sugar, another time sugar cubes and still another time brown sugar.

Always anxious to get out of the store, he never bothered to read the label on the can or box. It took weeks, even months before it dawned on him that he needed to find out what exactly it was that he was buying. The most embarrassing moment in his infrequent shopping trips came when he was trying to get paper napkins for his friends he had invited for dinner and he brought something he had no idea what it was until he opened the box. What came out were definitely not napkins he wanted to get. He read the box and realized it was meant for women. He could not take it back and had to throw it away. That day the seriousness of reading the labels came to him in its blatant shape. As time went by, he started to recognize certain brand names and he was able to shop with some confidence.

Since Saleem was cooking, he thought it was okay if he looked into the grocery bag. Right on top was a frozen banana cream pie. Saleem liked the desserts and this one was his favorite. He had liked it ever since he had tried it in the student union cafeteria.

Saleem found that everything he needed for making the dinner was there in the bag. It was four o'clock in the afternoon when Kader started chopping the onions as a suggestion that they could start cooking now. This way, they would finish early and they would have time to relax before Jenny arrived. Kader was using a cutting board that he could pull out from under the kitchen counter. Up until that day, Saleem had not known that there was a cutting board there. Every time he noticed something new, he wondered how much more he still had to learn. After the onions were chopped, the chicken carved and washed, it was time for the cook to step in.

Kader moved out of the way and Saleem took over the cooking area. He did not own an apron and so tucked in a kitchen towel instead into his belt to protect his clothing; this instantly transformed him into a chef. To his own surprise, he finished everything he needed to do in less than one hour. The chicken curry was simmering in the pot, the rice was cooking on low heat and the green beans were almost ready in another pan. He cut down the heat to low and after fifteen minutes he turned off all the burners entirely.

The clock showed that Jenny was not expected for another hour. Always keen to experiment with the novel recipes, he asked Kader if he had bought some yogurt recently. Kader came over to check. They found an opened plastic container half full of yogurt. The cook-in-charge looked at it, smelled it and decided it was good enough to use in *Raita* that his mother made by combining yogurt with grated onions or grated cucumber. They had onions. Saleem grated some in a bowl and added the yogurt. It did not seem to be enough. He poured some milk into the bowl, added a pinch of salt and black pepper and stirred it all together with a fork. He took a little of it in a spoon and tasted it and decided that a pinch of cumin would turn it into an authentic dish from Pakistan.

Kader opened the windows to let in some fresh air. He thought the aroma of the exotic spices might be strong for someone who was not used to them.

Just as it was getting to be six o'clock, there was a knock. Kader opened the door and there was Jenny. Jenny was of average height for an American girl; she stood at about 5'5" with short-cut brown hair. Saleem's first impression of her was that of a good-looking young woman with a friendly smile and pleasant personality. Kader took her coat and introduced her to Saleem.

"I understand you are a good cook and a recent arrival from Pakistan," Jenny said.

"A recent arrival, yes," Saleem answered, "but a good cook...you will soon find out."

Jenny, feeling a little uncertain in the new surroundings with unfamiliar smells floating in the air, sniffed, looked at Kader and asked, "It smells good. May I look at it?"

"It is all on the stove and hot in the cooking pots. We don't have serving dishes, so we will have to take the food directly from the pots," Kader told her.

Saleem interjected, "But if you want to look at it, it is here." He walked toward the stove.

Jenny followed him.

As Saleem carefully lifted the lid off the pot with chicken curry, a cloud of steam came up loaded with the spicy smell. Saleem and Kader both could read on her face that she was not quite ready for that.

"That looks very interesting," Jenny said as she backed away from the pots toward the living room. Kader showed her around the apartment and then everyone sat down.

Carrying out the conversation, Jenny said, "In this country, when people go to eat out, they usually start with a drink, which may or may not be alcoholic. What do they do in Pakistan?"

Kader and Saleem looked at each other and simultaneously said, "We talk." Everyone laughed. The initial sense of formality gave way to a lighthearted feeling of camaraderie.

Kader went to the kitchen and got Jenny a glass of water. "Here is our universal drink," he said as he brought two more glasses for himself and Saleem.

Jenny wanted to know what subject Saleem was studying and how long he had been in this country. Saleem in turn asked Jenny if she was from Oregon and the classes she was taking were for a degree. Over small talk, the three of them were better acquainted.

When it was time to eat, Kader guided Jenny to the kitchen where she helped herself to small portions of all the different foods that her hosts had made. Kader and Saleem followed her back to the dining table and they all sat down. The bowl with *Raita* was sitting in the middle. Kader explained what it was; she took a spoonful and put it on one side of her plate. Jenny was curious, yet careful, about all the different foods in her plate. Saleem briefly explained every item and what it contained and answered all her questions about preparing these dishes.

Jenny's first exposure to the chicken curry, when she caught a cloud of steam from the pot on to her face, had been overpowering, but now that she started eating it, she realized the food was not overly spicy. She liked what she was eating and said to Kader, "You know, I could easily get used to this."

"The credit goes to Saleem," Kader said with a slight nod toward his roommate.

When Jenny had eaten all that was on her plate, she asked if she could have some more. She got up and served herself a little of everything again. Kader wondered if she really liked the food or was just being polite. Saleem was happy that his cooking turned out to be palatable once again.

After dinner was over, Kader made some coffee. By now the banana cream pie had defrosted. Kader cut medium-size pieces of the pie for everyone and brought them over with the coffee.

"I did not know what to expect tonight, but I certainly had no idea that I would get such an elaborate dinner, including coffee and the dessert. Thank you both for this wonderful meal." Jenny said.

"Usually people say things like this when they are leaving. You are not leaving yet...? Are you?" Kader asked.

"No, no! It was such a good meal, I wanted to thank you right away before I forget what I wanted to say," replied Jenny.

Over the coffee and dessert, Jenny had been talkative. By now she was in her comfort zone. She pointed toward the empty chair at the table and said, "Next time we eat, we should try to fill all the four chairs. Saleem, surely you know someone you could ask to join."

Saleem mumbled and made excuses, "I am extremely busy at this point and have little time to make friends."

Changing the subject, Kader asked, "What are your plans for Christmas, Jenny?"

"I want to visit my parents," Jenny answered thoughtfully, "but it is such a long drive and the roads are generally covered with snow this time of the year. I never look forward to driving under those conditions and so, I may just stay here and take it easy." She looked up at the two and asked, "Do you guys have any plans?"

"Saleem is working hard. This is his first quarter, which is the most difficult for a foreign student," Kader answered. "And as for me, I am going to stay and not do much. I might meet with some of the professors, if they are around, and discuss some of my thoughts about my research project." Then, changing the subject again, he added, "We are also thinking of moving to another apartment. When we rented this one, we were in a hurry. During winter break, we might be able to find something cheaper."

"If you are looking for another place" Jenny replied, "I will keep my ears open and let you know in case I hear of anything,"

For a while, they talked about their experiences of renting apartments. Both Kader and Jenny knew a lot more about the problems with off-campus living. In Jenny's building, she said, it got noisy at times, especially when the kids on the ground floor had a party. Suddenly, she looked at her watch and realized how late it was—it was time she should be heading home. As she got up from her chair, she offered to help with the dishes. Both Kader and Saleem insisted that she was a guest and, according to their custom, guests were not supposed to do any work.

She thanked them again for the wonderful food and the good time she had. As she said her good-byes, she added that she would cook a typical American dinner for both of them soon. While Kader walked her to the car, since he was still feeling good about the evening, Saleem started to clean up the kitchen. He washed the plates and left them to dry. Soon, Kader was back and started spooning the various leftovers into the bowls to put in the refrigerator, and then he cleaned the pots and pans. He thanked Saleem once again for having cooked yet another great meal. He thought tonight's meal was by far the best yet.

Saleem smiled at him and said, "It was the company that made it so special."

CHAPTER 27

Since Saleem had started using Peter's method for studying, his grades gradually improved and he could tell the difference it had made in his entire learning process. Now, he was able to review his course work more rapidly and the questions on his tests were no longer as difficult as they seemed earlier. When he first started attending the lectures, he did not realize the significance of noting down all that was said in the class. Trying to understand the teacher, he listened with the thought of reviewing the textbook later on, but not all that was discussed in the class was covered in the book. Presently, while he was listening to the instructor, he was taking notes.

As time passed, he was getting a better and better grip on his studies in general. He felt confident that he would make it through the first quarter without failing grades. Still there was some chance that he might not make it, but he had stopped worrying. He had worried so much in the beginning of the school year that now he had just plain run out of worries. He was doing all he could. He was working hard, staying focused and not wasting any time. He wished to succeed; he wanted *God to smile at him.*

Just before the final exams, he made a promise to himself that if he passed all the courses, he would reward himself by buying a nice new suit. Using his newly learned method of study during finals, Saleem did well enough that he was able to improve his grades. He did not get any A's, which he did not expect because of his not-so-good performance earlier, but he managed to pass all the courses he was taking.

After the quarter was over, he was exhausted. Not only had he spent a lot of effort on improving his grades, the teaching assistantship required him to help correct the general chemistry exam.

The teaching assistants had to go through the final test of the general chemistry class of over three hundred students, in just one session. For this purpose, all twelve teaching assistants, Saleem included, assembled at three o'clock in the afternoon in a large room where Dr. Kramer announced, "We will all stay in here till we finish the job. Certain mistakes in grading were made last time. I do not want this to happen again. This time, two of you will check the same answer. Once the first round of marking is completed, I will call out the question number and the name of the student. If the two do not agree, we will discuss it until we find an agreement. We will adjourn for dinner for one hour at six o'clock and meet again at seven."

After he had finished explaining this complicated system, he asked if it was clear to everyone. It was definitely not clear to Saleem, but he decided that he would learn as they proceeded. Other assistants asked a number of questions and the answers cleared up some of Saleem's own concerns. Finally, Dr. Kramer said, "Okay, let's begin. If we still have problems, I'll explain as we go along."

Thus, they started the marathon session of grading. After about fifteen minutes or so, things progressed more smoothly. The process was slow, but thorough. At six o'clock, everyone got up and went to eat dinner. Saleem walked over to the student union cafeteria for his hamburger. They all returned at seven to resume their work. It was well past midnight when the group completed their work and recorded the grades of all the students. The quarter officially ended for Saleem and he was glad to go home.

He put on his coat and gloves and left the building. The cold and dark night embraced him outdoors. As he glanced down the parking lot, he saw another graduate student from Professor Hayden's group. The young man was about to get into his car when he recognized Saleem. He motioned for him to come over and offered to drive him home. Saleem gladly accepted. It had been a long day and he was exhausted. The roads were empty. The town was still aglow with Christmas lights everywhere. Somewhere, in the distance, Saleem heard a Christmas song. After a while, he realized the radio in the car was playing the music. His friend had turned the volume way down and that was why Saleem had thought it was somewhere far away. He knew then he was very tired and could hardly wait to go to bed.

CHAPTER 28

During the Christmas break, Saleem had decided to take time off from his studies and rest. With all students gone home, it was quiet on campus. Jenny, Kader and Saleem were all staying in Eugene, and as Jenny lived all by herself, she often came over to spend time with Kader and Saleem.

"Since none of us is celebrating Christmas," she said thoughtfully, "I suggest we do something together." She looked at Kader and Saleem and asked, "What do you guys think?"

Kader agreed, "Yes, let's all do something as a group." Then they both looked inquiringly at Saleem.

"But...I don't want to intrude," Saleem said.

"Then, if everyone agrees, we'll all go to Portland. I'll drive." Jenny said as she made decision for everyone. "We can go there a day before Christmas. I'd like you to see the lights in the downtown area and experience the last day of Christmas shopping in a city." She looked at Kader and Saleem and said, "You two can stay in the YMCA and I will stay at the YWCA. These places charge very reasonable rates. We can stay one or two nights, depending on how everyone feels. And Saleem, this way you will get to see some other place besides Eugene."

Saleem debated if he should go along with them, but both Kader and Jenny convinced him that he deserved a break after the grueling first quarter and he was welcome.

The three friends left Eugene on the morning of twenty-fourth after breakfast. They drove through the forested areas where the trees and the surrounding mountains covered with snow lighted up the scenery. Saleem had seen pictures of similar views on calendars that the Swiss pharmaceutical companies were distributing all over the world. But looking at photographs and being at the scene in person were two very different experiences. The passing panorama was real. Sitting in the back seat he was enjoying himself as a tourist in a dreamland. Such beautiful country existed not far from where he now lived; he found it hard to believe.

The drive to Portland took nearly two hours. Jenny seemed to know her way around town, which was helpful in finding a parking lot. After a short walk, they arrived at the center of town. The day was cold, but the atmosphere was warm and cheerful. The shoppers were rushing here and there, their arms loaded with all kinds of bags and boxes. Happy laughing children and their parents dressed in colorful clothes crowded the sidewalks. Some were out strolling like them, looking at the store windows and enjoying the sunshine. Saleem was delighted that he came along. Christmas music was everywhere and although Saleem did not understand all the carols, he nevertheless enjoyed himself enormously. He thought about India and how its music was different, mostly sad, especially the lyrics. Christmas time here in Portland was festive and the music was uplifting, which made Saleem happy.

They walked around looking at the store fronts. Jenny enjoyed her role as a tour guide, explaining to these foreigners, especially Saleem, how Americans celebrated Christmas; this was a special time of the year for her. She bought cotton candy and offered it to Saleem and Kader who promptly declined. They felt this was for children and not adults. To Jenny, buying cotton candy was like stepping back into childhood and she laughed happily between bites of the sticky fluff.

Downtown Portland seemed like one big fair. The aura of festivity brought back old memories again. He compared it to *Eid* at home, a celebration when every child and adult would wear new clothes and new shoes. Compared to Christmas, there was very little shopping on *Eid*, because presents were for children only and were usually in the form of money.

The visitors from Eugene were so absorbed, so lost in sightseeing that they did not realize they had been walking for over two hours until they were hungry, but at this hour every restaurant was packed with the families and the shoppers. It was past noon; Jenny suggested that they might drive a little farther from the downtown area. This way, they could see more of the town and probably find a place to eat. Kader thought since the weather was good and sun was shining they should enjoy this opportunity and walk rather than drive. And so the three continued on foot, enjoying the Christmas decorations and looking up at the trees adorned with ornaments and streamers between buildings. Jenny kept steering them toward the site where she had parked her car, thinking that if they did not find a place to eat soon, she would drive to a different part of town. Before they got to her car, they discovered a small restaurant that was not as crowded as the ones downtown and they all gratefully sat at a table. Saleem ordered a hamburger, a menu item he was now familiar with. Kader and Jenny shared a pizza. To drink, everyone ordered a soda.

On this trip Jenny had taken Saleem under her wings as if he were her younger brother who needed guidance. While she was enjoying her soft drink, she mentioned that most university students of their age would not normally have what they were drinking; if they were eating pizza they would order beer to go with it. Saleem remembered when he was working late in the lab, some students were taking a break, going out for pizza and beer—three words that seem to fit together. Saleem had not yet tasted the beer. He came from a country where alcohol was considered evil, and the stories about it were mostly about men getting drunk, beating up their wives and destroying their family. Everyone who drank alcohol was considered an addict. Thus, Saleem thought that no one drank for enjoyment, and men drank to get drunk, and he was not about to try it.

By now, Saleem had learned to tell if someone had had a drink. He could smell the alcohol on their breath from a distance. He knew Kader had beer occasionally because he had smelled it when he came in late at night. Saleem never said anything, but he suspected that his roommate did not buy the beverage for their apartment out of respect for him.

When Jenny was talking about the combination of pizza and beer, Saleem wondered if the two of them would rather have that drink instead of what they ordered. He mentioned this to Jenny, adding, "It does not bother me if you would rather drink beer."

"I normally don't drink alcohol until dinner time," she responded. "Please understand that in this country we do not drink to get drunk. Of course, there are always those who do not know when to stop. The drunkards. They are the ones giving beer a bad name."

Kader had been listening quietly and said, "The weather is really nice today. We should walk some more after we have finished lunch. And once it gets dark, it will be even nicer to look at the lights."

Jenny looked admiringly at Kader for changing the subject. She was, however, happy for saying what she did about alcohol, beer and drinking, because she wanted this young new foreign student to understand her position.

Kader's idea appealed to everyone in the group. As they left, they realized it was chilly outside. They walked back to where they had seen the department stores with the inviting window displays. Saleem had never seen anything like this before. In New York, he had been so fascinated by the tall buildings, the wide roads and the variety of cars, that he had not noticed much of anything else.

They passed a theater where people stood in line. The words "Biblical Times" and "King of Kings" caught his eye on the marquee. He had seen some movies of that era: *Quo Vadis, Samson and Delilah* and *Ben-Hur* were a few he remembered. He had liked them all for they were packed with extravagant action scenes, horses running, men fighting ferocious animals, Roman kings and queens walking through the gilded corridors. He assumed this movie would be similar. He suggested to Kader and Jenny that if they did not have any other plans, they might like to watch this movie. None of them seemed to know about the theme or, if they did, they did not bring it up. It was obvious, looking at the crowd near the theater, that it was a popular film. His two companions, however, did not show interest in a movie that would end late at night. They were more interested in being outside. And then they could always watch movies in Eugene at student rates

So, they walked around some more. Christmas lights were everywhere. Some storefronts had live men dressed as Santa Claus outside the entrance door, ringing bells and calling out HO! HO! HO! These men dressed in red suits wearing white beards were louder than the music being played. Jenny insisted that they go inside the stores and watch the crowds. She pointed out to Saleem and Kader that the shoppers they saw tonight were all procrastinators who waited until the last moment to do their holiday shopping.

There was so much to see, so much to observe. For Saleem, everything was new and fascinating. His two friends were afraid they might lose him in some store; they made a point to stay close. After walking around watching the lights, listening to music and visiting several stores, it got dark outside. They went inside a small place to eat. This time, Jenny and Kader ordered a pitcher of beer. Saleem by now knew that a pitcher meant a jug full of beer. He wondered why it was called a pitcher and not a jug…but then why were biscuits called cookies? The waiter brought three glasses, but Kader did not pour for Saleem. Saleem looked at the empty glass and was not sure if he should try some. His religion was not that was holding him back; it was his culture and the stories he had heard. Then suddenly he remembered Jay, who had once said he was not going to draw lines around himself in the new country. Saleem felt that he was drawing a line for himself here.

Hesitantly he asked Jenny and Kader if he could taste some of their beer. Kader poured a quarter of a glass without saying a word. Jenny raised her glass and so did Kader and they both said, "Join the club." Once Saleem took a small sip, he could not understand why anyone would want to drink this thing. Nevertheless, he managed to finish his quarter glass of beer over dinner. Tonight he broke a barrier—he crossed a line

It was almost ten o'clock now, but some stores were still open.

"Tomorrow, everything will be closed," Jenny said. "And the twenty-sixth of December, the day after Christmas is the biggest sales event of the year. We will have to see what we can do tomorrow and then hang out for one more night so that we can go to the sales. It is quite a sight to see, especially for someone who has never experienced it."

"We will see how it goes tomorrow," Kader said and Saleem agreed.

Jenny dropped Saleem and Kader off at the YMCA for the night and then returned to pick them up at nine o'clock the next morning. After breakfast, they decided to go to the zoo, which was one of the few attractions open that day. To their amazement, numerous families were enjoying their holiday at the zoo. Hot dog vendors were doing a brisk business. They came up to an ice-skating rink, something Saleem had never seen before. Fascinated, he watched the children and some adults twirling on the ice in tune with the piped in music. It was another sunny day and Saleem had a feeling of being in another world. They spent several hours looking at the various animals in the park. Lunch consisted of hot dogs al fresco.

Saleem decided he liked hamburgers better. To top off lunch, Jenny passed out gum sticks that would take care of the lingering taste of mustard and onions.

They had not yet made plans for the afternoon. The question of whether they would stay another night, or return home was still open. Jenny had her heart set on shopping for clothes and Saleem had in mind it would be a good opportunity to buy the suit he had intended to get as a reward to himself for passing grades. Kader did not have an opinion and said the he would go along with whatever the two decided. Jenny suggested that they all could drive to Salem, the capital of Oregon where they would see different decorations. From a telephone booth nearby, she called her friends in Salem. Her friends, who were teachers, were happy to hear from her and invited her and her foreign companions to come over and spend the night with them. The two roommates did not want to be a burden on anyone, especially on Christmas day, but Jenny convinced them that these were very close friends of hers. And they were Jewish; they did not celebrate this festival.

"They're actually looking forward to meeting both of you and I'm sure you two will like them," she said.

Kader looked at Saleem and they agreed to accept the invitation—after all, they were on vacation and they wanted to have new experiences. The trip took less than an hour on almost empty roads. Jenny located their place without any trouble. Saleem found the hosts to be engaging. Being high school teachers, they were interested in teaching the young and at the same time educating themselves. For that purpose, they had travelled far and wide.

They both had been to India and seen the Taj Mahal and many other places that Saleem had not even heard of. When they talked about the country of his birth, they were mostly talking of things that Saleem had never seen, or if he had, it was in a completely different way. Their impression of the city where he had spent four years as a student was so unlike of his own experiences that he felt they were talking of a different place. Learning more about life in that part of the world fascinated them, especially from those who came from there. Kader explained how lifestyles differed from town to town and that people spoke different dialects. If you traveled a hundred miles, he said, you might find another language altogether. Saleem and

Kader used English between them, because their native languages were different—the same went for foods and eating habits.

Talking about travels, Jenny's friends told stories of their adventures on their recent trip to North Africa. It turned out to be a pleasant afternoon for everyone and the time passed quickly. Soon it was dinnertime and the hosts insisted that they eat at their house. Sarah, Jenny's friend, had already started to prepare an Indian dinner while the three guests were driving toward Salem; she was looking forward to having company. Sarah showed Saleem the Indian cookbook she had bought in Delhi and told him that she often referred to it. "Tonight's food comes from one of these recipes," she said. Everyone helped setting the table. While they were getting ready to sit down, Saleem told Sarah that he started to cook only after he came to this country. His knowledge came from watching his mother prepare food for the family.

The food looked like what Saleem would make, but it had a different taste to it. Along with the dinner, the couple served water and milk.

After dinner, when all the dishes were washed and put away, the hosts set up a slide projector in the living room and showed pictures from their travels in Africa and India. When the images of the Taj Mahal came on the screen, they brought out how they were surprised that the building was so much bigger than what they expected it to be and lot more beautiful than its pictures. That had been Saleem's experience as well.

Busy talking and watching slides, everyone forgot about sightseeing. And although the hosts had boxes and boxes of transparencies, they turned off the projector when they realized that the audience was getting tired and losing interest. To end the evening, they served tea and hot apple pie with ice cream on top. Saleem liked this combination of hot and cold dessert.

The guests had their nightclothes with them. Jenny slept in the guest room. The hosts gave sleeping bags to Kader and Saleem, so they would not be cold. This time, Saleem knew how to use a sleeping bag. The night was chilly, but he kept warm and slept well.

Saleem, being an early riser, was first to wake up. As he took a shower and got ready, he was surprised to see Sarah was waiting for him with a cup of tea. She was an early riser too. He sat down with her and they started chatting.

She was interested in learning about all those difficult times for
his family during the partition of India and his moving to Pakistan.
During the conversation, she mentioned how her parents had suffered in Germany, how they had to move away and how they would
talk to her when she was a child about things they went through.
Her feelings he could gauge through her dark brown eyes. Now, an
anguish of grief he could see on her face, the look that he would
remember for a long time.

A bond was thus formed between the two—a bond that comes
through a common pain. At one point, she got up and hugged him
and kissed him on the cheek. For her it might have been a vent of
her feelings, an expression of sympathy, but for him it was a *kiss*. No
young woman's lips had ever touched his face. It brought out a sensation he had never ever experienced and his whole body tickled.
He felt awkward; he did not know what to do. He wanted to kiss her
back but restrained himself. The moment passed. She sat down and
started the conversation as if nothing happened. They talked about
their lives until everyone was up.

Later on when the guests and hosts were awake and ready, Jenny
invited everybody out for breakfast. They chose a restaurant not far
from where they were. Once seated, everyone received a menu. This
was not a great help for Saleem, but he started looking at the items
listed, partly out of curiosity and partly because it seemed the right
thing to do. Jenny raised her eyes and asked Saleem if he had ever
had pancakes with maple syrup. Saleem had not. Before leaving for
school in the morning, he prepared toast and a cup of tea in his
apartment. Mentioning the pancakes, Jenny said, "It is a common
breakfast in this country…for those of us who are not watching our
weight."

That was enough to persuade Saleem to order pancakes and coffee. He had abandoned the idea of drinking hot tea outside of his
apartment because it was never strong or hot enough for him.

Saleem liked the pancakes and thanked Jenny for her suggestion; he especially liked the melted butter and the smell of the maple
syrup. Others ordered eggs with toast, scrambled eggs, cereal and
muffins. Everyone had something different to eat; a cup of coffee
and a glass of water were the two things they all had. Since Saleem
was the most recent arrival in the US, they were constantly explaining
things that were new to him and he was, like a dry sponge, trying to

absorb as much as he could. During the last few days, he had gained a great deal of knowledge about American life by traveling and meeting new people.

They were a lively group. Saleem assumed that they all connected so well because everyone was young, open-minded and sociable. In the company of older people, he always felt their attitude to be polite, but patronizing. In this group he was comfortable and at ease. In this crowd there was a young woman who had kissed him. That memory lingered somewhere in some corner of his mind and kept coming back to him. They sat there for over an hour, just talking. He really enjoyed learning new things about the life of the young people and their habits in this country.

The experiences of the last two days made him marvel about how people coming from the different parts of world had so much in common—same joys, same grief. The only difference he noticed was the cultural background people grew up with that was unique to each of them. Diverse customs and habits might create insurmountable walls between some cultures. On the other hand, he thought, these differences could also open windows of opportunity for others to observe and learn from each other and expand their horizons—just as they did here at the breakfast this morning.

After leaving the restaurant, Jenny drove her friends back to their house. The three friends thanked their hosts for their hospitality. They in turn invited them to come back and visit anytime they were in Salem.

Back in Portland, Jenny knew exactly which department stores they would go to. Inside the stores a very different scene from that on Christmas Eve greeted them. Sale signs were posted everywhere. Clothes piled up high on tables near the entrances beckoned the customers to come and spend their money. In one store, they saw so many people gathered around some counters that it was hard to tell what was on display. People were acting as if this was the last day they could ever buy anything.

They finally entered a more expensive store. Here, in spite of the ongoing sale, things appeared calmer and under control. Saleem gravitated toward the men's section to look at different suits. Noticing a possible customer, the sales clerk took his measurements, picked two suits from a rack and laid them out side by side for Saleem to choose. He picked the dark navy blue outfit over the brown one and tried it on. It felt comfortable. The salesman commended him on his choice and sold it to him for a reduced price of thirty-two dollars. After Saleem paid, the clerk invited him to select a tie from the rack to match his new set of clothes, compliments of the store. Thirty-two dollars was no small sum for Saleem; still he thought he owed it to himself to keep his promise. These clothes would last him for several years anyway.

In the meantime, Jenny and Kader had made their own purchases. When Jenny saw what Saleem had bought, she asked him to hold it in front of him. She backed away a few steps and looked at it critically. "This is really cool," she said.

Saleem was confused; he thought he bought a woolen suit. He said, "No! No! I tried it on. It is quite warm. It is pure wool."

Jenny laughed and laughed while she explained what she meant by *cool*. They left the store with smiles on their faces. They were happy about their bargains and were glad to have stayed the extra day. Now it was time to head back to Eugene.

Saleem mentioned to Kader the next morning that he wanted to send Thank You notes to Jenny's friends in Salem and one to Jenny for driving them. He wanted to tell them how much he enjoyed himself and appreciated the hospitality. Kader felt that they had already thanked everyone in person, "No one expects Thank You notes from young people," he said, and Saleem believed him.

CHAPTER 29

During the semester break, Kader and Saleem looked for another place to live, but did not find one near the campus that would suit their purpose. On suggestion of their friends, who had been living in Eugene for some time, that summer would be a more appropriate time for their search, the two roommates postponed their efforts until then. They had become comfortable with their current accommodation and Saleem had a bicycle to commute.

More at ease in the new environment and confidence restored, Saleem now had a firm schedule for studying and other activities. During the week, he would have dinner at the apartment after he returned from college, alone or with his roommate, and then go to the library to study. Friday evenings he reserved for a movie—by himself if he did not find someone to go with. Saturday morning he would go to work in the lab. This was his way of staying in touch with his research project and the students who were in Professor Hayden's group. In addition, it gave him a chance to see the professor.

To an outsider his schedule might have appeared as if he was caught in a loop, doing the same things, following the same routine day in and day out, but a routine was what he needed in his life. After having a period of uncertainty and turmoil where surprises were the norm, he was now in a comfort zone where he knew what was around him, what was expected of him and what he was expecting to do next. He missed working in the lab, but he had learned from his experience and was astute to remember Professor Hayden's advice to put it off until certain requirements of his course-work were completed.

Time was flying by. Finals were over with, and summer was just around the corner. During the year, Saleem had gotten to know more students. Among them was a graduate student from Yugoslavia, Marco, who had the smallest car Saleem had seen in America, a Fiat 600. The Yugoslav and another member of Dr Hayden's group from Japan, Saburo, were planning to visit the Worlds' Fair in Seattle. There was room for one more person in the car and they asked Saleem if he would like to join them. The plan was to go through Mount Rainier Park and camp there overnight. Marco was an avid camper and had all the necessary experience for spending time in the wilderness. Saleem and the Saburo were both city people who had no skills or equipment for outdoor trekking. The only thing Marco expected from the other two was to pay for food and gas.

Saleem realized that he needed a break to recover from his demanding first year of graduate school. And to get ready to spend time on his project in the lab during the summer, he should refresh himself.

Saleem packed a small handbag with his clothes, a toothbrush and a shaving kit. They all set out early in the morning. He had not been out of Eugene since the Christmas trip with Kader and Jenny. Whereas everything was snow covered and frozen on that year-end trip, it was now green everywhere and the streams were alive with gurgling water. Seeing the waterfalls on the way, Saleem remembered his trip to Naini Tal with his father. As they drove, the rolling scenery changed from the gushing waterfalls to leisurely streams. It appeared to him that all that water Mother Nature had brought in the form of snow was now going back to where it came from.

Marco knew the area well and chose to drive through the back roads. To chart his course he carried a well-marked map. They stopped by different lakes where the calm water mirrored the surrounding mountains, adding another dimension to the ambiance. The mountains were as spectacularly beautiful as their reflection in the lake. The views were not wasted on Saleem, he felt refreshed and energized. Nature's display of serenity was doing its work on him.

Finally, five hours after leaving Eugene, they arrived at Mt. Rainier. Luckily, for the visitors, the peak was not concealed under the clouds that afternoon. She stood in front as a grand mountain displaying all its glory. As the evening sun moved in the clear sky, it illuminated the snow and the glaciers in ever-changing colors. The whole scene was breathtaking. Saburo, who had brought his camera, started taking pictures. Saleem picked a rock and sat down to enjoy the scenery. It was his first chance to be so close to a snow-covered peak, the peak reflecting the energies of the heavens and in his mind, at that time, he was the sole recipient. It felt good.

The days were long during summer, but eventually the sun set. They pitched their tent and set up the little cots and sleeping bags. Saleem was surprised to see how much his Yugoslav friend had managed to tote along in his little car. Of course, the small rack on top really helped.

The three friends unloaded the car, including an insulated box containing the hot dogs packed in ice. Marco had also brought some bread and canned baked beans. Saleem watched with fascination as his two friends built a fire for cooking dinner. He offered to help, but they did not seem to need him. "Well, you can clean up after the meal and wash the dishes," the Yugoslav told him. Saleem noticed they were not alone; a number of other families were also camping on the grounds. Tents of different sizes dotted the landscape. As it was a dark night, it swallowed the surrounding scenery, except for some camping lamps and some campfires, sprinkled here and there.

Marco heated the hot dogs first, and then the beans, using the same skillet. Although it was not easy for Saleem to use plastic forks and knives on the paper plates, the simple hot dinner tasted really good. Eating out in the open was an adventure Saleem would remember for some time. After dinner, it was his turn to clean up. First, he collected all the paper plates, the plastic forks and the wrappers lying around, and deposited them in a metal garbage drum provided at the campsite. Then it was time to wash the pots. The water was ice-cold and, once it hit the greasy skillet, it felt as if it came alive in his hands like a slippery fish. And before he could get hold, it went bouncing on the rocks. Marco knew Saleem needed the soap pad to wash off the grease. He brought it over and to Saleem's amazement, at the touch of the soap pad, the grease vanished as if it was never there. His hands were cold, but he felt he was able to help and he felt connected to the group now.

After dinner the three of them sat there watching the stars. The gallery of twinkling lights was on display. He saw the universe spread over him, noticed the big dipper and from this he could trace the pole star, the same stars that he had watched at night in India. At times like this, he wished he was an astronomer. Saleem had not slept under the open sky since he came to America. For a moment, he thought his parents might be looking at the exact same sky, but then it occurred to him that he was on the other side of the world and it would be daytime where his parents lived.

Certain events triggered his mind to remember his childhood days as it happened when he looked at the sky that night. Then for a short while, he would be back where he was born and all those family members and their memories would race through his mind. Being so far away from home—it always made him wonder if at any time in his childhood he ever thought he would travel such long distances for his studies to learn and see so many different things in a distant land—everything so foreign. He did not believe, nor did his parents ever think, he would move so far away from them. Going through these dreamlike moments, lost in the world of his own, he became unaware of his surroundings, as if his body and his mind were separated. Suddenly he realized he was cold and he was all alone. His friends had gone to prepare their beds to sleep. He got up and joined them. Luckily, they all had brought enough clothes to keep warm.

He slept well. It was warm inside the sleeping bag. His cot was light and narrow, but once he was in the bag, he did not need much space. The cot was there to keep him above the ground in case it was wet. In the middle of the night, he felt a small nudge and opened his eyes. Half asleep, all he could see in the dim light of the stars was an outline of an animal the size of a sheep. It was not far from him. There was some commotion, but not enough to make him get up. He went back to sleep. In the morning, there was much talk about a bear from last night. The garbage drum was turned over and trash was scattered all over the place. It confirmed for those who were familiar with wildlife that they had a visit from a bear. Saleem was not sure if the animal he had seen at night was the bear everyone was talking about, but it could have been. He had no idea that this animal could be dangerous. The only bears he had seen were in the zoo, or with those jugglers and magicians who went on the road shows in India, doing tricks with various animals. The performing bears, tamed like dogs, were not considered anything but gentle creatures and definitely never a threat.

At dawn, Saleem was awed at the sight of the snow-covered mountain. The early morning sunrays brought out colors in the snow that he had not seen the day before. Bathed in the light of the rising sun, the snow appeared in brighter shades than the previous evening. This awesome display of colors overwhelmed Saleem; he felt lucky to be here at dawn and to have watched last night's sunset.

Activity broke out with daylight and his two friends woke up as well. Marco built a fire once again to prepare eggs and make coffee. They all sat and had their breakfast around the fire. It was cold. Hot coffee tasted good. Saleem was again assigned to wash the skillet— this time he knew how to do his job. After breakfast, they packed their gear and left for Seattle. It did not take long to get to the fair. The fairgrounds were large and covered with booths that displayed lifeless industrial machinery idly sitting on concrete floors, and fancy goods decorated the stalls, where, programmed like robots, salesmen explained their function. There was much to see and do, but Saleem did not find it very interesting. Marco, however, wanted to see everything that was displayed. And Saburo took pictures wherever it was allowed. As a result, they visited several booths out of curiosity, and also because they had come so far to see it all. He would have preferred to spend more time at the campground in the mountains.

The only places that interested him were the Space Needle, a few fountains and the monorail, especially the Space Needle because he had heard that the circular top of the tower revolved. And the monorail, because when it moved, it felt as if it floated in air. From where he stood, he could not tell if any part of the Space Needle was moving. There was a long line of people waiting to go up on the elevators; Saleem and his friends decided to skip the ride, however, they did get a chance to ride the monorail. Later they visited the food court, where shops offered a large variety of international foods. When his friends ordered tempura chicken, he tried it as well. The food came with chop sticks, which he did not know how to use. The experience was novel but not what he would describe satisfying.

In the late afternoon, after they felt they had seen enough of the fair, the three friends drove back toward Eugene. In a couple of hours it started to get dark, Marco did not want to drive anymore and he did not trust anyone else to drive his car so they found a camping area where they stayed overnight. This campground had better facilities where they could use the showers.

Back at campus, the three settled their expenses. Saleem's share came out to be only seven dollars. This had turned out to be a most refreshing outing for Saleem, and better yet, it had not cost him very much. He thanked both his travelling companions, who had now become his friends, for taking him along. Certain moments during trip brought nature and him as close as he had ever experienced.

Once the spring quarter was over, the university grounds were very quiet. Saleem started looking for a place to live, something cheaper and closer to the campus. He found a number of vacancies and a few of them met his criteria. Saleem liked rooming with Kader, but the rent was rather high for him. Saleem told his roommate that he had found a more convenient, cheaper place near campus that he would be sharing with another Pakistani student. Kader had no problem with this, reminding Saleem that they both had taken this apartment when they were in hurry.

"If you found a better place, you should take it. We will still see each other and stay friends. As far as I'm concerned, I want to live closer to Jenny. Maybe we will even share a place together." Hearing this, Saleem was relieved in the knowledge that he had not caused any problems for his friend.

The new place Saleem moved into was different. It was an old two-story house with three apartments on the ground floor and two on the upper floor. Each floor had a bathroom. Saleem was to share the place on the second floor.

Since there were no classes to attend during summer, Saleem was able to dedicate much time and continue with his research project from where he had left off. Other students of Professor Hayden's group were also working in the same lab. He was pleasantly surprised to find that he knew a lot more about working in the lab than most of the other new graduate students, and this he attributed to his experience in the laboratory in Pakistan and what he had learned there from Dr. Jamal.

For some students, the lab work was as challenging as the course work was for him. In the same lab where Saleem was now working, two students, who were a year ahead of him and had finished all their requirements of theoretical courses, were also plugging away on their projects, but with little success.

One morning, they had to meet with the professor to discuss their work. When they came out from his office, each was holding a job application in his hands. The professor had pointed out that he had watched them work for over a year now and he had concluded they were good chemists, but research was not the right path for them.

When they were out of earshot of the professor, they let off some steam. They were angry and found fault with their assigned research topics. They were furious with the advice they received, but at no time did they question their own abilities. Not long after that, both of them left the university, angry and disappointed, with MS degrees. That day Saleem recognized the power of a university professor, and what it meant when *God was not smiling at you*.

Saleem spent most days and many nights in the laboratory where he got to know the remaining students. Saburo, the Japanese post-doctoral fellow whom he had gone to Seattle with, also worked in the same lab. They had felt comfortable together on that trip. One night, when both needed a break from work, Saburo asked Saleem if he would like to go out for a pizza. Saleem was always curious about these late night pizza parties, so he decided to go with his friend and find out what they were all about.

They drove in Saburo's old car. During the trip to Pizza parlor, Saburo told Saleem that he had paid one hundred dollars to a foreign student who had finished his degree and was leaving. *For that price, I could buy a car one day*, Saleem thought.

Arriving at Shakeys Pizza Parlor, a favorite student hangout, they found the place was packed with young men and women. The music, which he could hear as his friend parked the car, was loud and the vibrations of the perky mood hit him as he stepped in. Long wooden tables and benches sat on the floor for customers to sit, eat and drink together. Some were sitting at the tables; others were just standing, holding the beer mugs.

The place was very noisy. To talk, everyone had to shout, but it did not seem to bother anyone. As they found a place to sit, Saburo asked Saleem if he would like dark or light beer. Saleem had not realized they were going out for pizza and beer. He did not know the difference between the two types, so, on a whim he chose dark. His friend ordered a medium pepperoni pizza with a pitcher of dark beer.

He liked his pizza where every piece he ate the strings of cheese followed to his mouth. He doused it with crushed pepper; the heat of the spices enhanced the taste of the bubbly drink that his friend had ordered. The beer did not taste bad at all; actually it tasted rather good with hot spicy pizza and the mood that existed around him in the parlor. He drank two glasses and felt good when he left. Saleem now understood why college students were always talking about this combination. Food of choice for Saleem so far had been hamburger and Coca Cola, but once he entered the pizza parlor, he added the new combination of pizza and beer to that list.

CHAPTER 30

Soon September approached and it was Saleem's anniversary. One year ago he had come to Eugene. Reflecting on the events of the past year, Saleem realized how lucky he was. He had gone through some rough times, but he had survived and learned. He had an urge to do something special to celebrate. The only thing that came to mind that would not include others were the pathways he had walked when he first needed solace. He ambled over to the campus, looking to relive his first walk one year ago when he was new, in a mood to explore and had found peace of mind.

This time it was different; the newness was gone. The novelty was replaced by familiarity and memories. He had lived through some moments of agony during the past year. At the same time, he had found comfort in new friendships and through improving his grades. He recognized how all the adjustments to the new ways in this country had changed him in mind and spirit. He had adapted to the ways of life of the new land. One thing stood out the most; he was now able to drink beer—the mere thought of which would make him cringe in the past—without feeling guilty. He had succeeded to break through some lines around him.

In the course of first year, Saleem had made friends with Ken, another graduate student in his group. During summer, Ken got married and his wife joined him soon afterwards. Saleem thought of inviting the newly married couple over for dinner some night. He had been cooking now for some time and had developed enough confidence that he could attempt new dishes that he liked but did not know how to prepare. He remembered his mother making meatballs, each with a boiled egg inside of it.

Since he could now create recipes on his own, he decided he would try to make those for his friend Ken and his wife. The only way he thought he could cook this food was to wrap ground beef around the boiled eggs, bake these meatballs in the oven and then prepare the sauce with tomatoes and spices separately. At the end, he would combine the two in one pan and let the meatballs simmer long enough to absorb the flavor of the sauce. The whole process was going to be labor intensive and time consuming; still he wanted to give it a try.

Ken and his wife were from a small town in Kansas. Their exposure to foreigners was limited. Saleem and Ken had now known each other for almost a year, and during this time, Ken had learned many things about India and Pakistan from Saleem, but he had never been to Saleem's apartment. Ken's bride was new to Eugene.

Saleem invited the couple for dinner on a Saturday evening. When Ken mentioned it to his wife, she was curious to know more about India and Pakistan and looked the countries up in the world atlas. All she knew now of these countries was their geographic location. Coming to eat with Saleem, whom her husband described as a good friend, seemed like an adventure and a chance to learn about people from another part of the world.

Following his newly thought out recipe, Saleem prepared the egg-meatballs. On the side, he made some peas and rice. Saleem by now had acquired several serving dishes. He had already transferred the food from the cooking pans to these covered pots before the young husband and his wife arrived.

Ajmal brought flowers home from work, which he placed in the center of the table. When the guests arrived, they were surprised at the unexpectedly pretty setting. In addition to the lovely flowers, Ken's wife was visibly relieved to notice that there were forks and knives for everyone, which meant that she would not have to eat with her fingers. She was impressed and relieved. Someone had correctly told her that people in India and Pakistan ate all meals with their fingers, but she did not know that those who were living outside of the country had embraced changes in their ways. They had started to use silverware for dining.

The heavy smell of spices filled the air of the small apartment. This was foreign to the couple. As soon as introductions were over, they all sat down to eat. The food served was definitely very different from anything they ever had, known or eaten in Kansas. Ken noticed that the meatballs were rather large. The greatest surprise of the evening came when Ken cut up his meatball; he could not believe that there was a whole egg inside. Saleem felt that both, Ken and wife were so intrigued and fascinated with the idea of having an egg wrapped in meat that they forgot all about savoring the spicy flavor of the food. The novelty had definitely been a hit and they seemed to enjoy every bite. Saleem had bought a banana cream pie, which he served as dessert, and Ajmal made coffee for them. Ajmal and Saleem, during the conversation at the table, answered all the guests' questions about their homeland.

The couple stayed for some time after dinner, talking about the different ways of life in other parts of the world. The wife was surprised to learn that people coming from so far away were so much like those she had known all her life. The young couple found the experience remarkably educational and learned the kinds of things they would never be taught in a classroom. As they were leaving, the couple told Saleem and Ajmal that when they had first entered the apartment, the smell of the spices was new to them, which made them feel they had entered a different world. Now, after the meal was over, they were filled with understanding and appreciation for a different culture, a culture poles apart from their own. And they were appreciative they had been invited.

On Monday, when Saleem went to the chemistry department, he discovered that news of his egg-meatballs had preceded him. He was getting a reputation as a cook, although cooking was something he only started after he came to America. Even professor Hayden came to know about it. "I understand you are a good cook, Saleem," he said one day.

"I don't know if I am good, I just cook different kinds of meals," Saleem said.

"Someday you should come over, meet my family, and give them a lesson or two in your exotic cuisine."

"Most certainly," Saleem said. The subject never came up again.

Summer was over, the new quarter started, and everyone got busy once again. Saleem was now officially a research assistant. This meant that he did not have to teach or grade papers anymore. Now he could spend all his time in the lab. He knew this was where he wanted to be and it was in the running of the experiments that he was better than most of the other students. His professor knew that too. When he was a teaching assistant, he worked along with teaching assistants. But now he was involved in research and spent hours on his workbench with other students of Dr Hayden's group. In this group, the graduate students were working for their PhD. Several of the postdoctoral fellows who came from foreign countries were also part of this team. Saleem made friends with some of them and at least once a month, he would join them when they went out for pizza and beer.

CHAPTER 31

Over a period of time, Saleem got to know his new roommate, Ajmal, and some of his friends, who were all supporting themselves by working on or off campus. One of these friends, Ranjeet Singh was a Sikh by faith; everyone knew him as Jeet. During summer months, Jeet worked in hotels and private clubs in different towns and thus knew a number of people in the hospitality industry in the state of Oregon.

One Friday, just before school started for the fall quarter, Saleem came home early from the lab. As he entered the apartment, he found his roommate and his friend Jeet staring at a road map. They were planning an overnight trip. They invited Saleem to join them. Like everyone else, Saleem also needed a break. Before he committed, he wanted to know where they were heading and where they planned to spend the night.

"For the last two summers I have been going to this town where I work as a bartender. The owner likes me and treats me as if I were his son. I came back from there yesterday. He asked me if I would like to bring some of my friends along for the weekend. We can all spend the night at his house. The couple has no children, and they like to have young people around. I always stay with them. Their house is huge," Jeet explained, emphasizing the last word.

Although Saleem had been in the country for over a year, new situations still made him uncomfortable. He did not know Jeet very well, let alone the people where he would be staying. But then he reasoned, since Ajmal would be there as well, it would probably be all right to go. He never bonded with Ajmal the same way he did with

Kader, but now after living together for over a month he felt at ease in the new environment.

Feeling in need of some adventure, he accepted the invitation.

With their small bags packed, the three men drove off in Jeet's car, a two-year-old maroon Rambler of which he was very proud. It was a pretty drive on a winding road through the woods. They reached their destination within an hour and a half. Jeet parked the car a little distance away from the building and they all got out, stretching their legs. Jeet, closely followed by his two companions crunching gravel under their feet, entered the club as if he owned it. The place was nothing like Shakey's Pizza Parlor, the other place he had visited, which sold alcoholic beverages. The lights were dim; the music was there in the background and not in your face, as he had experienced earlier. Saleem noticed a long, well-polished wooden counter not far from the entrance; people sat there talking in low voices. The cigarette smoke was not heavy, but filled the air to a smellable degree.

The entrance of the three young men brought a new life to those who were there. The man behind the counter looked up and seemed genuinely happy to see Jeet. This had to be the owner, Saleem surmised. The man was short and bald. He wore a spotless white apron over a light blue shirt and a red tie. It looked as if he had just traded his jacket for an apron. Behind the bartender were rows and rows of bottles. He could see glasses of all shapes and sizes on the side, those hanging on a rack upside down like bats, fascinated him. Most people sitting at the bar knew Jeet too and seemed happy to see him. Jeet introduced his friends from the university to all those who were there. Being from the university carried some importance in this town, and being from a foreign country was unique. Saleem did not get anyone's name for he was too busy spelling out his own. After the pleasantries, the owner asked what they would like to drink.

"Scotch" said Ajmal. He did not seem to have to think about it. Or, he did when he entered the club.

"And how would you like your scotch, young man?" the bartender asked.

"On the rocks, please," Ajmal, answered with confidence. Saleem was impressed. He was not aware that Ajmal drank anything except an occasional beer. After Ajmal got his drink, the bartender directed the same question at Saleem.

Not knowing anything about drinks, he answered, "The same please."

Saleem had heard of scotch, but he had never had a chance to taste it. Before he realized it, he was holding a glass full of ice with a pale yellowish liquid in his hand, the smell of which he did not find particularly appealing. Finally, Saleem and Ajmal raised their glasses toward the bartender, thanked him and said, "Cheers." Stealing a sideward glance at Ajmal, Saleem noticed that his friend was as comfortable drinking the liquid as he had been ordering it; he had taken a sip and was rolling the liquid in his mouth and apparently enjoying it.

Saleem hesitantly took a sip. As it spread over his tongue, Saleem knew that this drink was certainly a lot different from beer. It was strong and he would have difficulty getting it down his throat. A burning sensation on his tongue numbed his taste buds; he could no longer taste anything except for the feeling of having a cold liquid in his mouth. He held it there and then slowly swallowed suppressing any reaction showing on his face. Before daring to taste his drink again, he waited until the ice melted and the liquid was no longer the ball of fire he experienced in his mouth. For a connoisseur it might not have been worth drinking, but the watered-down scotch for him was the only way to get it down. It took him forever to finish his first ever *real* alcoholic drink.

As the afternoon slid into evening hours, more and more members of the club started to arrive, some alone and some in pairs. For the most part, they were professionals: lawyers, doctors and businesspeople. Every time a new couple came in, the owner introduced them to Jeet's friends; all insisted on buying drinks for the foreign guests.

Saleem had the distinct impression that the whole town must know Jeet.

In spite of declining several offers from patrons, Saleem still downed two scotches and one martini. With time his taste buds got used the pungent feel and he started to relish the atmosphere. He liked the martini better, not so much for its taste as for the manner in which the bartender served it. First, he liked the shape of the glass, and secondly, he liked the olive soaked in that colorless liquid. By the time the martini had been served to him, he was on his third drink and in a different state of mind; this new experience was certainly enjoyable. To his own surprise, he was talking a lot more than usual. While chatting with a couple of the local people, he sat down at the counter and accepted one more martini. Since everyone wanted to talk with the foreign students, several couples came and sat next to him. Women seemed to be more interested than men were in finding out about these foreigners and their way of life in the faraway lands.

A woman in her late thirties came over and sat by Saleem. Talking about Jeet she said, "When Jeet started working here, he misinterpreted the affectionate ways of some women. He thought they were interested in a sexual relationship. Now that he has been here for a number of years, he understands the American women much better." This conversation took him to the memory of Sarah's lips touching his face and now he understood how some actions can be easily misunderstood. She looked into his eyes and asked, "How old are you?"

"Twenty-five."

"You don't look twenty-five. Well, you seem to be old enough to drink, but are you used to drinking? I mean…do you drink often?"

"This is my first time in a bar, and my first experience with real alcohol."

"I thought so…I suggest you stop now and eat some food. If you go on like this, you will get sick."

She reminded him of Jenny, who was always ready to take charge.

Heeding her advice, Saleem got up from the barstool and realized that feeling in his head was different than when he came in. An older couple who had talked to him at length about his studies and his plans was leaving at the same time as he stood up. The woman came up to him to say good-bye and kissed him on the mouth. This was the first time in his adult life that he had been kissed like this and he did not like it—from someone of his age it perhaps could have been different.

Before anyone realized, it was already past nine o'clock. The dining room closed at ten. Jeet suggested they should eat before the restaurant stopped serving and guided his friends to the dining area, which was a narrow room with windows on one side. Since it was dark outside, the only view was of some distant lights. The tables by the windows had light yellow tablecloths with matching cloth napkins. The china and the silverware reflecting the lights from the chandeliers decorated the place in front of every chair. The menu consisted mostly of seafood that Saleem did not know much about. He suggested Jeet should order for him whatever he was ordering for himself.

As a result, Saleem got a dish of rice and shrimp with bread and butter on the side. For drinks, they all chose water and coffee.

Although it was late and there were very few diners besides Jeet and his friends, the young waiters and waitresses were cheerful and full of energy, as if they had just come in. Some of them knew Jeet and while he and his friends were still eating, they started making plans for a party after they got off from work, which would be at ten o'clock. The food Saleem ate tasted exceptionally delicious, which he attributed to the effects of the alcohol he consumed.

As he enjoyed his food, he listened to his friends and wondered if he really wanted to party at this hour. He had had enough fun for one night. He was tired. His first thought was that he should ask them to drop him wherever they were to spend the night and then go have fun without him. The other option for him was to go along with them and be a spectator to what went on. The obvious lack of enthusiasm on Saleem's part or the fact that they were guests of the owner of the club did not water down their enthusiasm to satiate. They did not want to end their evening. After dinner they thanked the host—they were now ready to savor more fun. At ten o'clock the group exited the restaurant with an additional three people, one boy and two girls, who were to take them to a house where the party was on.

Stepping out of the restaurant into the cool of the night was a shock to Saleem's system. The dining room with its fireplace had been warm and cozy. Once outside, Saleem became aware that for the first time in his life, he was unable to walk in a straight line. The fresh air on his face felt good. Jeet, who was definitely sober for he had very little to drink, drove his friends a short distance following the car with the young people from the club. They parked in front of a house where the loud music was pouring through the closed windows. Saleem and his companions were ushered into a room bursting with young energy. The air was loaded with cigarette smoke and smell of alcohol. Beer seemed to be the drink of choice of this gathering. Saleem declined the offer. He had had enough for one night. He stood in a corner and watched what was going on. After some time, he realized he was disconnected with the crowd and went back in Jeet's car, which he found unlocked. His two friends, too busy enjoying themselves, did not even notice him leave. They found him lying down asleep on the back seat when they left the party past midnight.

A short distance away, the house was enormous—just as Jeet had described. After guiding Saleem and Ajmal to their rooms, he disappeared. Half asleep, Saleem went straight to bed. Aside from all the booze, he was worn out. Sleep was fitful; he kept waking up during the night. As a result, he got up with a major headache in the morning.

"Must be the alcohol last night," he muttered to himself as he touched his forehead. When he stood looking out of the window, he realized the drinks last night had left him with a miserable feeling this morning. He could not deny that he had a good time, but he was paying the price now. When he came the day before, he had no idea he would be drinking—definitely not to this degree. He faintly remembered coming out of the club feeling lightness in his head, where he could not walk in a straight line. If he saw someone in that state, he would judge them drunk. *So, I was drunk last night*, he thought. He did not want to do it again. For some it might be fun and for some an escape, but for him, he thought, he was pulled into it by the novelty of the situation.

He scratched his throbbing head then held it in his two hands and closed his eyes. Crossing lines was what he wanted to do but what he did last night was an immersion into something just for good time and went too deep inside into a territory unfamiliar. He was happy he did not embarrass his friends, or create a scene. From every situation he wanted to learn; he did learn his lesson and experienced something he knew nothing about. He promised he would be more careful…if there was another time. Not wanting to dwell on it, he went to the bathroom to take a shower.

The bedroom he slept in was on the upper floor from which he had unobstructed views of the valley—so different from where he lived in an apartment that provided views of the walls and the rooftops of other houses. Scattered over the hillside, he could make out some cottages. In the absence of breeze, the smoke coming out of the chimneys was rising leisurely in gentle curves and disappearing into the cold air. In the distance were mountains with patches of snow, but the ground nearby was free of the white powder and the grass appeared green to his tired eyes. He stood there watching and taking it all in. He did not know exactly where he was, but everything looked peaceful. It was a lovely morning.

After a hot shower he was refreshed and energized. He put on fresh clothes and felt even better. As he was getting ready to go downstairs to look for his friends, there was a knock on the door. Jeet was making sure everyone was up.

A little later, they all met downstairs. They badly needed coffee and something to eat to get over their indulgence of the night before. It was nine o'clock. The hosts, the owners of the house, had already left for work. Jeet knew the house and offered to make breakfast for everyone. But Ajmal wanted to buy breakfast for Jeet. So they drove to a diner that looked familiar, not because he had been there before, but because it was no different from the other restaurants Saleem had been to in the recent past. Whether he was in Eugene, Portland or Salem, Saleem felt that things were similar. Houses were of same style, and stores and eating places looked alike. Even the streets had the same names. That was America as he saw it.

A distinct aroma of coffee greeted them as they stepped inside the restaurant. A number of waitresses were busy serving customers, the atmosphere was cheerful with men and women eating and talking. A hostess who walked the three young men to an empty table handed them menus. Once seated, Saleem was relieved to notice that no one was curious about him or his friends in this small town. Just then a couple waved from a few tables away. The man got up and came over to say hello to Jeet and his companions. He was one of those they had met in the club the night before. Soon a young waitress took their orders. Saleem wanted eggs this morning. When she asked how he would like his eggs and he answered that he wanted them fried; she did not quite understand. Jeet knew what Saleem wanted and told the waitress to order them sunny-side up.

She smiled, looked at Saleem and said, "You are new here, aren't you?" She did not appear to recognize Jeet.

"There is at least one person in this town that does not seem to know you." Ajmal said to Jeet and they all laughed.

After breakfast, Jeet suggested they go to the laundry, where they would meet Darlene, the owner of the house where they were staying. They had not had a chance to see her yet; she had left the house very early this morning. The three of them wanted to thank her for the hospitality before leaving the town. When they walked into the laundry, they saw a middle-aged woman busy ironing clothes. She looked up, smiled, and stopped what she was doing. Jeet introduced

Darlene to his friends. She asked if they had eaten breakfast yet and inquired about their plans for the day. Saleem thought Darlene was a very pleasant motherly woman.

Satisfied that they were not hungry, she invited them on a tour of her workplace. Saleem got a chance to see the big ironing press she had been using earlier. The mechanized ironing of clothes fascinated him. He was familiar with the process but on a small scale, the ironing board and his little electric-iron which he acquired at a goodwill store for two dollars he used every week to press his white shirts. She also showed them the heavy-duty washing machines and the dry cleaning section, where in spite of the exhaust fans, that typical smell of chemical solvents permeated the air.

After chatting for a little while, they said goodbye. As they were leaving the store, Saleem wondered why someone who owned a club, a big house and a laundry, would be working so hard.

Saleem's new roommate had a strange habit; soon after reading he would tear up the letters from his mother. One day, thinking of his own mother, Saleem could not resist asking Ajmal why he did that. His answer was that mail piles up and eventually gets thrown away. The reasoning made sense, but still Saleem found it odd. Saleem's father was good at writing letters. He always answered his son's letters very promptly. His mother would let father and son correspond. Saleem had never received a letter written by his mother and always wondered how a mother would write to her son.

One day Saleem was in when Ajmal brought the mail when he came for lunch. Another letter from his mother came that day, Ajmal read it and, as usual, tore it up and threw it in the trash. Saleem once again was puzzled by his friend's action. He was curious.

After lunch, Ajmal had to leave for his job on campus. Saleem too had work of his own he needed to do. As he got busy, he forgot all about his desire to learn about that letter from a mother, which now lay shredded in a trash can. When he was about to leave, his eye caught a glimpse of those pieces right on top of the waste. The son in him urged him to go ahead and assemble those bits and find out what a mother was saying. Still he hesitated, asked the important question if it was ethically correct to read someone's mail. He knew it was not! He would not want anyone to pry into his private life. But then, it was a letter from a mother, a letter which for his roommate did not hold much value. In spite of the conflict going on in his mind, his curiosity won over his ethical sensibility. He went into the trash and picked up all those blue pieces of the ripped up letter one by one. For some, he had to dig under the refuse.

Not certain he had them all, he set his collection on the dining table and started assembling it like a jigsaw-puzzle, using words as his guide, to fit them together. The letter was in Urdu as expected. The words soon took shape and his excitement rose. It did not take long for him to get them in an order where he could read the beginning of the writing. As he started assembling from the top corners, the name of the city, Karachi, soon emerged. His ears were keen all this time for any sound of steps—Ajmal might come back to pick up something he forgot. He thought of locking the door but then decided not to because he never did that when he was in, except at night.

He expected a beginning, "my dear son", or something to that effect. What he found was, "My dear beloved, *the crown on my head*". The unexpected beginning confused Saleem. Never expecting such an unorthodox beginning of a letter from a parent, he wanted to read more. His inquisitiveness was now several degrees higher, the feeling of any guilt he might have had was now deeply buried under his intense concern to probe.

As the pieces fit together, he could now read and read it again. The letter was obviously not from a mother. It was from a wife, Ajmal's wife, a wife who longed for her husband's return, who was worried about her two children missing their father. The feeling of guilt, mingled with a sense of adventure, flowed through his entire being as he read those lines. All this would not have been such a shock, if Ajmal had not told everyone, including a girlfriend who visited the apartment often, that he was unmarried.

Suddenly, Saleem was struck by a wave of sympathy for a girl he hardly knew. This surprised him. He reasoned part of his compassion for women came out of his love for his mother. And that was perhaps why he was siding with a woman against someone he lived with.

Saleem understood he had broken a code. For him it was a troubling fact that he found something he was not supposed to know—using deceptive means—a reality he could not dismiss. The fact remained; he unintentionally discovered what he was not to know. Not to make it any worse, he decided he would never ever read a letter again unless addressed to him and never tell anyone about this one. In his mind, it was the best approach to minimize, if not undo, his feeling of guilt. Now that the pieces of the torn letter were back in the trash can, he could not bear looking at them. He pushed it under the table.

He felt differently about his friend. He had done something he thought was wrong but at the same time he had made a discovery. Useful it was not, but now he had secret knowledge, information he could not disclose. Ajmal's being married or unmarried did not affect anyone except his girlfriend. She, Saleem thought, might not like to continue a relationship with a married man, but with a tattoo on her arm she might be liberated to a point of not caring and carry on. All these thoughts, not in any way affecting his life, were fogging his mind.

Since he had acquired the knowledge, it made him look at everything Ajmal did differently. *He could be reading into things that did not exist.* Ajmal had not changed; it was Saleem who had doubts about his friend. Although how Ajmal lived his life was none of Saleem's business, still he was troubled by the fact that he had lied to him. Although he really would not call him a friend as he would his previous roommate, he was not a stranger. He was a man from his country; he was living with him. Honesty he expected from someone he spent so much time with. Living together they shared many things. With his discovery, he lost respect for him.

The letter revealed he was cheating on his family, not providing for them when they were expecting. They depended on him. He must have promised them, and God only knew what he had told them. He was no longer sure that his family was even aware of the fact that he was a student, spending money rather than generating any. His wife complained he was gone much longer than he had told her when he left. She understood he was leaving for a year of training, but now it was over two years. She presumed he was working hard for the family; still she was carrying out the responsibility of a couple alone. The language of the letter showed the woman was not well educated, but she was frustrated. She felt she had certain rights as a wife and he had responsibilities as a husband. She was living with her parents who perhaps had coaxed her to write the way she did.

From that afternoon when he made his discovery, he unconsciously censored his roommate's actions. He noticed patterns of behavior that were a little odd. He now paid attention to all items in Ajmal's mail, some of which he did not discard, and left them on the table. A number of printed brochures came for him in the mail. Saleem, curious about them, did not believe it was wrong to leaf through them when they were lying so openly—inviting him to browse. Why would his roommate get addresses of places where one could exchange wives or look for single women and escorts in different towns? Saleem had no idea. Ajmal who had lived in this country longer had told his roommate that the mail soliciting different types of trades and businesses was common in this country. Saleem accepted and added this to his memory bank as additional knowledge about the culture of this foreign land.

Saleem had also noticed his friend was bringing in new books and possessed a shelf full of them. He did not read them. His explanation was that the professor, when he cleaned the office, got the new editions, competing text-books for the courses he was teaching, considered them to be unsolicited material and threw them away. He felt bad about these books of knowledge discarded like this, so he provided them a home until he would give them to those who might need them.

He also occasionally brought orchids from the nursery where he worked and told Saleem that his boss wanted him to take them as a present for the girls he might know.

Saleem had not paid any attention to these things before, but now when he discovered how he had lied to him, he was looking for anything that appeared out of the ordinary, be it normal in the new culture he was now living in, or in fact something fishy. He possibly was seeing more than there was in those ghosts he was chasing.

He saw in a flower-shop window an orchid similar to what he had seen Ajmal bring in one evening. The price tag of ten dollars for a flower surprised him, especially when his bicycle cost him forty dollars. He no longer could say with certainty that the generosity of the nursery owner was the reason the orchids were acquired by his roommate.

The sleuth in Saleem was now defining everything in a different way. He felt his roommate was subsidizing his income by selling books he picked up and stealing those orchids from the nursery. But he wished it was his imagination. He had no desire to investigate any more; he had important problems in his own life that needed attention. The detective in him was distracting him from his work. Now he had a secret of his own, his knowledge about his roommate, he did not want to share with anyone.

Was he obliged to tell Ajmal's girl friend about her friend being married? The thought started to haunt him. He did not believe so. Wrongly or rightly, he did not want to interfere in the lives of other people, which could be interpreted as his lack of concern for them. Still, he believed everyone was responsible for their actions. If she had entered into a relationship with a married man, it was her fault. His own knowledge had come through unscrupulous means—probing into the life of a friend who perhaps trusted him and did not expect him to be snooping into his private life. The fact, however, remained that he had certain knowledge—obtained whichever way. Should he use it to help a young woman he did not know well? But the reality of the fact was that he did not want to betray his roommate more than he already had.

He was now a part of the deception, in a way. He, at times, felt bad about it. He rebuked himself for looking into the trash, finding and reading that letter which was not meant for him, sent his imagination flying in all direction, creating conflicts in his mind. Done was done! Now, he had no choice but to live with it.

Soon after returning from the trip with Ajmal and his friend Jeet, Saleem noticed a difference in his roommate's behavior. There was a certain formality and coldness in the attitude. It could be that Ajmal blamed Saleem for spoiling the party with those young waitresses at the resort, and he had decided the new roommate was not quite his type. Or, perhaps, Ajmal had found out about his reading of his mail; although he could not imagine how.

The fall term was just starting when Ajmal and some of his friends brought over some young girls, all freshmen, newly out of the restrictive surrounding of their homes, thrown into the liberal campus of the university. They were all trying to find themselves. Saleem had no information there was going to be party, though it was Saturday night. Since it was early, Saleem was still in the apartment when they arrived. The girls were so young, so immature. He felt out of place. All they wanted to talk about was having fun. One of them, an out-of-state student from southern California, got talking to him and explained about the gatherings she observed held in her neighborhood where the guests would throw their car keys in a basket as they arrived and when party was over they would blindly pick a bunch of keys and would go away with the car owner's woman for the night. Such were the topics of discussion, things explained for the benefit of a new student unaware of the culture. He was surprised, but not disturbed, and tried to imagine how it would feel if he was one of the attendees of such a function.

This party, though intriguing, he soon knew, would be a distraction for him. He could not deny he had a desire to experience the novel—the tantalizing temptations could easily weaken his resolve—he could feel it. It was a distinct possibility. That teased and worried him. He was afraid of these thoughts; they might seduce him, take him off-course and destroy his focus. Before he was drawn further into the mood of the younger students, he forced himself to get away. He decided to leave and went to the lab—to his work, his primary goal. They called him party-pooper. He did not care. His own expectations of himself and what his parents believed him to be made him triumph over his vulnerabilities: in the past, and again for now.

When he changed his first apartment, all he wanted was to save some money. He had no idea he was launching into a different world. Because when he came back home around two in the morning—he had purposely delayed his arrival—the lights were still on. Beer cans littered the place and a strange smell hung in air. The place was quiet but everyone was not gone. He found a girl sleeping in his bed. The same girl he had talked to when they all came in. He did not know if he should get in the bed too, after all that was where he slept every night. She was the only one from the group he had talked to before he left the party. For a moment, the idea stirred something inside him. Before his libido got the better of him, he moved away.

He spent the whole night in the living room where another body was stretched on the sofa. He dozed on and off on a chair. That night he decided he needed to move and stay away from this place. If he continued living in the same apartment he might get drawn into something unknown, things detrimental to his future, something he would regret. The drifting ideas bothered him. He had come too far, he had worked too hard to get where he was. He did not want anything to destroy it all.

Now, he was uncomfortable living where he was. He wanted to get away, he needed to find another place where he could concentrate on his studies, carry out his academic mission.

All he needed was a place to sleep and for this purpose he desperately wanted to contact someone. Jafar, from the Physics Department came to mind. He remembered Jafar taking him to his landlady. He got a lucky break. Jafar told him one of his neighbors was leaving. His landlady, whom he had already met, remembered him and readily agreed to let him in. Within a few days he was living in the new place—a one-room apartment on the second floor, which had a stove and a refrigerator. The bed folded into the wall. The place was comfortable, the landlady was friendly and above all he was living alone—like he did when he lived in the hostel in St. John's College.

Ajmal was unhappy when his roommate left, leaving him to find another roommate in a hurry—which he did.

A year passed since Saleem had moved away from where he was sharing the apartment with Ajmal. One day, walking on the campus, the two old roommates ran into each other. Saleem noticed a look on his friend's face he had not seen before. After the formalities of checking how each was doing, Ajmal told Saleem that he was thinking of leaving the university and going back home. He said it was to attend to family matters. Saleem, knowing what he knew, could understand. What Ajmal did not tell his former roommate was that he was being investigated.

A few weeks later he ran into Martha—Ajmal's girlfriend. From her he found out, Ajmal was no longer in the country—he was gone. She was justifiably sad and unhappy. According to her, he was charged for soliciting obscenity through the mail—some law that prohibited the exchange of those brochures he was receiving through the post office. They had found his address when those who were mailing the brochures were raided. His apartment was searched. In addition to the mail, they discovered a stack of stolen books. They took him in custody and sent him home—actually deported him. Saleem was sorry for what happened to Ajmal but was happy he was not living with him when all this occurred. He might have been caught up in the mess, for no fault of his. The girl mentioned nothing about his being married in Pakistan.

Saleem was so busy in his work he had no time to socialize. He found out through Jafar, now his neighbor, who seemed to have more time at hand, that the foreign-students' adviser, Dr. Brown, had invited

Pakistani students to his house for a get together. The professor was heading there as a consultant for six-months. The event was a social gathering and, at the same time, a fact-finding mission for the hosts. Before his departure to Pakistan, the professor thought he should pick up as much information as he could about the region—young people from the region, in his opinion, were a good source of knowledge. A total of sixteen students showed up—he counted them. Some he knew and some were new to him. His wife made Pakistani food for everyone.

As the dinner was over, Dr. Brown encouraged everyone to talk about their life at home. As the conversation warmed up, he asked if anyone wanted a beer. Not realizing it might offend some in the company, Saleem raised his hand. No one else did. He felt awkward, but he had expressed his intention and an open can was already in his hand. Too late to change the choice of his beverage, he pretended he did not notice the displeasure of some around him.

As the party was over, and students were leaving, he heard an older fellow Saleem had not met before, perhaps a new arrival, telling his friend how some people were so insensitive and careless to shame and dishonor Pakistan by drinking beer in front of foreigners. Saleem did not know who these people were, but it was clear that words were uttered for him to hear. The only way he could defend himself was by saying that beer was not illegal in Pakistan and if the law had changed since he left, he was not aware. But he did not want to get into an argument. He further heard, "As we know, drinking alcohol is a sin. And we need to project an image of our faith even if certain things are still allowed in Pakistan that our religion does not permit." The guy was one of those who came to study on a government scholarship. Ajmal thought the man was out of order, but he got in his car and left. He did not feel sorry for having a beer he enjoyed and was happy he was not among those who were so different from him in their thinking and wanted to impose their way of life on him, in the name of religion, as a matter of right.

The incident was unpleasant for Saleem but not something to dwell on. He put it away from his mind, keeping a reminder somewhere in his memory to avoid people from his country, especially those who had a beard. He really did not need new friends. He had come for a purpose and he was going to concentrate on his goal—he had come to learn, which involved certain changes in his life, and he was ready for that too.

Looking back on his days when he freshly arrived, he figured he was fortunate that per chance he had run into Kader when he arrived. Kader had taught him so much about the new life. They were so like each other. Sometimes he wished he had stayed put where he was, the same apartment the same roommate. Some students from Pakistan were so different that it made him wonder if they came from the same country he did. He considered himself privileged in the sense that he had parents who had liberal views about religion and social customs.

CHAPTER 32

Another year was ending soon for Saleem. At this point, he had finished most of the course work and was now spending many hours in the lab. He was not getting the results he was hoping for, but he was making other discoveries. His project had started with a specific objective, but was now headed in a different direction. Saleem kept Professor Hayden informed of his progress. They met quite frequently. One Monday, after they discussed the research project, Professor Hayden told Saleem that his wife was arranging an international student party and he was invited to the gathering. Saleem remembered the professor asking him about his cooking a long time ago and offered to prepare something for this get-together.

"No, no there will be too many people. You just come, meet some guests and enjoy yourself. We shall do it some other time," the professor told him.

Getting an invitation to his professor's home was a special occasion for him. Saleem was excited, but at the same time, he was a little uneasy about meeting people he did not know. Whenever he visited an American home, he was always sensitive to the fact that he came from a different cultural background where day-to-day life was very different. He did not want to create a situation that would be awkward for him or embarrassing to the hosts. Being in this country for nearly two years had taught him many things about the American way of life, mostly he had learned by observing others, including fellow students. However, he still sometimes found himself in unfamiliar territory. Yet the thought of being just one of many young guests from other countries was consoling.

The professor had asked him to come at five o'clock in the afternoon. To go there, he called a cab. In the meantime, he put on a clean white shirt, the suit that he had bought in Portland and the matching tie that the store had given him. He did not know how to get to the professor's house, but he trusted the cab driver to find it. He handed the driver a slip of paper with the address.

During the ride to the party, he saw parts of town that were new to him. His life had revolved around the campus because he was always busy, and a bicycle had its limitations.

The cab driver seemed to know where Pakistan was and was happy to learn more about it from his passenger. They had a pleasant conversation, which made the ride seem shorter than it was. The driver parked the car in front of a huge house behind lush lawns. Beautiful flowers the likes of which Saleem could not name, except of course for the roses, lined the front of the house and the walkway. Tall trees surrounded the property, which added a feeling of mystery and privacy to the house.

Admiring the landscape as Saleem walked toward the entrance, two other men who looked as if they were from Africa joined him. They were well dressed. One of them even wore an overcoat, or was it a raincoat? Saleem could not tell. The professor and his wife were at the door greeting their guests. The men arrived ahead of him. They shook hands with the professor and his wife, at which point Mrs. Hayden asked if she could take the man's coat. Saleem heard that and thought he had to take off his jacket too. He started to unbutton, but Mrs. Hayden told him that he could keep the jacket on. She had been collecting long coats and raincoats. Saleem made a quick mental note of the difference between a coat and a jacket for future reference.

Professor Hayden now introduced Saleem to Mrs. Hayden. All she said was, "Nice to meet you Saleem, my husband talks about you."

He took it as a compliment and moved on because someone else was behind him. To one side of the foyer, he noticed a small table with nametags. He found his name and pinned it to the lapel of his jacket. With his name on his jacket he felt he had an identity. He was happy he would not be spelling his name to those he met at this party.

Saleem proceeded to follow the murmur of voices. He noticed some foreign postdoctoral students from the department standing around, chatting. He noticed he was not the only one wearing a suit and tie; it seemed all very formal.

A number of young men and women from different countries were standing holding drinks in their hands. Some young women had the national attire of their country. A Chinese girl was dressed in a red gold-embroidered dress buttoned to the chin; an African woman wrapped in most colorful clothes was walking around with a drink in her hand. Saleem remembered the professor telling him that it was a party for the students from abroad. The atmosphere was international, although there were just as many Americans as foreigners, some young, some not so young.

Through a large window in the living room, Saleem could see the backyard with more green lawn and tall trees. The room must have been quite large because it did not feel crowded, even though there were about thirty people there. Some younger servers were moving among the guests with trays holding an array of snacks and drinks. Saleem picked up a glass with an orange-colored liquid. It turned out to be a fruit punch. A drink in hand, he walked up to the small group known to him from the chemistry department. It was the first time for all of them to be in their professor's home and they were being very cordial and proper.

Just as people usually talk about weather when they have nothing worthwhile to say, the chemists in the room started talking about chemistry.

A little later the hosts moved away from the door. All the guests had arrived; all the nametags on the table were gone. People in small groups were now chatting mostly with others they already knew. The professor and his wife moved about the room, talking to people, taking one or two from one group and introducing them to another, the name tags announcing their names. Saleem was happy he did not need to pronounce his name every time he met someone new; still a number of guests asked how he said it.

Soon the chemistry group was split and Saleem ended up with one of the professor's neighbors. From him Saleem learned the professor's wife was an active volunteer in an organization that extended to other countries. "They are older people who have time on their hands. They collect used articles for people who lost everything in catastrophes like earthquakes, typhoons or other such tragedy. They have a warehouse where they keep the donations; they sort them and have them ready for an emergency shipment. The organization has volunteers in foreign lands that cooperate with the local group.

The institution is in its infancy, but they hope to get more people to join them," he told Saleem. They chatted some more about politics in India and Pakistan, and to Saleem's surprise, he found the man to be very knowledgeable about that region.

Finally, it was time to eat. For this purpose, four tables were set in the living room. The seating was assigned by name. Saleem found his name and sat down. To the seated guests Mrs. Hayden announced that each person should pick up his or her plate and go to the kitchen. The food was typically American; a large table held platters heaped with turkey meat, roast beef, roasted potatoes, vegetables, and green salad. Butter and rolls were set on each table.

With food on his plate, when Saleem sat down he counted seven additional guests were sitting at his table. John, the man he had talked with earlier was one of them. Judging from his accent, Saleem presumed he was from an East European country. The seating arrangement was in a way that men and women alternated; on his left side was a young woman from Kenya and on the other side sat a woman from China. They made small talk about how long they had been in America and what they were studying.

Saleem always had a problem talking to strangers, so for the most part it turned out to be a quiet dinner. The older man at their table tried to keep the conversation going, asking questions or telling the young men and women things about Eugene, Oregon or America. The talk drifted from one topic to another. Soon the subject was LSD and its use by young people. Everyone had read about it or was familiar with the drug and had an opinion. The University of Oregon was a liberal campus with a number of students from California; however, Saleem did not know anyone who was experimenting with these drugs in the student body. But then, he mostly knew graduate students who were past the age where peer-pressure or curiosity got the best of their judgment.

Professor Haydens' neighbor John, looking at everyone and at no one in particular, said in a serious tone, "The media tends to make a big deal about things considered sensational. LSD is a very controversial drug these days and it gets far more coverage than the birth control pill, although the pill will have a long-lasting effect on society and LSD will soon be a thing of the past."

The discussion about the pill and LSD was getting everyone interested at Saleem's table and just as people were warming up to the topic, a woman's voice asking for attention came over. "Two of the four tables have a bowl in the middle. These bowls contain gift-wrapped objects. Please pick one up and unwrap it. Inside, you will find a small present with a name attached. Present this gift to the intended person. I hope you will get to meet other people this way. If there is anyone who has not finished eating yet... please excuse me! I did not mean to interrupt your dinner."

However, everyone was done and those who had bowls on their table picked up one piece. Saleem's table had a bowl. The package he picked contained a little toy car and a name, Theresa Jafrey.

Saleem now had to find Theresa Jafrey. He knew the individual of this name had to be at one of the tables without a bowl.

Mrs. Hayden's voice came up again, "If you cannot find the person, you need to look harder because everyone is here and we want you to talk to and meet as many people as possible.

Everyone got up and started to look for someone to give the present to. Saleem walked here and there, bumping into young men and women who, like him, were also looking for a name. He ended up on the other side of the room, but did not find Theresa Jafrey.

Mrs. Hayden saw Saleem wandering around, wrapper in hand. She came up to him and read the name on the gift box. She looked around the room and said, "She is here. This game was her idea... Where are you, Terry?" she half shouted.

Out of the kitchen came a beautiful tall girl. She walked over to where Mrs. Hayden and Saleem were standing. Mrs. Hayden introduced them to each other. Looking at her, Saleem thought he had met or seen this girl before, but he could not place her. Terry, however, knew who he was; he was the man who had given her a ride from the infirmary to her dorm. She also knew he was a graduate student in the chemistry department; he had told her so that morning. She had actually been hoping he would be here today.

"Here is a car for you, Theresa Jafrey," Saleem said handing her the present.

"You don't recognize me, do you?" With a twinkle in her eye, Terry said. "I'm the girl from the infirmary."

"I thought you looked familiar, but I couldn't place you. It seems so long ago. It is so nice to meet you again," Saleem said as he shook her hand.

"And… your name is Saleem," she pronounced slowly reading it from his nametag.

Now, he remembered who she was. He also recalled what the cab driver had said about her. That day, he had not been feeling well and she too had been sick. He had thought about her briefly, but there were so many other more important issues on his mind. He had been busy with his studies and the thought of a girl, no matter how beautiful, was hard to fathom. Tonight was different. He was in a better place now; he felt more secure and confident. And he was attending a party.

She was wearing a dark blue dress; her light brown hair was tied in a knot. He guessed that she was about five eight. She inquired about his program in graduate school. He asked her about her studies. She told him she had to drop out for one quarter because she had gotten ill, but she recovered and hoped to make up all the time she lost. To Saleem, she looked healthy, and actually beautiful. They were still talking when Mrs. Hayden's voice came up again. "Dessert is ready, and there is coffee also… for those who drink coffee."

As she passed by Saleem and noticed that he and Terry were still talking, she said, "She must have really liked your present. She hardly ever talks to anyone."

Terry said, "We found out that we had met before."

"Oh, how interesting," Mrs. Hayden said as she went into the kitchen.

Both Terry and Saleem took coffee and a piece of cake from the center table and then sat down together. Saleem told her of his former difficulties and that he was doing well now.

"Call me Terry, all my friends do," she said.

They could have talked some more, but Mrs. Hayden directed everyone to change partners. Then John came up to Saleem, laid a hand on his shoulder and said, "I see, you've met my daughter." It appeared John was going to say more but the music started to play and center of the room was prepared for dancing by moving furniture around.

Saleem knew nothing about dancing, so he just sat down on a chair and watched. He saw Terry dancing with someone he did not know; they seemed to be having a good time. He drifted to the other room where the professor had set up a slide projector telling stories about his hunting safari in Africa.

It was now past nine o'clock and the guests had started to leave. Mrs. Hayden asked Saleem, if he had a ride home. Saleem told her that he took a cab to come.

"So many people are here; someone should be going in your direction. Let me check," Mrs. Hayden said and disappeared. In the mean time, Saleem noticed Karl, one of the postdoctoral fellows in Hayden's group, was looking for him to check if he found someone to take him home. Karl told Saleem he could ride with him. Saleem was happy to find a way of getting home on his own and told Karl he would meet him outside right after saying good-bye to the professor and his wife. They both needed to acknowledge their hosts. They found and complimented Mrs. Hayden for arranging such a lovely dinner party and thanked her for inviting them. Saleem wanted to say good-bye to Terry also, but he did not see her.

By the time Saleem got to his apartment, it was nearly ten o'clock. After the party his room felt so quiet. Saleem picked up an old magazine and took it to the bedroom. He tried to read in bed, hoping he would fall asleep. Meeting Terry had been the highlight of his evening and he was excited. He could not sleep as he kept thinking about her. While lying awake, he was telling himself, *She is too pretty and she is too young. She perhaps has a boyfriend. Forget her and go to sleep. You still have a long way to go to finish what you came here for.* The idea he needed to keep his goal in focus kept repeating in his mind until he fell asleep. His neighbor came home late and then Terry's image kept appearing again. He did not get to sleep well that night.

The next morning he woke up tired. It was drizzling outside. He made himself a cup of tea, put on a raincoat and went out. He decided it would be good for him to walk to clear his mind. For a while he did not open his umbrella. Mist of raindrops sprayed his face and the fresh morning air worked wonders. By the time he reached the lab, he was refreshed and ready to do some work.

Karl was already at the lab. The radio was tuned to an FM station that played classical music. Saleem found it very appealing this morning. Karl told him that he usually had difficulty going to sleep after a party, so he had decided to come and work at night. Soon he would go home and sleep during the day. As Karl got ready to leave, he asked Saleem if he would like to join him for breakfast. Saleem thought about his cup of tea earlier, but he could have something to eat now. They were not sure whether the student union cafeteria would be open this early or if they needed to go somewhere else. It was Sunday morning, so they decided to go off campus. Since Karl had a car, it posed no problem.

Karl, a postdoctoral fellow, had gotten his degree from Heidelberg and was here for one year to get some experience while he planned to see the country. Since the two men were at different stages of their careers, Saleem was trying to get a degree, Karl already had one and both were working on different projects in the lab. Karl and Saleem had never spent much time together. Karl was soon to go back home; he had already been here for over ten months.

Eating their breakfast of cinnamon rolls and coffee, they stayed in the restaurant talking for over an hour. Among other things, Karl told Saleem about his student life in Germany and inquired about Saleem's research project and his life in India and Pakistan. Surprisingly, Karl was quite well-informed about the partition of India, the ethnic riots and the killings that followed. When Saleem described how he lived through that period he found his friend to be a good listener. As Karl dropped Saleem off at the lab and went home to sleep, getting out of the car, Saleem said, "If you decide to sell your car when you leave, please let me know." Karl nodded and drove away.

The rain had stopped. Saleem did not go back to the lab directly; he walked around a little more, enjoying the fresh outdoors. Today, he was elated. It was a wonderful feeling. Something he had not experienced in a long while.

When he had attended college in Agra and started going to the movies, he fell in love with many movie stars on the screen. He knew that he let himself fall in love easily and if this were happening again, it would pass as it did in the past. With these thoughts on his mind, he went to the lab and got involved in his experiment. Later, he spent some time in the library to carry out some literature search concerning his project. The time passed quickly and it was dark before he realized it—he even forgot to eat his lunch.

With spring came the rains. Rain in Eugene was seldom heavy. Usually in the form of a light drizzle, it fell often. These rains were the life of the lush green lawns and flowers. But he missed the summer monsoons of India where a mass of dark clouds came rolling in, announcing their arrival with roaring thunder that shook the earth, bolts of lightning that split the skies and poured buckets of water. When he had arrived and the sky calmly got cloudy, the light sprinkle of rain was romantic, like for those who had seen too much sun and longed for shade. As the time passed, he wanted sun back in his life.

These days Saleem was spending most of his time indoors in the lab or at the library. In the library one afternoon, a few days after the party at the professor's house, someone tapped him on the shoulder. He turned around and to his surprise found Terry standing there, looking as beautiful as he had remembered her. She was dressed in jeans and sneakers. His heart started to skip beats again. He had made a conscious attempt to put her out of his mind, but he must have failed.

"I looked for you after the dinner, but you disappeared without saying goodbye," she said.

"I was catching a ride home with a friend. I did look for you… Sorry," Saleem answered.

"Well, now that I bumped into you, I want you to come and have lunch me," Terry said. "I will buy. Remember, you took me to my dorm when I was sick? I think it's time I did something for you." She wondered if she was being honest with herself. The words coming out of her mouth could be construed as: I want to spend some time with you. Is he getting my message? Perhaps not, was what she thought now. She knew she had not been herself since she met him at the party, but she did not care.

Saleem felt uncomfortable to have a girl pay for his lunch, but he also did not want to argue. The two of them walked to the student union cafeteria. It was not quite noon, so there were enough seats available in the dining area. They found a quiet corner table and sat down with their hamburgers and glasses of milk.

Saleem did not like cold milk in the beginning when he arrived in America. In India and Pakistan, milk was always boiled and then served hot. Saleem had thought that it was done for hygienic reasons. But he learned that older people held a strong belief that cold milk would make them sick, whether it had been cooked before or not. As a result, his mother would never let him drink it cold. After coming to America where everyone drank milk right out of the refrigerator, Saleem had developed a taste for it. Still, sometimes he would warm it up and drink it before going to bed. Etched in his mind somewhere was the thought that hot milk made you sleep better.

Terry wanted him to tell her more about his life. Saleem said that he was going to ask her the same thing but, since she had asked first, he was glad to report that he was doing much better than when they met in the infirmary. "I was going through some serious difficulties with my studies when I met you the first time, but I've managed to survive and hopefully will be able to get my degree in two years or so. I'm working hard and Professor Hayden has been very helpful. It was his advice that saved me. Otherwise, I might have flunked the first quarter and then I would not be sitting here talking with you today. It was the fear of failing that made me ill. That's why I was in the hospital where we met that morning."

She listened without interrupting him.

For some time, they both sat there, eating in silence. Saleem wondered if she really wanted to know all that. Finally, he said, "Now it's your turn. By the way, I met your father at the party."

"I don't know how much you want to know about me... My last name throws people off because I look like a typical white American girl, but my father came from Kashmir. My mother is from England. My father got his education in England and had been working there as an engineer when he met my mother. They immigrated to this country and made it their home. My sister and I were born in California. I have a twin sister. We were still very young when we all moved to Eugene. You didn't get a chance to meet my mother at the party. She had a cold and couldn't come."

She stopped for a while as if she wasn't sure she should continue, but then decided to add, "My father and I get along very well, but with my mother...it's a different story." After another pause she said, "As you know, I'm a sophomore now and hopefully will finish college about the same time as you. During the summer, I intend to intern with the local newspaper and do some babysitting. I have also worked as a waitress from time to time. My mother wants me to assimilate in the American culture, by which she means that I should go to parties and have a boyfriend... Now I've told you the story of my life. I don't know why; I just wanted to." She blushed and looked down at her plate.

He wanted to tell her that he liked her father and now knew why he was so well informed about the India-Pakistan political situation. Instead, he asked if her sister looked like her. Eating and talking about each other, they sat at the table for over an hour, interrupted occasionally by Terry's friends who were passing by. It was now time for her to go to her class and for Saleem to return to the library.

"I hope to see you again soon," Saleem said to her as they were leaving.

He was pleasantly surprised to hear her say, "I'm sure you will, I still want to know more...about your life, I mean."

Saleem felt as if he were in a different world, walking on air. He had never ever spent so much time with a good-looking girl. Granted, he had thought about the young woman after they had met in the hospital. And he had briefly fantasized about her after accidentally meeting her again at the party, but he was not going to do anything about it. And now she sat with him and they had talked as if they were old friends. What a wonderful day this turned out to be. This was a good omen. Surely, his luck would now turn and soon his experiments would start showing results. At least he was hoping all these things would happen. Suddenly, he realized he forgot to ask for her phone number. Being what he was, he told himself, *If this relationship is meant to be, it will, and, if not, nothing can be done about it.*

Still, thinking about her, he went back to the same place in the library where she had found him. His reading material was still lying open on the table, just as he had left it. He sat down and started turning the pages without being able to concentrate. All he could see in front of him was her face. He closed his eyes. The face was still there. He placed the journal back on the rack, and went outside to clear his mind. He just loved to walk on those narrow winding pathways on the campus, which weaved around buildings and lawns.

He still had a lot of work left to satisfy the requirements for his degree. He had come too far to be swayed by his emotions. He could not afford to waste time thinking about girls in general or this girl in particular. With a struggle going on between his heart and his mind, he slowly ambled back to the lab and tried to focus on his immediate goals. He sat down at his desk, folded his arms and reminded himself about the reasons he had come to this country. He had accepted the challenge and he would meet his goals.

CHAPTER 33

John was not Terry's father's real name. His actual name was Jaan Mustafa Jafrey, which over a period of living in the English-speaking world morphed and changed to John. His father's family was friends with the influential Nehru family, the Kennedy's of India. They all were from Kashmir. When John finished his engineering degree, his father wanted him to stay in England, take a job and get some experience. While working in London, he met a young woman, Bernice, who was an office employee. Bernice liked his dark hair and his not-so-white complexion. She thought he was very handsome. She also knew that he came from a rich family in India. They fell in love and were soon married.

John liked living in England. A number of young people from his part of the world were residing in or near London, the children of rich and privileged in India. He would meet with some of them on a regular basis and discuss current events—politics of their homeland. They exchanged their thoughts and fears about what would happen to India after the British left, and they talked about the war that seemed imminent in Western Europe. Bernice was not interested in politics and felt as if she was in a foreign land when John's friends visited him, which was often, talked in their own language, and got excited when she had no idea what they were discussing. Occasionally, they would notice that she was there, they would switch to English. Still, their thoughts she could not share. Her views of England were very different from theirs. In her mind, England was the most powerful country in the world. It did colonize a large part of the world, but she did bring a glimpse of modern technology to many of these countries. In retrospect, she realized that she entered this marriage blinded by young love, which she now regarded as infatuation. Now she started to see things differently. She saw her husband as an Indian and herself as British—one of the Brits who ruled India. And at times she would let her husband know of her thoughts. Argument would follow.

With time, John came to realize that his interests in politics were hurting their relationship and their marriage might not last unless they made significant changes in their lives. As long as he stayed close to his Indian friends, they would get together to discuss the current political situation. In order to safeguard their marriage, which for him was an institution of family, he decided, and Bernice agreed, to move to America. She wanted to put a distance between him and his friends. The United States was the land of opportunity where both of them would be foreigners. They could start a new life together. Soon after the decision was made, John found out that the American companies were looking to hire engineers from England. He interviewed, got a job and the couple moved to California.

As an engineer John earned good money and Bernice, because of her accent and British manners, became popular in the neighborhood. John had a busy schedule and his job often required him to travel. She spent her days with her new American friends. He still missed England and those discussions he enjoyed with his countrymen, but he had little time to dwell on anything besides work. And he was grateful that his wife was happy in her new environment. The California sun had put a smile on her face.

John also got to know other engineers at work. He quickly found out that Americans worked longer hours than Europeans did. They were also more open and friendly. It was easy to form new friendships, but their interest in international politics was limited.

After renting for a little over a year, he and Bernice bought a house. Having more room now, she started inviting her friends from England to come and visit them in California, which they did. They pointed out to her how she had changed—her accent, her manners were now very American. She knew her American friends did not think so.

Bernice wanted to have at least one child, but she had been unable to get pregnant when they were in England. Now, after a year in California and just prior to moving into their new home, she found out that she was expecting. When the doctor gave her the good news that she was expecting twins, she was thrilled, if a little worried about taking care of two infants. The pregnancy was without any complications and she gave birth to two little girls whom they named Theresa and Mary.

Watching over twins became a problem. She found it difficult to tend to the needs of not only one infant but two. The pattern of her life changed. She wanted to get together with her friends as before, but looking after the babies and with her husband frequently away on business, she had no time to spare. This took a toll on her. She started to get depressed. She could not cope when the babies cried; sometimes she would cry with them.

Her neighbors noticed that she would go out shopping, leaving the daughters all alone at home. Understanding her tribulations, they offered to assist her with the children. She was reluctant to accept at first, but soon she realized that some help was needed for her own mental health and also for the children's welfare. To give her a break from her tiresome schedule at home, one of her friends would watch the girls for a few hours, while the others would take her out to lunch or they would go see a movie. These outings were therapeutic for Bernice and slowly she started to get over her depression.

John recognized what was going on at home. He did whatever he could to give Bernice a break from the rough routine of looking after two young children.

In the meanwhile, an opening came up in the state of Oregon where John would be in the office most of the time. Bernice liked the idea of John not travelling so much. They moved to Eugene, bought a house and settled down. Like a caring father, he loved his girls and wanted to spend as much time as possible at home.

Life started to improve for Bernice. She too loved her daughters and felt she should do all she could to give them a good life. But, she missed the good old days and her former social life. She had put on weight during the pregnancy and found it difficult to get rid of it. She stopped looking into the mirror and started dreaming of the day when her daughters would be old enough to go to school and she would have some time to herself.

As the girls were growing up, they were developing noticeably different personalities. Twins, everyone said, would be so much alike that only their parents would know who was who. As it turned out, the girls were very different from each other, not only in looks, but also in temperament. They had so little in common that people had trouble believing they were twins.

Everyone around her told Bernice that children grow up fast, and before long, she would miss them. But for Bernice time had slowed down since she had her daughters. Those first six years after childbirth were the longest six years of her life. The girls needed to be watched all the time. Oftentimes, they were sick and required visits to the doctor.

Their pediatrician was an older man who always told Bernice that once the girls grew up she would look back on this period of her life and miss it. "It is natural for a mother to love and cherish her children. You should take pleasure in it so you will relish this moment of your life in future. This is your opportunity to enjoy watching them grow up and develop into young women," he told her.

She was not convinced. The burden of responsibilities seemed unbearable, with no end in sight.

Finally, the girls started school. Now, she had gotten so used to having them around that she missed them when they were not with her. She would drive them to school in the morning and pick them up in the afternoon. She worried about who was taking care of them at the school. The girls made friends with other children in their class and the parents of these children became her friends.

Thus, Bernice started to have a new circle of acquaintances and more free time. She felt that she was getting back to enjoying life again. During the past six years, she had gotten more mature. She believed that people took her more seriously now that she was a mother of two. Before she had her children, she considered herself a girl; now she was a woman. For the first time, she started to feel a sense of accomplishment in her life when she looked at her daughters. Child rearing had brought in her a sense of authority. She had spent six years telling her children what to do and now she transferred this habit to adults as well. She started having opinions about things and expressed them as if she were an expert.

John took a great interest in parenting his daughters, and thus he exerted as much influence on their character as Bernice. Terry was closer to her father and Mary gradually became more like her mother. Terry did not like to put on makeup; Mary, on the other hand, always had her nails painted and would show off those colorful ends of her fingers in school. John disliked makeup on young girls, but Bernice thought it looked good on Mary. He had learned long ago that it was better to go along with his wife's decisions if he wanted to have peace at home.

Bernice started to get restless. She had never liked to stay too long in one place. Living in a house for too long made her feel as if she was growing older with the house; new living spaces made her feel younger. She was ready to move and this time she had a good reason and her husband's support. Her daughters were soon to attend high school and the area high school was not rated high academically or socially. John wanted the best for his daughters. He was interested to send them to a good school that would prepare them for college. Bernice located a house in a neighborhood where most people were well-educated professionals and the area high school had a good reputation. Just about, everyone who graduated from there went to college. Her concern for the daughters was not only education, but also finding them good boyfriends that eventually would lead to good husbands.

Once they settled down, Bernice had no problem making friends with the new neighbors. Having two girls in the school opened up many doors through their new schoolmates. She found her British accent was still a plus, especially in a neighborhood of educated middle-class Americans. And she was readily accepted by the area residents. People were curious about the interesting family where the father was from Kashmir, mother from England and the two daughters who appeared to be typical American teenagers. Several families in the neighborhood wanted to make their acquaintance.

John was happy to meet new people with whom he could have intelligent conversations and others who liked to discuss world politics—his favorite subject. He found most of his new friends to be open minded and accepting of his liberal views on religion. Like him, his neighbors were born into a religion, but they were not rigid in its practice. Professor Hayden and his wife were one of those couples in the neighborhood. Mrs. Hayden liked the girls, especially Terry who always acted like a mature, responsible person. Mary, she thought, was a nice girl with a wild streak.

It was becoming clear to both parents that Terry would definitely go to college. Mary, if she went to college, would only go with the goal of finding a husband. By the time they graduated from high school, Mary had a steady boyfriend.

When both sisters were accepted by the university, the parents celebrated the event by inviting neighbors to a dinner party. Terry opted for journalism as her major and Mary chose home economics.

To have more freedom and experience life, the two sisters moved into the dorm. One night, Mary and some of her friends in the dorm were going to a party. Mary invited her sister to come along with them and have some fun. Terry thought she should go because the classes had not been in session long, and her sister was already turning into a party girl. She went to this gathering of young students intending to look after her sister. Once there, Terry felt uncomfortable in this setting of wild people and loud music; she stayed close to Mary and her boy friend, Eric.

Because Terry had come alone and did not know anyone there, several young men approached her. Some were too old for her and some too immature. With so many young people in a small space, the apartment got hot. Terry was thirsty and accepted a drink from one of the hosts. But the drink did not agree with her and she started to get sick. There was so much smoke in the room! Her head started to spin.

Mary noticed that there was something wrong with her sister, so she asked Eric to take them back to the dorm. But Eric, unwilling to leave the party, suggested that Mary and her sister should go outside to get some fresh air. When the two sisters were outside, it got worse for Terry. She started to throw up once, twice, and then one more time.

In the mean time, a neighbor had complained about the loud noise. In response, a police car appeared. The officer knew that students get noisy and came, not so much to break up the party, but to tell them to keep it under control. He saw the two girls outside, passed them without saying a word and went directly to the door. A boy answered the sharp knock to check who was calling. The officer stepped in to tell everyone to cut down the noise. Once inside, he noticed that some of the kids were too young to drink. He was going to overlook it this time, but he pointed out what he had seen and, in a terse voice, warned them that if they did not quiet down he would come back and check their IDs to see if they all were of drinking age. As he was leaving, he said, "If you guys are smart, you will keep it quiet, but if I get another complaint from the neighbors, I will bring along my partner and we may have to take some of you with us." This put a damper on the group.

During this time, Terry had become very ill and Mary had to insist that Eric drive them to the hospital. She did not want to call her parents and worry them. Besides, she would have some explaining to do. Hoping to avoid additional scrutiny, Eric suggested that they take Terry to the college infirmary and let a doctor there look at her. All three of them drove to the infirmary. The doctor checked Terry's pulse and her blood pressure. He looked into her pupils and checked her temperature. After the examination was over, he asked Mary to tell him what happened. He listened carefully to Mary's brief explanation and decided that it was nothing serious; the worst was already over. Turning to nurse he wondered aloud, "I hope we aren't having an outbreak of this flu on campus."

"I wouldn't worry yet. On weekends we always get a few cases like this," the nurse answered.

The doctor suggested Terry should spend the night at the hospital for observation. The nurse wrote down the phone number and address of the parents, in case they needed to be called. She then handed Terry a can of 7-Up and a paper cup. Terry was already feeling a little better. She had a few sips of soda and then lay down on the hospital bed.

In the morning, Terry shared a cab with a young foreign student. She liked him more after he would not let her pay for the taxi; it was so much like what her father would do. After she left the taxi and went inside the dorm, she looked for her sister, who was supposed to pick her up from the infirmary. She found her deep asleep; it was Saturday, a day of rest for Mary. Not that her sister ever worked hard. Terry decided not to wake up her sister and headed for her own bed. She had not slept much the night before and felt drained.

CHAPTER 34

Although more than a year passed before they would meet again, Saleem and Terry occasionally wondered about each other. Terry knew that the young man who had given her ride to her dorm was a chemistry graduate student and Jim Hayden, her neighbor, was a professor of chemistry. She thought it might not be too hard to find out who he was and how he was doing. One night, when the Haydens were at Terry's house for dinner, Jim mentioned he had a new student from Pakistan working for him. He brought it up, thinking John might be interested in meeting someone who so recently came from the region of his birthplace. However, John did not show any interest; mainly because of the age difference. Also he did not find much in common with the young people from Pakistan or India whom he had met in recent years. He had been away from that part of the world for so long that he no longer had much in common with the Indians and Pakistanis, especially in view of his being married to a British woman and having lived in the United States for umpteen years.

The only person in the room who was curious about this student kept quiet. She had met someone like him after being hospitalized, a fact of which her parents were still unaware.

When John first met Saleem at the party for foreign students, he remembered Jim telling him about the one from Pakistan. He did not bring it up then and, as far as Saleem was concerned, he did not even know who John was or where he was from.

At the same time, when Saleem saw the name Theresa Jafrey, it did not mean anything to him. He assumed that the last name could have some association with the region where he grew up. However, when he laid eyes on Terry and her father he concluded that these people were not what he thought they might be. He liked Terry and her father because of what they were; where they were from did not matter to him. He especially liked Terry because she was the young attractive girl, the one the cab driver once had mistakenly referred to as his girlfriend. He still remembered that day.

Toward the end of the party, when John saw Saleem talking to his daughter, he had a flashback to his own younger days. Suddenly, he saw himself in Saleem. He came over and reached out warmly toward him—his daughter noticed that.

Even though Terry and Saleem liked each other, neither knew how the other felt. Both were committed to their studies. Any romance would be a distraction at this stage.

Two weeks passed since Terry had taken Saleem to lunch. As she walked towards her classroom, on a whim, she decided to go through the chemistry building. As she crossed through the main entrance, there was Saleem on his way to the library.

"What a surprise to run into you like this," Saleem said. Spontaneity took him over as he added, "Maybe we should get together for coffee sometime."

"How about this afternoon? I'll be done around three. If you have time, we could meet in the student union at 3:15?" She tried to sound casual, not too keen.

Saleem said, "I would love that. I'll make time."

They parted, unaware of each other's emotions.

On the way to class, Terry wondered if it was true what her father once told her about men. He had said that it was difficult for them to show or express their feelings, especially men from the East. She assumed that she was not the only one who had thoughts about him; he had to have some inkling of how she felt. He must, otherwise he would not have asked her for coffee. She made up her mind to find out what was going on, how he thought of her.

When Terry entered the cafeteria, Saleem was already there waiting for her. They sat at the same table where they had lunch together. She remembered telling him a lot about her family and herself. She hardly knew anything about him, besides his being a graduate student who had some difficulties in the beginning of his studies and had now settled down. Other than that, she knew little of his life.

They both sat there, looking at their coffee cups, wondering how to start a conversation. Terry finally asked, "So, tell me something about you growing up in India and then moving to Pakistan."

Saleem did not remember if he had told her anything about his past. He wanted to. He started from his childhood memories; they were dear to him. He told her about his father and mother, and about his experiences at school. He stopped and asked, "Do you really want to know all this? Am I not boring you?"

"No, no, I want to know. This is so interesting. I wish my mother would tell me about her life as a child in England, or my father of how he grew up, for that matter. They never talk to Mary or me about their past, which is a shame. Please tell me more, I'm interested … honest I am. I really want to know," Terry insisted.

This encouraged Saleem to tell his life story, his school days in India, his college, and then moving to Pakistan. He could go on and on, but made it as short as he could; still it took an hour.

When he was talking, the words were coming to her as if they belonged to her. She knew she had them registered somewhere between her heart and her mind. Now, they were part of her soul. They were bonds between him and her through certain subliminal communication. The more he talked, the closer she felt toward him. She wondered if he was aware how his facial expressions changed as he narrated his life—sad at one time, happy at another. She had never listened to someone like this before. In his accented English, words poured out of his mouth, which took her to a different world. A world of dreams. A world of romance. A world she had never known.

Was this the beginning of something new in her life? she asked herself. When he was talking about his father going to jail she had an impulse to kiss him to let him know that she cared. But then, that would not be proper, so she let it go. A strange wave of happiness came over her and she suspected she must be falling in love with this man. There had been boys in her life during high school, boys who declared their love and devotion and who sent her flowers on the Valentine's Day. In each case, she questioned her own feelings and in each case came to the same conclusion—she did not share their ardor. This time it was different. Deep down inside she felt the stirrings of a new sensation. She was still uncertain what Saleem thought of her. As she was listening to him relate his life stories, she felt she was discovering her own roots—the roots through her father.

It was not like it was the first time anyone had told her his life story. It was not like she had never read a similar account in a book. This was different. This time as his narrative was making headway, she had a strange feeling that she was going to be a part of it someday

Before long, numerous students came in, and it led to an increasingly high noise level in the cafeteria.

Terry and Saleem had been so lost in each other's conversation that they were unaware of time and their surroundings. It was already past five o'clock. Terry jumped up and said, "I hate to leave, but I'm meeting with a girl at six to discuss our homework that is due tomorrow. However, I would love for you to meet my parents. I know they'd be interested in hearing about your life, too," she lied. She knew her mother would not want to hear about anybody's life, especially that of a Pakistani student. Her father might. "Now that I know where to find you, I'll come down to the chemistry building more often. And when I open the door, you will be standing there just like you were today."

Saleem got up, "I had a great time…look forward to seeing you soon again"

They shook hands and Terry left. His eyes followed her all the way to the exit door; she turned around and looked back at him.

Saleem was so overwhelmed by his own feelings that he did not want to go back to the apartment. He wanted to be alone. He wanted to relish every moment of the past two hours. He did not want to lose this sense of elation that Terry had brought out in him—he wanted to relive the past hours if he could.

Terry's thoughts on the way to her dorm were very similar. All she could think about was Saleem. In her thoughts, she and Saleem were walking hand in hand along a mountain path where the air was filled with fragrance of the grass and flowers were blooming all around her. She had never been there before. This had to be love, she thought. She had the urge to tell someone that she was in love. The only person that came to mind was her sister. She needed her tonight. When she got to their room, her sister was not there. Putting her romantic mood aside, Terry met her classmate and the two of them concentrated on their homework.

After they finished their homework, Terry walked back to her room. When she entered the dorm room, she saw Mary hunched over a book. "Mary, I need to talk to you. Sorry, it can't wait," she said abruptly.

Mary was alarmed and thought there must be an emergency. It was unlike Terry to be so worked up.

"I'm in love!" Terry blurted out.

"What? What are you talking about…? Did I hear you say that …? You are in love?" Mary raised an eyebrow.

Terry was quiet for a while and then answered, "Yes, I think I am."

"Wow! Who is this guy? Do I know him? Does he know about it? How did it happen?"

Terry told her about Saleem. Mary vaguely remembered her sister talking to a lanky young man, a foreign student, at the Hayden's party. After thinking for a while she said, "You know, Mother might have problem with that. She wants you and me to marry one of those rich neighborhood kids. She has perhaps already picked out a couple of them and is planning to manipulate us into thinking we chose them ourselves."

"Yes, I know. I just had to tell someone and I know I can trust you. Please don't tell anyone about it…for the time being. Maybe I'll manage to keep it from Mother until summer vacation when we all can handle a crisis more easily without disturbing the schoolwork. As for Saleem, he perhaps has some idea about my feelings, but I haven't said anything to him and neither has he. I believe he does. I hope he does."

They were both quiet for some time.

Mary broke the silence, "I know you had to tell someone and I'm glad you told me. I suggest you cool it for a while and let it sink in. Maybe it will pass. Think about all the consequences before you do anything further."

This was sound advice. Terry was surprised to hear the words coming from her sister. She thought, *She would have said the very same thing, used the very same words, had the roles been reversed.* She developed a new respect for Mary, whom she thought of as a person incapable of having a serious thought. However, for Terry this was a matter of heart. Rationality seemed out of place.

After having this conversation, both of them were too excited to concentrate on their books. Mary had not only been surprised by the news, she detected something strange in Terry's voice, something she had never heard before. She would have never expected her ever-so-rational sister to put her studies at risk for a boy, a boy from the third world yet, who was at least four or five years older than she was. Also, she was worried how her mother would react when she found out about Saleem. She concluded that her sister was emotionally exhausted and confused.

Saleem, unaware of what was going on in that dorm room, was still walking around to get his own mental upheavals under control. He did not eat dinner, went back to the lab, and tried to concentrate on his work. At midnight, he joined some of the others students who were going to the Shakey's for pizza and beer, hoping the vibrations of the youth in this place of fun and noise would take his mind off Terry. And to a certain degree it did.

Back in his apartment Saleem's mind drifted back to the girl again. He wanted to see Terry to tell her how he felt, but he always had difficulty expressing his feelings. He closed his eyes and tried to visualize telling her he loved her—could not do it, even in his imagination. Fear of rejection made it even worse. He did not know what to do. He needed to talk to someone; he needed to tell someone, but whom? His friends Kader and Jenny came to mind.

Saturday morning, Saleem called Kader and asked him if he could meet with him. Kader, Jenny and Saleem met for lunch at a small downtown café. They had not seen each other for some time. Once they sat down at a table, it felt like old times. Saleem found out that Kader was busy writing his thesis, and had an offer from UCLA for a fellowship after he finished his program at the University of Oregon. They also talked about their plans for the summer. Finally, it was Saleem's turn to unburden his heart. He told them about meeting Terry, his feelings for her, and his confused state of mind.

Jenny immediately saw herself in the role of an advisor to this young, vulnerable man. "Look Saleem, I think I can take care of this for you. I can at least find out if this girl is aware of how you feel and, if she is, what her thoughts are…Where does she live?"

Kader interrupted, "I think, we should let Saleem decide if he needs any help. He might have come to talk to us just to clear his mind." Turning to Saleem, he said, "You and I have known each other since we both arrived in Eugene. If you need advice or help of any kind, I'm here and I'm sure Jenny will help in any way she can." He stopped, looked at her and smiled, "You already heard her plan for solving your problems." They all looked at each other and burst out laughing.

Saleem was grateful to have his friends as a sounding board. As they finished their meal, they promised they would keep each other up to date on their activities. Jenny also reminded Saleem that they had four chairs in the dining room, if he ever wished to bring Terry over. She repeated her offer of help in any way she could. Kader paid the tab.

Talking with his friends and the ride back on his bicycle made him feel better; a burden had been lifted off his mind. He decided that he would tell Terry how he felt. He must get it off his chest. If her response was negative, he would get over it and go on with his life. On the other hand, if she shared his ardor, he would be one happy man. Not knowing was unsettling and was interfering with his studies. How to find her was the big question now. In the meantime, he needed to get control over his mental state. Rushing into things was not a part of his character; he decided he would wait until he met her again. Then when he met her what would he say, he was not sure. Should he just declare his love or not use the four letter word at all and talk about what he was going through? He could not make up his mind and decided to leave it until the opportunity demanded a decision.

He did not have to wait long. On Monday, he ran into her as she was passing through the chemistry building on the way to her class. He asked her when she would have time to talk with him, and they agreed to meet in front of the building again at noon. As it happened, both showed up fifteen minutes early. They were both anxious and acting awkwardly, not knowing how each other felt.

She hesitantly asked, "So, what did you want to talk about?"

"Things," he said. "Do you mind walking with me around the campus? I don't want to go to the cafeteria."

"We're on campus," she said, "Let's go."

They strolled down a curved path, he with his hands in his pockets, she holding her notebook across her chest, no one saying anything for the longest time.

He finally gathered up all his courage and said, "Terry, I don't know how to say this…" He hesitated for a moment and then blurted in a low nervous voice, "I have fallen in love with you." The words were finally out. Unaware of how she would react, he pulled out his hands in front as if he wanted to cover his face. "Okay…I said my piece," was all he could add.

The words sent her world spinning with happiness. Not knowing what to do, she took his hand and squeezed it gently. The touch of her hand, a touch he wanted to feel, sent a spark tingling through him from head to toe.

She had tears in her eyes when she looked up at him. They walked around holding hands, saying things to each other without uttering a word, lost in thought and wondering what to do next.

"Terry, you have not said a thing."

Terry looked into his eyes and said, "I am so...I can't talk. But I'm glad you told me. I wanted to tell you the same, but didn't know how. I love you too... I love you so very much!" She was quiet for some time to collect her thoughts and then said, "Remember the first day we met in the hospital, and when you wouldn't let me pay for the cab? You acted so much like my father would. He and I are very close." Holding his hand, she looked into his eyes and added, "When I heard the Haydens were giving a party for foreign students, I hoped you would come. I wanted to meet you again."

They walked quietly for a while. She, being the more expressive of the two, poured out her emotions in a low voice as it was meant only for him, "And when I saw you that night in your dark blue suit, something inside me said: Terry, is this the man you have been looking for? I didn't know what to say, but my heart said, yes!"

Suddenly there was a sense of closeness between them as formality melted away. This was a new feeling for both of them...a feeling they both longed for but were unaware of. Whipped by emotions they both felt exhausted.

Being not very good at expressing his feelings and spilling out his heart, Saleem's words took another direction, "Now that I know how you feel, I hope to sleep better tonight. The confusion... the agitation...the questions...the answers. All that was going on in my mind was driving me crazy." A weight lifted off Saleem as they headed back to where they had met for this vitally important conversation.

"You're lucky, Saleem. You don't have my mother to deal with. But I will handle it my way—in due time." She did not want to leave him and he did not want to let go of her hand, but he did let go without ever realizing what he did when he thought he saw some other students come by. Indoctrination of his past—no display of affection in public—took hold of him.

Terry noticed it and understood. Both had afternoon sessions planned. As she was leaving for her class, Saleem said, "I have a few friends who would like to meet you."

"You already told them about me?" Terry asked coyly. She seemed happy and then added without waiting for a reply. "We will figure out when you can come home and meet my parents."

She wanted to kiss him before they left, but she was not sure how he would respond. She knew her father disliked the parade of love in front of people. So she just squeezed his hand and turned to leave.

Saleem went to his apartment. He had not spent much time there lately. On his way, he relived the events of the past hour, the events that were so vibrant that living through them was bliss once again. He had a sensation he could not describe. He had feelings he was unaware of. He wanted to tell the whole world, but also had an urge to keep it as his own secret. The air around him was glowing with his aura, but no one else could see it. His life seemed more precious today than it had ever been because a girl loved him and he loved her. He had a sense of fulfillment today.

Because Saleem was an early riser who did his best thinking in the morning hours, he always went to the chemistry building before eight o'clock. Normally he rode his bicycle, but this morning he decided to walk. After the events of the day before, his mind was still reeling with thoughts of Terry. If he ever could control his feelings, he wanted to analyze his own actions of the past few days. His sentiments were overwhelming his thinking. His rational side was telling him that he did not really know the girl; the emotional side would counter this by saying that it was not important at this point. The only thing that mattered was the fact that he cherished her. His feelings were outweighing his thoughts and he was happy to be in love. By telling her of his love, he had affirmed what touched his heart—he was in a new phase now.

At lunchtime, Terry came over to the lab. She looked different to him, different from the other times when he had seen her. Or, was he looking at her differently? Trying to stay calm and collected he asked, "How did you find out where I work"?

"I have been stalking you for the last two years," she said with a mischievous smile. "Just kidding. Your professor is our neighbor and a family friend. I've been here a number of times. How about lunch?"

They strolled together to a place nearby. As they were walking, he told her, "If it is all right with you I would like to call you Theresa instead of Terry. The first time I found out your name I learned it as Theresa, and when you came out of that kitchen door looking as beautiful as you are, I associate that girl with Theresa more than with Terry."

"The things you say, Saleem, make me fall in love with you all over again. Promise me you'll never stop saying things like this to me. Of course, you can call me Theresa…it is my name."

Changing the subject she said, "I would like to see where you live".

"I live in the lab." They both laughed.

"And I would like you to meet my sister".

"She's your twin? Will I be able to tell who's who?"

"We are twins but very different from each other."

On that note, she left for her class.

On their next meeting, Saleem told her that he would like her to meet Kader and Jenny. He told her about these friends and how Kader had always been like an older brother to him. He was the one who had brought him over to the hospital that night. Jenny, Kader's friend, was a wonderful person who was always ready to give advice, whether you wanted it or not. He added, "They are a lively couple, you will like them. My other friends work in the lab and you will gradually meet them too".

Professor Hayden noticed that Terry was often in the chemistry building. Once she actually stopped by his office to say hello. Then one day, he saw her and Saleem going out together. He mentioned to his wife how Terry was spending time with Saleem. Mrs. Hayden, remembering the night of the party how Terry had talked with Saleem, wondered if he fascinated her. "He is a few years older, and she is mature for her age—that makes them a good couple," Mrs. Hayden said.

"I wouldn't go that far, but they do look nice when they are together," her husband answered.

"If something has really been brewing between these two, I wonder how her mother will react when she finds out…knowing her mother and how she thinks," Mrs. Hayden said.

"I like the young man. He's smart and very good in his lab work, he will soon have enough work for his thesis," the professor said. "But I haven't told him this yet."

"Do you suppose it would help the kids if we invited Saleem over to cook, as we once planned, and invite the Jafreys along? This way they can all meet in an informal setting. I like the young man and you know how much I like Terry. I'd like to help her all I can," Mrs. Hayden said.

The professor thought for a while and said, "I'll wait for the right time and see what I can do."

In the meantime, Kader and Jenny wanted to meet Terry and asked Saleem to bring her over for dinner. Saleem now had a car, the old black Volvo Karl sold him at a good price when he left to go back to Germany. Saleem picked Terry up at the dorm and looked forward to introducing her to his closest friends.

Jenny, who had a gift of making other people comfortable, took Terry by the hand and showed her around the apartment just to make her feel at ease and welcome. When they came to the kitchen, she said, "I've been telling Saleem to find someone special so we can fill all four seats when we have dinner. I'm so glad he brought you here this evening to sit in this fourth chair with us."

When the two women came to the living room, Kader told Jenny, "Did you know that I played some part in Terry's being here tonight?" Before Jenny could ask how, Kader added, "I took Saleem to the hospital where he met Terry for the first time."

"Okay, I'll give you some credit." She clapped.

Soon everyone was clapping and laughing. Terry was happy to meet these people; a feeling of congeniality and acceptance filled the room.

Kader never claimed to be a good cook, so Jenny had prepared the entire dinner of beef stew. She had salad and bread on the side. For drinks, she served beer, coffee and water. Jenny asked Terry if she would like beer. Terry declined, saying she would have water; she needed to wait a little longer for alcohol. While at the table, Terry noticed that Kader and Saleem always talked in English.

First, she wondered about that and then asked, "Both of you come from Pakistan, but I notice that you talk in English. Is it because of Jenny and me?"

"No, no we speak different languages. I speak Bengali, the language of East Pakistan and Saleem speaks Urdu, the language of West Pakistan. The only common language we know is English," Kader explained.

Both Kader and Jenny were interested in Terry's studies and about her plans after she got her degree. Terry started to realize that Saleem's friends knew a lot more than she did, but they were very nice and she never felt intimidated or patronized in any way. The dinner ended, as usual, with Saleem's favorite dessert: banana cream pie and coffee. Throughout the evening, Jenny had steered the conversation to include Terry.

In the end, everyone had a good time and Saleem drove Terry back to her dorm.

CHAPTER 35

With the discovery of their love for each other, Terry and Saleem wanted to be together. Terry especially wished to be with or around him all the time. But they understood that they both had responsibilities. Their commitment to their studies was serious and they each had set a specific goal that they intended to reach. Saleem was spending more and more time in the chemistry building. Professor Hayden noticed him working long hours, which led him to believe that his young student wanted to finish soon.

One day, Saleem and Terry were eating lunch in the cafeteria when he noticed the professor come in. It was now over two years since that day when the professor had sat down with Saleem as his adviser to discuss the problems with the new student. The professor, just like last time, got his tray with food and headed to where they were sitting. He said hello to both of them, asked if he could join and sat down without waiting for an answer.

While looking at Saleem he said, as if reminiscing, "Last time, when I had lunch with you it was some time ago and things were different then. This time, I am here entirely for social reasons. Remember, last year, or was it at the beginning of this year, that I asked you to come to our home sometime and let us taste some of the famous foods you cook that we have heard so much about? If you think you can tear yourself away from the lab for a few hours, my wife and I would love to have you over. And would you please cook one of your favorite dishes, so we know what makes everyone crave about your food? We would also like to include our neighbors for dinner."

He looked at Terry and added, "Your parents would like to join us...wouldn't they"?

Terry said, "I know, I would…but for my parents, you may want to ask them yourself."

"Oh, that's good. Then we'll leave it to Saleem. He will tell you when it's convenient for him, and you will pass it on to my wife. She'll take care of the rest," Professor Hayden said.

They talked a little about weather and other trivial things. As he was finishing his meal, the professor looked at Terry and said, "I notice you often in the chemistry building these days. You should consider taking a course or two in Saleem's field of interest. Then you can help him type his thesis."

Terry blushed and said quickly, "I plan to type his first draft anyway, even if I don't know much chemistry."

The professor smiled at both of them as he got up and left.

Saleem and Terry sat there in silence before she spoke, "Am I spending too much time in your lab? I hope I'm not keeping you from your work. If I am, please let me know."

"You needn't worry on my account because I am doing really fine. I have a few more requirements to fulfill and then it would be all lab work; the lab work and research is what I enjoy the most. I find the research part of my program sometimes frustrating, but never difficult." He felt confident that he would finish within his set time, if not earlier. "Did you hear what Professor said about typing my thesis? I suppose I'm getting there."

When Terry was alone, she wondered why Jim Hayden asked her about typing Saleem's thesis. Afterward, she mentioned the conversation to Mary. Mary reminded Terry about their earlier agreement of introducing Saleem to their parents during summer vacation, not before. Terry remembered and made up her mind to tell both Mrs. Hayden and Saleem that the best time for dinner at professor's house would be after the final exams.

Saleem and Terry continued seeing each other on a regular basis. She started to go to movies with him on Saturday nights where they would hold hands. He took her to his favorite spots on campus and, if it was not raining, they walked hand in hand, laughing and running after each other like children.

It was a tradition in the Jafrey family to get together for lunch on Sundays. Sometimes, Terry or Mary was not quite up to it but they always made a point to be there at the usual time. It was on one of those regular Sunday lunches that her mother asked Terry, "So, how is your new friend, Terry…? I guess he works for Jim Hayden. Isn't he from India or Pakistan? I don't believe I have met him." Their mother's statement took both sisters by surprise and for a moment they did not know what to say.

Terry finally spoke, "Oh, he is okay."

"You must be wondering how I found out." Her mother paused and then continued, "Eric mentioned to his mother that the three of you had lunch with him. I hadn't seen her for some time, but yesterday I bumped into her at the grocery store."

She did not say any more and both sisters were thankful for that. Their lunch had gone as usual where their father inquired about school and informed them about world politics. Their mother told them about the neighbors, particularly about the neighborhood boys who had gone to high school with the twins, mentioning especially those who were going to the prestigious out-of-state universities. Some of them would be coming home soon for summer.

John proudly showed the girls the new plants in his garden and the new grill he got. He promised to barbeque some chicken for them next Sunday, weather permitting. Terry talked with her father, while Mary and her mother were in the kitchen. Drifting into his past, John told his daughter about living in Srinagar, a city in Kashmir, not far from the Dal Lake and going on boat trips with his parents. And how as a child, in summer they would go to different gardens, the gardens that were full of flowers whose fragrance still lingered in his memory. The girls noticed their father, as he was getting older, was talking more and more of his childhood days.

Terry asked him if he would ever go there to visit his birthplace and see his relatives. "It may connect you with your younger years," she added. She even offered to go with him, if he would like her to.

John had occasionally thought about going back for a visit, but he always put it off. The distances were great and the political situation in the region was unstable. However, the main reason he never went back was that he feared nothing would be like what he remembered. He was not the same person as when he was young. His parents were no longer living and he was afraid he would not be able to relate to the changes that had taken place over time. He remembered the Kashmir of the past—the past that was not present. Present day Kashmir was a battleground. He was content with his memories—pleasant and beautiful—they were always with him, as long as he could talk with someone about them. After the girls had moved out, he was lonely. He loved to read when home from work, but the house was not the same without the girls.

Terry felt sorry for him and wished that he and her mother had a better relationship. To her, it seemed her parents were getting old but were not getting old together.

Mary came outside to tell her sister that they should leave as it was getting late. They both had classes to attend next morning. She also wanted to speak to Eric as to how his mother came to know about the lunch with Saleem. Once back in their dorm, Mary related to her sister what she and their mother had talked about. First, Mother wanted to know who Saleem was—incidentally she kept on calling him *the foreign student*—what was his relationship with Terry and what Mary thought of him. As far as Mother was concerned, it was a bad idea for her daughter to have any kind of a relationship with a boy from a different cultural background. "She will bring the subject up with you after finals, when we both move back home during the summer." What her sister was telling her was what Terry expected from her mother, but she trusted their father would intervene and back her up as he always had in the past.

Once they got done talking about their mother, Terry got busy with her books. The thought of seeing Saleem the next day excited her and soon Mother was no longer on her mind. She had not seen him for the last two days.

Finally, the spring quarter was over and the campus became quiet. It was that time of the year again when the two sisters moved back home. Terry was not looking forward to spending the summer at home with Mother, but she did not have a choice. She was still financially dependent on her parents. Sometimes, she envied those kids in college who lived on their own, doing part time jobs that meant cutting down on credit load and prolonging studies, but they had the freedom she longed for.

To get her mind off these matters, she went to talk to Mrs. Hayden and asked her if she still wanted to have that dinner party Jim had talked about and, if she did, she would like to help in any way she could.

Mrs. Hayden asked Terry, "Do you think it's a good idea to have this get-together? Jim and I talked about having a social event to help the two of you...you understand when I say the two of you, I mean you and Saleem. We were hoping that bringing Saleem into our home and introducing him to your parents, especially your mother...in a casual way...it might help. I really want to have all of you over and if you believe it would bring everyone closer, we could plan a date." She looked at Terry who did not say anything. She continued, "Well, today is Tuesday. Would this coming weekend be too soon for you and your family?" She went up to her calendar to make sure there were no conflicting engagements for her or Jim. Finding none, she called out, "This coming weekend would be fine with us."

"Thanks, Evelyn, for your help and all the things you do for me. I'll check with Saleem and let you know tomorrow," Terry said.

"That's fine. I'll wait to hear from you then," Evelyn said. "And once you confirm it with Saleem, I'll invite your parents."

The only way she could talk with Saleem was to go to his lab. Terry found Saleem busy on his bench wearing his safety glasses and a lab coat. She stood there until she got his attention. It took him a minute or so before he could get to her. As he asked her to come and sit down, she said," I came to tell you that there is going to be a party this coming Saturday at the Haydens' where you will be the chef. I'll have to let Evelyn know if it's still okay with you. Remember your professor talked about your cooking one time when we were eating lunch."

Saleem went to his desk and looked into his papers, as if he were checking his schedule and said, "I have no cooking assignments that night."

She laughed. "Perhaps, I won't be able to see you until then. Oh, yes, Evelyn also asked me to tell you to make a list of grocery items you'll need for your recipes and give it to your professor."

When Saleem had a chance to see his professor he told him he would get what he needed and would do part of the cooking at his place and finish it at his house.

Professor Hayden said, "Don't forget to tell me how much it costs, because I want to reimburse you. I know how much money graduate students have, I was there once myself."

Early Saturday morning, Saleem went to the store and purchased ground beef, eggs, onions and garlic. He had all the other spices that he needed. Remembering the success of the egg-meatball dinner that he cooked for Ken and his wife, he thought he should repeat the same menu; the only change he would make was that instead of having a full egg inside, he would use only one half of a boiled egg to keep the size of the meatballs smaller. Recently, he had seen a recipe for a meatloaf in a magazine and figured he could use the same ingredients for making meatballs—his food was now acquiring an American flavor.

Saleem got busy early in the morning and finished everything he needed to do before noon, took a shower and leafed through a magazine until it was time to leave. He drove to the Haydens' house and got there just a few minutes prior to four o'clock. Evelyn and Terry were already expecting him. The professor was in his library, reading or dozing off, no one knew

While Terry helped Saleem bring everything into the kitchen, she told him that she would like to help him and possibly learn a few things from him. Terry knew the kitchen well and everything was stored. She told him that her parents were coming at 5:30. Since everything was halfway cooked, there was plenty of time to finish the meal. As Saleem was arranging his pots and pans, he gave Terry a large onion to peel and chop it finely, if she could do it without cutting herself or tearing up her eyes.

She looked at him and said, "Yes Boss! Is it all right to grate it?"

"Yes, if it's easier for you."

While Terry was taking care of the onion, her eyes stated to tear and she almost grated her fingers. Unaware, he chopped a few cloves of garlic. She watched him brown the onions in butter and pull out a bunch of spices from a bag he brought with him and sprinkle them over to onions, add some yogurt and tomato sauce, and stir it together.

He looked at Terry's eyes and said, "I should have taken care of onions. I am sorry. Well, we'll let it simmer for some time and then add these meat balls to it and leave everything on low heat till it is time to eat. We'll turn the heat off at five and it should be ready by the time the guests arrive." He had already prepared peas, potatoes, and Raita—that was yogurt with grated cucumber, a pinch of salt, black pepper and a dash of cumin. Terry noticed how focused he was when he was doing things and finished everything as planned in less than an hour.

He asked, "Evelyn has already taken care of the drinks and dessert…is that correct?"

"It has been taken care of," Terry answered.

Just as they were talking about her, Evelyn walked in. She had not come into the kitchen since Saleem and Terry brought things in from the car. She sniffed and asked Saleem what the spices were.

He showed her what he had brought in. To demonstrate her knowledge of different seasonings, Evelyn opened the cabinet door and showed him a rack full of nice looking bottles of spices. They looked so clean, as if no one had ever used them. Some of them, he noticed, had never been opened.

"Use whatever you like from here," she said. "By the way, what are we eating?"

"Terry has been helping me and she will show you what we have done so far."

Terry showed Evelyn the meatballs, rice, vegetables and spicy yogurt to go along with the food.

The professor emerged from his study around five and said, "I smell some exotic food."

Saleem said, "I hope you and everyone like it."

They all sat down in the living room. Saleem wondered how everything would turn out. *Whenever he made food for his fellow graduate students, they all liked it.* He just hoped everyone would be able to eat what he cooked. He made those meatballs just so that if the food was not to some one's taste, at least it would be novel.

They all came over as planned and Saleem met Terry's mother for the first time. She was a middle-aged, good-looking woman with a stern face. When introduced to Saleem, there was a hint of a forced smile. Jim and Evelyn noticed that and so did everyone else. John had already met Saleem at the party and greeted him cordially. Evelyn was a gracious hostess, told Bernice that Saleem was Jim's student, and added, "Jim thinks highly of him and soon he will get his PhD."

"So, you plan to go back after you finish and help your countrymen?" Bernice asked Saleem in her typical British accent.

"At this point it's hard for me to say anything with certainty. I will decide after I have finished. I'm keeping my options open," Saleem said.

Before she could ask another question or say anything else to Saleem, John intervened, "Where did you learn to cook, Saleem?"

Saleem told him that he had never cooked until he came to this country. He had watched his mother cook when he was young and when he came here, he started cooking out of necessity.

Jim interrupted, "Organic chemists are always heating and boiling. It's easy for them to cook. I'm not saying all chemists are great chefs, but Saleem seems to be…from what I hear…and we will find out today." He looked at Saleem and smiled.

Evelyn served drinks with help from Terry and her sister. Soon afterward, they sat down for dinner. Evelyn noticed that Saleem had transferred the food into covered serving dishes and set them on the table. When everyone sat down, Evelyn, who was sitting at one end of the table, asked Saleem to do the honors of explaining what he had made.

Saleem, as he took the covers off, explained that he made rice with small amounts of curry powder to give it some color, then there were the peas and the potatoes and finally, there were the meatballs. He intentionally omitted any mention of eggs inside of them.

The food was passed around the table, starting with Evelyn who was first to serve herself and Saleem would be the last. When everyone had filled their plates, Professor Hayden said, "I want to thank you, Saleem, for taking time off from your studies, coming here to introduce us to your country's food and giving us all a chance to be together."

At this point, they cut open the meatballs, because they appeared to be larger than usual. The reaction around the table was not very different from what he had experienced when he had served similar food to his friends. Having egg wrapped inside meat was unexpected for everyone.

John mentioned he had eaten something similar in his early years in Kashmir and he helped himself to a second serving of rice and meatballs.

Even Bernice seemed to be amused and had a smile. "These seem to be modified Scottish meatballs," she said. No one was familiar with this dish, so the subject was dropped.

The dinner went surprisingly well. Terry was relieved that the evening was going well so far, while Mary was quietly praying that it would work out well for her sister. She had started to like Saleem not only because of her sister but because she found him to be a decent person. He always treated her with respect, as if she were a grown-up woman.

Evelyn was interested in finding out more about the food she was eating. Saleem who was sitting next to her explained that he was born in Northern India. He thought the Mugals, who ruled India for a length of time, introduced this type of food to that part of the world, especially the meat dishes. "Now as I learn, there seems to be some Scottish influence as well," he said as he looked toward Bernice. "But what I made today is what I saw my mother cook. I used whatever spices I could get locally."

Everyone at the table was listening to Saleem except for Bernice, who was trying to ignore him and looking for something in her purse.

Terry noticed her mother, but she admired the way he explained things to a bunch of old people…his poise…his confidence—the reasons she utterly adored him.

After the main meal was over, Evelyn and the two sisters got up, cleared the table and brought over dessert, which was an apple pie and vanilla ice cream. Evelyn said, "I thought the food would be a lot spicier than it was and that's why I got ice cream and pie to cool the palate. But we like the apple pie anyway, and I hope you will too."

After dessert and coffee, as they all got up, John walked over to Saleem and thanked him for making the dinner. "The food was so similar to what I ate as a child that it took me back many years."

Then they talked about places in India. When Saleem mentioned that he was at Aligarh Muslim University, John got excited and told him how so many of his family members were connected to that institution and he warmed up to Saleem. John started telling him about his boyhood years in Kashmir and his subsequent life in England. He was talking about how religion had played an important role in politics in the Indian subcontinent and had in fact resulted in the partition of the country.

Saleem mentioned that his father was very open-minded; still he had supported the formation of Pakistan. He also mentioned his uncle Shams who was a skeptic where religious beliefs were concerned.

John told Saleem that he also found it difficult to accept some of the logic behind religious ways of thinking and he would have liked to meet his uncle Shams so they could exchange their views.

Jim and Evelyn watched John animatedly talking with Saleem and then looked at each other and smiled. Bernice, who was busy telling Evelyn about a sale she went to the day before, was either oblivious to what was going on around her or was pretending to be.

The two girls were telling Jim what they did in school last year and what their plans were for the summer. They all seemed to be comfortable at the Haydens' home. Evelyn had that rare quality of setting the pace of her parties and of putting guests at ease. Even Bernice was happier when she left than when she had come in.

It was getting late and it was time to leave. The girls had cleaned up the kitchen. When they were drying the dishes, Mary smiled at Terry. "Father and Saleem seem to be getting along really well. They seem to have things in common to talk about."

Terry said, "I wish mother, too, would open her mind one day".

"And what was that Scottish meatball thing she brought out? I don't remember her mentioning this ever before or ever cooking it for us… I will never understand her." Mary said.

When Evelyn came in and saw the clean kitchen, she gave them both a hug and thanked them, "Sometimes I forget you're not my daughters." She turned to Terry. "Saleem is a nice young man. I liked him right away when I first met him, and now that I've gotten to know him a little better, I like him even more."

Bernice thought that Saleem and Terry were alone in the kitchen together. She asked Mary to go and help her sister. Mary knew that her sister and Saleem had already put everything in the car and were still outside having their private moment, but she obeyed her mother and stayed in the kitchen until Terry came back.

During the time when Terry and Saleem were alone, she told him how proud she was of him for handling everything so well. She kissed him good night and went back into the dining room before her mother came looking for her.

When the Jafrey family was back at home, which was in walking distance from the Hayden house, John still excited about the party, mentioned how much he enjoyed the evening and the food. Looking at Terry, "I liked Saleem. He is an open-minded boy. I like that in young people."

Bernice stayed quiet. She had noticed that there was something going on between her daughter and the young man. She had noticed how they looked at each other. She had so many plans for Terry's future, but none of them included Saleem.

CHAPTER 36

The first chance Terry had to sit down with her mother alone she asked what she thought of Saleem. She wanted to clear the air by telling her mother how she felt about him.

"I am not in a position to judge anyone and have no opinion. I don't know him".

This irritated Terry, but knowing her mother, she could tell it was her way of controlling the situation. "You always told us what you thought of people you met for the first time, you must have formed an impression of Saleem. You must have. You are my mother, and I would like to know what you think of someone I like… I may even be in love with him."

"Ah ha, so that's it! I did not realize things have gone that far. I have a piece of advice for you, missy," Mother said.

Terry looked at her as if saying, "Let's have it,"

This got Bernice started, "You know I have dreamed for you two girls to be completely assimilated within the culture of the country where you were born and we all live in. One reason why we moved to this neighborhood was so you would meet the right kind of young men for your future. You may have a career or not, that is up to each of you. Saleem does not fit into that equation." She softened her tone and continued, "He is a foreigner and he comes from a developing country. For all we know, he may go back and leave you here. I don't want you to get hurt."

At this point, Terry wanted to interrupt, but decided to wait until Mother had finished her tirade.

Bernice continued, "When your father and I got married, we knew we were in love. He wanted to go back home but couldn't because

I did not want to live in India. We never discussed these issues in detail, but I could feel he was unhappy. We immigrated to this country to start all over again, but he still missed his Indian friends. I feel that we both made a wrong decision that robbed us of the happiness we had hoped for. I don't want you to make the same error and be miserable all your life. You and Saleem are so much like your father and me—two people with different backgrounds. Take a close look at us. Why would you want to make the same mistake? It did not work for us. Learn from it, Terry. Forget Saleem. You will get over him."

After Bernice had finished, a speech she had been preparing since she saw Saleem and her daughter together, she slid back in her chair, just as a trial lawyer would after presenting a case against an offender. In this case, she was the judge and the prosecutor.

Now it was Terry's turn to defend herself and her friend. She would have liked to point out that, she, Terry, was very different from her mother and so the parallels drawn did not apply. But by now, Terry was angry. She felt her face and her ears were on fire. She knew when she was in this condition, her logical mind did not work well and if she talked, she would blurt out words she might regret. So she held back and said, "I need to think about what you've said, Mother. I'm tired."

Bernice felt she had scored a victory and went to bed satisfied.

Terry, on the other hand, saw a completely different picture. Terry saw her parents in a very different light. She felt her mother's argument was not honest. It was obvious that her parents were not happy, but it was not her father's fault. It was her mother's attitude that created problems. In Terry's opinion, her mother regretted that she, citizen of a ruling country, married a man from a colony. Her mother felt superior to her husband; although when they married, he had a far better job and position in a British company than she did. He was far better educated than she was. These thoughts were crowding Terry's mind when she went to bed. She did not sleep well that night.

"I understand what you were saying last night," Terry said when she was alone next morning with her mother after breakfast. Sitting at the round table in the kitchen with her arms and elbows on top, "I know you want to protect me, and everything you said is true. However, you are comparing me with you, while we are talking about a different era. You and I are different people, born in different decades. We think differently because you grew up in England, whereas I am an American. I don't think that Saleem is in any way inferior to me. If anything, I find him to be superior in knowledge and in experience. I would trust his judgment anytime in any matter concerning my life. You said you made a mistake. If you are unhappy, it is because you do not want to leave father, and at the same time, you don't want to change your attitude toward him. I believe he still loves and cares for you. He always puts your desires ahead of his. And it's not because he thinks that you're English and he is Indian. It's because of his love. He adores you, Mother. And if you ever returned his affection you could be a happy woman." As Terry finished, she noticed her mother's face had turned red. She thought she had touched a nerve when calling her English and her father Indian.

There was a moment of silence. Her mother got up, poured herself a glass of water and sat down again. "Terry, you have to understand that I am your mother and my concern is about your future and it is my responsibility to protect you, and I will…in a way I see fit. I'm talking from experience and you are talking with emotions. That boy is bad news for you. I'm not saying he isn't a good person. All I want you to understand is that he comes from a different culture and it will be difficult for you two to adapt to each other. You might think that because your father was born in India you have something in common with Saleem, but you were not born there and you have grown up in an entirely different society, a society where men and women can talk and discuss problems as if they were equals. Men from his country are not used to that. Why make life more difficult than it is, for you and for others who care for you? Have you ever given it a thought that you may be looking for a father-figure in him?"

Terry did not know how to answer without confronting her mother, but she felt this thing needed to be resolved quickly, and today was as good a day as any. Controlling her anger as well as she could she said, "Mother you have to realize that I am over eighteen. You have always accused me of being too serious for my age—and of not enjoying life. And now you tell me my thinking is flawed." She stopped for some time, but not long enough to let her mother interrupt her. "I don't understand what you mean when you say that you will do what you see fit. Would you please explain?" She was annoyed by her mother treating her like a child and by the threat. She added

before her mother could get up to leave, "I am not going to stop seeing Saleem. I don't know where our relationship will take us, but I
know I love him."

To her mother, Terry suddenly appeared as a child throwing a
tantrum. "You are angry, and cannot see things clearly. We will discuss
the matter later." And with that she walked out, leaving Terry alone in
the kitchen. Terry was too irate to think beyond her mother's unrea-
sonable words.

Mary came in and sat down next to Terry. "I didn't hear the
whole conversation, but I think I did get the picture. So, what are you
going to do?"

"I don't know. I'm angry and I can't think clearly. I wish I could
see Saleem. But first I need to figure out what I want and what my
options are."

"Don't you think Father should know about all this?"

"This is pretty much between Mother and me. I don't want Father
involved in this—at least not at this point."

"You know, I'm on your side. If you ever want to talk or want me
to do something, let me know. I'm here." Mary lightly tapped her
sister's shoulder as she left the room.

Terry sat in the kitchen alone for awhile, drank some water and
went to her room. Her feelings wounded, her mind in turmoil, Terry
lay in bed concocting ideas, which her rational self was trying to
suppress. She would have liked to move away from her mother but
stomping out of the house would not only look childish, it would
be foolish, since she had no place of her own. She had saved some
money, but it was not enough. It was summer vacation and all of her
friends, except for Saleem, were out of town. Above all, she wanted
to act like the adult mature person she thought herself to be. She
realized that independent living in an apartment was not affordable
at this point in her life. Several questions popped into her mind and
options started to take shape. But she could not come to any definite
conclusion as to what she needed to do. She even rejected the idea of
meeting with Saleem. Suddenly, she felt unloved and insecure. She
wanted to cry but to her crying was a tool of the weak. Her defiant
eyes put a stop to the haze of her tears.

Her mother was lost in her own world, trying to work out the
challenge put out by a grown child. Then she remembered her own

life at that age and how she would defy her mother and wanted to have her own way. But, a voice inside her kept on telling her what she was doing was right. Girls at her daughter's age do not know what is right and what is wrong. If she had listened to her mother, she might have had a different life—better or worse she could not say. Facing the dilemma, she was not sure what to advise. She had already said her piece. Going back to discuss the issue again would be yielding to a stubborn child and she did not want to that. And she was determined to save her girl.

As time passed, some choices became clear to Terry. She believed she had certain rights in her parent's home and that her mother could not throw her out, especially since her father had always sided with her. She would simply stand her ground; maybe her mother would come to see her viewpoint. And in case she decided to leave, she would do that in her own time when she was prepared and ready.

It was Sunday, and her mother had prepared lunch for everyone—as she always did. They all ate together. To Terry the food tasted different, as if it was spiced with anger. Still Terry acted as if nothing was wrong. She did not want her father disturbed by her problems.

Unaware of what was going on between mother and daughter, John brought up how nice the party had been last night. He enjoyed it so much that he suggested they should have one where he would prepare the food. They could invite the Haydens and some friends of the girls.

When he asked Bernice to decide what would be an appropriate time for this, she proposed that, since they just had been to a party, they should wait for two to three weeks if they were to include Haydens. To Bernice the idea of an outdoor party was attractive; it would provide her a chance to invite some of the young men who were at home during the summer. Three weeks time sounded good to everyone and together they set a tentative date.

As they were leaving the table, John asked her daughter to invite Saleem. "It would be good for him to get out of the lab and see another home in America."

Through her looks Bernice sent a message of disapproval, but stayed quiet.

Terry had not gone to see Saleem since the party, and he had not called her. Her mother thought she was getting through to Terry.

Not mentioning her concerns about her mother's meddling, Terry had told Saleem that she would not be seeing him as much during the summer. Saleem thought that would be all right with him. This way he would spend all his time in the lab and try to finish as much of his work as he could.

The local paper, where Terry had applied for a job, offered her work as an intern. She knew they did not pay well, but the work was interesting and it could prove to be helpful in her career later on. Her sister Mary found a job in a restaurant. Both sisters made about the same amount of money. Terry was working to save money. Mary, on the other hand, was making money to buy new clothes and new shoes.

One evening on her way back, Terry chose to stop by the lab and see Saleem. They had not seen each other for over a week now. After a few tender moments, they went out for a meal. From a telephone booth nearby, when she called her house to tell her mother that she would not be home for dinner, she had a feeling of liberation while Bernice felt she was losing control over her daughters.

Terry had not told Saleem anything about her recent confrontation with her mother. She was in a dilemma; she did not want to have secrets from him at the same time she did not want him to think that he was the cause of troubles between her mother and her. As they were eating, Terry mentioned in passing that her mother and she were having some problems, but it was not unusual.

To bring a different subject into the conversation, she mentioned that her father had enjoyed his cooking so much that he wanted to have a party of his own where he would cook and Saleem was invited. She said she would let him know the time and date soon. She also gave him her phone number at the newspaper office and asked him to call her some time when they could go out for lunch.

As she was leaving, he told her how he missed her and that he kept himself busy to keep his mind occupied. "I'm planning that someday we can arrange it so you will be with me all the time," Saleem managed to say.

Terry answered, "I'm working on it too," kissed him and left.

Saturday at five in the evening was a convenient time for everyone to come to the dinner party at the Jafrey home. On the way over, Saleem remembered his mother's counsel about when you go to someone's house for the first time; always bring something along for them. Heeding to her advice, he bought a bunch of flowers for Terry's mother. Since the Jafreys did not live far from Haydens' house and Terry had given him directions, he had no problem finding it. He arrived a few minutes after five. As Terry opened the door, she thought he had bought the flowers for her and whispered, "Thanks, but give them to mother, please."

He found Bernice in the kitchen and handed her the bouquet. Bernice was surprised and genuinely smiled at him for the first time and thanked him.

Bernice had invited another couple and their son, Jeff, who was going to college at Berkley. Jeff and Terry had known each other in high school. He had taken her to the prom. She wanted to give another chance to this possible relationship. In her mind they made a handsome couple.

Terry introduced Jeff and Saleem, "Saleem meet Jeff, an old friend of mine who is going to Berkley and plans to go to law school." Turning to Jeff she said, "This is my friend Saleem who is working for his PhD with Professor Hayden. The professor says he's almost done."

Just as Terry was finishing her introductions, the Haydens walked in. Evelyn came up to Saleem and as she shook his hand she said, "There is our favorite young man, a chemist, who knows how to cook."

Saleem was shy. He was not used to getting much attention. He saw Mary and Eric and went over to talk to them.

Soon, Terry and Jeff also moved where the other young people were standing. Jeff started telling them about life at the Berkley campus. He was defending the students there by saying that it was only a small number of students who were taking part in activities that some considered out-of-line and were getting attention from the media. The majority of the students was serious about their studies and worked hard.

Jeff's father, who had traveled to India and the Far East, walked over and joined the group. He looked at Saleem and said, "I would say you are from India or Pakistan."

"In a way, I am from both places. I was born in India and came to this country from Pakistan."

When he found out Saleem had gone to college in Agra, Jeff's father started naming all those places tourists make a point to visit but natives leave for another time, which never comes.

Saleem was not comfortable in this house. If it was not for Terry, he would not be there. Bernice's eyes seemed to follow him and he did not find any friendliness in them. Terry's father was outside preparing food. He used it as an excuse to go out to the backyard to say hello.

John was happy to see him and said, "My cooking is not as creative as yours was a few weeks back."

His cooking might not have been creative but he certainly had dressed for the occasion. An apron and the chef's hat made him look like the part he was playing. He was turning pieces of chicken with a long pair of tongs and rolling the hot dogs on a grill, which was spewing out a mixture of steam and smoke. All his attention was taken up by the food he was preparing for the guests.

Saleem wanted to leave him alone. As he turned around to go back to the house, he was surprised to see Terry standing behind him.

"Hey Mister, you stay with me and don't wander around. You are my special guest tonight." She walked back with him to where Jeff, Eric and Mary had formed a group of their own.

Jeff was interested in finding out more about India and Pakistan from someone who had lived there. In his view, his father's version of these places was that of a tourist who saw what he was shown and did not include life experiences of the country. He was not interested in historical sites; he wanted to know more about the people there. Jeff and Saleem talked for quite some time. Saleem explained what he could. He enjoyed talking about India and Pakistan—for him, it brought back memories of home. Saleem and Jeff seemed to like each other and discussed meeting another time.

When the food was ready, the guests found it placed on a long table. The women served first, the men followed. To Saleem, it appeared more like a picnic than a dinner. He picked a piece of chicken and a hot dog, took small servings of potato salad and baked beans. There was no Kashmiri touch to the food but then, nothing in the house was from Kashmir either.

Terry's mother pretended to be busy, but Saleem could tell she was ignoring him and watching him at the same time. She was disappointed that Jeff seemed to have taken a liking to Saleem.

By the end of the dinner, Bernice knew that her strategy of rekindling an earlier flame between Terry and Jeff had failed. Most people who knew the young graduate student in chemistry seemed to like him. Having a heart-to-heart talk with Saleem crossed her mind, but she put it aside for now. She did not know him enough and doubted she could convince him to see her view of the situation. She was getting frustrated. She was so used to having her own way in family matters.

CHAPTER 37

During his once-a-month trips to the bank to deposit his check, Saleem would pass by a jewelry store never caring what they were selling. Recently, he had started to look into the window where the rings were on display. One ring in particular caught his eye. It had a round diamond that sparkled in the light. A price-tag was attached, but no matter how hard he tried, he could never read the amount on it. He had never been interested in any type of jewelry before and paid little attention to what anyone was wearing. But he understood the significance of rings in the society he was living in—they symbolized relationships—and relationship was on his mind these days.

One day, unconsciously drawn by the desire to look at the ring again and the curiosity about its cost, he found himself standing next to the counter inside the store. The man, owner of the shop, walked with him to the window, took out the piece and informed Saleem that it was $400. The jeweler then carried it over and to accent its quality he laid the ring on a piece of black velvet. The man was in his fifties. He had owned this shop for the last twelve years, but had never known a foreign student come in to ask about any of his wares.

"Do you plan to take it back home for someone, or does the young lady happen to live here?" he inquired. Saleem did not want some stranger prying into his life and did not answer. The man realized that his question was awkward and quickly rephrased, "I'm sorry, I did not mean to meddle, I only asked because if the young lady happens to live here she might want to take a look. It is an expensive gift and she will be wearing it all her life."

This seemed reasonable, and because the tone of the salesman's voice was now soft, Saleem calmed down.

"But how would I surprise her, if we shopped together?" After a couple of moments, he added, "Well, let me think about it." He thanked the jeweler for showing him the ring and for his advice.

He had gone in just to find out the price of the jewelry, but now he was facing other questions. In essence, the purchase of a ring would signify an intention to change his life; he wondered whether he was ready for this adjustment. In essence, was he ready to get married? And if so, would she marry him? These questions kept popping in his mind. Fantasizing about his future, lost in his thoughts he went back to the lab.

Once in the lab, he found his work bench reminding him of his first priority—his degree. This was what he came for, and this was what he wanted to be done with as soon as possible. He wanted to finish one thing so he could take the next step. With this in mind, he brought himself back to the world of chemical research.

He started to spend more and more time in the lab. His hard work was paying off; he was beginning to get results, results that were worth publishing. Still, he was not content with his situation, he missed not seeing enough of Terry, and that was hard on him. In spite of him being very busy the summer appeared to be long and neverending. She was still living at home and working for the newspaper. She would drop by on Fridays and occasionally they ate together or went to a movie.

He also knew that she would soon be living on campus again and then he would be able to see her more often. By the time the summer was over, he understood that he needed her in his life. Without her, his life was incomplete. He decided that he would ask her to marry him. But how? He did not know. This was a big step for anyone, but for Saleem it was a giant leap. Then came the doubts again about whether he was ready or not.

Whenever Saleem was downtown, going to the bank, or going to the movie, he would unconsciously pass by the jeweler's window, stop and look for the ring. As if beckoning him, the ring was always there. He had started saving money in the past few months. He did not know exactly what for, but now it was becoming clear to him that he wanted to buy the ring for her.

Terry's twentieth birthday was more than a month away. He thought he should invite her to go out for dinner before she or her parents made other plans. When Terry told her mother that she was going out on her birthday with Saleem, it was not what Bernice wanted to hear. She was planning to have a party that would include boys from Terry's high school days in the hope that she would reconnect with someone more suitable than her present friend. She was also against her daughter going out with a young man on her birthday—especially with that man from Pakistan again. In addition, she worried about girls being alone with boyfriends on their birthdays, because she thought things might get out of control; she remembered her own younger days and told her daughter about her fears.

Terry was getting weary of her mother's attitude. She started looking for an apartment. She connected with one of her friends who was also going to be a junior in the college and wanted to move out of the dorm. Since the school had not opened yet, the girls found a place without much difficulty. The place was tiny but it was a small sacrifice for the independence she would have from the constant supervision of her mother. Terry had saved enough money by now that she could afford a place of her own and would not have to depend on her parents for all her financial needs. Her sister preferred to remain at the dorm.

A week before school opened, Terry told her mother that she was moving out to live in an apartment with a friend. The look on her mother's face made her say, "No, it is not what you think. I'm going to share an apartment with Tara, a friend—a girl."

Her mother was unhappy. To her it seemed safer when the two sisters lived together in the dorm. She knew Eugene was a quiet place. She was not worried about her daughter's physical safety she just did not want her to make decisions on her own.

However, Terry was over eighteen and knew that her father was on her side. Bernice felt helpless. She was upset with Terry, which was common these days. But, she tried to be gracious and helped her daughter move to the new apartment. She certainly did not want Saleem to drive Terry. When they arrived at the address, they found Tara had already moved in; she came outside to meet her friend's mother.

With Tara's help, Terry removed her belongings from the car and carried everything inside. She then invited her mother to come in and see her new place that was part of a large house. It had a small living area with a stove and a sink in one corner. The bedroom and the attached bathroom that the girls were to share had no windows.

However, the living area had a large window facing the street and a small one over the stove looked out at the backyard of the house. In the kitchen the appliances and the heavy drapes on the window were all unanimously telling the same story—their old age. Mother, as she concluded the tour of the living space, wondered why anyone would leave the comfort of home and for that matter organized life in a newly built dorm to live in a cubbyhole like this. To Terry it was her first step in her quest of freedom from her mother's everlasting rants about her relationship with Saleem.

The house belonged to a widow who lived in the other section of the building. She had certain restrictions for her renters: no smoking and no parties. Neither of the girls smoked. Unknown to Bernice, the place was in walking distance from Saleem's apartment. That was a definite plus for Terry. It was also not far from the newspaper office where Terry had interned. It was convenient in case she found a job with them. Tara had a phone installed and told Terry that she could use it for local calls any time she wanted to.

Tara knew about Saleem, but had not met him yet.

CHAPTER 38

A day before her birthday, in spite of the jeweler's earlier caution, Saleem went to the store and asked the clerk about the payment policy. Recognizing Saleem, the man replied that they preferred the entire amount in cash. The bank was not too far away, so Saleem walked up there to withdraw the money. Since the sum was rather large, he was asked to show his driver's license and ID card. With money out of his bank account in his pocket, all sorts of doubts, fears and hopes crowding his mind, he returned to the jewelry store.

The man took the ring out from the window and cleaned it before he placed it into a small box with its lid open for Saleem to see. He thought it looked very pretty. As the salesman filled out a receipt, he said, "Young man, I like you. So, I'm giving you a receipt with which you can return the ring, if you needed to for any reason. Just bring it back within one week, together with this receipt, and there will be no questions asked."

Saleem handed him the money. Parting with so much money, making the biggest purchase of his life, made him wonder why and what he was doing. But on the outside he was calm.

The man put the box in a small paper bag, handed it to Saleem and said, "Congratulations, to deserve this she must be a very special girl."

Saleem and the store owner thanked each other and shook hands. As he walked back to his apartment, he thought that no one, except for the shopkeeper, knew what he was carrying inside his jacket: a ring in his pocket and a song in his heart. It felt as if his feet did not quite touch the ground.

Back at his apartment, the doubts crept in—part buyer's remorse, part uncertainty about his decision. That night he tossed and turned in his bed, wondering about the timing, whether he acted rightly or wrongly. He had no idea how Terry was going to react to his proposal—that was if he was able to muster up enough courage to propose in the first place. Then there was the question about his parents' possible disapproval. They believed in arranged marriages. To them a young man going out and find his own wife was unheard of. Finally, the morning came and the day was October 10—Terry's twentieth birthday. He could not shake certain ambivalence about his feelings and he found it difficult to focus his thoughts after that sleepless night.

Whenever his mind was not clear, he went out for a walk. It usually helped him sort things out. He chose his favorite paths on the way to campus. It was still early in the morning and the sky was cloudy. There was a cold mist in the air. He passed by a maintenance crew working on the lawn and tending the flowers. This time, even the brisk morning walk did not bring the results he desired. His brain did not seem to function properly. He found himself in the same uncertain state of mind as the night before. He went back to the apartment, dropped onto the bed and fell asleep. When he woke up again, it was already eleven o'clock. He had slept for three hours. He felt better after taking a shower. As he walked over to the lab, his mind suddenly cleared up. There was no more confusion. He had decided to do whatever felt right for the moment.

To celebrate the twins' birthdays, their parents took the girls out to lunch. They presented Terry with a watch, and Mary received a small transistor radio. Mary had bought a sweatshirt for Terry, and Terry had gotten a pair of gloves for her sister. After lunch, a waiter set a small cake with twenty lit candles in the middle of the table. A few more servers joined him, stood around in half circle and sang happy birthday to the girls as they blew out the candles together.

Saleem returned to his apartment at five o'clock, took another shower, changed clothes, and with the ring in his pocket drove to Terry's place. On his way, he bought a bunch of long-stemmed red roses. She was looking out the window and when she saw the familiar Volvo pulling in at the curb. She flew out of the house. She wore a light blue dress that she had bought just for tonight.

Saleem nervously stepped out of the car, handed Terry the flowers, and wished her a happy birthday. Terry wanted him to come inside and meet her roommate. Tara was standing in the middle of the living room, waiting for the two to come in. Tara could immediately see why her roommate liked Saleem. She too was a little nervous when Terry introduced him to her, but she quickly got over it and shook his hand. Both girls admired the flowers and stuck them in a long-neck wide-mouth bottle—a student-vase.

It was October and the days were getting shorter. Terry and Saleem left the building together. As they got in the car, he kissed her on the nose, telling her he did not want to smear her lipstick. She laughed. She told him all about her day, the lunch with her family, and the presents she received from her parents, her sister and her roommate.

"Saleem you are spending too much money on me, the flowers, the dinner—all in one night. Are you sure it is not too much?" she said as he parked the car in front of Mazzi's, a fancy Italian restaurant. It was a weekday and the place was not crowded. The couple was seated at a table by the window. The lights in the restaurant were low and in the background one could hear music. The atmosphere was conducive to a romantic supper.

They had not seen much of each other during the summer because both of them had been busy and Terry was staying with her parents. As they sat down and ordered the food, he told her about what he was doing in the lab, but she was more interested in hearing stories about his childhood. Among his favorite stories of younger days was his adventure when he went hunting with his uncle where they mistook a cow for a tiger but luckily did not shoot it. Terry having no experience with guns or hunting could not relate to it but found it amusing. He then changed the conversation and told her, "I really missed seeing you.

Terry returned the sentiment, "I wish I could spend every day with you. But," she sighed, "I am happy at least to be with you tonight. And why shouldn't I be with you after all it is my birthday—a special day in my life. I'm no longer a teenager".

As they were relishing their dinner, his nervousness was gone now. He tried simply to enjoy the moment. He felt the ring in his jacket, but decided it was not the right moment. They sat across, looking into each other's eyes. He saw her as a happy girl who was enjoying her life. He did not want to change her into a woman with responsibilities. He liked her just the way she was tonight. Tomorrow would be another working day for them, so they decided to leave soon after they finished their dessert, which he had insisted on because it was her birthday.

As they left the restaurant and got into the car, it started to drizzle. They drove back to her apartment in silence. Before she got out of the car, she looked at him tenderly; they both had their eyes closed as they kissed goodnight. He felt he was somewhere—like in heaven. And she wanted this moment to last forever. As he walked her back to the apartment, it was raining. He protectively put his raincoat over her as they climbed the front steps. Their bodies were touching and neither wanted to part.

"I wish this would last forever," she whispered looking into his eyes.

He held her tight and they kissed again before she was gone. As she closed the door behind her, she danced and shouted, "I am in love, I am in love!"

Tara's voice from bedroom brought her back to earth, "I hear you! I hear you! I am so happy for you," Tara said as she came out and hugged her.

Saleem went back to his apartment with the ring still in the little box.

CHAPTER 39

The next day, Terry showed up to go for lunch with him. She gave him the phone number of her apartment and asked him to call her sometime to get together, or just to talk. He had never been comfortable talking on the phone, so he knew he would not use that number very often. She thanked him for the dinner and the beautiful roses, which looked just as fresh this morning as they did last night. She said, "It was one of the best days of my life. I turned twenty and my mother was nice and polite, in spite of my upsetting her original party plans for Mary and me."

"I'm sorry…it seems I'm the problem between you and your mother. At times I feel she does not like me.

"Sorry, I brought my mother into this. I love you and I would do anything to keep us together. My mother is a difficult person. Her problems have nothing to do with you or me. Maybe I shouldn't say that about my mother, but she is her own problem. The relationship between her and me has never been good. I'm more like my father. I must have his Indian blood in me that makes me do things she doesn't approve of," Terry said.

They looked at each other, her eyes full of tears. "I didn't mean to hurt your feelings. I love you. I'm just too rational. I tend to analyze instead of opening my heart and express my feelings. I came close to suggesting something crazy last night, but my head overruled my heart once again." He knew what he meant but noticed that she was blushing.

Changing the subject, she went on to explain that she had more expenses now as she lived off campus. For that reason, she had applied for a job at the newspaper.

Looking at her new watch, she realized it was time for her class and she left. On her way to the class she was thinking of the recent conversation and felt that she and Saleem usually seemed to talk about things in a serious manner. She accredited it to his influence on her and also because of her growing older. This was a sign of dependability in him, she believed.

In the evening when Saleem went home, he felt very much alone. He pulled out the ring, held it in his hand, and then he looked at the receipt, which included the words, "Full refund if returned within one week of purchase." He examined the ring closely, liked it even more than the first day he laid eyes on it and decided to keep it until a more appropriate time. He bought it for someone special who was going to get it one day. For the first time he realized that by purchasing the ring he had dared responsibility. He had taken matters in his own hands.

He was aware that if he was at home, his family would first discuss the issue, and if and when they arrived at a decision, his father would go to the girl's family and ask for her hand for his son. He would not buy the ring; they would. He was doing something on his own that he had never seen done in his family. To be able to give a ring he bought to a girl he chose, he would have to cross another line. But he did not know how or when.

Now, his problem was where to keep it safe until that suitable moment arrived. He put it in its little brown bag, stuffed it back into the breast pocket of his blue suit, and tried to forget about it.

Since it was getting cooler and rains were falling more frequently, he was spending more and more time inside the lab and the library. He was gradually completing the requirements of his program, one by one. The professor had always been friendly towards him, but he had felt new warmth since the dinner party when Saleem cooked for them.

Terry had managed to get a part time job with the newspaper. They met for lunch on Fridays only, and occasionally they would go to see a movie on a Saturday. Since she was a junior with a full load of course work and was working, she did not have much time to spare. Both of them were so focused on their studies that Saleem started to wonder if the right time for giving her the ring would ever come. The days seemed to be flying by fast.

CHAPTER 40

Another year had passed and Terry was now a senior and her twenty-first birthday had come and gone. The ring had stayed in its brown envelope with him all this time. He started to wonder if he would just keep it forever. It already had lost its newness while waiting for Saleem to pick up his courage to propose.

His world had now shrunk to his apartment, the lab and occasional meetings with Terry, the only break in his routine—a routine in his life he needed to be productive and focused.

At times, Terry wondered if they were drifting apart. But then she reminded herself that her friend was mentally engaged on getting his degree. During her relationship she had discovered that no one, herself included, could distract him from this goal; any possible future with him would have to wait until he had his PhD.

The holiday season was approaching. One day in early November, Professor Hayden told him, "I have asked all of my students who are to finish soon, to come over for Thanksgiving dinner and you're invited. The time is set for five o'clock, but you may come at four, this way you'll have a chance to meet our son and his wife who will be there."

Saleem was glad to accept the invitation. Also, he could not get over what he heard his professor say. He was close to achieving his goal.

For the special occasion Saleem put on a white shirt and his only blue suit. As he was putting the jacket on, he felt the ring. When he reached his professor's house, Evelyn greeted him affectionately. She introduced Saleem to her son David and his wife Claudia. The couple had driven from San Francisco where David worked as an electrical engineer. David and his wife seemed close to Saleem's age. They were in the process of describing their life in San Francisco when Terry walked in, followed by her family. She was wearing her dark blue dress.

Same house, same girl, and possibly same dress, thought Saleem as he remembered the first time he had set eyes on her at the Haydens' party for foreign students a couple of years ago. He remembered how she had walked from the kitchen into the living room and how mesmerized he had been.

Something was happening to him. He started hearing music, a music he never heard before, and everyone in the room disappeared, except for Terry. Completely oblivious to his surroundings, he asked her to stand still, walked up to her, pulled out the ring from his pocket, put it on the palm of his hand and extended it toward her. "I am going to do the craziest thing I have ever done in my life. I am asking you if you will marry me."

Terry froze and then, stunned, she said, "Yes. I was wondering if you'd ever ask."

She picked up the ring, gasped and then quickly put it on. After that, she just stood there and did not know what to do.

They both were in another world, intently staring at each other when from afar he heard Evelyn's voice saying, "Saleem, you may kiss her now!"

The two of them embraced while everyone clapped and cheered. She looked at Saleem, then back at the ring, and said, her voice quivering, "This is so beautiful!"

Saleem heard hands clapping around him but he was not sure, whether he was dreaming or if it was real. He was in a daze.

Just as all this was going on, a bunch of graduate students, the friends who were also invited walked into the house. They heard the clapping and thought the party had started early. As they came into the living room, their eyes fell on Saleem, frozen and holding hands with Terry.

The only person in the room who was unable to share in the excitement was Bernice. She was sitting on a chair with a glass of water in her hand. Saleem and Terry also noticed that Bernice just sat there, unable to take part in this most important moment of her daughter's life. Saleem looked at John; he was smiling. He came over to Saleem, put his arm around him and said, '*Mubarak ho*' which meant congratulations in Urdu. These were the first words he had heard her father say in any language other than English.

For a moment, the party turned from a Thanksgiving feast to an engagement gala for the two young people—favorites of so many in this house. Although Saleem had been thinking about proposing for a very long time, carrying the ring around in his pocket for over a year and waiting for the right moment to pop the question, he was still amazed at what he did. It was as if someone else had done it for him. He had asked her to be his wife in front of all these people. Something happened to him when he saw her tonight. He felt neither shy, nor bold; he acted as if he were in a trance—in a different world.

Meanwhile, the professor was grilling vegetables outside in the backyard when he heard the clapping. He, being unaware of what transpired inside his house, was glad that his guests were having a good time.

Saleem found out from Evelyn where the professor was. Anxious to tell him what just happened in his home, he took Terry by the arm and they went outside looking for him.

As soon as the professor saw the beaming duo and the ring Terry had on, he understood the reason for cheering. He put down the skewers and extended both arms toward the young people, saying, "So, that's what the clapping was all about. Saleem, you chose a wonderful girl. Congratulations! What a wonderful day for an engagement! Go enjoy yourselves, I will be done shortly."

On their way into the house Saleem said, "I wish I could calm down and concentrate on others and the party. Do you think you can?"

Looking into his eyes Terry said, "I don't know...I'm trying. I will go directly into the kitchen and try to help get the food ready, as I promised. That is why I came early. *Came early to help...got engaged instead...*" She kissed her ring.

As they re-entered the living room, everyone cheered again. This time Saleem and Terry both smiled back, their faces radiating happiness.

Saleem went up to Evelyn and said, "I apologize for causing commotion in your house today. I had wanted to do this for a long time now, actually more than a year, but somehow I never had the nerve. Today, something came over me and took control. I hope I didn't disrupt your dinner plans." To himself he wanted to say, I am so glad I did it!

"Don't be silly. We are honored that it happened in our house. I'm very happy for both of you. You know how much I like Terry. She's like a daughter to me. My husband and I are very fond of the two of you." Then she said, "Did you tell Jim?"

"Yes, I did, and thank you for being kind and understanding. I will always remember this moment in your house," Saleem said.

Before Terry went back into kitchen to help Mary, she closed her eyes and took a few deep breaths to calm herself.

Her sister looked at her and smiled, "I could see it coming, and I am happy you guys did it." She looked at the ring again and said, "Oh, my God this thing is not cheap… Terry you did good!"

David and Claudia congratulated Saleem. Then Claudia said, "We didn't know we were here to witness this important moment in your life. We got married two years ago, and we're very happy we did." She looked at her husband and back then added, "We hope you will be happy too."

Soon, Jim brought in the turkey, all cooked, lying on its back on a silver platter. The sisters had been helping the hosts with the main dishes. Everyone was now admiring the Thanksgiving dinner, as it came together on the large table. Saleem and Terry, however, were still caught up in their own private world—the moment that had brought them closer together in their life.

Once everyone was seated, Professor Hayden performed the ritual of carving. Just as he must have done in the past years, Saleem thought.

David was sitting next to Terry and was telling her about their life in San Francisco. Terry was listening, but her mind was somewhere else. Claudia was asking Saleem questions about India and Pakistan. She mentioned that she and her husband were thinking of taking time off next March to travel to Singapore and India.

The dinner was elaborate and as they all ate, it got quiet around the table. For dessert, there was a choice of apple or pumpkin pie. Pieces of pie were offered with or without ice cream, followed by coffee. Toward the end of the meal, the professor raised his glass and made a toast to Saleem and Terry's happiness.

While the women were busy clearing the table and carrying the leftovers into the kitchen, Saleem thought it was time to go and talk to Terry's parents. He did not see them and was told that they had already left. He was disappointed.

It took Evelyn, and Claudia, with the help of the two sisters, some time to take care of the leftovers and clean up in the kitchen. In the meantime, the professor, his son and students retired to the living room. He poured some cognac for those who wanted to drink and then lit a cigar for himself. Later on, he was going to show some slides. His students noticed that he did not talk chemistry in the house.

Once Terry was done with things she wanted to take care of in the kitchen, she and Saleem asked Evelyn's permission to leave.

"I am so happy for you two! And let me tell you again how happy I am that this important event took place in our house! Go and enjoy your evening. You sure have some planning to do." She said as she walked them to the door.

Mary left with the couple because she needed a ride home. She had seen her parents leave early and assumed that her mother had developed one of her famous headaches.

After dropping off Mary, Saleem and Terry drove to her apartment. Once inside, Terry turned on the lights, put her hand directly under the light bulb of the table lamp and looked at the ring again, "This is so beautiful. I wish your parents were here to see it. When did you get it?"

"I got it a day before your twentieth birthday and planned to give it to you that night, but it did not feel right. I guess I was thinking too much," Saleem replied with a shrug.

Suddenly it occurred to Terry what he had meant the day after her birthday when he told her that he was going to do something crazy. "I clearly remember what you said the day after my birthday. But I didn't understand what you meant." She was silent for a moment and then said, "You mean, you have had this ring for over a year and I knew nothing about it? Did anyone know?"

"No, not a soul… Except for the man who sold it to me."

"What you were going to do on my twentieth birthday and what you did tonight is not crazy, it's adorable. You have made me the happiest girl in the whole world. Thank you, Saleem!" She wrapped her arms around him and kissed him.

She looked at the ring again; she could not get over it how it sparkled in the light. Saleem told her about his conversation with the jeweler, mentioning how the store was willing to take the ring back for whatever reason within one week. "When I didn't give it to you, I wondered if I should take it back. But then I kept it."

"I am so glad you didn't take it back." She looked down for a moment and then thinking about her sister's words: *this thing is not cheap*, looked back at Saleem and said, "You have spent so much money on me. You must be broke by now."

"Don't worry about me! I had been saving money for this ring and my father had sent me some when I just came. Besides, this is a once in a lifetime event."

Her roommate Tara had gone home for Thanksgiving. Now, they were alone and they were engaged. An awkward feeling existed between two of them. They had never been all alone in the privacy of an apartment, all to themselves. They were unsure how to react.

She broke the silence, "What would you like to do…? I could make you a cup of tea. Both my parents come from tea drinking countries. I really know how to make a good cup of tea." When he did not answer, she said, "I suppose it is all right to start living together now that we're engaged. Call me old-fashioned, but if it is okay with you, I would like to wait until we get married. I hope you don't mind."

He laughed. "I didn't know you had tea and our status on your mind." He bent down and kissed her. "I like the way you think and, yes, I would like some tea…please."

As she was about to put water on the stove, the telephone rang. Terry wondered who would call at this hour. She picked up the phone; it was Mary. She heard her say that their mother was in the hospital. She had had a mild heart attack. Mary was calling from the hospital ward. Terry told her sister she would be there as soon as she could.

As she changed her clothes, Terry asked Saleem to drive her to the hospital. The ride took less than ten minutes. They found John and Mary sitting in the visitors' lounge. Terry rushed to her father, "How is mother? I feel terrible, I feel guilty. I'm so sorry. I might have caused her being here tonight," in her anxiety she blurted out.

She was about to cry when her father put his arm around her shoulder. "Calm down. It's not so bad. You didn't do anything wrong. If your mother doesn't agree with what you did, it's her problem. Don't blame yourself for her condition. In fact, I approve of what you did. Mary and I are happy for you two." After a while he added, "The doctor is still with her, but a nurse who came out earlier said that her condition is not serious."

They sat there without talking, waiting for more news. Waiting for someone to come out and tell them that she was well.

To be in a hospital lobby was a first for Saleem. He found it depressing to look at the long gloomy faces of the people who were sitting around in anticipation, some anxious, others resigned. White uniforms dashed around purposefully, like in the movies. The atmosphere was somber and gloomy.

After a while, a doctor emerged and came to them to tell John that his wife was not in any serious danger. Apparently, there was no damage to her heart. She was resting now. "You can go home and come back to see her in the morning," the doctor said.

They all got up and started walking slowly toward the parking lot with their heads down as if weight of gloom hung around their necks. They all seemed worn out. John abruptly stopped and looked at Terry. "Your mother has a family history of heart disease. She has had high blood pressure and high cholesterol for a long time now. She takes medicines for both. What happened, happened. You didn't cause it. So, don't blame yourself. We will come back tomorrow. And I suggest you come and stay with us at home tonight."

Terry looked at Saleem and said, "Will you drive me and stay with me for a little while, if I go home?"

Saleem nodded. "Of course, I will."

In silence, they continued toward their cars. As they drove to Terry's home, Saleem said, "I don't know how much you know about heart attacks. These episodes do not just happen. They are caused by hardening of arteries, which develops over a long period. The deposit of plaque and narrowing of the arteries can cut the blood supply to the heart muscle. They can also do the same to the brain, causing a stroke. The doctor said it was a heart attack, not a stroke. Chemical processes in your mother's body caused this blockage over some time. As your father said, it did not happen because of what took place tonight. There is a remote possibility that it did…but very remote. According to your father, your mother has a family history of heart problems… And the most important thing is that she is going to be all right."

Terry was quietly listening, hoping he was right.

When he had finished, she said, "I'm impressed! But how do you know all this?"

"My father wanted me to be a doctor, so I read up about different ailments. Tomorrow, you can ask the physician, he will tell you pretty much what I said."

They were finally at the Jafreys' home. As they entered, the house appeared empty and quiet without Bernice; the lights in the house seemed dimmer and the air seemed heavy with angst. John asked if Saleem would like tea.

Saleem realizing that John wanted some company said, "Yes, please."

The girls went to the other room, where they talked about the events of that night. Saleem and John went to the kitchen where John prepared tea. They took their cups and sat down at the dining table. "I am glad about you and Terry. By now, I'm sure you've noticed that Bernice and I are not the happiest couple in the world. The fault lies with both of us. She wanted things her way and I let her. But I resented it, and resentment created a gulf between us. We tried moving from one place to another, hoping that each new environment would somehow mend what was wrong with us. We never sat down and talked about the problems—we carried them along from one location to another. I was always afraid that the marriage would break down if I sat down with Bernice and told her what the real cause of our unhappiness was. That, I did not want, because of the girls. They are precious to me and I always wanted to give them the best." He was quiet for some time and then spoke again, "I don't know why I'm telling you all this. Maybe, because I now look at you as a part of the family, or perhaps you helped me connect with my past. I see myself in you. I hope and pray that you two will be happier than Bernice and I have been." As he finished, his voice was shaky and his eyes were wet.

Saleem did not say a word. The two men finished their drink in silence.

John got up and said, "Thank you for listening to me. Now you may go and check on Terry."

Saleem thanked him and said, "This was the best tea I've had since I left Pakistan."

Saleem did not know where Terry was; the house was unfamiliar to him. He walked to the door where he heard muffled voices. Soon after he knocked on the door and heard Terry say, "Come in."

He pushed the door open and walked in. The room had a bed, a table, a chair, a number of pictures and some posters on the walls. He found Mary sitting on the chair and Terry lying on the bed.

"I'm glad you are here," Terry said.

Mary said, "Me too". and added, "Father needed to talk to someone—a man from outside."

"I am a man from outside, trying to get in," he said with a smile.

The way the words came out made the girls laugh.

Looking at Terry he added, "Well, it's getting close to midnight. I should go back to my place. Tomorrow, I'll call to find out how your mother's doing. I'll be glad to come with you to see her, but at this point, it may be better if you went without me."

Both sisters walked him to the door after he had said good night to John who remained seated on the living room couch.

Mary remained with her father while Terry went out to see Saleem off. She looked at the ring again, "What a night!" she kissed him. "Mother's illness put a damper on everything, but I will always love you, no matter what."

He answered, I love you and I always will". And thinking about all those events of the day he drove away.

Mr. Jafrey, flanked by his two daughters, arrived a little after eight at the hospital the next morning. They were able to go in and see Bernice. Terry thought her mother looked pale, but she was talkative as usual. The family stood around her bed. She told them she was feeling weak, but otherwise she was ready to go home.

The nurse came in and told John that the doctor had recommended to do a few more tests today and then he would decide if you could take her home. Mother smiled at the girls and raised her arms for them to hold. The girls sat down one on each side of the bed. Terry said, "I am sorry…I caused all this."

"No, don't blame yourself. I need to take better care of my body and watch what I eat. Your father and I should also start walking… this was a warning. Hopefully it will not happen again. Let me look at your ring." She pulled Terry's hand toward her. "Oh, it is beautiful. I didn't get to look at it last night." Mother's eyes and her facial expression told a different story. Yes, it is a nice piece of jewelry, but why are you wearing this thing?

To Bernice it was merely a piece of jewelry, and a mark of defiance. For Terry, it was a symbol of love, love that had given her a new life.

As they were talking, the doctor came in to tell them essentially the same thing the nurse had already mentioned. "She's looking good," the young doctor said with a big smile, which she returned. He was not the same as the one they had seen last night. This doctor looked as if he was from India. He spoke with a British accent. "Most likely she will be able to go home this evening. She needs to rest—with minimal physical exertion. Also, for a few days she needs to avoid all excitement." He shook hands with John, and bid good day to the girls and Bernice.

Soon after the doctor left, the nurse came in and told them to come back in the afternoon. The staff needed to prepare the patient for additional tests.

As they were driving home, no one talked. Bernice and her illness were on their minds and each one coped in a different way. After a while, John said to Terry "I suppose you want to see Saleem. We could drive by where he lives and drop you off, or pick him up and take him home with us."

She appreciated her father's thoughtfulness and gave him directions how to get to Saleem's apartment.

Saleem was surprised to see the whole family standing in front of his door. "How is your mother?" he asked Terry as he invited them all in.

She is feeling much better and she might come home this evening. John answered as he looked around the small apartment and asked Saleem, "Would you like to come with us for the day; we would drop you back on our way to pick up Bernice later on".

Since it was the day after Thanksgiving and there was not much else to do, he agreed. They all left in John's Buick. Terry and Saleem sat in the back seat.

As the Buick started to move, everyone credited Saleem's presence with the positive change that occurred in the car's otherwise dismal atmosphere. Now, each person had something to say.

Mary turned toward the back seat and spoke first, "Saleem, we saw a young doctor who looked just like you, handsome, not as tall as you, but tall enough—"

Terry interrupted, "Don't drool over him. He was wearing a ring."

"You should meet him. You might know him," Mary said.

"Do you know how many people live in India? Millions! There is very little chance that I would know anyone from there that I meet here," Saleem said. After a while he added, "I take that back. I did meet someone I knew, the very first day I arrived here."

"So, there is a chance that you may know him," Mary said.

"Mary liked him and would like you to introduce him to her, but unfortunately for her, he appears to be married," Terry teased Mary, emphasizing the word married.

They arrived at the Jafreys' home. None of them had had anything to eat this morning and it was getting close to lunchtime. The two sisters were no expert cooks, but they knew how to prepare eggs, pancakes and, of course, sandwiches. John and Saleem opted for eggs and pancakes.

As the girls were busy in the kitchen, John asked Saleem about his studies and how much more time he needed to complete the program.

"Normally, it takes four years, so I am hoping to finish by the middle of May," Saleem answered.

"I imagine you want to get married soon," John retorted.

"We haven't had a chance to discuss it yet, but the whole idea of getting engaged was to live together as a married couple," Saleem answered.

The sisters called out that lunch was ready. Everyone moved to the dining table. John passed the plate to Saleem first and insisted that he should eat well. The conversation became lively during the meal. John brought out that he had never had pancakes until he came to this country, did not like them at all in the beginning, but now he loved them.

By the time the meal was over, all plates were empty. John showed Saleem around the garden and the things he had recently planted. Before they knew it, it was time to go back to the hospital.

They dropped Saleem off at his apartment and went to pick up Bernice. Bernice looked pale and tired, but she was eager to go home. She did not say much on the way home. Terry wanted to go to her own apartment and promised to come home later.

After her father dropped her off at her place, she decided to walk to Saleem's place instead. She was sure that she would find him there.

He and Terry had not been alone together for more than a few minutes since he gave her the ring. They had many things to sort out and a future to plan. With this in mind, they decided to walk to the campus where everything was quiet and the streets were empty. People stayed inside, mostly feasting on turkey leftovers. It was peaceful.

Saleem motioned toward an empty bench. "I'm going to inquire if there are any vacant apartments coming up in the married student housing complex. They are convenient and the rent is reasonable."

Terry, miles away in thought, did not immediately reply.

"You agreed to marry me last night, didn't you?" Saleem kidded.

She looked at him as if she just woke up from a dream. "Of course we could get married right now, if you wanted to. It's just that my mother's illness has been bothering me. I know she didn't plan to get ill, but she always manages to steal attention when someone has an occasion to celebrate. She does it to Father all the time, and now she did it to me. She tried to take away from me the most important moment of my life. I know, you probably think what I'm saying is unfair, because you love your mother. But you do not know mine. She is different."

Saleem looked directly into her eyes and said, "Your mother did not deliberately cause her problems last night, but I promise you that we will make up for all the things that were lost in your life." He put his arm around her. "And another thing, let's not rush into anything. We will get married when you are ready." He added, "By the way, I need to send a picture of you to my family in Pakistan. They'll want to see who I'm getting married to."

They sat there for some time, content to be together, until it got cold.

"I don't want to go home, I want to be with you," Terry sighed, her head still leaning against his shoulder.

"I want the same, but if anything happened to your mother tonight and you weren't there, you'd never forgive yourself. Remember, the doctor said she needed to avoid stress, and your staying with me would surely be stressful for her. Let me drive you back to your home so your mother knows where you are."

He drove her to the parent's house. As she climbed out of the car, he said, "I plan to be in the lab all day tomorrow. Come on over if you have time." As he went back to his apartment, he did not know what to do. He did not want to go to lab that night. He went to watch a movie instead.

Even though it was Saturday, it seemed like any other workday in the research lab. When Terry came in, everyone congratulated her and all the girls wanted to see her ring. Terry started to feel important. She was getting special attention. Except for her mother, everyone wished her well and had only positive things to say about her engagement to Saleem. And when they heard the story of his proposal, they invariably said, "Oh, how romantic!" Terry began to feel that being engaged had somehow elevated her status.

CHAPTER 41

When Tara returned from her visit and found out about the engagement, she insisted on hearing every minute detail of how it happened. Terry related the whole story of how Saleem had pulled out a ring from his pocket and asked her to marry him in front of all those people at Professor Hayden's house.

"I almost passed out, and I don't remember what I said. I must have said yes and put the ring on, because here it is." She raised her hand toward Tara's eyes.

Tara told her, "I like Saleem. He is smart, he will soon have a PhD, and he will get a good job. He will make a good husband and be a good provider. Congratulations! I think it is all wonderful."

Terry's mother had not said a single word about Saleem. John brought up his name a couple of times during the dinner on Sunday night when both girls were home. But Bernice just ignored it and never commented one way or another. Still worried about her illness, they just let it pass and talked about other things. Terry had so many exciting thoughts about her future, but she also did not say anything. After dinner was over, she returned to her apartment. Mary went to her dorm.

Now the parents were alone. John decided to take care of his wife and did all the chores in the house for the next few days. He cooked and served Bernice and tried to be mindful of her wishes. Neither of them brought up the touchy subject—Saleem.

Five days later, John drove Bernice to her doctor's appointment. After the check-up, the doctor pronounced her fully recovered and told them that she could resume her normal activities at home and do whatever she wanted to. The doctor also recommended that they both engage in some form of physical activity—daily walks together would be a good start. Bernice was to lose some weight and watch her diet.

As they drove back home, she whined about the depressing atmosphere in the hospital and all that went on during the Thanksgiving dinner. John brought up Saleem and asked his wife if she was ever going to accept him as a son-in-law.

"To be honest, I don't like him," she replied. "He may be a good person, but he is not the right man for my daughter. He has taken our daughter from us, and he has turned her against me. She does not listen to me anymore. I just don't see him the way you do."

John quietly listened to her ranting. Once they were home he finally said, "You do not like Saleem because he reminds you of me. Isn't that the truth? We've been married nearly thirty years and you still have not come to terms with it. I love you. I always have. If you really dislike me, why did you stay all these years? For the past few weeks, your behavior has been atrocious."

He was quiet for a while and waited for an answer. When Bernice did not respond, he continued, "No one takes our children away from us. They move away when they grow up. That is just how life is. If you are graceful about it, they will be close to you. But if you are spiteful, as you have been toward Terry, you may not see them again." He looked at her to see if she would speak. "Perhaps you did not leave me because you were afraid to be alone. If that is true, it is an awful reason to stay together," he said in a harsh voice.

"We have been married for a long time now. People get used to each other over time. The novelty wears off. Relationships get rusty, and I am not the only one responsible for what has gone wrong with our marriage," Bernice answered. "I loved you when we were young, but we got side tracked into other things…started neglecting each other…"

He interrupted her, "I never stopped loving you. The only mistake I made was that I should not have given in to all your whims. I should have stood my ground."

Suddenly, she was fearful that he might leave her, "I don't want to lose you. I need you. If you really love me, you will stay. I will try to be the way I used to. Don't ever leave me. Please."

He was quiet for some time and then said, "I have decided to sleep in a separate room from now on. This will give you a chance to think things over. I also don't intend to continue living with someone who looks down on me. Perhaps things will change. I don't know…" He got up and left.

She sat there, stunned by her husband's words. She was more shocked than hurt by the truth that had finally been said out loud. In the past, she had always gotten her way in this relationship; this was the first time that her husband talked back to her. She started to cry. It helped a little. Deep inside, she recognized he was right. He had seen things much more clearly than she realized. She was aware that she had stopped respecting him; that was why she could no longer love him. But then she wondered, had he not stopped respecting himself by always agreeing to everything she wanted, instead of standing up to her once in a while? She was lost and did not know what to do next. Did she want to win him back? Would he be willing to try again, or was it too late already? Was Saleem planting ideas into her husband's head, or was he going through a mid-life crisis? She just could not think straight right now, and she started to cry again, silently, until she fell asleep.

Because of the difficulties with her mother, Terry did not want to see her any more. She even began to doubt that her mother's heart attack had been real. In her mind, it was possibly her mother's way of drawing attention away from her daughter, because she had dared to do things against her wishes, challenge her judgment by getting engaged to a foreign student.

Christmas was approaching, and the festive lights and music made Terry feel better. For her, the period between Thanksgiving and New Year's was her absolute favorite time of the year.

For students at the University the holiday season consisted of taking the finals for the fall semester. Terry was busy studying for the exams. Saleem saw less and less of her the closer it got to the exams.

By the time Terry finished all her final examinations, it was already mid December. Right after that, she needed to buy presents for everyone, including Saleem this year. She did not think he celebrated Christmas, but she wanted to get him something special that would also be useful. She bought him a woolen scarf and a pair of gloves.

When she gave him the presents, well before Christmas Day, he thought that it was done out of a sense of respect for his background and not wanting to offend him in any way. He told her that he liked to celebrate any and all occasions, as long as religion was kept out of it.

She was pleased to hear what he said, his words mirrored her own beliefs and she knew it was true of her family as well.

Because of the problems between Terry and her mother, not to mention between the parents themselves, Terry did not enjoy the holiday season this year. She did not find much pleasure in shopping and parties.

"By the way, I have signed up for the married student housing unit, and there are going to be two units available at the beginning of next semester," Saleem told Terry. "I'm hoping we can get married and start living together, because I miss you and I want you to be with me as my wife." The thought of living together as a married couple so soon was exciting and lifted her spirits.

CHAPTER 42

Terry and Saleem celebrated New Year's Eve with other graduate students, some of whom were married. Their New Year's resolution was to cross the barrier—a legal declaration of being husband and wife—that was keeping them from living together. The wives of the other graduate students encouraged them to carry out their plans and promised help in every possible way.

When the government offices opened on January 3, they both went to the courthouse and found out where to get the papers to fill out for a marriage license. To prove they were of legal age, Terry had brought her driver's license and her birth certificate. Saleem showed his passport and driver's license.

Within a few days, their marriage license arrived by mail. Now, they had sixty days to finalize the process. Terry called her father and told him about it. Her father mentioned that her mother was still not well, and he would give her the news at an appropriate time. But from his voice, Terry could tell how happy he was for her.

John then asked, "What are your plans…for the wedding, I mean.

Terry informed, "Saleem and I are thinking of getting married in the courthouse. Under the circumstances, it seems like an appropriate decision.

He told her, "Your mother and I had always thought of giving you a proper wedding, but in the present situation, a court ceremony sounds like a good idea to me. Your mother is not able to enjoy anything these days, but you know that you and Saleem have my blessings. I am sorry that I will not be there to celebrate, but my thoughts and my best wishes will be with you." Why he would not be able to attend, he did not say. He started to choke, and could not continue.

He did not tell her that he and her mother were not talking these days.

As a wedding present, he bought them $1,000 in travelers' checks, which they could use in any way they liked.

Kader and Jenny had moved to Los Angles. After finishing his PhD, Kader had worked with a professor at UCLA for a year, and now he was with a financial firm. Jenny had also finished her Master's degree and was now working for an insurance company. When Saleem called and told them that he and Terry were getting married in the courthouse, Kader immediately said that he and Jenny would be there. Saleem thought they should get married on January 10, because Terry's birthday was October 10. Ten represented a lucky number in his mind. Unfortunately, January 10, 1965 turned out to be a Sunday when the government offices would be closed.

So Terry and Saleem, calendar in hand, drove to the courthouse to set an appointment with either the judge or the county clerk. They were able to pin down a date on Friday, January 15 at 4 p.m.

Saleem called Kader and relayed their wedding date. Kader and Jenny managed to fly in and were there as witnesses to their friends' marriage ceremony. Mary and Tara were also present. The ritual took place in the least romantic setting of a dark wood paneled court-room. It lasted just a few minutes. The witnesses and the judge signed the marriage certificate, and the court clerk validated it with a stamp. The judge declared them husband and wife.

The newly married couple and their friends left the courthouse and headed for the same restaurant where Saleem had taken Terry for dinner on her twentieth birthday. Kader informed the group that he was the oldest of them all and had a job. He would therefore be paying for the wedding dinner.

Mary and Tara had not met Kader and Jenny before, but they had heard about them from the bride and groom. All six of them were seated at a large round table.

Kader solemnly announced, "This dinner is to honor the bride and groom. You are all my guests tonight. Saleem and I met just as we arrived in Eugene and we have been like brothers ever since. Jenny and I are happy to be the witnesses to this momentous occasion in the life of this wonderful couple. Let us wish them happiness and a wonderful life together."

During dinner, the waiter picked up from the conversation at the table that he was serving a wedding party. As a surprise at the end of the meal, the restaurant presented them with a wedding cake, which had been hastily assembled in the kitchen by laying a smaller cake on top of a larger one.

Kader was going to pay for it, but the manager refused and insisted that it was compliments of the house. Kader added a generous tip to the bill in appreciation of the thoughtfulness and great service.

They all enjoyed themselves and were happy to have been included in the celebration. Some of the patrons in the restaurant, when they saw the wedding cake, came over and congratulated the bride and the groom.

As they were walking toward the parking lot, Jenny got between Terry and Saleem and took their hands into hers. She looked Terry straight in the eyes and pronounced, "You are a lucky girl, Terry, to have a man like Saleem. I have been advising Saleem since the day I met him. Now I give his hand to you and appoint you as his adviser in the future. All these men need women advice-givers." She laughed and the whole group joined her.

Kader and Jenny were going to spend the weekend in Eugene; both of them had friends there. They planned to fly back on Sunday. Everyone thanked the couple from L.A. for the dinner and for coming to town for this special occasion. Saleem promised to come with Terry and visit them once he was settled in his job. Then they said their good-byes.

After everyone left and the newlyweds were alone, it finally sank in that they were indeed husband and wife. Terry knew she had alienated her mother, but she felt good that she had held her ground. The thought came to her mind whether she did what she did because she wanted to stand up to her mother, or if she married for love. She was happy; she had waited for this day for some time, but inside there lingered some sadness. She wished her mother would see her way.

Beyond this point, they had no plans.

In the car, Saleem turned to Terry and asked, "What do we do now?"

Terry said, "We have $1,000 that my father gave us as a wedding present. We can do whatever we want with them. We can spend all or part of it in next two days. You decide. You are the wiser one."

"After this wonderful day, I don't want to stop celebrating. Let's do something special for the next two days and then start a new routine on Sunday, when we get back," Saleem said.

Terry looked at him and smiled. "And, how do we do that?"

"I saw a Holiday Inn sign not far from here. We could go there and check in for tonight and in the morning decide what to do next."

Neither of them had much experience with staying in hotels or check-in procedures. Saleem had stayed in a hotel in New York City, and he vaguely remembered the signing-in process. He parked the car in front of the entrance, walked up to the reception desk, and asked if they had a room available for two. Since he was wearing his suit, he looked very respectable.

The clerk had him fill out a form and looked at his driver's license. The charge was going to be $15 for the night, which Saleem paid in cash. He had taken out $100 from the bank the day before. The clerk produced a hotel map and pointed out to Saleem where the room was located and where he could park his car. He then handed him a key that had big metal piece attached to it. The number 117 was etched into it in large numerals.

Saleem got into the car and drove around the building to a spot that was close to their hotel room. Terry had not brought any change of clothes with her. Saleem had thrown some underwear and two pajamas in a handbag. Just in case she needed one.

The newlywed couple stepped inside the hotel room. It was their first time alone since the ceremony and they were self-conscious. He put his arms around her and whispered, "I love you, Terry, and I always will."

Terry undressed in the bathroom and took a shower. She stepped out again, wrapped in a towel, and climbed into the bed. Saleem showered and emerged from the bath, dressed in his pajamas. He carefully entered the bed on the other side. The festivities of the day and the newness of their status as man and wife caused them to be nervous, yet excited. As he moved toward Terry, Saleem reached over and turned off the table lamp.

There was special buoyancy to their walk the next morning as they entered the breakfast room. The pair exhibited a new closeness and intimacy with each other. As they sat facing each other, morning sun shining on her face and her hair, he saw in her a person as beautiful as he had ever seen before. His new future, his heart knew, was starting that day.

"You must be on your honeymoon," the young waitress exclaimed in a low whisper with a knowing smile as she looked into their glowing faces.

"We got married yesterday…in the court," Terry murmured. The server frowned. Terry laughed nervously and added, "But it isn't a secret." She extended her left hand for the young girl to get a better look at her wedding band.

Pancakes and eggs never tasted better than on this glorious morning. Terry wanted to give Saleem the traveler checks she was carrying in her purse, but Saleem told her to keep them because he still had enough money to pay.

During the meal, they discussed what they wanted to do that day. Saleem said, "I don't know about you, but I would like to check out and move to our new place. Once we are settled, you can go back to your classes on Monday."

Terry looked at him and said, "You are good. You read my mind. I was thinking the same thing. I cannot spend another day in these clothes. Let us go back after we're done with the breakfast."

Saleem was relieved. Wearing the same suit two days in a row was getting to him too.

Mary told John about the details of Terry's ceremony in the court. He was disappointed that he had not been able to attend his daughter's wedding, but he knew that one day he would make it up to her. Neither Mary nor John mentioned any of this to Bernice.

CHAPTER 43

Without knowing, Bernice had become an outcast in her own family. She started to realize that unless she changed her ways she was heading to lead a very lonely life in her old age. Her charm had faded with her youth; it was not easy to make new friends now. She knew how difficult it was for a single old woman to have a decent living as she thought of her own mother. She dreaded the idea of being single and alone in the last years of her life.

Terry had made no effort to see her mother. She did think it would be proper to inform her of her new status, so she mailed her a small note. That was when Bernice found out that her daughter had gone ahead and done what she was determined to do. When Bernice saw John, she showed him the note.

"Yes, I was told a few days ago," was all he said. He never talked much before, but these days it was as if he counted each word.

The winter quarter brought many new things into Terry's life. She had a husband now, a new apartment and they were enjoying life together. Both made an effort to adjust to each other's ways, and felt responsible for the other person's happiness. Time passed quickly and before Saleem and Terry realized it, the winter quarter was almost over. While Terry had been studying for her exams, Saleem was busy organizing his work.

At the start of the spring quarter, Saleem had all the material together for his thesis. At the same time, Terry had started thinking about typing the manuscript and getting it organized in her mind. She was almost finished with her work at college. She needed only six more credits to complete the requirements for her degree. She had time to spare and started thinking about finding a temporary job and found one in a restaurant not too far from where they were living. She was determined to provide all the support Saleem needed during the final lap of the race toward his goal—the PhD degree. His four year work was about to end. She started typing his thesis. Working together they were developing a closeness they never had before.

And then she missed a period. She was worried; a pregnancy was not something she was looking forward to at this point in her life. In her mind, a newly wedded couple needed to go through a transition from courtship to a life of being husband and wife, time to know each other in the new role. Pregnancy would certainly disrupt her life and complicate her plans.

During the tests, when she discovered she was not pregnant, she wished she had waited to tell her husband about her condition. But it was too late. She was frustrated with herself. He had started to treat her as if she was pregnant and brought over catalogues of toys and other children needs to show her, which was not what she wanted. She was annoyed but would not show. Her inner self wanted to hear someone say she was not pregnant. On her way home that night, she was trying work out how to relay the news to her husband.

When she returned from her work he was home. As she entered he asked, "How did it go"?

Terry knew he was not asking about her work; her sister who had given her ride home had put the same question a few minutes ago. She was exhausted and she was confused. At this point, a repeated four-word query sounded like an interrogation, "Well...I'm not pregnant. You will have to wait a while for a child to play with." She blurted out and could hear anger in her words. Her tone of voice surprised her. She knew she was angry but could not say why. The only reason her mind could provide for her manner and the way she spoke was the thought put in her head by her mother that a wife in Pakistan was supposed to have a child as soon as possible after marriage.

The realization that her mother still influenced her thinking troubled her that a seed planted by a parent was corrupting her thinking was a revelation. This was all she could think in her frustration. *Would she ever be free of parental control?* she wondered. At the same time, Terry felt she had snapped at her husband for no real reason. She was angry at herself and was taking it out on poor Saleem.

She felt awful. She started to cry, her tears gushing, tears that she needed to cleanse herself of her mother's lingering influence.

Saleem did not understand what was going on. Not knowing what to do or say, he put both arms around her and held her close. They stood like this for some time without saying a word. He kissed the top of her head and then put her face in his hands and kissed her wet eyes.

She felt comforted and reassured. Holding her husband she tightened the embrace, as if she wanted to squeeze out her mother from their married life.

Saleem, for his part, realized that the situation was beyond his understanding. As they released each other, he was puzzled and wanted to say something profound, but the moment passed and he could not think of anything to say.

Once Terry got over her emotions, she felt drained. She kicked off her shoes and dug her toes into the shaggy pile of the soft carpet, the only new thing that came with their apartment. It felt good under her tired feet. Her feet released from constraint of shoes made her feel at home. She went into the bathroom and splashed cold water on her face. It cooled her burning eyes. A mirror was mounted right over the sink. She was afraid to look into it; she feared she might see her mother standing behind her with a look on her face: I told you so! She took a few deep breaths, and flushed the toilet for no reason. Deep breathing and the sound of gurgling water calmed her down further. When she came out she was herself again; but for a little sadness on her face there was no sign of annoyance anymore.

As usual, the take-out boxes of Chinese food that Saleem had picked up for dinner on his way back from the lab were tightly packed. While her husband took a quick shower, Terry heated the food. The aroma from Kung Pao chicken, Szechuan beef and white rice revitalized her appetite. It made her realize how hungry she was in spite of the late hour. To make up for the unpleasantness of the early hour, she took out her prized gold-rimmed china she had recently purchased from an estate sale and set up places for two with a candle in the middle of the round table—the table that wobbled to acknowledge the occasion. For the first time she saw the flame reflected in the gold rim as a belly dancer twirling in the sea of fire. Her mood suddenly brightened.

By the time they sat down and had their dinner they had forgotten about the *situation* they had and were acting again like two people in love. They stayed there at the dining table and told each other about their day. It was past eleven by the time they went to bed. Saleem was soon snoring while she lay awake thinking how to avoid the repetition of the scare of the last few days.

CHAPTER 44

Saleem brought his notebooks home; the notebooks, written in long hand, contained all the work he had done in the lab since the start of his graduate program. He explained to his wife how like the chapters in a book, the dissertation was to be presented in separate parts: the first part would contain the object and aim of his work; the second part would describe the methods and procedures used. In the following part, he would discuss his results and lastly, there would be the experimental details.

Terry, not being a science major, did not clearly understand how to best organize her husband's work. She went to the department library to see how former students had formatted their theses. From reading some, she was able to create a layout in her mind for arranging the work at hand. This was her first exposure to scientific writing. What surprised her most was the fact that all the sentences were in passive form. Instead of saying I (we) added compound A to compound B; the sentence would say A was added to B. The entire work was presented in an impersonal manner. When she came home, she asked Saleem why the experiments were written in this manner. Saleem had never thought about that; he had simply accepted it as the proper style in scientific writing.

Terry was thinking aloud, "It appears to me that no one wants to take responsibility for what they have done."

Saleem did not agree with that. "But, they always put down their name on the scientific publications, so everyone knows who did the work. But I will ask my professor when I see him," he added, but never got around to doing it. The question remained unanswered.

She pointed out to him that there were structural chemical formulas to be drawn that went beyond her limited knowledge of chemistry. He would have to do that himself or sit next to her when she drew them and help her understand what she was doing.

"We will do everything together. This way I can spend more time with you and also it will make us a team," he said. "I really appreciate what you're doing…all the effort you're putting in. It saves us a bunch of money too. Since we are saving money here, I think you should quit your job at the restaurant. We can manage with what I get, and we still have some savings."

Terry liked the idea. She never enjoyed working as a waitress; someone was always looking at her in a way she did not like, and some customers were just simply unpleasant. She was going to call the owner and tell him that she was to quit, but then, on second thought, she decided to go there and tell him herself. He had been nice to give her a job when she needed work.

With time on her hands, she immersed herself in Saleem's project. He had stopped going to the lab and they spent most of their time together. They were enjoying themselves. It did not even seem like an effort. It was fun.

They had started going out for lunch to a Chinese restaurant not far from their apartment. For the first time in his life, Saleem was having a good time being a student. This was the last quarter in college for both of them. With Terry's help, he was done sooner than he had expected. He took the first draft of his typed thesis to Professor Hayden so he could read it and make corrections. Normally, the professor would be too busy to read and edit the work of his students. The task would be assigned to one of his post-doctoral fellows. But because his wife had so much affection for Saleem, Professor Hayden decided to make time and do it himself.

"Is your wife helping you with this?"

My wife…? I am married…? Realizing he was, he said, "Yes, she is. She is the one who typed it all."

"Today is Tuesday. Let's meet again on Friday at ten in the morning and we will discuss if there are any changes to be made."

Saleem thanked him and left.

When the other chemistry students saw Saleem's typed thesis, they asked if Terry would type theirs as well.

"You will have to ask her yourself next time you see her. She comes here all the time," he answered.

After meeting with the professor on Friday, Saleem was able to incorporate all the suggested changes and the final copy was ready. In the acknowledgements, which he wrote at the end all by himself, there were only two names, his wife's and his professor's. The dedication was to his parents.

Terry asked, "Do you really want my name there?"

To which he answered, "Without you, all this would not have been possible."

She happily took complete charge of getting the copies bound and the title printed on the cover. Of all the graduating students in the lab, he was the first one to submit his thesis.

With Saleem's work done, Terry found time to type and prepare a final draft for two other students. She had experience and the task was not difficult. She made some money.

Terry's parents had not seen their apartment. Time had passed and Terry's anger toward her mother had subsided. She called home one day and it happened that her mother picked up the phone. Terry politely said to her, "Saleem and I would like you and father to come over and have dinner with us. We would like you to see where we live."

Her mother accepted, "We would love to see you both and visit your place."

Terry thought Saleem was too busy to cook, so she bought some take-out dinner and only had to prepare a vegetable dish. The parents arrived on time. The dinner table was set for four. Terry had laid out her gold-rimmed china and the elegant glasses. By sticking pennies under one of her table legs, she made sure that it would not wobble.

Bernice was impressed with how well they had done and John was excited to see them both. The parents still had problems communicating together, but they decided not to dwell on them, at least for tonight. The children were unaware of what was going on between Bernice and John. Outside the home, their parents successfully presented themselves as a well-adjusted couple.

Saleem showed them around their small apartment and pointed out how it was conveniently located close to the stores. He also explained to them how the building housed mostly married graduate students, and so it was quiet and safe.

"Did you get this china as a wedding present?" Bernice asked.

"No, Terry bought it," Saleem said.

"I got it at an estate sale. Saleem really likes the gold-rim on the plates," Terry added quickly.

Bernice was proud that her daughter had inherited her own good taste. Terry told them that Saleem had nearly completed all the requirements for his degree and that they would soon leave for California. John was immensely happy to hear that and told them how proud he was of them.

Bernice was incapable of showing any warmth. But she did congratulate Saleem in advance of his final achievement. It turned out to be a pleasant evening.

"Mother seems to be getting over her frustration with me," Terry said after her parents left. They had promised to see each other again soon.

For John and Bernice, this had been the first night out together since the incident when he had told her what was on his mind. During this time of separation, both of them had realized that life alone was something they did not know anymore. When they got home, they were talking like two friends who had not seen each other in a long time. Both were ready to resolve their problems, but neither one wanted to give in.

That night, John found Bernice in his bed in the middle of the night. They both felt how much warmer a bed could be when they were together.

In the morning, when John got out of bed, breakfast was waiting for him on the table. "Thank you Bernice, it was nice of you to make breakfast and wait for me."

"I know, I have not been a good wife, but I will try, if you can bear with me a little longer. You have to understand that you allowed me to act as I did for a long time. So, it will take time for me to change, but if you can be patient, I will keep on trying."

John looked at her. She seemed sincere and she looked prettier than in years. He smiled at her, reached out to hold her hand wondering if he had rediscovered the woman he loved. And knowing well that people do not change, he said, "You are a very beautiful woman, Bernice."

Bernice wanted to hear this from her husband for a long time and more often, but being a man he never thought much of it.

He had not learned to say, "I love you." In his opinion, if he loved someone he would show that by his actions not by words. Words had little substance, he thought. Anything can be said without following it up by action. Words need to be supported by actions, but the actions did not need words to give them meaning.

But his wife failed to see what he was doing for her. Or, he was doing it for so long that she had taken it for granted. She longed for words that never came.

Different cultures emphasize different aspects in lives of people. In the home where he grew up, it was very uncommon for a man to say he loved a woman. This was something women said to their children. John was always doing things for his wife. He would buy flowers and gifts for her when he felt she was down.

But it was not enough for her. She wanted to be told; she needed affirmation. In her culture she had seen and heard these words so often that she expected to hear them from him, her husband, as often as he could say them. This was one medicine she needed for her insecurities.

She remembered when her father left her mother, all he had told her was, "I don't love you anymore." She was afraid, if someone was not saying it and she was not hearing the word "love", she was unloved. Words were as important to her as his actions. She even hinted this to her husband, but he never caught on to it. She would sometimes wonder if she ever left him would he ever say, "I love you, don't leave me." She was not quite sure. And she did not want to go that far to test him. He did care, she knew, and that had to be enough for the time being.

The final day arrived, the special day for which Saleem had worked hard for the last four years. He put on the only suit and tie he had. With all the good wishes from his wife, he drove to the Department to fulfill the last requirement of his degree—appearing before a committee to defend his thesis.

As he was standing outside waiting to be asked in, he all of a sudden had a flashback to the past when he was waiting outside to be interviewed by Sharma Gee to take an exam to start his formal education. Today he was taking his last exam of the formal education that he had started some twenty years ago in a land on the opposite side of the world.

Saleem was nervous as before when he entered the room, but when he saw the friendly face of his professor, his confidence returned. They asked him to present a brief summary of what he did, which was followed by questions. No one asked a question he could not answer. It appeared to him that they had already approved his work and the process was a mere formality.

As he thought the session was over, one member of the committee, a professor of physics asked him if he would explain why he did what he did.

The response that came to his mind right away was that he did it to complete the requirements of his degree, the same reason he was there at this point answering questions. He started to say, "I was assigned this problem by my professor." But when he looked at the expression on the faces of the committee members including his research adviser, he could see that they wanted something more— something more profound. Therefore, he continued. To dress up his answer, he added, "I started to work on this project to fulfill one of the requirements, but my interest and curiosity grew as at every step the failure or success of an experiment gave me a direction. The interpretation of the results made it challenging and stimulated my thinking. As I got more involved, I learned more and finally was able to make a small contribution to the knowledge of chemistry. My contribution may not be large, but I do have a feeling of accomplishment." To him it was a rhetorical question that needed a rhetorical answer. He stopped at this point to once again look at them as if asking if his answer was acceptable.

They all seemed satisfied. In an hour, it was all over. As they emerged from the hall, they shook his hand and called him Dr. Shah.

Once he was alone he had a feeling he never had in the past. He knew he was happy, but this was happiness like he had never experienced before. In a flash, he lived through all those moments of bliss he had ever known in his life. One memory after another passed through his mind's eye, bringing in those past events, which were a source of joy at one time or another. And the sense of achievement erased all those periods of agony, and patched all cracks of disappointment he had experienced through this not-so-easy path to his goal.

He yearned to sit down to absorb it all, but at the same time he wanted to run home and tell Terry. On a whim, he stopped at the tobacco shop. He knew Terry could not handle smoke, but that did not stop him from buying a pipe and a pouch of tobacco.

Instead of using his key to enter the apartment, he knocked.

Terry opened the door and saw Saleem standing on the stairs, pipe in his mouth. She understood—Saleem now had his PhD!

He opened his arms wide and said, "We did it!"

She ran to him, tears of joy blurred her vision. From the corner of his eye, he could see the dining room table had been set with the gold-rimmed glasses and plates.